Storm Surge

Weather Gods Book 1

Melissa Gunn

Melissa Gunn

Cover design by Getcovers.com

Storm Surge

ISBN 978-0-473-56597-8 (Paperback POD)

ISBN 978-0-473-56598-5 (epub)

ISBN 978-0-473-56599-2 (kindle)

ISBN 978-0-473-61580-2 (Hardcover POD)

For Isabelle and Élise

CONTENTS

AUTHOR'S NOTE

This book is written in New Zealand English, so expect more 's's and 'u's than you might be used to.

It is set in an alternative near-future world much like ours, with the effects of climate change, but with demigods, shifters and other supernaturals.

CHAPTER ONE

AUTUMN

I t was just another wet day in October when Freya's house fell into the sea.

Freya had not paid much attention to the recent weather warnings. She'd been too busy playing with her new black and white kitten to notice much of anything, although it was a shame that the wind and rain meant she couldn't play outside. She picked up the kitten and squeezed it gently, glad that it was safe inside with her.

"You stick with me, Mr Fluffbum," she murmured. "It's too wet for girls and kittens out there. And you really don't want to get too close to those waves." The kitten squirmed out of her arms and ran under the bed.

"Oh, no, Mr Fluffbum. I need you to stay with me." Freya got down on her knees and peered around to locate the kitten. Her long, mousy hair fell irritatingly into her eyes as she did so. "Come on, puss, come out."

There was a clatter outside her door. Her mother was hurriedly piling food and bedding into wine boxes, running in and out of the house with their worldly possessions as Freya tried to coax Mr Fluffbum out from under her bed.

"Come on, you silly furball. There's nothing to find under there except dust bunnies. And you can't eat *them* when you catch them."

The kitten ignored Freya, intent on stalking something unseen. As the kitten pounced at last, a sudden 'crack' resounded through the small cottage. Freya jumped, bumping her head on the bed.

"Ow! Mr Fluffbum, did you hear that? It didn't sound like thunder." She kept talking aloud in an effort to keep calm. It worked a little, but her voice was unsteady as she continued talking to the kitten.

"What *have* you caught under there? Show me." The kitten was now lying on its back, scrabbling at something that might have been small and furry, but was still mostly invisible under the bed.

Rubbing the sore spot on her head, Freya squinted at the creature Mr Fluffbum had captured. In her effort to discern its shape in the shadows, she failed to notice that a large crack had appeared in the floor behind her. She shuffled backwards to try to get a better view of what the kitten was doing, and scraped her knee on the new crack.

"This house is just full of nails and cracked bits," she said.

Mr Fluffbum appeared near the edge of the bed, chasing a small hairy item that moved unexpectedly under its own power.

"Wow, I haven't seen a house hob since we arrived here. Good find. Now chase it closer to me..."

In typical feline fashion, the kitten immediately batted the hob back under the bed. Freya sighed dramatically, and crawled under the bed in pursuit of her uncooperative kitten and its prey.

"Come on, Mr Fluffbum. It's time to go. Mum says the storm should be gone by tomorrow, then we might get some sun at last. That would be nice, wouldn't it? Although then I suppose I'll have to try and stop you from chasing birds again. I didn't appreciate the sparrow you brought me last week - you know they're endangered, don't you? Well, I guess you don't; you're a cat. You probably just thought it was lunch. Endangered, tasty lunch."

"Freya! What are you doing still inside? I told you to get out over an hour ago. Forget the cat. We have to get out *right now*! The house is going to go!"

Her mother stood in the doorway, blond hair darkened and bedraggled by rain, thin face marred by frown lines, her usually carefully tucked blouse half pulled out. Freya noticed that her mother's hand on the door frame was trembling.

"I can't leave Mr Fluffbum!" she cried.

"You can't stay in here. Quick, out now. No arguing."

Freya lunged for Mr Fluffbum and grabbed him firmly by the scruff of the neck before running out into the hall, her heart pounding. She and her mother raced for the front door, bumping awkwardly into each other and off the walls as they ran. Freya stumbled as the floor beneath her began to tilt wildly and a terrible screech filled the air as the cottage's foundations gave way. Panic gave wings to her feet as she leaped through the open doorway, her mother a heartbeat behind her.

They came to a halt on the far side of the crumbling asphalt road from their cottage. Freya's older sister Tammy was loitering there, an anorak hood covering her pale hair, ripped jeans so full of holes that she might as well be wearing shorts. Freya could see her dad further down the street, shoulders straining his wet shirt as he carried a large box away from the cottage.

"Thank goodness *you* did as you were told," Danae addressed Tammy in obvious relief.

Tammy shrugged.

"Not much else to do out here," she said.

From the street, Freya could see how the waves had undermined their small white-painted cottage where it sat perched at a jaunty angle on the cliff, leaning towards the waiting sea. The other cottages on the seaward side of the street sat a little further back than theirs, and it didn't look like those dwellings would be badly impacted by the waves. Not today, at any rate.

Who knew a storm surge could affect us up here?

It was clear from the tilt of the house that the foggy layer of sea spray on the windows would not be a concern for long now. Her room, closest to the sea, would be the first to fall. She and her mother had escaped just in time.

A thought struck Freya.

"Mum, did you get my books out?" she asked. "I didn't have a chance to, with Mr Fluffbum under the bed."

"No, Freya. I got *you* out. The books were less important."

"But they were library books!" cried Freya, starting towards the house again.

Her mother grabbed her arm, fingers digging in like claws.

"No, Freya, you can't go back in."

The wind buffeted Freya, unexpectedly strong. Salt spray lashed her cheeks, blown off the waves surging inches below the cliff top. Freya turned side-on to the wind while she adjusted her hold on Mr Fluffbum. A bigger splash soaked her legs - that last wave had over-topped the cliffs, gushing through the gaps between the houses. A dreadful sucking noise filled her ears as the wave retreated, and the house tilted further. Another wave swelled over the cliff and Freya backed up hastily, nearly fast enough to avoid being dragged by her mother's still-clutching fingers. The library books were beyond help now. Freya's retreat was halted by the low brick fence around their opposite neighbour's property.

One more wave came and went, and the whole cottage tipped more drastically, timber creaking, leaning into the sea's embrace. When that wave retreated, the cottage went with it, like a toy being sucked down into an emptying bathtub. The sound as it disappeared was more of a crunch than a splash. Somehow, that made it more final.

Freya and her sister crept closer to the cliff-edge to get a better view of where the cottage had landed, leaving their mum trying to cover a pile of their things with a small blue tarpaulin. The thin tarp kept catching the wind and blowing off the pile.

"Wow. It's like a jotunn dragged it into the sea! How cool!" said Tammy.

Freya nodded in gloomy agreement. It did look as though a giant's hand had helped their house down the cliff. But...

"I wish it hadn't gone over with my books. Do you think the library will charge me for losing them?"

"Oh Freya, never mind the books. Just *look* at it. How many people can say they've barely escaped their house falling off a cliff! I'm posting this on Flimflam for my friends to see."

"But Tammy, don't you mind? How can I get Mr Fluffbum settled enough to sleep on my bed?" Tears threatened to spill out of the corners of her eyes, and she squeezed them shut for a moment, wanting to appear as adult and carefree as her older sister. Then the realisation hit her, and she lost the battle with her tears.

"My bed was still in there! I don't have anywhere to sleep!" As always, it was the little things which broke her resolve. Large-scale catastrophes, Freya could deal with, keeping calm while those around her panicked. A house? No problem. But lost books and no bed? Now *that* was a problem. "Oh, Mr Fluffbum. What will we do now?"

As Freya's tears were alternately whipped away by the wind and then blended with the persistent rain, Tammy gave her a quick squeeze around the shoulders with one arm. This was as close as she came these days to the bearlike sisterly hugs she used to give Freya when they were smaller.

"Never mind, Frey-frey. We'll be in a mansion before you know it. Or more likely another tumbledown house too close to the sea. But we'll be somewhere. Cheer up and enjoy the view, now. Just think, you won't have to worry about cleaning those salty windows anymore. People pay money for experiences like this, you know. I wish I'd filmed it with my phone; we could have sold the footage. Evidence of climate change and all that. We could've been famous!"

"Don't call me Frey-frey, I'm not a baby. And your phone would have run out of charge before you could film it anyway. You're always running out of battery. Anyway, everyone knows about climate change, I mean, it's hard to miss. Especially when your house drowns because of it." Despite her sister's annoying attitude, Freya leaned against Tammy in an attempt at reassurance - whether for herself or her sister, she wasn't quite sure - before Tammy shoved her gently away.

"Sure, it's totally obvious. But honestly, haven't you seen some of the stupid memes on Flimflam? Like the one where climate change activists and flat-earthers are put in the same boat to go swim the rising seas till they go off the edge? Climate change is so last decade, even though it's getting worse. But I think a good house-down-the-cliff movie would get people's attention."

"Maybe if you gave me your phone and got yourself a new one, I could see those memes on Flimflam myself. And message my friends, like you do."

"*So* not happening. You're way too young for a phone. According to Mum and Dad, at least. Plus you only ever talk to your cat these days. You ought to work on that. But we should be calling a news station, getting some attention, not standing around gloomily in the rain. I'm going to try and get some photos at least. If Mum lets me any closer to the edge, of course. Honestly, if it wasn't such a cliché, I'd say she was like a mother hen."

Perhaps I am too young, maybe that's why I'm not excited about this. I don't have a silly Flimflam account to pay attention to, or post to house-destruction videos on. And no-one talks to me at school, that's why I only talk to Mr Fluffbum.

Freya didn't understand Tammy's careless attitude towards their home. Home meant books, her bed, her favourite corner with cushions in it for reading on. Freya herself was beginning to feel like she was floating away, as rudderless as the bits of her house she could see washing away below.

What was a person when they had no home? How do you define yourself without walls?

She shivered. The rain was coming down harder than ever. Mr Fluffbum meowed plaintively.

"Don't worry, Mr Fluffbum. We'll find somewhere soon. I hope. Surely the sea gods don't hate us that much."

"It's a goddess in these parts," said Freya's mother, Danae, from just behind her. Freya jumped in surprise. Danae had abandoned her efforts with the tarp to intercept Tammy, who was indeed trying to get better photos of their ex-cottage as the roof began to float away.

"Don't you remember? We talked about it when we moved in. Anyway, don't talk about *them* here. We're too close, they'll hear us. And they're all in a rage these days, what with the plastic crisis, the oil spills and the collapse of the fish stocks, so hush." Her mother's voice was harsh with stress and the tarp in her hand fluttered loudly in the wind.

Freya's dad loomed suddenly near, bearing another box away from the seaward side of the road. The box was plastered with 'fragile' and 'this way up' signs beside a picture of a wine bottle. He took the blue tarpaulin from Freya's mum and secured it quickly around his box.

"Listen to your mother, Freya. With *her* family background, she ought to know about the fishing crisis. Although *I* think it's a god behind this storm," he said, shooting a challenging glance at Freya's mum.

Freya wondered at the accusation in his voice. Her mum never said much about her family, who'd moved countries a long time ago, leaving Danae alone here in Britain. Or maybe Danae had moved here by herself. Freya wasn't quite clear on the details.

"Does it matter whether it's a god or a goddess? That's still our cottage down there in the waves," Freya said, attempting to smooth troubled waters.

"It certainly matters to them. But don't worry, we'll find somewhere to go," said Danae, ignoring Dion's comment.

Freya thought her mum was trying to put on a brave face, focusing on the opinions of deities to avoid the disaster zone that was now their house. Freya had never seen one of those deities her mother was always telling her and Tammy about. She wondered if such beings really existed. If they did, they weren't on her family's side right now.

Freya watched gloomily as what had once been her bedroom wall flaked off into the waves. The interior plasterboard submerged briefly under the sea, then reappeared with a single strand of seaweed draped over one corner. She could see her wallpaper. Off-white with small diamonds of blue, it contrasted sharply with the brown seaweed. The next wave sucked it further out to sea, where crest after crest broke over it until Freya could no longer see it. She suddenly remembered the house hob. Could it have escaped the sudden destruction? It was hard to see how. She gulped and crossed her fingers that it hadn't gone over with the cottage. Hobs were supposed to bring good luck to a house, but today's one certainly hadn't brought any.

It was the middle of the afternoon when the cottage was washed away for good. A group of neighbours who had helped rescue furniture stood around, watching it go. Freya thought she and her family should be fortified with popcorn as they watched their former life wash away in the storm surge. That would go well with Tammy's photos for social media.

The whole family stood together now, watching the destruction. Their nearest neighbours were glancing sideways at their own houses, perhaps wondering if they were safe. Freya's cottage had been the closest to the cliff-edge though; no-one else would be out of a home today. When the drama was over, the neighbours edged away. Nothing could make it clearer that they would be offering no further help today.

Freya watched them go resentfully, only now realising that she was soaked to the bone and cold. Mr Fluffbum scratched irritably at her as she held him too tightly. She had just realised how close she had come to going into the sea along with the cottage.

"Come on then, Tammy, Freya. Come on, Dion. Let's see if we can find somewhere to stay before all our things are ruined by the rain. Oh, what shall we do first?" Despite her obvious fluster, Freya's mum took charge. She kept up a constant monologue of suggestions, complaints and recriminations.

"I knew the place was too good to be true. It was too cheap. Not that we could have afforded anything more expensive. But we'd settled in here, my plants were growing well. I wish..." Her voice wobbled momentarily, before she regained a veneer of calm, leaving whatever she wished unsaid. She addressed her husband, who was standing a few feet away, looking out to sea with a frown on his face.

"Dion, help me get something covering the pillows, they'll be sodden else. Or the food, we can't use wet flour. Tammy, get your things covered. We'll need to get everything moved by nightfall, or lose them. This isn't a great neighbourhood. I know the neighbours helped us move our things out of the house, but just wait and see what happens after dark. Or rather, let's not. Freya, get that cat into a box or something and help, now."

"But Mum..." Freya's voice trailed off as she realised that she didn't have much choice. Tammy didn't say anything as she piled her few possessions into a rucksack. Her face was pinched, lips pressed tightly together. Freya decided against complaining to her. She didn't look like she would be sympathetic to anyone. Maybe she was still wishing she hadn't missed the opportunity to film their house being washed away.

Freya's dad stood with his hands in his pockets, ignoring the goings-on as the family tried to figure out what they could take with them. His brown hair was black with rain, and droplets ran down his face unheeded. He was the one who had found this house, had enthused about the sea view and the good fortune that they could afford the rent. It was clear now that the rent had been low for a reason, and the sea view was all too visible with the cottage no longer blocking it. Surreptitiously looking at her dad's thunderous expression as she cast about for a box that might hold a squirming kitten, Freya decided that she wanted to speak to him even less than she wanted to complain to Tammy - even though her dad was usually her first choice of confidant.

Finding a reasonably solid box under a soggy duvet, she manoeuvred Mr Fluffbum into it, not without difficulty, as he somehow managed to get both front paws stuck on the sides of the box as Freya slid him in. Even after she'd tied the box with string, a white-mittened paw slipped out through the top of the box as Mr Fluffbum explored his new string toy. Despite the disaster that had struck their family, Freya couldn't help but grin at his antics. The world couldn't be all that bad, not when there were kittens like Mr Fluffbum in it.

Freya bundled up her wet duvet into a parcel. Perhaps they could dry it out somewhere, later. Now that she'd removed the duvet, water dripped into Mr Fluffbum's box. He yowled irritably.

"Sorry. I'll get you somewhere dry soon," she promised the kitten. She looked over at her sister, who was juggling mysterious jars into her bag.

"So, Tammy, if you wanted to sell a video of our house being destroyed, why *didn't* you? I mean, you have a phone. And photos too now, assuming your battery lasted. According to Mum, the storm surge was forecast. Someone knew it was coming, even if *we* didn't expect the surge to carry the house with it."

Tammy was silent a moment, then muttered.

"I don't know who I'd send it to."

"Well, any of those friends who are always texting you, maybe?"

"They wouldn't care. They're mostly trolls anyway. They don't go near the sea. Though I guess they might have to if it keeps rising."

"Real trolls?!" Freya asked, disbelievingly.

"Well, part-trolls, at least. You wouldn't believe how many half-breeds I've met at high school. I'm sure the PE teacher is a werewolf too. No pure human could be *that* keen on ball sports."

Once again, Danae passed by at an inopportune time, this time carrying a tray full of seedlings that she'd evidently rescued from their house's former site.

"Tammy, how many times have I told you not to call people half breeds and weres! It's rude, it will get you in trouble - with me *and* them - and it's probably not even true," she said.

"Oh, it's true, all right. But they're sort of friends, so surely I can call them what they are?" Tammy said.

"No, you can't. No-one is supposed to know about people like us. If you bandy about phrases like half-breeds, either they'll think you're racist, or they'll guess the truth. Neither is a good outcome, so kindly find a new description, whatever your friends are."

Tammy rolled her eyes when their mother turned her back.

"I don't see why we're always so shrouded in secrecy. It's not like we have anything to lose by being known. I mean - look, we can't even save our own house. It's not like we'd lose power by telling."

Freya glanced around quickly to see if their mum was in hearing distance. She wasn't.

"Don't say that to Mum, Tammy. She'd probably go spare if you did, right now. But... I wish we did have power. Enough to save my books, and not have to hide what we are." She looked down towards the site of their cottage again and felt a niggle of guilt about that hob. "Enough that finding a hob meant the cottage wouldn't get washed out to sea without warning!"

"Oh, don't I know it. I don't think hobs could manage that much though. They're small fry, power-wise. But if I had power like those stuck-up deities, I wouldn't waste it on washing away some innocent demi's cottage just because you had an argument with their oh-so-glorious ancestors."

Tammy glared at the waves as though her stare alone would hold back the sea.

"Are we truly demi-gods then?" Freya asked. "Or demi-goddesses, anyway?"

"Sure we are. Can't you feel it in yourself?" Tammy struck a dramatic pose, arms raised to the sky, ignoring the rain dripping off her nose.

Freya wondered when her sister had stopped minding the rain. At one point she'd had quite a water phobia. "That sounds rude, Tammy."

"*So* not what I meant. If you don't know yet, you'll have to figure it out when you're older. Not my job."

"Alright, don't give me a straight answer. You do know that I still don't know what power I'm supposed to have, right?"

"You're supposed to figure that out when you go through puberty, Freya. Ask me again when you're older. Just be glad I figured out the rain issue for us."

Freya couldn't remember much of an issue with rain, except that there was usually too much of it. And she *really* didn't want to discuss puberty with Tammy out here on the streets. She pursued another topic instead.

"So who had an argument with a god then? Do you know? I've always wondered why we don't move away from the sea."

"Mum's never quite told me, but as far as I can gather, her ancestors were in some argument with a sea god. Or maybe goddess. Probably a god, the way she always goes on about the important difference between gods and goddesses. But I don't know why we don't go inland either. Especially now!"

"So, the gods are real, then?"

"Frigg, yes. Better not let Mum hear you asking that. Bastard gods. Fenris' teeth, I wish they weren't real."

After a moment, Freya attempted to defuse her sister's anger with distraction. Although she was angry herself, it also seemed a dangerous emotion here on the edge of the cliff, so near the sucking waves and whatever gods or goddesses they might be hiding.

"So. Anyway. What *are* part-trolls like?" Freya was processing her sister's earlier comments about half-breeds.

"Oh, you know. A bit hairy, the girls too, not just the boys. Arms like spaghetti, keen on rock music. Surely, you've seen them at school? And there were those werewolves in the last town, too."

Freya shook her head. "I'm never sure what I'm seeing."

Tammy warmed to her topic. "There was one in my class last year who turned up to all the school discos in pink pyjama shorts and an orange muscle top. He just stood around waving his arms in the air in time to the music though, so no harm done except to fashion and my nostrils. That troll's B.O. was something else. To be honest, from what I can see, half-trolls are pretty much what Mum tells us they are. But don't tell her I said so, she'd rub it in for years."

"Do all the part-trolls have bad taste in clothes then?"

Tammy nodded, her eyes on the sea.

"Far as I can tell they do. That was a supreme example though."

"Tammy, why are we talking about trolls and their fashion choices?"

"You got anything happier to talk about?"

"I guess not."

"There you are then."

CHAPTER TWO

AFTER THE DESTRUCTION

It took the family till after nightfall to find an emergency shelter. By that time, they'd left Freya's dad guarding the damp pile of their rescued belongings, and gone on foot to see what they could find. What they could find, as it turned out, was one room in an old, damp bed-and-breakfast, tucked into the cramped streets away from the beach. Its peeling exterior held nothing more promising than a faded sign advertising 'vacancy'. They had to pay up front for a week's lodging, which took most of the cash they had, or so Danae said. There was a double bed and a fold-out couch in the single room, so at least everyone had a bed to share. And while it was musty and dank, it was certainly less damp than their house must be at that moment.

Apparently, in order to stay at homeless shelters, you had to tick a number of boxes. Freya's mum had been complaining bitterly for the last couple of hours about how Freya's family did not meet whatever those criteria were. Freya wondered how much worse things could get, compared to losing your home off a cliff. Looking around at the faded walls of the room they had found themselves in, Freya decided she didn't want to know how much worse it could be. Apart from anything else, Tammy hadn't yet revisited their conversation about trolls. That alone was cause for celebration, no matter how crummy the walls of their temporary abode.

"Freya, Tammy, you'll have to find something to eat from your bags. I hope you still have some snacks left in there. I'm going to go back and get your father. One of the neighbours might give us a lift with all our gear."

Freya noticed her mother wasn't complaining about their former neighbours' propensity to steal, now. But...

"Mum, I didn't have a chance to grab any snacks. And I'm hungry. Mr Fluffbum is too."

Her Mum looked at her sadly.

"Oh, Freya. I only have things that need cooking, and nowhere to cook them. You'll have to share with your sister, assuming she has anything. I have no clue what that cat can eat though. Tammy?"

Tammy muttered darkly under her breath, but rummaged in her bag and fished out a bent flapjack, still in its packaging.

"Here. But I don't have many more, so don't complain when it's gone. I guess the cat can lick up the crumbs, if you don't mind him being poisoned by chocolate."

She tossed the package to Freya, who nearly caught it.

"Gaia wept!" she exclaimed as she fumbled it from the floor. Hunger and shock were setting in, now that they had stopped moving.

"Freya!" exclaimed her mother sharply. "We can't afford to anger any gods. No swearing, remember?"

Unexpectedly, Tammy intervened.

"Oh, come on, Mum. After what happened today, surely a little swearing isn't going to attract any more godly notice? It's not like she's standing at the sea, shouting, like Dad probably is right now."

Danae looked like she might argue the point, then her face crumpled.

"Oh, I know. I'm sorry girls. It's just all too much, right now. Look, do your best with the food. At least there should be breakfast food downstairs in the morning. Not that we'll be able to eat half of it, as usual. The cat might eat eggs, Freya. And Tammy, you're probably right about your father, which is all the more reason for me to go fetch him now, before he says something the goddess can't forgive. Just... look after each other, OK?"

"Yes, Mum," they chorused. Their mother was always enjoining them to look after each other. The repetition made everything seem a bit more normal.

Once their mother had left the room, Freya tore into the flapjack.

"Do you want my cat poisoned?" she asked Tammy, with her mouth full of oats and sultanas and only the tiniest flecks of chocolate.

"I'm not answering anything while you show me what you're eating. Finish your mouthful *then* ask, or I'm not talking to you."

Tammy turned her back meaningfully. Freya obediently swallowed (she *was* hungry, after all), then repeated the question.

"Look, Freya, I don't mind your cat in principle, but I was never allowed the dog *I* wanted, so it doesn't seem fair. So, since you're the one with an extra hungry mouth to feed, you'd better get busy finding something to feed it. I've given you what food I could spare. Maybe next time we have to leave somewhere in a hurry, you can remember to grab some food too."

Freya felt that Tammy was being spiteful, but she couldn't argue about the food. She *hadn't* thought to bring out any, not even for Mr. Fluffbum. As though on cue, a complaining wail emerged from the box in which she had smuggled her cat into the bed and breakfast. Pets weren't allowed, of course.

"Shut him up, Freya," hissed Tammy, sounding catlike herself. "They'll kick us out if they find out you have a pet in here."

"I don't know how to make him quiet. He's hungry." Nevertheless, Freya hastily opened the box.

Mr Fluffbum leaped out gracefully, but spoiled the effect by landing on the edge of a bed, slipping backwards and scrabbling at the covers. Freya laughed, but Tammy glared at her.

"If that cat scratches the covers we'll have to pay for them, you know."
Freya subsided guiltily.

"Here, puss. Come sit down with me." She patted the bed beside her, and for once Mr Fluffbum complied with the suggestion, stalking along the bed and sitting with his back to both of them. He washed a paw and used it to groom his ears.

"At least he's not making a noise, now," said Freya.

"Good. What happens when he needs to use kitty litter again and there isn't any?"

"I'll teach him how to use the toilet. I saw that on a video once, it should be possible."

"Better hope it is. Because there's an awful reek coming out of that box already."

Freya leaned over to look, but recoiled.

"Ugh. That's disgusting. No wonder Mr Fluffbum was yowling, anyone would hate being stuck in a box with that smell."

"Clean it up, quick. I can't stand it over here," complained Tammy.

Reluctant to deal with her cat's mess, but knowing she had no option, Freya picked up the box and held it at arm's length.

"OK, open the door. I wish this place had an ensuite."

"Yeah, me too. Then I wouldn't have to smell that filth while you get it out the door."

When Freya returned from emptying out the box - she'd left the box itself outside - she had to close the door after herself to stop her cat escaping.

"No you don't, Mr Fluffbum. We have to stay here for now."

Tammy flopped backwards, her head thudding onto the pillow with a dull sound. She pulled out a flapjack of her own - chocolate coconut, a better flavour than the one she'd given her sister, Freya noticed.

"I can't believe I'm stuck in this room with you and a cat. I was supposed to go out tonight, you know. I actually had an event in my social calendar. For once," said Tammy.

"It's not my fault the house washed away!"

"Yeah, yeah, I know. It's just my luck though. I managed to line up a date with someone who wasn't a troll, and some stupid goddess gets in a snit and destroys our house."

"Ooh, who was this non-troll? A werewolf? A demi?"

Tammy had often bemoaned her luck (or lack of it) when it came to dates.

"Neither, thank you very much for your confidence in me. He was an actual human. A genuine non-hybrid, as far as I could tell. As rare as hens' teeth, as Mum would say. OK, so maybe a demi would look better, but this guy is a much better option. Not as hairy as a were or a troll, plus no pack to annoy. No chance of angering his ancestors with an accidental curse, either. But now here I am, stuck with minding you while Mum yells at Dad for getting us a rental on a cliff. Missing my first decent date in months."

Freya hesitated, then suggested to Tammy,

"You could still go. I don't mind being by myself. I'm old enough now."

Tammy sat up, suddenly alert.

"Really? I mean, sure, I think you're old enough too, but does Mum? She's going to be pretty mad at everyone for a while since her plants went over the cliff with the house."

Freya patted the cat, who was urgently nudging at her hand. She didn't want to be alone, but she did have Mr Fluffbum with her.

It's worth a couple of hours of loneliness if it means I avoid a week of Tammy complaining.

"I'm sure I can handle Mum. Or I can blame you, of course."

Tammy glared at her sister. Freya laughed at the expression on her sister's face.

"Kidding! I've got Mr Fluffbum for company. You go. Otherwise, I'll never hear the end of it. And you might never meet another pure human again. It's the first time you've talked about one, anyway. Mind you, I'm pretty sure I haven't met anything other than pure humans."

"I won't remind you about the werewolves in the last town then. You're not so bad as a little sister, sometimes. Well then, I'd better start getting ready."

Freya watched her sister's hasty preparations with mixed feelings. She was sure Mum would be mad at both her and Tammy - but Tammy was always wanting to go out and socialise. And Freya *was* old enough to look after herself, she was sure. Especially when they had only a single room to live in. Keeping Tammy in would make everything worse. Especially when Dad got back. Tammy and Dad were a volatile combination. Dad always seemed to feel that he should exert control over his older daughter. Tammy objected to any form of control vociferously. Tammy didn't keep her frustrations to herself, as a rule, and she was in prime form to argue with everyone. On the other hand, now that her plans were back on track, Tammy hummed to herself as she gave herself a quick wash using the ancient pink porcelain sink that made the room a more inconvenient shape.

"So, does he have a name, this human guy?" Freya asked idly, as Tammy moved on to adding mascara to her pale lashes.

How did she manage to pack mascara in that frantic flight from our cottage?

"Not one I'm going to share. The less you know, the less you can tell," said Tammy.

"Oh, come on, Tammy, we're not in some murder mystery. I'm pretty sure no-one's going to torture the name out of me - not even Dad!"

Tammy laughed, which had been Freya's intent. Their dad was more likely to exit a room himself than argue back with Freya. For some reason, Freya had always been able to talk Dad around to her way of thinking. Tammy called him a slitherer-outer - when she wasn't arguing with him.

"Oh, all right. He's called Dan, and he's an ecologist. Or possibly biologist. Something like that. I met him after school a few weeks ago," said Tammy.

"How come you always seem to have time after school, when I'm doing homework with Mum?" Freya was more interested in unfair treatment than in Tammy's boyfriend.

"I've already learnt all that stuff. Anyway, as I was saying, Dan's out here doing repairs on the wildlife rescue place, so maybe he's a carpenter who happens to like animals. Anyway, he was going to show me some of the wildlife tonight. You know, the nocturnal things like badgers and bats and foxes. It seemed like a good opportunity to move things along. Then this stupid storm blew up and ruined a perfectly decent house - don't tell Dad I said that. But I figure we've secured what we can from the storm, so my time's my own. Don't tell Mum, will you?" Tammy finished applying eyeshadow and moved on to shaping her lips with a red pencil.

"I have to tell her something, she'll ask where you've gone. Though at this rate, she'll arrive back before you go," said Freya.

Tammy checked the time on her phone, which was plugged into a wall socket to charge, and swore.

"Frigg. I'm going to have to run. And I hate running. Look, tell Mum I've gone to talk to a friend. It's true enough. See you in a bit."

Tammy finished her lips with a dark red lipstick, then dashed out the door with her half-charged phone, leaving Freya alone with her thoughts and her cat.

"Well, Mr. Fluffbum. Was that the right thing to do? I know she would be insufferable if she stayed here, but will she be safe out in a storm with some biology student or carpenter?"

Mr Fluffbum paused in grooming his black and white fur and looked at her long enough to blink once, slowly.

"I hope that's a yes. I wish I could understand your thought processes. Mind you, that would be a big jump from the way things are at the minute. I'm not sure I understand anyone else's thought processes right now. Why would Tammy want to go out on a night like this, right after we lost our house? I wish Mum and Dad would get back. I didn't think I'd miss Tammy - she's out so much anyway - but it's pretty lonely here after all. Even with you."

Freya curled up as close to Mr Fluffbum as she could without disturbing him, and tried to imagine that this cramped room was her own. Even when she closed her eyes, she couldn't manage it. The bed was too hard, the smells were all wrong. But she must have gone to sleep eventually.

CHAPTER THREE

NIGHT WAKENING

That night, Freya dreamed of tsunami again. She'd had recurring dreams of giant waves most of her life, ever since a real wave had plunged her into the water when she was small. Freya didn't know how old she'd been when the wave rolled her, but the memory was still crystal clear. She'd been playing in the waves, jumping with them as they rolled into shore, letting the swell of water help her to defy gravity. Suddenly, a huge wave had risen before her. She'd tried to leap with it, but it curled over her head, momentarily encasing her in a tube of air surrounded by water. She could see the sun glinting through the sea above her head. A few tiny fish were visible, silvery sides flashing. It was beautiful.

Then the wave broke, flooding her air-filled tube, and Freya was tumbled over and over, white foam filling her eyes as the wave battered her against the sandy bottom. She couldn't tell which way was up. Her need for air burned in her, her instinct telling her to breathe while her brain told her to keep her mouth shut against the roiling water. She didn't quite manage to obey her brain. Salt burned the back of her nose as she choked on seawater. She started to panic and flailed wildly, forgetting her swimming lessons completely. A moment later, it was over, the wave receding and leaving her gasping on wet sand. She'd been unable to stand up before the next wave flowed around her, this one not so large, but still terrifying to the recently submerged Freya. Somehow, she found her feet and ran from the oncoming tide, collapsing again when she was halfway up the dune, well out of reach of the waves.

Freya woke up, gasping as if she'd been running from the waves again. The dusky spider-speckled ceiling came slowly into focus as she lay on her back fighting for breath. Mr Fluffbum nudged her hand for attention, and she gratefully patted the cat. As she regained breath control, her reasoning brain woke up.

It's just because of what happened to the cottage, she assured herself. *Nothing to worry about here. We're much farther from the sea now.*

Freya lay in the dark, listening. All she could hear was rain pattering on the window.

"Mum? Dad?" There was no answer. Freya sat up. Mr Fluffbum twitched an ear but remained still, a dark blob on the pale coverlet of her bed. The room was poorly lit, but Freya could see a couple of motionless shapes on the biggest bed, separated as far as the still-narrow bed would allow. At least her parents appeared to have made it back. But why hadn't they woken her to ask about Tammy? There was no sign of her sister in the room. Freya wondered where the boxes and piles of their things had ended up. How late was it? Surely Tammy should be back by now. Moving slowly to avoid bumping into things, Freya still managed to walk into the end of an unseen box. She muffled a curse, barely, as the hard edge caused a shooting pain up her shin. So that's where the things were. Her parents stirred briefly but subsided without fully awakening.

Freya crept closer to the window. Where *was* Tammy? And why had Freya woken up? The rain was tapping softly against the window, nothing like the earlier deluge. Just as she was noting that, a sudden gust of wind made the rain batter noisily. Was that the noise that had awoken her? She didn't think so. Life in their cliff-top home had meant she was used to the sound of battering rain at night. She shivered. It still didn't look like good weather to be outside in. Had Tammy gotten safely to the wildlife centre? Perhaps she hadn't noticed how late it was. Lightning split the night and thunder rumbled. Freya gasped; her heart thundering almost louder than the storm outside. The lightning had momentarily been tinted red. And just outside the window, the flash of light had illuminated a figure peering in. Freya jumped back.

Without any desire to go closer, but equally unable to relax when she knew there was someone outside, Freya edged closer to the window again. Predictably, she could now see nothing outside. The dark skies and rain combined to make it impossible to identify anything. There was a scuffle beside her as Mr Fluffbum leaped onto a conveniently placed box to peer out beside her. Lightning flashed in the distance, and Freya was afforded a momentary view. Moving away in the direction of the retreating storm was a lone figure. The reflections of streetlights on the wet ground made it look like the figure's feet weren't touching the ground.

"Now that is just odd. I'm going to have to ask Mum a bit more about storm deities in the morning. I wonder if Tammy knows anything?"

Freya considered for a moment. She shouldn't go outside at night, by herself. But she couldn't leave this mystery unsolved. Not with Tammy still out there somewhere. She gave Mr Fluffbum a quick scratch under the chin.

"What do you think, Mr Fluffbum, shall we go see who's walking in the storm? It seems an odd thing to do. I don't know if I mean someone walking around or us going out to check. Maybe both. Oh well, everything else is strange tonight, why not that too?" She edged over to the door, attempting not to bump into anything else, then opened it with care, trying not to let it creak. She had to go down badly lit stairs - mercifully carpeted - in order to reach an outside door.

How on earth did someone manage to look in the window on the second floor?

Peering out the front door, cold night wind touched her cheeks, and a spattering of raindrops dampened her clothes. She hesitated. She couldn't see the figure anymore. She should simply go back to bed. Mr Fluffbum pushed past her and set off down the steps in the direction of the beach.

"Oh, no, let's not go out there!" Freya said in dismay.

The cat ignored her and continued.

"Really. Sometimes I see why people get dogs, at least they occasionally listen to their owners."

Mr Fluffbum paused to give her a glare as though he understood exactly what she was saying.

"Sorry, I still love you, Mr Fluffbum," said Freya.

The cat continued on his way. Freya followed the cat, who led her almost all the way to the beachfront before pausing. Freya wondered why he persisted through the squalls of rain, but she kept at his heels through the maze of bungalows and guesthouses that lined the streets of their coastal town. They were at the edge of the town when they stopped, further away from Freya's ex-cottage than she'd realised. Here, instead of a cliff, gentle sand-dunes backed the beach, followed by an encampment of holiday and caravan parks. The tide had gone out in the hours they'd taken to find the bed and breakfast and move their things. The waves thundered at a safe distance now, though they were still intimidatingly large.

Freya followed the beach path through the dunes and paused to look out to sea. She was slightly sheltered from the wind by the dune to her right. She couldn't see her ex-cottage at all from here, which was probably a good thing. She thought she might slip back into tears if she saw its familiar roof being pounded by waves again. What she could see was distracting enough. Over the sea, thunderclouds reflected the orange glow of streetlights from the town for a short way, before receding into darkness. Where visible, the underside of the clouds looked like it was boiling. Occasional lightning strikes lit up the sky. The wind whipped through the marram grass with a thin keening noise, audible between the crashes of the waves. Windblown sand bit into her pyjama trousers.

Running along the beach towards her were a small group of what looked like young boys about her size. Their tops were off, and they seemed to be racing each other. Red storm light flickered around them, though the storm itself held no such light. They caught sight of Freya, and veered towards her. She took a step back uncertainly, and tripped over her cat.

"Why did you bring me here, Mr Fluffbum?" she muttered. "There's weird people." Mr Fluffbum looked up at her and twined around her legs, purring.

One of the boys arrived ahead of the others. He stepped forward, taking on the role of spokesman. This close, she could see he was probably her age, older than she'd first thought. He was whip-thin with wiry muscles in his arms and his ribs were showing. Dark curly hair blew into his eyes and he impatiently shoved it back.

"Hey, cat-girl, you don't belong out here tonight."

Ignoring the insult, Freya tried to reply with dignity.

"Well hello to you, too. I live in this town; I'm allowed to be out here." She was defiant in the face of opposition, no matter that she'd been wondering if she should be here a moment before.

"There's 'allowed', and then again, there's 'why in Tethys' name are you on the beach in a storm when *we* are racing'. But, since you're here, you must be here to race us. 'Cos we don't need cheerleaders. Join in! Come on, last one to the lightning is octopus bait."

Baffled, Freya watched the whole troupe of boys wheel around and race for the sea, where the lightning flashed down obligingly. She felt no inclination to join them, even when the leader turned and beckoned to her. Lightning was deadly, she knew. It would be crazy to run towards it, even if it wasn't over the sea. And surely, if she didn't go near the waves, she couldn't be octopus bait? Who were these crazy storm-racers?

As the boys reached the waves, she expected them to splash in, running through the breakers like surfers would. Instead, they ran on, leaping waves but skimming over the surface. They were clearly more than just crazy boys.

Thunder rolled, echoing along the empty beach. For a moment Freya thought she could see Thor with his hammer in the thunderheads.

No, I must be imagining it. No-one's seen Thor for centuries, only his offspring. Or so Mum says.

She shook her head as if to negate the thought. She could hardly see the boys now; the waves were high out at sea. Just as she thought this, she once again glimpsed the leader, racing back towards her, so fast he was on the sand by the time she'd identified him. He raced up to her, panting, and suddenly grinned.

"Sorry you wouldn't race tonight. I guess since it's your first time out we shouldn't make you octopus-bait though. See you again some time, maybe? I'm Lio. Apeliotes, really, but I prefer Lio. 'Cos otherwise they'd call me Ape, and who wants to be called that?" He stuck out his hand, and Freya belatedly realised he meant for her to shake it. She did so, feeling his palm unexpectedly warm and real against hers.

"I'm Freya. Sorry, I don't think I can join in with your sort of race."

"No problem. I just thought it might be fun. Another time?" he asked again.

"Er, sure. Sometime," Freya replied, while privately deciding that she should definitely stay inside at night in future. Even though it might be good to talk to someone other than her family for a change...

Lio looked like he could hear the lie.

"I won't make you run over the waves if you do."

"Oh, good. I suppose that would help. A bit," said Freya.

"Well, look out for me after storms then. I'd better catch up with the others, now. Till next time."

He turned away again with a wave, and was off, fast as the wind. Freya was left alone with her cat once more.

"Well, Mr Fluffbum, was that why you brought me here? To meet someone? Or were you just after some fish?" Freya asked.

For Mr Fluffbum was crouched on the sand, sharp teeth ripping into a small, shining fish that Freya was sure had not been there before. Perhaps Lio had brought it. That would be better than her cat eating something old and smelly, anyway. She waited impatiently for her cat to finish the fish, feeling the cold bite of the wind through her thin pyjamas now that she was still. The cat completed his meal and began washing his face with lazy licks of his paw.

"That doesn't look like it would end up with a clean face, you know."

Mr Fluffbum ignored her comment and continued his ablutions. At last, he was done. Freya was shivering by then. Together they walked back to their temporary home. It felt like it took forever. Freya was glad to snuggle under the blankets to warm up when at last they got home. It took her a while to drop off, as she considered her unusual evening out. At least Mr Fluffbum had got fed. Finally, sleep claimed her.

It seemed like only the next moment that Freya was awoken by a clatter at the door to their crowded room as Tammy returned and promptly fell over a box.

"Be quiet, Tammy. You'll wake Mum and Dad," muttered Freya.

"Surely this is more stuff than we had at home?" Tammy complained in a hissing whisper. "Oh, Freya, did I wake you up? Sorry. I have had the best time, thanks for being a sport this evening. Shame about having to come back here instead of having my own bed to fall into, though. I could get truly cross at that sea goddess."

Freya yawned, then stared at her sister as her words processed through a sleep-dazed brain.

"What time is it? And what would you do? I mean, if they're real, then goddesses are a fair bit more powerful than we are. We're only demi-goddesses."

"Yeah, yeah, and our powers are that of demis, far less than full-blood deities, I know." Tammy used the shorter, easier-to-say term of demi to refer to their demi-goddess nature. "Doesn't stop me from wanting to do something amazing though. One day I will, just you wait. But meanwhile, I am all for having fun, and fun is what I have had. Pure humans are so innocent. At least at first."

Tammy grinned, the faint light in the room showing the white blur of her teeth. Freya shook her head.

"Should I ask, or is it yet another of those things I am too young to know about?"

"Oh, definitely too young. But you should go visit the wildlife rescue place anyway. You'd like the animals, seeing how much you like that cat of yours."

"Er, Tammy..."

"Yeah?"

"Did you see anyone hanging around here, before you came in?"

"Other than me and Dan, I don't think so. But there were storm sprites out earlier. You know, the ones you get with lightning. I avoid them if I can. They used to tease me when I was about your age, trying to get me to run races with them. As if even a demi could win in a race against one of them. Why, did you see one?"

"Maybe. Yes. That's probably what it was," said Freya doubtfully.

"Oh well. Like I said. Avoid them if you can. Mum always said they were bad news."

There was a creaking from their parents' bed as someone turned over.

"Ugh, it's too weird having all of us in one room. I'm going to sleep."

Tammy turned her back on everyone and drew the covers on the sofa-bed over her head. Freya sighed, and followed suit. There was too much weirdness for words, tonight.

CHAPTER FOUR

DIFFICULTIES AT THE GUEST HOUSE

The next morning was chaotic. The cramped room was overly full with four people and a house worth of belongings in it. Everyone was grumpy from lack of sleep and displacement. Even Mr Fluffbum seemed out of sorts, with no regular cat food to start his morning. Freya managed to improve her cat's mood by salvaging some boiled egg from breakfast. Her mum and dad hardly spoke, passing salt and pepper fiercely to each other. Freya was amazed at how much anger could be expressed with a polite gesture. Tammy slept through the breakfast hour, then woke up late, hungry and demanding food.

"And where were you last night, young lady?" Dion frowned at Tammy, hands on hips as he watched her fumbling through her bag in search of something.

"None of your business, Dad. Maybe if you spent more time paying attention to us instead of to your wine magazines, I'd want to tell you."

"None of your lip, young lady. I asked a reasonable question, and you can give a reasonable answer," said Dion.

"Why should I? You never do," countered Tammy.

Danae interrupted.

"That is quite enough. Did you even think about what you were doing, leaving your sister by herself in a strange place? Anything could have happened to her. You're grounded for the next week, do you understand? And the next time you're left in charge of your sister, you stay with her."

Tammy opened her mouth to argue.

I don't want to be stuck in the middle of this, thought Freya. She avoided the rest of the argument by sneaking back into the breakfast room to procure cereal for her sister, where she was caught by the proprietor as she came in to set out the crockery for the next day.

"No breakfast outside the hours of seven and eight, thank you. And no coming into this room unless you're with your parents." The short, plump proprietor had grey-tinged skin that looked unhealthy in the morning light, and a steely voice. Her hair stuck up in tufts wound around with what were probably meant to be jaunty ribbons. Freya was terrified of her. After that, Freya refused to do anything else for her older sister.

"Go yourself if you want milk. I don't want to be yelled at by that gnome."

"Freya, don't call people gnomes unless you've asked them their heritage. She could just be one of Hera's clan. Though she's not house-proud enough." Danae frowned at the musty walls. Freya grinned to herself. Her mother was so easily distracted by trying to diagnose people's demi-heritage.

After breakfast, her dad was on the phone, arguing with his boss from the snatches of conversation that Freya overheard.

"But I can't just head off on a buying trip now. I don't even have a house for my family." There was an angry pause.

"Yes, yes, I know you depend on me, but so do they."

An even longer pause.

"Well, if you put it like that, I suppose I have to," said Dion.

That didn't sound promising. Her dad worked with wine companies, and often visited the large vineyards of the south. Sometimes Freya wondered why they didn't all just move south too. But her mum had always vetoed such suggestions.

"It's too expensive, for one. And your father's bacchanalian tendencies would overwhelm us, for two."

Freya had never quite dared to ask what bacchanalian tendencies were. She suspected it was better not to know. When she was smaller, Danae had explained that Dion was a demi descended from Dionysus, god of wine. That made perfect sense to Freya, given her dad's job, not to mention the amount of time he spent in the pub. But as she grew older, she was beginning to realise that an affinity for grapes was probably not all he'd inherited. She didn't want her golden world view to be clouded by dark hints, so she ignored them when she could.

Her mum pulled out her ancient laptop, and started searching rental adverts. As she often did, she kept up a monologue as she searched.

"It's such a shame we can't get back the deposit for our house. That would make it so much easier to find somewhere new. After all, it's not our fault the goddess was angry."

"Isn't it?" Tammy was lying on their shared bed, giving herself a manicure.

"No, Tammy, it's not. Even if my father was a fishing magnate."

"What's a mag- thing, Mum?" asked Freya.

"A big boss. Your grandfather ran the biggest fishing company in the southern hemisphere, before it went bust."

"Is that why we don't eat fish?"

"It's part of the reason. The issue was more that when your grandfather's company did go broke, it wasn't for any mundane reasons. Rather, the local sea goddess took offence, and expressed that in a very real and direct way. At least the plague didn't get him, I guess. Anyway, my mother figured all this out after his ships went down, and she taught me. So now, we're watchers. Messengers, if we could get someone to listen. I've pretty much given up on that. I'm not cut out to be a journalist. We're not responsible for what happens, but we are supposed to keep an eye on it. There was another oil spill last month, I expect that didn't help. And cod stocks have never been so low, despite the fishing bans."

Overwhelmed by this flood of information on a subject her mother usually avoided, Freya focused on the easiest-to-target part of her mum's speech.

"You always talk about cod. As though we cared about some fish or other."

Tammy made horrible fish-mouths at Freya, who flapped her hands back.

"You should know enough to care, that's why I tell you. Anyway, as I was saying, someone could have killed a dolphin with a trawler, that often brings on deity-driven storms. And if we're the only deity-descendants in the area, we get the blame. Or possibly it's more personal, thanks to your grandfather. His ships did come this far north, so I suppose he could have angered this goddess too. Be that as it may, what we need now is somewhere to live. Oh, what about this one... seaside apartment... no, I guess that wouldn't work. Let's give that sea goddess some space for a bit. We do need to keep an eye on things near the sea though."

"Why do we, Mum? Surely we've just seen that seaside dwellings are a bad idea?" Freya was indignant.

Tammy chimed in.

"Yeah, and haven't we known that for like, my whole life?" She blew fiercely on her freshly painted nails.

"Tammy, don't blow that stuff my way, it stinks!" Freya protested.

Their mother ignored the minor squabble and continued with her exposition.

"In that the sea has been encroaching your whole life, yes. But the situation has been going from bad to worse, and the sea gods and goddesses need to be placated, if this whole sea-rise issue is going to be resolved."

"I thought that was due to climate change? That people made?"

"Yes, but climate change isn't just some human waste issue. The gods and goddesses don't like what humans have done to the world. Don't you listen to the lessons I give you?"

"We can't avoid your lessons, Mum. You go on and on." Tammy waved her arms around to indicate how long their mum went on for.

"It sounds like I need to go on more, if you haven't got the basics right yet," said Danae.

"I'm just telling you what we learn at school," said Tammy.

Freya nodded. She was also confused by the difference between what her mum said and what school told them.

"School doesn't teach you everything. It's too human-centric. Now, I have a house to find. Ah, how about this. It's another row-house, I hate that, being so close to others, but it's a bit inland. Not too far from the sea, but inland. Plenty of countryside around it."

Tammy made a face. Freya made one back.

"Stop grimacing, girls. It's cheap, so there's a chance we could afford it. Dion, are you off the phone yet? Look at this place, shall we see if we can get it?"

"Sorry, Danae. I've been called away by work. You'll have to manage the next move. Choose something in our budget."

"You're going away *now*?" Danae's face was somewhere between disbelieving and furious.

Dion shrugged.

"I have to if I want to keep my job. It's not for long, just a couple of weeks."

"I know we need the money, but that's just the worst timing. Can't they wait? It's only wine."

"Danae, there is nothing *only* about wine."

Freya tuned out. This was an old argument, with no ending in sight.

An hour later, Danae had narrowed her search to a small selection.

"This one I found earlier looks best. But we'd have to move north."

Tammy was less than pleased.

"You mean I'd have to change schools? Seriously? I have *just* got a good group of friends here."

Freya wondered if it was the school friends Tammy was worried about, or the mysterious Dan. Their mother was not sympathetic.

"You can take a bus, I expect. Or get used to a new school. Oh! Cursed Fafnir. It's got a huge up-front deposit requirement. We'll never manage that. I suppose we can try to find somewhere else cheap, locally. Come on, Dion. You must have some opinion?"

Their dad looked up from his perusal of a wine trader magazine he'd picked up somehow. It seemed like an odd thing to have rescued from their now-destroyed cottage.

"Yes, yes, local would be good. Close to the station."

Freya was sure her mum rolled her eyes at that unhelpful response.

"Well, we'll see what we can do, but I expect you'll have to bus to the station. Hmm. What do you think of staying in a beachfront holiday park over winter, girls?"

"Sounds chilly." Freya pulled a blanket over herself to demonstrate. The cat who had been sitting on the blanket stalked away indignantly. "Sorry, Mr Fluffbum. I didn't see you there."

"I've had enough of the beach, Mum. Isn't the loss of a house a huge sign that we shouldn't be so close?" Tammy was always more to-the-point than Freya.

"Yes, but surely a cabin with separate rooms is better than trying to live on top of each other in this one room, don't you think? And it's not actually on the beach. That's just marketing."

"I guess."

Tammy's response was lukewarm, but Freya had to nod her head in agreement. She wanted more space after just one night. Though she wasn't keen on being near the beach, either.

"Well, I'll make the call now. It would mean we wouldn't have to leave this town right away; you could keep going to the same school for a bit, girls. Would that make you happier, Tammy?" said Danae.

"I suppose. I still don't see why we don't move further from the sea, but anything is better than more time in the same room with my entire family."

"That's unkind, Tammy. I know it's difficult to share such a crowded space, but please don't make it worse with your attitude."

Tammy flounced out of the room, but returned a few moments later in a completely different mood.

"I can't believe it, Freya, she *must* be a gnome!" she giggled.

From outside their cramped room, the voice of the proprietor could be heard, a flat, grumpy intonation.

"No breakfasting after hours, young lady. I know you can hear me. Breakfast is between 7 and 8am, no excuses."

Tammy had covered her mouth and was letting forth small, explosive gasps as she tried not to laugh. Freya caught her eye and indicated the pillows on the bed. Tammy buried her face in them, her shrieks of laughter still audible despite her attempts to muffle them. At last, she subsided.

"Sorry. It was just so funny."

Freya rolled her eyes.

"Sure, Tammy, get us chucked out of this place, why don't you?"

"I'm not trying to, but I was just nipping into the breakfast room to get something else to eat, and she emerged from under a rug! I mean, really under it! I don't know what she was doing there. It was like some horror movie. Except that her crazy hairdo got caught in those stringy bits along the edge of the rug, and she just stood there fighting with it, before she saw me. I just ran, but oh, it was so good." She buried her face in the pillow again.

"Seriously, Tammy, she came out from under a rug? That's not gnomish behaviour. More like... oh, I don't know. Mum, what lives under rugs?"

Their mother, who was holding a phone to her ear, threw a harried glance their way and shrugged.

"Dust mites? Hush now, I'm on hold."

Tammy collapsed in giggles again, and even Freya couldn't resist a chuckle.

"A bit bigger than that, Mum. More supernatural," said Tammy when she'd recovered.

"Oh, probably a kobold, then. You girls will have to be polite, or we'll all suffer."

"But aren't all kobolds short hairy men, Mum?" Freya was curious. They'd only covered kobolds briefly as homework.

Danae covered the phone with her hand for a moment.

"And what species continues to exist if it's all made up of hairy men? I thought you'd done more biology than that, Freya."

"I thought they could be like aphids, with virgin births. Look, Mum, no need to go into more details. We don't get sex ed until next year at school."

Tammy and Freya exchanged looks - Freya embarrassed, Tammy still barely holding in hysterical laughter. Trust Mum to go straight into unnecessarily gritty detail. Their mum had always had a bit of a thing about equality in mythology. Usually, it made Freya laugh. Today was no exception. She lost her embarrassment in a gale of giggles. Finally, when Danae appeared ready to throw her phone in exasperation, the sisters settled down.

"Alright, Mum, we'll be polite. Won't we, Tammy?"

"Sure, sure." Tammy's casual hand wave didn't bode well for her politeness, but it was the most assurance she was likely to give.

CHAPTER FIVE

A NEW HOME

T hey'd ended up moving into a glamorously named 'beach chalet'.

"Honestly, it's just a fancy name for a shed with bunks and a kitchen," grumbled Tammy as they struggled to spread their rescued things out.

"At least it's got more than one room." Freya had to share a bunk room with Tammy, and there had already been a tussle over who got the bottom bunk. Freya had won because of her cat not being able to climb ladders. She was sure Tammy had wanted it because it was easier to slink quietly out of a bottom bunk.

"That's true. I am so glad we don't have to share with our parents anymore," said Tammy in heartfelt tones.

"Because you find it hard to sneak out?" Freya was suspicious of her sister's motivation.

"No, because teenagers aren't supposed to share a room with their parents. *And* because it's hard to sneak out." Tammy smirked.

Freya threw a pillow at her, which Tammy easily batted aside. The pillow fell on an untidy stack of belongings which hadn't yet found a home. The stack promptly fell over with a crash.

"Girls, I hope you're unpacking, not fighting." Danae looked through the door frame. There was no actual door, which made any sneaking out pretty much moot.

"It's hard to unpack when there's nowhere to unpack into." Tammy immediately went into offensive mode, perhaps hoping to avoid being told off. Freya took a different approach, and picked up the first object she could put her hand on. Lifting a piece of ragged fabric, she waved it in her mother's direction.

"Where do you want this, Mum? Isn't it your old cloak?"

"Oh, so it is. What was I thinking? I can't believe that old thing got rescued and not my new one. That one's practically rags already."

Mission distraction, successful. Freya exchanged a slightly smug glance with her sister.

"But don't let my things get in your way, girls. Put anything of mine in a pile on my bed. You'll need to make some shelves out of the boxes, or something like that."

When they had finally found homes for the random assortment of gear they'd ended up with, Freya and Tammy headed outside. There wasn't much to look at. There was nowhere around the beach chalet to grow a garden, even if it had been allowed. Grass stretched desert-like between their abode and the identical, uninhabited one next to them. Beyond that, the land was increasingly bare and sandy as it led towards the sea. Like most of the holiday parks and mobile home lots in the area, the 'beach' part of the name was something of a misnomer - the beach was several hundred metres away. Freya was secretly glad of that. Her tsunami dream had been recurring with depressing frequency since their cottage fell into the sea.

Their diet was low in green things as a result of the lack of garden, but Freya's mum was the only one to lament that fact loudly. In times of plenty she was wont to force salad on all her family. Freya missed the salads, but didn't want to tell her mother so. It would make everyone feel worse.

Their dad was especially disgruntled on his return from his wine-selling trip. Freya never heard them arguing, but she could feel the tension between her parents increasing daily. She wasn't sure why - they'd been together all Freya's life. But something seemed to be wrong between them apart from the daily grind of working and feeding the family. She and Tammy were doing the dishes - by hand, the chalet didn't possess even last-century technology like a dishwasher. Their parents had walked off in different directions a few minutes earlier.

"Have you noticed the way Mum and Dad are acting, Tammy?"

"Hard not to, isn't it?" Tammy handed Freya a dripping cup.

"Yes, but aren't you worried?" Freya grabbed the cup, a moment too late to stop it dripping sudsy water on the floor.

"They'll figure out whatever it is themselves. They're adults, it's their job. Besides, there's nothing we can do, you know if we say anything Mum will just get uptight and Dad will say he's got an important work call to make."

Freya reluctantly agreed. That was exactly what had happened the few times she'd tried to ask her parents about the way they were acting.

"Anyway, I'm busy working on my own relationships, I don't want to have to think about our parents having one. I mean, ugh! This place is too small for anyone to have a relationship, *I* think." Tammy demonstrated the smallness of the chalet by gesturing around with her dripping dishcloth.

"Ugh, stop it, Tammy. You're not still seeing Dan, are you? I thought he went back to wherever he came from. London, or somewhere."

"Leeds, Freya, big difference. Yeah, he went back. Such a waste. But he's coming back soon to do more restoration work, he says. Of course, there's a new guy at school, too. Only just a demi, his ancestry is so long ago. But he's an Eros demi, so he's pretty hot."

"Surely everyone will be after him with that sort of background?" Freya might not be interested in boyfriends herself, but she knew that Eros had been the god of love.

"Yep, that's why I need to work on the relationship."

Freya sighed. This was such a typical Tammy-attitude.

"Tammy, do you ever stick with one person? I get dizzy with the number of people you get to know in a month."

"Where would the fun be in that? You're only young once."

Freya thought, once again, that she should be the older sister, not Tammy. Tammy just seemed so... lightweight. Maybe that wasn't quite the right word. She, Freya, was serious by nature, and found it hard to be as light-hearted as Tammy. Maybe this was just Tammy's way of dealing with the strangeness of their life. It worried Freya deeply.

"Sure, Tammy, but you could try sticking with one guy for, oh, a few months. Just for the novelty. Though I guess given we're moving again soon, there's not much point in my suggesting that."

"No point at all. Cheer up, Freya. One day you'll be as old as me, and think of the fun you'll have if you lighten up a little." Tammy pretended to toss a plate Freya's way. Freya grabbed it out of her hands.

"I don't think I want to lighten up that much. I'd float away. I'll just grow into a little old cat lady, thanks."

"You're going the right way about it. From what I hear, you only talk to people about that cat of yours."

"Sure, but what else can I talk about? It's not like everyone at school knows we are demis. Not even the trolls know that. And Mum always tells us not to let anyone know, in case they try to take advantage of us."

"Yeah, yeah, I know. Frigg knows what she thinks they would do, apart from say we're crazy. Maybe she just doesn't want us committed to a mental hospital.

Or given medication, or something. But seriously, try talking about something else. It might even get you some friends."

Freya turned away, feeling tears prick at her eyes. She desperately wanted friends. She just didn't know how to get them. Somehow, she always said the wrong thing at the wrong time. She talked about her cat because it was a normal thing, something other people might relate to. Unlike their foraging ventures to stay fed, their hasty removal from the bed-and-breakfast before their paid time was up because Tammy *had* offended the kobold lady who ran it, or worst of all, their mother's certainty that their house had been washed into the sea by an angry North Sea goddess. OK, that last bit was probably reality too, but she didn't have to like it.

"Oh, never mind, Freya. You'll get there one day." Tammy put her arm round Freya's shoulders in an attempt to cheer her up. Unfortunately, her dishcloth was still in her hand, and it dripped over Freya's top.

Freya shrugged her arm off.

"Tammy!"

"Just figure out what mask you're prepared to wear, one that people can relate to, and you'll be fine. That's what I do."

"A mask? What, like paint and papier mâché? I don't see you doing that."

"No, dummy, not an actual mask. A pretend mask. One in your imagination. You, know, like playing charades, just keeping your character going all the time." Tammy demonstrated, passing her hand over her face and changing expressions.

"Gosh, how comforting. So, I just have to not be me, and I'll find some friends? Not what I need to hear, Tammy."

Freya tossed her tea towel at Tammy and stepped away from her sister, balling her fists hard enough that her nails bit into her palms. Surely, one day, she could find some friends who accepted her for herself. Surely.

CHAPTER SIX

A FAMILY FRACTURE

As Freya, Tammy and Danae reached the door of the chalet after a rare shopping trip, they gratefully lowered their heavy bags to the slightly damp ground. While they removed their muddy shoes, a burst of off-key song reached their ears.

"Dad!" yelled Tammy, without reducing her volume to allow for nearby ears. "When will you learn to sing in tune?"

Freya rubbed the ear nearest to Tammy.

"When will you learn not to yell with us beside you?" she muttered.

"Dion, have you been to work today?" Danae's tone was sharp, as it always was when their dad had obviously been drinking on the job.

"No work to go to today."

"Well why not? You had a job yesterday, didn't you?"

"Been let go. Not enough vintners in this part of the world, apparently."

"Surely no fewer than there were last week? I thought vineyards were a growth area, what with the warmer climate? You didn't say anything about this, this morning."

Their mother's voice was strained, her rising anxiety apparent.

"Nothing to say, was there. I guess all those vintners think they can sell their product themselves. Let 'em learn. They'll come crawling back when they find no-one wants their vino. I give them a week. Or a month. Not long, anyway." Dion's voice was slurred, one word blending into the next.

Freya looked at her dad in horror. She'd never heard him sound as bad as this.

"Girls, take our food into the kitchen. Get yourself something to eat. Dion, come outside. We're going for a walk. Take an anorak, it's chilly out here." Danae was sharp, commanding as she rarely was.

To Freya's surprise, her father did as he was told, pulling on his shoes and a coat from beside the door. There was a lost look in his eyes that was unfamiliar, and deeply worrying. She stepped back to let him pass her.

"Go on in, Freya. See what you and Tammy can make that tastes good. Think of it as a challenge," said Danae.

"But I want to talk to Dad-"

"Make the dinner, please, Freya. Your father and I are going to have a bit of a talk."

Her mother was determinedly positive now. Freya took one more look at her dad, and scurried inside. Whatever they were going to talk about, she was pretty sure she didn't want to hear it. As she closed the door, she could hear her mother's voice rising, anger or anxiety or both lending a sharp edge to her tongue. She blocked her ears as she ran to the kitchen. It didn't help.

For weeks after the shopping day, their mum and dad hardly talked. Family meals were tense, Tammy's comments about her day falling on apparently deaf ears, Freya's hesitant queries unanswered.

Freya came home from school one day to find things missing from around the chalet.

"Mum! We've been burgled!"

There was no answer from Danae.

"Mum's not back yet, obviously. What's the problem?" Tammy appeared, still wearing her high school uniform.

"There's things gone."

"Who would bother to burgle us?" Tammy said rhetorically. "It's not like the thrift shop wants their things back."

"But there's stuff missing."

Tammy accompanied Freya on a tour of the small house.

"You're right. There *is* stuff missing. But it's a weird selection. I don't think a burglar would take some cans of baked beans and the tin-opener." Freya bit her lip. Tammy was right - but that meant something big was wrong.

A hunch struck her, and she went to their parents' room. There, she opened the drawers on dad's side of the bed. Empty. Freya gazed at the bare wood of the bottom of the drawer, hoping that it would be a trick of the light, and in a moment, she would see it magically refilled with her father's worn clothes.

Freya had no such luck. Staring at the dusty wooden drawer, Freya wished fiercely that they lived in a world where that sort of magic existed. Instead, it was all hiding talent, pretending to be normal, while struggling to get enough to eat. She blinked back tears as she heard her sister enter the room. Together, they stared at the empty drawer. Its emptiness seemed a betrayal.

"Did he hate living with us so much?" she whispered.

Tammy replied in a tight voice.

"I think he just hated being poor. And jobless. Maybe he found some way to support himself in the lifestyle he wished to be accustomed to. Without us. Oh, Freya." Tammy's voice wobbled. The girls exchanged a rare hug. "What will Mum say?"

Freya snorted.

"Probably something like 'pass the salt, Tammy, you're the closest one'. It's not like she's said much more than that, recently. I'm sure you've noticed the deadly silence at dinner."

"Hard not to notice. I wonder what Dad did, to annoy Mum so much?"

"Somehow, I don't think Mum's going to tell us."

In the event, their mum didn't say anything, at least not to Freya. Freya wondered if she talked to anyone about her husband's disappearance. Her mother was tight-lipped and grimly silent for a long time afterwards. As predicted, Danae refused to answer questions about Dion.

"But will he come back?"

"I doubt it." Dirty dishes plunged into the sink with a violent splash.

"Will we get to visit him? Where is he, anyway?" Freya took the clean dish thrust at her and wiped it dry.

"I doubt it, and I don't know." Another dish plunged to its watery fate a little too hard, and cracked in two.

"Gaia wept, now look what I've done." Conversation closed.

CHAPTER SEVEN

AUTUMN

"Yum, sheep sorrel!"

Freya pounced on the tiny leaves half-hidden in the short grass, and picked one leaf off each of several plants before stuffing them in her mouth. The delicious, sour tang was one of her favourite flavours. Certainly better than the dreadfully bitter dandelion salad their Mum had made last week. They'd been supplementing the family's now-single income by foraging for food, led by Danae, who had substituted herblore for their usual after-school lessons with barely a blink.

"Freya, leave some for me." Tammy shoved her sister aside to gather her own mouthful.

"Don't be greedy, I'm hungry too, you know."

"You're always hungry, even after we've had a charity food box delivered," Tammy said.

"I'm growing faster than you." Tammy couldn't argue with that, thought Freya. Tammy hadn't gained height in a year.

"Outwards, yeah."

"You're not one to talk."

The sisters' casual bickering was interrupted by a distant call.

"Freya. Tammy. Make sure you bring something home."

They sighed as one.

"Yes, Mum."

"OK, Freya, back to the job then. If you can keep yourself from eating everything," Tammy said.

Freya picked just one more tangy leaf to soothe her empty stomach. She loved food foraging when she wasn't hungry, but there hadn't been any food in the community pantry yesterday, so there had been nothing for breakfast this morning. A handful of sheep sorrel was tasty, but hardly filling. She dutifully picked a few leaves for her bag. She looked ahead along the flat country road they were following, overhung with shrubs, and was rewarded with a much tastier sight.

"Look, wild walnuts!"

"Hardly wild if they're beside a road leading to the local hall," Tammy said.

"I don't care, they'll taste good."

A car approached from the distant town, and Freya averted her eyes, pretending to be just enjoying a country walk with her family.

Nothing to see here, we're not freaks eating wild food.

Freya hated people thinking she was odd. It was bad enough *being* odd.

Once the car had passed, Freya ran along the road towards the leaning old walnut tree, which had evidently kept growing after being partially blown over in some earlier storm. It was pinning a fence almost to the ground, in addition to overshadowing the road they were following.

"Thank goodness it's autumn, I don't think I could have waited for the nuts to fall if we'd found this tree in summer."

"In summer we had a house and a garden. And normal food."

"Well, yes. But walnuts are pretty normal. Hazelnuts, too."

Freya gave up on arguing with Tammy, putting her efforts into collecting as many of the smooth, green-husked nuts as she could. The high winds last week had obviously blown a lot of walnuts off the tree, as the husks were beginning to split, revealing glimpses of a pale, wrinkled brown shell underneath. Freya pulled the husk off one nut, and cracked the shell between her teeth before prying out the nut meat. Tammy asked her dryly,

"You know they have to dry before they taste good, right?"

"This tastes good even if it's not ripe yet." That wasn't quite true, thought Freya, grimacing at the faintly bitter skin around the nutmeat, but she was hungry enough not to care. Walnuts, even not-quite-ready walnuts, were much more filling than sorrel. She noticed that Tammy had also paused to open a nut.

"This takes me back." Their mother's voice was bemused. Both girls turned to see their Mum had caught up to them. "We went foraging all the time during the pandemic."

Freya sighed to herself.

Here we go again.

"We know, Mum. You've told us a million times, that's why you know how to forage, you would have starved without whatever that book was. Blah, blah, blah," said Tammy.

"Don't be rude, Tammy. And aren't you glad of it now? We'd be much hungrier if I hadn't taught you how to find your own food," said Danae. There was a wobble in her voice that made Freya's insides squirm.

"I suppose. But it's not a pandemic now, we just lost our house. And couldn't we have called on a house hob or something? They're supposed to keep the occupants of their houses fed, aren't they?" Tammy said.

"Well, if we had a permanent house that might work." Danae's voice had a sarcastic edge now as well as a wobble. Freya wished Tammy hadn't mentioned anything. But her Mum continued, voice rising.

"If you don't mind being fed on earthworms, then yes, I suppose we could have done that. Personally, I prefer not to rely on a supernatural being with badger taste buds, that we don't even have around right now."

Danae turned away, her lips so firmly pressed together that Freya was sure she was trying not to cry. After a moment in which Freya could hear her breathing heavily, she turned back, apparently pretending nothing had happened.

"And I'm just as glad it's not a pandemic again, it was so crowded with foragers back then. Plus of course, there were people getting ill everywhere so we had to be extra careful with washing our gleanings. With just us out here, we have more to choose from, and we're unlikely to get ill unless some angry demi with pestilence in their past curses us. Here, fill this bag with nuts, this tree could keep us in protein all winter if it comes to that." Danae thrust a large paper bag at Tammy.

Freya shuddered. She hoped it did *not* come to that, however much she liked walnuts. The last few weeks had made her acutely aware of how much she liked regular, store-bought food. In contrast to her daughters, their mother seemed to be revelling in the opportunity to revive her old skills, and she reminisced constantly.

"You know, now is one of the best times to be foraging for food. There's so much still available. Now spring, that's the real hungry season. You wouldn't think so, would you? But it's too early for most things to be ready, just a few greens and suchlike. I never thought I'd be sick of asparagus, but I was that year. Now, look, here's another treasure!"

A little way past the walnut, Freya saw her mother reaching over a fence to a short bush with large leaves and small brown roundish things on it. "What's that one?" asked Freya warily. Treasures these days were not always what they seemed.

"It's a medlar!" Her mother smiled. "Something sweet to eat, if we wait for the fruit to blet."

"What does blet mean when it's at home?"

"Er… hmm. To soften with age."

"You mean *rot*, don't you?" Freya scowled at the innocent-looking brown fruit.

"Well, in a way. But it's good. I've had it before."

"Mum, that's so disgusting. You want us to eat rotten fruit, now? Ugh!"

Tammy made exaggerated retching noises. Freya snickered. While she didn't want to eat rotten - no, *bletted* fruit either, Tammy's reaction was so typically overstated.

"What if that wildlife-tending friend of yours offered you bletted medlars. Would you eat them then?" she asked Tammy.

Tammy lifted her chin airily.

"Dan wouldn't offer me rotten fruit in the first place. He has higher standards."

"Well, Miss High Standards, how about Freya finishes collecting walnuts while you and I get those hazelnuts further along. They should be ready by now. If you are lucky, we'll find some pheasant berries too. You can be the taste tester. If you're extraordinarily lucky they'll be ripe. And meanwhile, how about you tell me about this Dan character? I don't believe you've introduced me."

Tammy looked daggers at Freya for bringing up Dan in front of their mother. Freya looked the other way, and continued collecting walnuts. She wondered what pheasant berries were like. It sounded like an unripe one would not be a treat. She could hear her Mum and sister arguing as they advanced towards the hazelnuts. She didn't like Tammy keeping secrets from their parents, but she didn't want to be a snitch, either. Tammy had explained several times in the past that such actions were frowned upon, especially by big sisters.

"Dan's just someone I met at school, Mum," explained Tammy.

Freya opened her mouth to protest this lie, but shut it again. Tammy would definitely call her a snitch if she told her Mum that.

"And what sort of demi is Dan, then?" Danae's voice was alert.

"He's not a demi. Or a were, or a troll. Just a human."

"Well, that's a rarity. I hope he's a nice boy, not hanging with vamps or anything?"

"Ooh, Mum, I would never go out with someone who was 'hanging with vamps'. Anyway, no-one says that anymore. You're so out of date."

"Well, what do they call it now? Update me."

"It's called bleeding up, Mum. And anyway, I don't know anyone who does that. It's a gross idea, who wants to be food?"

"I'm glad to hear we are in agreement with that, at any rate. So, speaking of food, that's all the hazelnuts picked." She called out to Freya. "Have you got the walnuts?

"Yes, Mum."

"Good. Freya, have we got enough salad leaves yet? No? Then everyone on the lookout for fathen or nettles, we can have cooked greens at least. Though it's a bit late for nettles. And there could be apples in the hedgerow, that would be better than pheasantberries."

"You want us to eat nettles now? That's taking hunger a bit far, isn't it?"

"Do you want to eat or don't you, Tammy?" Danae asked.

"I want to eat real food."

"This is as real as food gets."

"Then I want fake food. In a packet," Tammy said.

Near the damp ditch, Freya had found something else that looked familiar. She picked the frondy leaves on their crunchy stem and waved it proudly.

"Look Mum, celery. We could have soup with this, right?"

Freya quite liked soup, it was a comforting food, especially with fresh bread to go with it. Now, she held out the vegetation she'd found for her mother to inspect.

"Not that one! Freya, that's not celery. That's deadly poison. Hemlock water droplet. Put it down and we'll find somewhere to wash your hands. But better look closely at it so you'll see the difference, next time. I don't want any of *that* ending up in our soup! We'd all be in hospital or worse."

Freya dropped the offending plant as though she'd been burned, a curdling anxiety forming in the pit of her stomach at the thought that she had almost poisoned her family. Though the crisis had been averted, the feeling stuck with her, a nagging guilt that spoiled her enjoyment of the day.

The small family trudged on through the chill autumn day, gathering and gleaning. It took several hours before they had enough food to satisfy their mother, by which time they'd ventured far through the countryside beyond the town, and it took them another hour to get back to the holiday home they'd moved into after their time at the bed and breakfast had run its course. The chalet was a slight improvement on the mouldering bed and breakfast, but only in that they no longer all had to squeeze into one room. The owner of the chalet had explained that the reason they were having it cheap was because it was the off season, and they'd be cleaning the shared toilet block themselves. Freya thought the holiday park owner was definitely part troll - or possibly a descendant of Charon. He certainly seemed miserly enough to be a descendant of the stingy river-guarding god.

CHAPTER EIGHT

WINTER

"**I** heard Mum talking to Dad on the phone last night." Tammy leaned towards Freya conspiratorially.

Tammy and Freya were trying to make dinner with a can of beans and an assortment of foraged greens. Danae was still out, working late as she had done often in the last few weeks.

"Wait, what? How do you know it was him?" Freya glanced around to be sure they weren't being overheard.

"She used his name, idiot child."

"I'm not an idiot, and don't call me a child!" She raised her arm, mock-threatening.

"Yeah, yeah. But do you want to know what she said?"

"Maybe..." Arm lowered again, Freya leaned in.

"She said, 'I've had enough of your running around town' - something like that, anyway - 'The girls and I will figure out a way forward ourselves. If you had thought of us before you went off, you'd have stayed home.' So, you know what that means?"

"That you eavesdrop on private conversations?"

"No! If she wanted it private, she shouldn't have been talking outside my window. No, it means that Dad has gone off with someone else. Can you believe it?"

"I don't want to believe it."

Freya put her hands over her ears. She didn't want to know if her dad had major personality faults. He was still Dad to her, and she missed him.

"Oh, spoilsport," said Tammy, but she walked over to the kitchen counter and started hunting for other things to eat. She didn't try to tell Freya any more about what things their dad might have done.

The year drew on and the days grew darker.

"There's nothing growing but toadstools out there now, Mum" Freya complained one bitter afternoon.

"And it's too cold," added Tammy.

While it wasn't raining, the air was chill with a promise of frost. Outside, the long grass on road verges had died off. Even the late harvest apples were long picked.

"Hmmm. I don't want you going after mushrooms, even if we could do with the food. There are too many poisonous ones that look similar to the edibles. At least to the uninitiated. Very well, we'll get back to your history and theology lessons. I haven't taught you much about that since we left the cottage on the cliff. It does mean less to eat today, though. We could be down to cattail tubers soon."

We haven't had home lessons since Dad left. Apart from foraging lessons, of course. Freya knew better than to mention her dad now.

"Do we have to have lessons? Couldn't we just read a book where it's warm?"

Freya was dressed in all the clothing she owned; the chalet wasn't warm except in comparison to outdoors. She tried again to avoid work.

"I'm sure Mr Fluffbum would like the company better if we're quiet."

"You can read books *after* lessons. Your cat will just have to wait for his chance at quiet. Have a walnut and let's get started."

"I have school homework to do," announced Tammy.

"Well, that's a first. Alright, since you're so keen on working, you may do your homework. Freya, come over here by me and we'll go over the Norse gods."

"I need to find something for Mr Fluffbum to eat, though, Mum. He came in with a vole yesterday, I'm sure it's because we aren't feeding him enough and he's trying to hunt. It took me ages to catch it again after he let it go," said Freya.

"At least he cares enough to try and feed you, Freya."

"Ugh, that's gross, Mum!"

"So, Norse gods."

"Oh, alright." Her attempt at diversion having failed, Freya surrendered to the inevitable.

One good thing about the beach chalet was that it wasn't too far to go to meet Lio. She'd followed Mr Fluffbum to the beach most nights after they moved to the chalet. Some of those nights, Lio was there. Freya had been shy, hesitant to talk to him at first. But since he never pushed her to do things she didn't want to, and always had something for Mr Fluffbum, she'd come to look forward to his presence on the beach.

Of course, going to the beach wasn't Freya's idea of fun these days, especially not in the dark of winter, but she had to keep Mr Fluffbum fed somehow. Curiously, he turned his nose up at walnuts. Whenever a storm rolled through the area, her cat led her to the door at night.

"Honestly, Mr Fluffbum," Freya whispered to her cat on one such night, "why do you always choose the times I'd rather be at home in bed to leave the house? I thought cats liked comfort."

Her cat blinked, the glow of his light-reflecting eyes briefly quenched, and scratched at the chalet door again.

"Oh, all right. But it's freezing out there." Freya stepped into her wellies and slipped an anorak from the hook by the door, but waited till she was outside to put it on. It was too noisy, the fabric crackling and liable to wake someone, if she put it on inside. Tonight, it was sleeting. She was both soaked and chilled by the time she wrestled on the coat. She pulled its hood well down, and hoped this trip wouldn't take long. She couldn't wait to get back into her warm, cosy bed.

Down by the dunes, Lio appeared as he invariably did on such occasions, with fish for her cat held in one hand. He was alone this evening, his racing cronies nowhere in sight. The tide was in, so there wasn't much space for racing along the beach - the waves encroached on the dunes at high tide. Lio crouched down to offer the fish to Mr Fluffbum, who took it delicately in his teeth, then turned his back to eat in privacy.

Freya took the opportunity to duck into the small shelter provided by a rare salt-tolerant shrub that was growing on the edge of the dune. She huddled under her anorak, and was relieved when Lio sat down beside her, blocking the wind a little more.

"How do you do that?" she asked him. "How do you and your friends run on water?"

She felt, rather than saw him hunch down miserably.

"They're my brothers. And we all have the gift from our father." His mouth snapped shut audibly.

"You must be demis, then," Freya ventured. Lio didn't reply.

"I wish I knew how to do something like that. I know my family are demis too, but no-one ever tells me anything more than that. How am I supposed to know what powers I might have? I'm old enough to start getting powers now, but nothing's changed."

A particularly savage gust of wind threw sleet at them like needles. Freya covered her face with her arms and hoped it would pass soon. At least it was dark enough that Lio couldn't see her embarrassment at bringing up such a personal issue.

Beside her, Lio – who at least had a top on this evening – shrugged.

"I can't remember being taught that. I guess my brothers and I traded secrets a bit – but mostly we just played tricks on each other."

"Typical boys."

Freya could hear the smile in Lio's voice as he replied.

"Yeah. And I still don't know how to do half what they can. We're all different, though, maybe we can't do what each other does."

"I'd settle for being able to do anything. Anything at all," Freya said. "The way things are now, I might as well be human."

Lio laughed aloud.

"It must be odd living amongst humans all the time. No wonder you have trouble figuring out what your powers are. I guess you can't practise out in the open?"

"As if. I'd be grounded for life if I tried. If I had something *to* try. All I'm allowed to do is identify other demis – and then avoid them," Freya complained.

"At least your parents care. My dad doesn't care what we do." Lio sounded as though that was a problem. Freya noticed that he didn't mention his mum.

Best not to ask about that, she thought.

"Do you think you could teach me anything?" she asked. To Freya's disappointment Lio shook his head.

"I haven't a clue about anything other than wind and storms," he said. "And I can tell that's not your specialty."

Freya leaped eagerly on the clue.

"Do you know what powers I have, then? My mum descends from Freya, and my dad from Dionysus. But Mum does plant stuff, and Dad sells wine. Not exactly the stuff of gods."

Lio shook his head again.

"It's too hard to tell when you're a mix," he said. "I only know you're not like me, not a descendant of Aeolis."

Freya drooped, feeling the bitter cold more now that her bubble of hope had been burst.

"Are you ever here when the weather is good?" Freya asked Lio wistfully, hugging herself tightly to keep in any vestige of body heat.

"No, worse luck. You'll only find me on the edges of the storm. It's a bit rubbish, but that's my life."

"Wow, that *is* rubbish. For me, too. If I have to go down to the seaside, I'd rather it was in good weather. I hate storms."

Lio shrugged. "Sorry. If it helps, it's great to see someone else out here who isn't a deity or one of my cousins."

"Thanks. I think. But if you manage to come on a sunny morning, I'd be just as happy," said Freya.

"I'll bear it in mind, assuming I get any power over my life some day."

Lio looked so downcast, even in the dark, that Freya couldn't help but feel sorry for him, even as the wind buffeted her hood off, exposing her face to the freezing rain.

"Oh. Well, good luck with that, I guess. I'd like some power over my life too. Coming out here is about the only thing I get to decide to do, and even that's governed by Mr Fluffbum. Thanks for keeping him in fish, by the way. We don't have anything at home he can eat, except when we get cat food in a charity box."

"He seems to enjoy my offerings. And it never hurts to keep a cat happy." Lio smiled at the cat, who was now performing his after-meal grooming, licking his paws and swiping them over his face in the lee provided by their bodies.

Mr Fluffbum twined around Freya's legs, then Lio's, and then turned away to lead Freya back to the chalet.

"See, even now I'm being bossed around!" Freya laughed a little, although she was serious.

"You'll never be your own boss with a cat around," called Lio, as Freya rose and followed Mr Fluffbum back over the dune. She waved a hand in acknowledgement. Even if it came about by the whim of her cat, Lio's help with feeding Mr Fluffbum was about the only bright thing in her life at the moment.

CHAPTER NINE

SPRING

The main street was strangely unchanged, Freya thought. Surely, a storm that washed away a family's house and tore apart their lives should change more than just that house. Freya and her Mum were walking around the town on a Saturday morning, looking for examples of practical theology. Freya was enjoying the rare opportunity to spend time with Mum *without* having to look for food, though she'd die rather than say so. Tammy had vanished on errands of her own that morning.

"I wish we got to do more of this. It's much more fun being out and about looking for demis, than it is sitting around talking about them."

"Yes, but you have to know what you're looking for, before you go looking." Typical Mum-brand circular logic. "Now, tell me when you think you've spotted a non-mundane."

"What about that old man? He could be a relative of Woden, couldn't he?" Freya tried to indicate the person across the street without pointing. She felt silly, indicating with her chin.

"What makes you think so?" Mum never let Freya get away with a simple yes or no answer.

"Umm... he's old?"

"Anyone can be old, Freya. Try harder now."

"Er. OK. Um... Well, the big black birds embroidered on the back of his jacket seem like a bit of a giveaway. And oh, I don't know. He looks sort of like a know-it-all."

"The phrase is 'wise'. And the big black birds are ravens. But don't let him see you staring." They hastily turned off the main street. The old man in question was looking at them suspiciously.

"Why don't we make friends with other demis, Mum? Wouldn't it make sense to know more people like us?"

"That's never ended well for us in the past. It's best to stay underground, so to speak. Just another ordinary family." Danae glanced behind them and increased her pace.

"Surely ordinary families don't move as much as we do?" Freya was panting a bit as she tried to keep up with Mum's long, not-quite-running strides.

"Perhaps not. I believe they don't have angry goddesses destroy their homes, either." Danae turned a corner, dodging a wind-blown sheet of newspaper as she did so.

"That doesn't seem fair." The paper Mum had dodged wrapped itself around Freya's legs. "Ugh!"

"Come on, Freya, forget the rubbish. We've been spotted, and we need to get out of here. The last thing we need is a confrontation with some know-it-all Wodenite demi."

"Why?" The question was mostly a gasp for air.

"Because Wodenites think any descendant of Freya is honour-bound to do what they say, and I will not put up with that. Especially since they usually want to re-enact some shamanic rite or other. Definitely not what I want to do with my life - or yours." Danae grabbed Freya's hand, and they broke into a run. Freya wasn't sure what her Mum was trying to tell her, but fear gripped her throat as she was tugged along.

Around another corner, the familiar town seeming all too small with its limited turnings and short streets. The two of them drew up short as the old man who might be a demi appeared suddenly in front of a bakery a few shops down from them. A bus drew up across the road in a screech of air brakes.

"Quick, let's get the bus." They crossed the road hastily and leapt up the steps of the bus.

"Two please," gasped Freya's Mum as she scrabbled for her purse.

"Where to?" the bus driver asked in a grumpy voice.

"Oh. Um. Two stops along, please." Danae seemed flustered, almost dropping her bag as she fumbled for her phone to pay for the bus. Freya looked out past the driver's balding head, and saw the Wodenite crossing the road, too.

"M- mum. He's coming." She could hardly get the words out, anxiety tensing her jaw muscles.

"Is it time to leave, driver?" Danae's voice was tense but controlled.

"All in good time." The driver closed the bus doors, but sat reading from a clipboard for a minute. The old man appeared at the closed door and tapped at it. The driver looked up, shook his head meaningfully, and engaged the engine. The bus lurched forwards abruptly. Freya staggered against her Mum; Danae grabbed for a handhold. Through the bus window Freya saw the old man raising his hand, looking bewildered. To her relief, the bus surged around a corner without slowing to pick him up.

"Come on, Freya, we may as well take a seat." Danae waved Freya further down the bus. Freya took staggering steps towards the middle seats - one, one two three, lurch, one two. She grabbed the handle attached to a seat opposite the back door and swung herself in. Thump. Danae made a more graceful entry beside her, and the tension seemed to drain out of her.

"Sorry about that, Freya. It's not often Wodenites actually do follow us. But I met one once who wouldn't give up, and it's given me a real dislike of them." Danae glanced out the window, apparently checking that the coast was clear.

"What if he was an ordinary old man wanting to catch the bus home?"

"Well, then he'll have to catch the next bus. We'll stay on one more stop. Just in case."

Freya suspected Mum wasn't telling her everything. It seemed odd to go out looking for other demis, but then run when they approached.

"Are there any demis that are safe to spend time with, Mum?" Freya looked back too, and was reassured to see the usual assortment of people out shopping. No bird-embroidered jacket to be seen. Of course, it was hard to spot anyone between the racks of clothes designed for a warmer beach than theirs, stands of postcards and huge signs advertising all-day breakfasts to the tourists.

"I guess most of them are probably safe. A lot don't even know what they are. Our family is unusual, you know. We *know* about our demi heritage on both sides. That's why Di-" Danae broke off. Freya was sure she'd been about to mention her dad.

"Are you ever going to tell us why Dad left, Mum?" Freya pounced on the idea.

"It's nothing I want to talk about. Just... well. Just remember it wasn't your fault. Right, here's our stop. Off you get, Freya."

Typical. Mum's saved by the stop.

Freya felt her face set in a mutinous expression, but she followed her mother off the bus and didn't revive that line of conversation. They'd alighted from the bus outside the main village, but still a reasonable walk from their home. They had to pass several holiday parks and a mini-golf establishment before they reached the park that housed their chalet. Plenty of time to grill Mum about demis before they got home.

"So... if you avoid demis, how did you meet Dad?"

OK, so maybe she wasn't totally leaving that topic behind.

"I don't want to talk about that now, Freya. Maybe when you're older." Danae's voice was tight and she increased her pace.

"But Mum-"

"I mean it, Freya. Now, what do you know about the descendants of Woden? Since there's clearly one in this town, give me a rundown on them."

"Oh, Mum." Freya looked away, towards the succession of empty holiday parks that lined this road. They'd be busy in summer, but now they were desolate.

"Now, please." Mum's face was set in hard lines. It was clear she wasn't going to discuss Freya's dad anytime soon.

"OK, but I seriously think we need to know how to meet demis, Mum, not just how to recognise and avoid them. I mean, since there's apparently so many out there, we can't keep running all the time."

"I suppose you will meet other demis one day. Maybe you have already at school. There's no need to rush things though. And as I've told you earlier, most of them don't know what they are. It's the ones with more recent ancestry who have more obvious features. And there are some odd societies who keep themselves to themselves. But I hope you don't meet any of *them*. They tend to inbreeding."

"If that's what I think it is, I really don't want to know, Mum."

"You don't. So, Wodenites. Go."

As Freya recited the sum total of her knowledge of Wodenites - the descendants of Woden, or Odin - she considered the reason they were out together today. This trip reminded her of why she missed Dad so much. If Dad had taken her out, they'd be making sandcastles on the shore, or eating chips somewhere. In contrast, Mum always wanted to teach her just a little more. There never seemed to be time for fun. Even more so now that Mum's job was the family's only income.

To be fair, practical theology had always been Freya's most interesting home lesson. When she was younger Freya had had to memorise endless lists of gods, goddesses, minor deities and sundry supernatural beings, as well as their attributes. Once she remembered those lists by heart, Mum led them into long discussions of what attributes might indicate that a person was descended from which god or goddess. As they were doing now, they then went out looking for examples. Freya could handle bookwork if she had to, but practical was so much more interesting.

Sometimes, especially as she got older, it was embarrassing to be seen out with her mother, especially when Mum gave people odd stares. But at the same time, she learnt to pick out the descendants of all the Greek deities like Dad, the Norse ones like Mum, the Celtic ones, Indian subcontinental deities (although she had a hard time keeping those straight, there were so many), and all sorts of varieties in between. Because of course, humans being human - or partly human at least - there was no reason for someone descended from one set of deities to marry only other similar descendants. The resulting polyglot was confusing.

"Why aren't we home-schooled, anyway, Mum? I mean, we spend so much time learning stuff with you. We hardly ever get time to be like normal kids. If we were home-schooled, we might have time for regular stuff."

"You know why you have to go to school, Freya. First, I have to work, or we don't eat. Second, we live in this world with other people. Not all of them are demis like us, not even most - or at least not in a meaningful way. You have to know how to get along with other types of people so you can make your way in the world. Now, name the five most common crosses of deity and their identifying traits."

Freya sighed, and recited the requested list. There was the mini-golf place. They'd be home soon.

"Yes, but is that the same everywhere?" she asked once she'd finished the list.

"No, it depends on which country you're in, and which city or town, too," said Danae. "So, remind me what we have in this town."

"Hardly a town by the time we get out here, Mum. But it's mostly trolls, kobolds, and assorted water demis. In the last town there was a were-pack, and they tend to drive everyone else away. Like they drove us away."

Her mother grimaced, but didn't disagree. The move that took them to the cliff-top house had not been a pleasant one.

"Are weres always like that pack?" asked Freya.

"We avoid them for a reason. When we can."

"But didn't you tell us that were-packs were supposed to be about family and order and that sort of thing. Why don't they want to include others?"

"Sometimes they do. Usually, other weres. As demis, we aren't part of their family structure. Now, how do you identify a troll-descendant without talking to them?"

Subject closed. As usual. Even after their hurried departure from a cheap rental in a town to the north, her mother had not been prepared to discuss details of weres. As she listed the ways to identify if someone had troll in their DNA (usually running an estate or with inherited wealth, often unpleasant, usually engaged in subjecting others to online harassment - nothing that would overtly make them any different to anyone else) Freya wondered what Mum was hiding. If anything, her mother's avoidance of the subject made Freya more interested. If only there was an easy way of getting real information on non-mundane subjects. Sure, the internet abounded with stories about weres. However, most of it was pure fantasy as far as Freya could tell.

Take that myth about werewolves only coming out on full moon nights. Freya knew through bitter experience that werewolves were out and about at all times of the month. Freya thought perhaps they should have known that werewolves inhabited that town. It was right there in the name, Wolverton, and in the 24-hour, 7-days a week gym with a large signboard outside stating 'Wolf's Gym'. The large wilderness reserve around it also made it perfect for werewolves.

"So, if wolves like hierarchies, I guess that's why they were in the police."

"Yes. Most of the army is made up of weres too. People who like to know where they stand in relationship to each other."

"People who don't mind being told what to do?"

Freya's Mum laughed.

"Yes. Not like you. Or me."

Freya nodded in emphatic agreement. While she was usually quiet about it, she did *not* like being told what to do.

I didn't realise Mum noticed that.

"So, since the werewolves were the bosses of the police in Wolverton, they must like hierarchy too, right?"

"That's right. I'm sure they must have had some heritage from a law-loving deity too. Iambe, perhaps, or Athena. Some deity without a sense of humour, certainly."

"You know, Mum, even though we lost our house after that, I'm glad we moved from Wolverton." Freya leaped over a puddle that spanned the road, ice riming its edges. It might be spring, but it hadn't got warmer, yet. Her mother picked her way around the edge more circumspectly.

"Me too, Freya. Having them visit the house every week with a different excuse was draining. And when after all that, they said the house was contravening all sorts of bylaws and we had to move out - well. It was a blessing that your father found the clifftop house."

Rather than argue with the authorities, the family had moved on to yet another town, another new school, a new job for Freya's mother.

"How do you manage to find jobs, every time we move, Mum?" Freya swatted idly at the skeletons of teasels by the roadside.

"It's not so bad when you have essential skills. There's always a need for people who can grow plants as if by magic." Danae grinned at Freya, acknowledging that her skill with plants was *actual* magic. "And of course, my resume is filled with people who give glowing references, because once I'm in the door, people see results. You have to remember that a lot of it is attitude. Turning up at the door of a polytunnel complex doesn't do any good on its own. Learning to pull off the right attitude at the right time can be the difference between being run off the property with dogs on your heels, and being offered a job on the spot. I prefer the latter, so I learnt. Of course, having the skills and power to back up the attitude once you have the job is important too. If you're lucky and end up with the power, you might be able to do that too. I think Tammy has something similar, but not quite the same as mine. You - well, I just don't know what you've got, yet."

Freya felt let down. Just when Mum was finally telling her useful things about demi powers, and she had nothing to offer about Freya's own powers. When would she ever learn how her powers worked - or even what they were? At this rate, she'd end up knowing all about werewolves and trolls and nothing about herself. Mum looked at her with a faint smile and gave her long braided hair a gentle tug.

"That's partly why you need to stick with school - sooner or later, you'll find something that calls your power. You just don't know what it's going to be. So, let's get back to the lesson. Tell me what you know about cofgodas and tresgu, and tomorrow we'll go for another walk and see if we can spot anyone descended from one of those."

"Oh, Mum, I can't remember what cof-whatever are. Have I even learnt about them yet? And would we ever see one around here?"

"It sounds like you need more lessons at home."

"No, I don't, Mum! I have school homework to do, too."

I never have enough time to do the things I want to do.

"Oh, well, we'll have to be moving on from this town soon. It's not long till the beaches start drawing summer crowds, and we can't stay on at the chalet then. I've lined up somewhere cheaper for us to move to, further north."

"Do we have to move?"

"Yes. Sorry Freya, no arguments, please."

Freya drooped. While their precarious existence in the chalet wasn't ideal by a long way, she had begun to hope that maybe this time, they could stay in one town, not move on from places grown familiar and therefore loved.

"Never mind, Freya, perhaps there'll be some kids you can be friends with in our next town."

"How can I make friends with anyone? I never have any time, either I'm at school, working, or I'm at home, working. Or I'm looking for something to eat."

"Talk to people at school, Freya. I'm not there, I can't do it for you."

Freya kicked viciously at a stone on the road, and missed. The rest of the walk home was silent.

CHAPTER TEN

SUMMER

They went north before the summer crowds arrived. One town further up the coast, so that Freya's Mum could keep her current job. Another house near the sea, but not on a cliff this time. The new house was in a run-down part of town, graffiti on many walls, litter blowing in the streets. It was too far to get to their old school, so Freya and Tammy had to change schools. There had been arguments before they moved.

"But *why?* I can walk to school," said Tammy in an aggrieved tone.

"It's over an hour on foot and we don't have a car," said Danae.

"Children in developing countries walk that far all the time," said Tammy.

"You complain when you have to walk ten minutes," observed Freya.

"I could catch a bus," said Tammy.

"With what money?" asked Danae, putting her hands on her hips.

"I could get money."

"With a job?"

"Maybe."

"I'm not going to have you doing anything illegal, and that's all there is for someone your age around here, at least out of harvest season. You'll go to the local school." Danae turned away from Tammy. Case closed. Tammy exited the room with a huff. But Freya couldn't leave the subject yet.

"But Mum, I don't want to leave here. Why do summer visitors get to move in, and we have to move out?" she said.

How do I feed Mr Fluffbum if I have to move away from Lio's beach?

"Summer visitors will be paying more than us." Danae's lips pressed tightly together, as though she wanted to say more but was stopping herself.

"Can't we pay more, too?"

"No. Not with your father gone."

Freya hesitated, then asked in a small voice;

"Can't Dad come back? I miss him."

Danae's eyes seemed to flame for a moment; she took a deep breath in through her nostrils. Freya stepped back, uncertain what to make of this reaction. Danae started speaking in an intense, upset voice that Freya recognised from her mother's telephone arguments with her Dad.

"Your father will not be coming back. I told him when he left that if he was going to another woman, he could consider himself no longer part of the family. He's spent the last three years having an affair under my nose, and I am not standing for it any longer. So no. I'm sorry you miss him, but he should have thought of his family before he went wandering."

Freya opened her mouth to protest, then shut it again. There was nothing she could think of to say, the hurt from her mother's words spiralling into an amorphous ache in her stomach.

It was hard to settle into a new school. Few of their clothes had been rescued from the clifftop house, and they had no money for new ones. Freya found herself dressed in second-hand clothes from thrift shops once again - which she didn't mind, except that the kids at the new school often recognised the clothes and teased her about wearing their cousin's cast-offs.

Freya's Mum spent more time drilling her daughters on plant recognition than on deity recognition, in the short period between her getting home and darkness falling. That puzzled Freya until she and her sister were sent out on their own to forage what they could from the countryside outside their town. With only one income, food was even less abundant than usual. Anything edible they could find added to their meals. In the weekends, Freya was pressed into helping her mother set up a new garden in the thin strips of soil around their new house. Somehow, nothing Freya planted managed to grow. Perhaps it was merely that her plantings were on the shadier, drier side of the small yard. Maybe it was something more.

"How come my plants never look like yours, Mum? I planted beans right next to your row, and none of mine have appeared."

"Perhaps some mice found yours."

And got full before they got to Mum's row? Sure.

"But why is it always my plants that die?"

"I don't know, Freya. Maybe your demi abilities aren't plant-focused. You may have some other talent you haven't identified yet."

"But we need food. Everyone needs food. So why can't I grow it?"

"How about you and Tammy go out foraging? There's probably some hawthorns ripe by now."

Freya went, feeling inadequate. What sort of descendant of a harvest and fertility goddess couldn't grow food?

If only we didn't keep moving, I might be able to get a part-time job to pay for a phone, thought Freya. *Then I could use the phone to identify food plants, and I wouldn't keep nearly poisoning us all. And we'd be less hungry, too.*

Of course, what with all the extra-curricular schooling her mother put her through, she didn't have much time for a job as well as school, even if jobs for young teens were available in their latest insignificant town. While the subjects she studied at home tended to be more interesting than those at regular school, that interest was offset by the hours her mother kept her at it.

"Mum, I think I'll scream if I have to recite how to overcome frost giants once more. I know how to do it if I have to, OK? And it's not like we even have frost giants here. They've all moved north, or out to Iceland, or wherever. I don't *need* to know how to defeat a frost giant."

"You'll be happy when you come up against one and know what to do, though."

"Can't I learn how to make a cornucopia, instead? That would be more useful, Mum. We could use more food around the place."

A horn of plenty would be awesome. No foraging required.

"I've told you before, I don't have any Greek or Roman heritage. A cornucopia isn't going to work for me. So, I can't teach you how to make one. Your father might have known how, but he never told me if he did. Since he's not here, we have to get food the hard way, by growing it ourselves or picking it. Now, since you mention Iceland and you know all about frost giants, tell me about the huldufólk."

It seemed Freya was stuck with reciting Icelandic folklore this afternoon. She sighed dramatically, but complied. She probably shouldn't have reminded her mother of her father's heritage, however indirectly. Anything to do with her father, or his Greek heritage, made her mother grumpy. At least lessons meant she escaped the persistent drizzle outside. It did mean staying in the mouldy-smelling living room, however. Sometimes there were no good options. She sighed.

"Huldufólk are usually hidden. Some people call them elves, but others think elves and huldufólk are different. We don't care which is which unless they are causing problems with humans..."

"And why does it matter which is which, Freya?"

"Umm. Some of them are good at growing things, I can't recall which. Oh, that's right, elves are smaller. I've seen a picture somewhere of a cat on some elf houses!" She stroked Mr Fluffbum, who was curled up beside her. He started purring.

"Oh Freya, you and your cats." Her mother laughed; her grumpiness forgotten for now. "Alright, so elves are smaller. You'll have to study up on what beings can help to grow things. That's useful to know. What plant is considered to be a sign that elves are near?"

Freya made a face at her mother.

"You and your plants, Mum! It's lords and ladies, isn't it? That one with the leaves that look a bit like sorrel."

"Yes, and you won't forget that one in a hurry, will you?"

The memory of burning mouth and lips after biting into the leaves of that toxic plant one hungry afternoon was indeed etched into Freya's memory.

"No. Never."

"Right, moving on. You've covered what you remember about huldufólk, as little as that is; what about volcano gods?"

"Oh, Mum," complained Freya, "volcano gods are even less relevant to me than frost giants. We don't even *have* volcanoes in this country."

"Not here, but plenty of other places in the world have them. And you know that where people go, their gods and the descendants of those gods go with them. Why, in the country I grew up in, volcano gods were so thick on the ground every tenth person was descended from one!" Danae was more animated than usual when she talked about her country of origin.

Freya rolled her eyes. She didn't quite manage to escape her Mum noticing.

"Be polite, Freya," said Danae sternly.

Tammy spoke up from across the room where she'd been glued to her phone all afternoon. Somehow, she managed to avoid half of their Mum's grilling sessions.

"Come on, Mum, we know you come from far away, where the things invisible to see are different from here. You've told us often enough we could recite your story backwards."

"Yeah, Mum. No volcanoes here, no volcano gods. Right?"

Their mother was clearly hurt, the corners of her mouth turning down, but she drew a deep, steadying breath.

"Just because you've lived in this country all your lives, doesn't negate my experience. Also, people come from all over the world, so you could meet a volcano god or his offspring anywhere, not only near a volcano. And why are you still on that phone, Tammy? I told you to go read a book, or do your homework."

Tammy sighed loudly and pointedly.

"All right, Mum. I'll listen to a book. Reading's too hard. I don't see the point of homework though."

"Tammy," said Danae, a warning in her tone.

Tammy rose and went to dig her laptop out of her bag, flipping it open as she sat down again.

"Good. Now, Freya, sit still and tell me about volcano gods one more time," said Danae.

Seeing her mother close to the edge of anger, Freya took a breath herself. Things were so different now, without their Dad. She missed him taking her out in the weekends. He always used to take them for chips on the beach. And every time, he ended up talking to dozens of people Freya didn't know, but he seemed to be great friends with. She wondered for a moment if her Mum ever got to talk to other adults these days. Maybe not. Maybe that was why she spent so much time giving lessons to Freya and Tammy.

"OK, Mum. Here's what I know..."

CHAPTER ELEVEN

AUTUMN

The long, empty summer passed slowly. Freya hadn't managed to make any new friends at school before the summer holidays, so she was forced to hang around at home, or go for walks by herself. Tammy could sometimes be persuaded to play games, but she spent more time on her phone than talking to her sister. Freya was almost glad when autumn and school came around again.

The skies were grey and stormy on the first day of school. Tammy and Freya had to walk home despite the weather; Tammy met Freya outside the gate of her school. The wind was whistling through narrow streets. Rubbish piled up in sheltered corners and the promise of rain was in the air.

"This is sprite weather," remarked Tammy. "We should look out for them."

"Are you sure that's a good idea? Aren't sprites dangerous? Like the volcano gods Mum is always going on about?" As usual, Freya took a more cautious approach than Tammy.

"Sprites are a totally different kettle of wool."

"I think you're mixing your phrases."

"Doesn't matter. The point is, they're not so much fun. So, when I say look out for them, I mean look out for them so we can avoid them."

Freya looked at her sister curiously. Tammy wasn't the sort to avoid any being, as a rule. Tammy saw her looking.

"What?"

"Nothing."

"Look, I was out in a storm once and got shocked by them. It wasn't a fun experience and I don't want to repeat it, that's all."

The rain chose that moment to fulfil its promise, and the girls broke into a run. There was a flash, thunder rolled, and a red light flickered off to the right.

"Faster, Freya! There are sprites around for sure." There was another flicker, to the left this time. "Fenris' teeth! I don't want to get caught out here with them. Can't you run any faster?"

"No, I can't! I'm puffed!" More thunder, and Freya felt a sharp pain zip through her heel.

I'm sure I haven't been hit by lightning; I'd notice that more. Wouldn't I?

Freya glanced back, and there was a flickering red-hued figure behind her. Not the same as Lio back on the beach, after their house had been washed away. This figure was less human-looking, more elemental, if that was a word.

"Is that a sprite then, Tammy?" she gasped.

Tammy looked back.

"Yes!"

Freya found she was able to run faster, after all. She twisted and turned through the streets, feet pounding on the asphalt. Tammy overtook her, and Freya felt another of those unpleasant shocks. She found another reserve of speed. At last, their home was in sight. They tumbled through the door and slammed it shut behind them. Tammy sank down with her back to the door. Freya followed suit.

"And *that* is why I don't like sprites," said Tammy.

"I see what you mean." Freya shivered. She hoped she never encountered sprites like that again. "Can sprites kill us?"

"Not as far as I know. But I've never waited around to find out."

Tammy scrabbled at her school bag, and pulled out her phone.

"Why the hurry with the phone, Tammy? I'm pretty sure you're not supposed to have boyfriends home on weeknights."

Tammy directed a brief glare at Freya.

"I'm not trying to get hold of a boyfriend, I'm checking that it still works, dummy. Electric shocks aren't good for phones."

"I guess not. How did you get that phone, anyway? It's not fair that you have one and I don't."

"I didn't get it from Mum and Dad if that's what you're asking. Thank Frigg, it's turning on. I thought those sprites had shocked it dead for sure."

"And where would you be without your phone. Oh, I know. You might actually talk to us in the evening instead of being on your phone all the time." Freya wasn't sure if she just wanted more of her sister's attention, or a phone of her own. *Perhaps attention* and *a phone would be good.* "So, if you didn't get it from Mum, who did you get it from?"

"Not a pesky little sister, that's for sure."

"Come on, Tammy, tell me. Or I'll ask when Mum's here. And tell her about that new Min demi."

"You wouldn't!"

"Would, too."

Tammy looked at her consideringly. Freya looked back, trying to look fierce. The effect was ruined by Mr Fluffbum sauntering down the hall to sniff disapprovingly at Freya's wet bag. He looked at her questioningly.

"Sorry, Mr Fluffbum. It's not dinnertime yet," said Freya.

The cat turned his back, sat down and stuck up a hind leg to clean.

"I guess it doesn't hurt to tell you," said Tammy, ignoring the cat; "after all, you'd only tell your cat. Dan gave me the phone when I first met him. He was getting a new one from *his* parents, and he gave me his old one so we could talk. OK, nosey?"

"If that was all, why the big deal?"

"Because I told Mum it was from a school friend. So, keep it to yourself and your cat, alright?"

"Alright." Since Tammy had gotten her phone from a boyfriend, there was no chance of Freya getting one from their Mum. She sighed. No chance of a phone, sprite-shocks in the storm, and what was the bet that there was no food left in the house, either? It wasn't shaping up to be a good afternoon.

The wind was still howling when Freya woke up in the night. Mr Fluffbum had leapt onto her bed and was walking to and fro on top of her, instead of curling up as a welcome warmth beside her.

"What is it, Mr Fluffbum?" she muttered. "I'm still trying to sleep here."

Mr Fluffbum's claws needled her sharply and she sat up abruptly.

"Frigg's chariot, that hurts!"

Having got her attention, the cat leaped off her and walked to the door, looking back expectantly. Freya groaned.

"Don't tell me you're hungry now. We won't have money till Mum's been paid. And the shops aren't open in the middle of the night even if I had money for cat food."

Mr Fluffbum uttered a short, plaintive meow and scratched at the door.

"OK, I'll let you out. Maybe you really do need to catch your own food."

Stepping carefully so as not to wake Tammy or Danae – most of the floorboards had their own individual creak – Freya made her way to the front door, following Mr Fluffbum's gently waving tail. Waiting for her cat to go out into the heaving night air, Freya wondered if Lio was out there somewhere. It was certainly a stormy enough night for him. When Mr Fluffbum stepped out, she followed – keeping a sharp eye out for sprites.

It wasn't far to the sea – too close for comfort, in fact.

At least we're not right on the cliff anymore, Freya reminded herself as she skirted the neat hedge that divided the shore road from the seashore. Mr Fluffbum had slipped underneath it, of course. On the far side of the hedge, the beach stretched out into the distance, the tide out, only small rivulets wending their way to the sea. Here and there, white shells half buried in sand gleamed in the light from seaside houses. At first, Freya thought she'd followed Mr Fluffbum for no good reason, but then a flickering in the distance resolved itself into a solitary running form.

Lio. Freya felt a smile tugging at her lips. At last, someone who she could talk to without holding back or pretending to be something she wasn't.

When Lio at length jogged up to her, she was barely surprised when he offered her a half-wave before bending down to present a small, gleaming fish to her cat.

"Are you always prepared for cat-feeding?" she asked.

Lio grinned.

"I'd like to say yes and claim higher knowledge, but it would be a lie," he replied. "I saw you in the distance, and luckily there was a shoal of fish nearby. Small ones, of course. We don't get the big fish anymore; they've all moved north or been fished out. But I don't think your cat minds."

They both looked at Mr Fluffbum, who was making toothy inroads to the fish.

"I almost think he prefers your offerings to cat food," Freya said.

There was an awkward pause.

Talk about something other than your cat! Freya berated herself.

"Do you know what to do about sprites?" she asked.

"Avoid them?" suggested Lio.

"Easy to say, but how do you do it? You must come across them all the time, since you're always in storms."

"Rubber soled shoes," Lio said, waggling a foot in demonstration.

"That's all? Seriously?"

"Nah, they're just too scared of my Dad to come after me," Lio said. "But the rubber shoes help too."

Freya rolled her eyes. *Not much help there.*

"Any progress on finding your powers?" Lio asked.

"If only," sighed Freya. "I keep hoping it'll become really obvious one day. But no luck yet." She crossed her arms, tucking in her hands. Her second-hand pyjamas were no match for the wind that howled along the empty beach.

"You'll figure it out," Lio assured her. "Every demi does, if they have enough power. And I'm sure you do."

"I hope so." *So much for someone I can talk to about anything, this is just as stilted as the conversations at school.*

"Tell you what. If you haven't figured it out when I see you next, maybe we can do some experiments. See what you can and can't do."

Freya felt a flicker of hope at the thought.

"That sounds great. Can't we start now?"

But Lio was shaking his head.

"Can't you feel the change in the wind? This storm is on its way out. And that means I am too. See you soon!" Lio touched her arm, so briefly she wasn't sure it had happened, and ran off in the direction of the distant sea.

Every stormy night after that, Freya slipped out to see if Lio was about. Often, he wasn't there, and Freya felt foolish for having left her warm bed for a cold beach. But a few weeks shy of winter, with the wind the only reason there was no frost on the ground, Lio was there, skimming stones from the thin strip of sand between the seawall and the sea. The beach was hardly there when the tide was in. Freya crouched down beside him, her nose already numb with cold.

"How can you stand to stay still when it's colder than the lowest level of the underworld?" she asked.

"I never notice the cold. Lucky, really, or my life would be a good deal less fun."

"And fun is the most important thing?"

"Some days, it's all there is," Lio said seriously.

"Well today, there is more than fun. Can we do some experiments to figure out my powers?" Freya was half hopeful, half full of trepidation. What if they tried and nothing happened? What if she had no powers to find? Her sister had been well into discovering her own powers by Freya's age.

Lio stood up and stretched.

"Now that *does* sound like fun," he said.

A chilly half hour later, Freya wasn't sure that it was fun at all. Lio had had her brush her hands over plants, lie on the earth and speak to it, jump through gusts of wind, hold rocks and hum to them, and finally wade into the waves on the very edge of the sea. None of it had made her feel like she was brimming with power, and the last effort had left her soaked and shuddering with cold.

"I haven't tried you with fire," Lio pondered out loud. "But fire's tricky to experiment with. It doesn't seem like a likely power for you with your parents, either. You might have some sort of trigger that you need to use, too. And the possibilities for that are endless." He shrugged, lifting his arms helplessly. "Sorry. Maybe we can try again another time."

CHAPTER TWELVE

SPRING

After the storms of autumn and winter, it was a surprisingly dry spring. Freya hoped that this meant she'd find some outdoor-minded people to make friends with. After all, she could talk about plants, and they weren't surrounded by the mysteries of the demi-world. But before the spring was well advanced, Danae announced that they were moving again.

"I've got a better job, girls. And I won't be sorry to move out of this house." Danae looked at the graffiti-covered walls with distaste.

They took a bus to the town where the new job was located, carrying their things in a random assortment of bags and suitcases. Freya had managed to acquire a second-hand cat cage from someone's dumped rubbish. It certainly made it easier to carry Mr Fluffbum with them, though the cage bumped painfully against Freya's legs as she lugged it along on the long walk from the bus stop to their new abode. Distressed wails emerged at regular intervals.

"Sorry, Mr Fluffbum. We'll get there soon. I hope."

Both Freya and Tammy were unconvinced by their new cottage when they arrived at last. A two-story red brick building at the end of a road on the outskirts of town, it was identical to every other house on the street, except that it was missing several tiles from its red roof. The garden around it was overgrown, a mass of weeds obscuring any landscaping that might once have been present.

'It's very cheap," said Danae as the family stood outside the house, looking at it in some dismay.

"It's lucky it's been so dry," said Freya, noticing some of the missing roof tiles in the grass beside the front door.

"Mum, exactly how much are we paying for this dump?" Tammy's voice was sharp. She didn't wait for Danae's reply. "Too much, I bet. Did you actually sign a contract? Are we stuck here?"

"Of course, I signed a contract, Tammy. You don't get to rent a place unless you do. For your information, young lady, we're here for six months, at least. It depends on if I can get a better job again. If I manage that, we won't stay long - or if we do, we'll make sure the landlord does some repairs. Meanwhile, we can make it clean at least."

Tammy sighed dramatically.

"I *suppose* the weather's warming up. Honestly, Mum, does this place even have running water?"

"There's a stream nearby..." Danae's eyes glinted. Tammy didn't notice. Freya did, and held her tongue.

One, two, three and...

"Mum!" Tammy was outraged.

"Of course, it has running water, Tammy. It may not be warm water, of course. I'm not sure that the hot water tank is working. Your father was always better at checking on that sort of thing."

"Wow, did you hear that, Freya? Mum admitted Dad was good at something!"

"Oh, shut *up*, Tammy. Don't make things worse," said Freya.

"Girls, stop bickering and let's get to work on the inside. Freya, there's some old cloths in the kitchen, you can start cleaning there. Tammy, you can start in the bathroom. You've always had more water affinity than me. Get some water flowing in there."

"Are you telling me I can invite water nymphs into the bathroom?"

"No, Tammy, I'm not. I'm telling you to clean the bathroom the old-fashioned way, with soap and water. No nymphs inside, thank you. We'd be washed away in no time."

Tammy stomped off to the bathroom. Freya put Mr Fluffbum's cat cage on the floor in the corner of the kitchen.

"You won't be in there too much longer, I promise. We need to get everything clean first, then you can explore inside."

The cat meowed piteously for a while, before giving up and curling up to sleep.

Fifteen minutes after they'd started cleaning, a tremendous gurgling sound began from the bathroom. Danae, who'd been battling the mould in the bedrooms upstairs, called out.

"Tammy? Is that you? Freya, go check on her, please."

There was no answer from Tammy, but the gurgling transitioned to splashing, then a dull thumping came from the bathroom door. Freya dumped her ragged cleaning cloth on the kitchen bench - the surface must be decades old; it wouldn't suffer further from having a dirty rag on it - and went to investigate. She took the nearly full spray bottle of sugar soap she'd found under the sink. Maybe that would speed up Tammy's cleaning, assuming that was what was causing the noises.

"Tammy, are you in there?" There was no answer, but more thumps sounded on the door. Freya tried the door. It seemed to be locked. "Tammy, what are you doing? Look, I'm coming in. Can you unlock the door?" Still no answer. Freya considered her options. There was an outside window to the bathroom, but it was small. Too small for someone her size to get in and out of. That wasn't going to do much good. She looked at the sugar soap in her hand. Useful, yes, but maybe not what she needed right now. She went back to the kitchen, where a box of food sat, yet to be unpacked. A nearly full packet of salt was wedged between cereal and a paper bag of dried herbs.

Yes, that might help. I'm sure Mum said salt was good for removing negative energy, and it sure sounds like that's what there is in there.

Freya pulled at the packet, which stuck. It came unstuck all at once, pulling the herb bag out with it, and ripping it open. Both she and the kitchen floor were showered with salt crystals and green flecks.

"I only just cleaned that floor!" Freya glared at the speckled floor, before scraping together the remaining salt that had hit the bench rather than the floor. It was speckled, too. "Oh well, I guess a few bits of fennel in the salt won't hurt."

She marched back towards the bathroom. There was water spurting through the keyhole and out from under the door, now. The long, dusty carpets in the hall were history, judging by the squelching as she walked on them.

No great loss, I guess, thought Freya, observing the ugly pattern on them.

"Hold tight, Tammy. I'm trying to help." There were more muffled gurgling sounds. "What are you *doing* in there?"

"'M fine," came Tammy's muffled voice.

She doesn't sound fine. I'd better do something.

Freya unscrewed the spray-cap of the soap bottle, poured the remaining salt from her palm into the bottle, and replaced the cap. She shook the mixture up, gave an experimental squirt towards the floor - it needed a good clean, too - and raised the bottle towards the bathroom door's keyhole.

"Stand back, Tammy."

Pushing the soap bottle against the keyhole, she gave three quick squirts. The water stopped trickling. She gave another squirt. The water started to slow its progress from under the door.

Maybe I need to put some spray down there, too.

She bent lower, and gave a few squirts of salty, soapy, herby solution to the crack below the door. The water stopped flowing altogether, and the gurgling sound resumed. "Tammy, are you OK in there?" The gurgling stopped at last, and Tammy's voice, rather fainter than usual, replied.

"Er. Yeah. Fine. Give me a moment." There was a silence punctuated by muffled thuds.

"What are you *doing*?"

"Nothing."

The door opened a crack, and a bedraggled Tammy looked out. She was wet from head to toe, and her usual artfully enhanced face had makeup smudged across it.

"Bathroom's clean," she announced in bright tones. Freya opened her mouth, then closed it without saying anything. She didn't want to be a nag, not when her sister was pretty much the only near-aged company she had. But it was quite clear to her that Tammy had ignored their mother's injunction against using water nymphs as cleaning aides.

"Good," she said. After all, what more was there to say?

Later, they hung up all the soggy carpets outside, hoping that the uncertain spring sunshine would dry everything out by sunset.

Mum shouldn't have been surprised that Tammy didn't listen. After all, she doesn't usually.

Their mother did seem surprised though. Her admonitory lecture had begun when she came downstairs to find out what the thumping had been about, and hadn't finished yet. From behind the longest rug, part of Tammy's face appeared. She saw Freya on the other side of it, and winked.

No, I don't think Tammy's listening now, either.

As it turned out, Freya loved many things about their new town. It was further inland, for a start, and the hills were novel after so long in the fens and broads. But she couldn't tell kids at school about nymphs in the bathroom, or making her first feathered cloak from collected feathers, or identifying demis by the subtle clues in their behaviour or dress. That meant that once again, she had no friends at school. And it was too far to get to a beach to meet Lio.

"Honestly, Tammy, how does Mum expect me to make friends when I can't tell them anything about who I really am? How I spend my time after school? It's not like I can invite anyone home for a quick lesson in deity-recognition. Even if I wanted to, Mum never agrees."

Tammy shrugged.

"I don't try. Friends come; friends go. It works out. They don't need to know my innermost secrets, or even my outermost ones. Just be yourself, your mostly-human self, I mean." There was a sudden glint in Tammy's eye. "Of course, that could be the problem. Maybe you're just too 'I'm more deified than thou'." She didn't finish the sentence as Freya leapt at her, mock pouncing like a cat.

"OK, OK, calm down. I'm teasing you. I know it's tough coming to a new town. Think of me, I haven't got to see Dan in weeks. I have to break in a whole new crowd."

"But that's just it. How do you always manage to *get* a crowd?"

It was Tammy's turn to shrug.

"It takes more time in some places. I mean, look at me, I'm having to clean bathrooms in order to get company here."

"That didn't work out so well for the rest of us." Freya had not enjoyed lugging wet carpets around.

"Maybe you don't remember, but we had some history in the town on the cliff, people knew us a bit. We were there for a couple of years, after all. Tell you what, stick with me for a bit, this weekend. You'll fit in sooner or later, but there's some things I could do with your help with, when we get some time off."

"I'm guessing that if it's something you want to do, I won't enjoy it. No thanks."

"Just help me out this weekend, and I'll show you what I mean. No need to be lonely when you're descended from Freya and Dionysus."

Freya hunched her shoulders.

"Maybe I like being lonely. Anyway, I've got Mr Fluffbum."

"A cat is not an excuse to have no friends, Freya."

CHAPTER THIRTEEN

SPRING

The weather warmed up enough to dry out the inside of the house as well as the outside. Their mother had picked up a few extra hours work in a nearby horticultural centre, leaving Tammy and Freya on their own a lot. She was going in for a morning's work this Saturday, which would mean money for groceries. Tammy was officially in charge of Freya. Freya was still slowly eating breakfast, trying and failing to convince herself that a bowl of porridge was delicious without milk and sugar.

"And no leaving Freya alone, this time," cautioned their mother as she stowed a wrinkled apple in her bag for lunch. Freya glanced up at her in surprise. Had her mum noticed Freya being left alone when her sister went out? Mum usually seemed oblivious to that sort of thing.

"You'd know where I was if I had a phone," Freya suggested.

"Maybe so, but who's going to pay for one?" said Danae.

Money is always the problem.

"I'd have more friends if I had a phone, too."

"If they are only not your friends because you don't have a phone, they're not worth having as friends."

That was depressingly true, but it didn't help Freya feel any better.

Phones are pretty much essential for life, why doesn't Mum realise that?

"Enough about phones, Freya. Stay with your sister, and I'll be back in time for dinner. The shift shouldn't go on any longer than that. Look after each other, girls. I've got to go now, or I'll be late."

Freya watched her mother's retreating back for a moment, feeling her tension release as the front door closed. This was the first time in a while they'd had a whole day to themselves to explore the surrounding area without being pressed into finding food as well, or having to sit through extra lessons. The sky was blue, and the hills were inviting. It was too good an opportunity to miss. She took the last bite of porridge and stood up, shoving back the rickety chair that you had to sit on just so, or it wobbled unbearably.

"Come on Freya, hurry up!" Tammy was waiting by the door.

Freya shoved a couple of precious flapjacks into her rucksack, double checked that she had a water bottle, and added a light coat.

"I am hurrying, I'm just packing a few things so we don't have to survive off the land today."

"Oh, alright. I'm not in the mood for whatever's growing at this time of year anyway." Tammy returned to her phone.

Mr Fluffbum sauntered over to investigate Freya's rucksack, and rubbed against her legs.

"Sorry Mr Fluffbum, you can't come with us this time. You look after the house." Last time Freya had let Mr Fluffbum wander, he'd disappeared for hours, then when she returned home from a fruitless search for him, she'd found him gnawing on the remains of a brownie. Now, Freya didn't trust Mr Fluffbum at home unless he was shut in. One mangled brownie was one too many as far as Freya was concerned.

"We're going out for a walk, not on a camping trip, Freya." Tammy was obviously impatient to go, waiting by the front door and flicking irritably through some app on her phone, glancing up at Freya from time to time as though she was an irritating intrusion. Tammy's phone was so frequently in her hand that it was practically an extension of her sister. "Come on, slow poke," Tammy said when Freya finally joined her. "I found something interesting to check out, but we won't get to see it if you don't get a move on."

Freya looked at Tammy in surprise.

"I'm not convinced it's something I want to see, if you're so keen. Can't we just see if there are lambs on the hills, that sort of thing?"

"*Boring.* Come on, you're always wanting me to do things with you. This is your chance."

"I guess."

Freya hastily slid her feet into dishevelled trainers, wondering what Tammy was so animated about. Usually, she protested at having to look after Freya. She certainly didn't want to show her things.

"I'm ready."

I hope this is going to be worthwhile. Maybe I'll see some lambs anyway.

Tammy led her away from the town - their cottage was on the edge of town, but not far enough out to be considered a country house. They passed the town's allotments, verdant with spring growth. Freya spotted young onions, crawling tendrils of peas, and lush potato tops. She craned her neck, trying to see their plot from the road. Had the lettuce sprouted yet? She'd spent the past week helping her mother do the weeding after school. She hadn't been thrilled about being pressed into helping to destroy plants, but she was glad that her mum was enjoying herself, humming as she worked – such a change from the bitter lines Danae's face had often assumed in recent months. The allotment gave Freya something to do after school apart from worrying about whether she'd make any friends. It was also a less tension-filled pursuit than demi-hunting expeditions, the only other thing her mum seemed inclined to do with her these days. She wished her dad was around still, to take her out for chips and feed the gulls. That had been a much more relaxing way to spend an hour or two.

Tammy hustled her past the allotments, seeming anxious not to be spotted.

"Come *on*, Freya," she repeated. "We're not stopping to garden; we've got better things to do."

She led the way up the hill, pressing on faster than Freya's still-shorter legs could manage, then waited at the top of the slope. There, she pointed to a stile leading into the fields. A walkway went through the valley and disappeared into some woods near a stream in the distance.

"That way. Quickly though, there were cows in here last week and I don't want to be bothered by them. There might be a bull."

Freya hastily climbed over and half-walked, half-ran in the direction Tammy pointed. She didn't want to be bothered by a bull, either. They reached the next field without incident, and without glimpsing either cows or bulls, to Freya's relief. She didn't mind them, exactly, but they were so big and curious. There *were* sheep, and lambs, too.

"Oh, look, Tammy! Lambs! They're so cute, the way they bounce over the grass."

"I guess. They don't do much for me."

Freya was disappointed when Tammy hustled her past the lambs.

Over the next stile, and they were closing on the woods. The sky was mostly blue on this spring morning, a welcome change after a week of rain and grey skies. The sound of the swollen stream rushing through its bed reached their ears.

"Nearly there," Tammy encouraged Freya. Tammy left the path right at the edge of the woods, leading the way behind some bushes which hid them from the road. She seemed to be taking care not to be seen by anyone.

"We are allowed to be here, aren't we?" Freya asked nervously. She didn't want to be shouted at by some irate landowner.

"'Course we are, it's a public footpath. I just don't want anyone joining us."

Freya wondered who might join them in such a lonely spot. Sure, there were always ramblers, but not many bothered to come near this village. It wasn't renowned for anything in particular. Tammy set down her own bag by the stream edge, and told Freya to do the same. There was a bare patch of ground there, too trodden down by cows to grow things. A small weir slowed the stream just after the bare patch, and the sound of water rushing over it was loud in Freya's ears. Beyond that, the stream disappeared into the trees, dark and uninviting. Freya shivered, although it wasn't cold.

"Alright, now has Mum taught you anything about Norse magic or summoning yet?" Tammy asked. Freya shook her head.

"Just demi-spotting and folklore. You've been in the room half the time, surely you know that."

"Me being in the room is not the same as me paying attention," said Tammy. Freya rolled her eyes.

"I keep hoping Mum's going to tell me more than myths and how to identify other demis. But she's always too busy or too tired, these days," she said.

"Well, then you'd better listen up. This is probably the most fun thing you can do with a summoning, but Mum won't tell you about it. It works best with more than one of us, which is why I need you. And don't tell her I told you, or else!"

Tammy was fierce, her gaze holding Freya's eyes until she nodded.

"Right. The first thing you should know is that you definitely do need to follow the rules. Do everything I say, and nothing else, got it?"

Freya nodded again, an unexpected thrill coursing through her. What was Tammy going to show her? Would she finally learn something of her own powers? Perhaps Tammy would know a trigger that Lio hadn't been able to think of. She felt a pang of loneliness, knowing that she was too far from the sea to see Lio.

Tammy selected a long stick of fennel from the weedy area at the edge of the field, pulled a pinecone out of her jacket pocket and lashed it onto the fennel with some lengths of ivy from the edge of the woods, then returned to the stream's edge.

"This part I learnt from Dad when he was celebrating a big wine sale one time. It's Dionysian, sort of. I'm pretty sure Mum never, ever does this. This is top-notch fusion, not traditional Norse stuff. Although it's got a bit of that, too. And I don't want you blabbing to her, OK?"

Freya was more concerned with Tammy having learnt something from their dad that he hadn't shared with her. How come she hadn't been included?

"When did Dad teach you? He never taught me anything about his demi heritage."

"He probably thought you were too young. It was a couple of years ago, at least. And you were probably out with Mum."

"And he didn't argue with you? Wow."

"Well, I guess he showed me because I was arguing that he never taught me anything, but that's not the point."

Tammy found a section of bank where the young grass was still thin, and drew a circle in the dirt around herself and Freya.

"Stay inside the circle. Don't even poke your finger out, or I'll be going home alone to tell Mum you were eaten."

Freya's thrill turned to dread; a cold hand clenched in her stomach.

"Should we be doing this then? If it's so dangerous?" She hated the quiver in her voice, but couldn't quite control it. "I'm pretty sure it's illegal to let your sister get eaten while you're in charge."

"Don't be such a wimp. We'll be fine if you follow the rules. But I think you should know about this, and Mum won't ever tell you. And like I said, it's fun. So, as your big sister, it's my job to educate you about the possibilities. Just stay in the circle." Tammy was dismissive, despite the danger she'd just highlighted.

"I don't want to be eaten."

"So, stay where you are. Next thing. I'll be making a song-web. Don't say anything, or make a sound. Not this time. Hit the wrong note at the wrong time and my song-web won't work, so sit still and listen."

Freya nodded once more, afraid to say anything that might make whatever this was go wrong.

"OK, Freya. Last thing, if anything *does* go wrong, there's a packet of salt here." Tammy pulled a paper sachet of salt from her pocket and deposited it in Freya's hand. "If it looks like something is going to eat either of us, throw the salt on it - without letting yourself out of the circle. I'll go out, but don't you. I have experience. You don't. I've waited till I could bring you for this summoning, and I'm not sure exactly what we'll get. But salt should sort it out if it's not as fun as I think it will be."

Freya obediently clutched the small paper packet of salt. Her sweaty hands dampened the packet. She hoped that wouldn't affect any anti-eating properties it might have. Wasn't salt usually used as a *seasoning* for food? Maybe whatever Tammy was going to call was like leeches, which curled up and dropped off when sprinkled with salt.

"All set. Let's do this!" said Tammy enthusiastically.

Tammy turned away from Freya to face the stream. Her eyes were alight, her whole body seeming to vibrate with suppressed excitement. Freya wondered what could possibly be so exciting - and so potentially dangerous. She almost missed Tammy's first notes, as she started to sing. Tammy was quite quiet about it, despite her evident excitement. Tammy held her phone near her mouth, recording herself sing. Freya saw her stop the recording after a few low notes. Then she switched to playback mode, and as the recorded notes played, she sang in counterpoint. She repeated this a few times, till the recording was almost a chorus. Glancing at Freya, she put a finger to her lips, and sang one more time along with the recorded song. At first Freya was too busy watching her sister with envy to notice anything else. Her sister's voice was rich and full, especially in chorus with herself, much more resonant than Freya's own.

How did she learn to sing like that? I've never heard her singing at home.

However, after a few minutes of listening to what she assumed was what Tammy meant when she said a song-web, Freya realised that something was happening in the stream. Immediately above the weir, a sort of whirlpool formed in the muddy brown stream. It deepened improbably given the size of the stream itself, then inverted into a watery tower, so abruptly that Freya gasped.

Tammy glanced at Freya again, irritably. She gestured for Freya to cover her mouth with her hands. The watery tower moved out over the bank in front of them, forming itself into a humanoid shape as it did so. A large humanoid shape, with a horse's head and chains around its arms and legs, all outlined in brown water. Little wavelets muddied the bare areas of the bank and swirled the low vegetation in circles. The edges of the water-being lapped around their drawn circle. The being looked at them with an expression that forcibly reminded Freya of her father in a bad mood, despite being made of muddy water.

"Why have you disturbed me, young ones? Is your mother near? You are clearly not of an age to be useful to me." Its voice was full of rushing sounds like the stream was making, which made it hard to understand.

Tammy looked profoundly irritated. Freya tried not to giggle.

"I am *so* old enough. I'm practically seventeen," said Tammy.

The being, who must surely be a river god, shook his head.

"No. You are too young to master the power you have summoned. Release me."

"Why should I?" Tammy said rudely.

"Because if you do not, we will be here for a good few years until you are old enough that you *can* deal with the likes of me. I can wait. Can you?"

Tammy did not look happy. This experience was clearly not going as she had anticipated.

"Don't you want to be released from your chains?"

"Yes, but by one who can survive the consequences of releasing me. You, girl, are not that person." The being rippled. Freya looked away for a moment, feeling dizzy.

"What consequences?" asked Tammy.

"If you were old enough and trained enough, you would know. Release me."

"I don't see why I should." Tammy looked mutinous.

"Maybe one day you will return without your sister and I will take you. Maybe another will do so. But now, alas, I must wait. Release me. Find another of your own age. I am not for you."

What does that thing mean, take Tammy? Freya wondered. She didn't dare ask, though. She didn't want the grumpy water being paying her any attention.

"Not likely. And what's my sister got to do with it? How do you even know she's my sister?"

"Without her power, I would not have come today. Except perhaps to take you and your power for myself."

Well, that answers that question. But what power is he talking about? I didn't even sing.

The river god didn't answer Tammy's other questions. Instead, it drew more and more water into itself, losing much of its shape in the process. It now towered over them, surrounding their circle on all sides. There was a tiny hole in the water where Freya could see the sky, with its head in the centre. It no longer looked remotely humanoid. It looked as though they were about to drown on dry land.

"Freya, the salt. Now!" Tammy commanded her. Freya wasn't sure that throwing salt was going to help at this point, given how grumpy the being was already. But she also didn't want to deal with an irate Tammy, so she tore open the salt packet and threw it. As the salt crystals hit the watery being, the whole thing abruptly washed back into the stream, drenching them as it fell out of shape, back into regular water. The drawn circle was washed away, leaving them alone on a muddy bank, gasping with the shock of cold water. Tammy looked at Freya, then away.

"Just don't say anything, OK?" she said bitterly.

On the way home, chilly and wet, Freya asked;

"Why did you think it would be fun?"

Tammy looked at her, then away.

"Last time, with a different stream, the river god was younger. And... fun. You know."

Freya didn't know, but she thought she might have an idea of what Tammy meant, given Tammy's interests.

"So, the last one didn't cover you with water and ask for Mum?"

Tammy laughed aloud.

"Well, I did get covered with water. Thank goodness that doesn't hurt anymore. But no, the last one certainly didn't ask for Mum. Definitely not." She smiled to herself.

"And last time it really was fun. Next time, we won't go after a big rainstorm. I've never seen a water deity get so huge. And I probably shouldn't have chosen a section by a weir, either. Being chained up like that is bound to be irritating to a kelpie or naiad. It was good you threw the salt, too. He was too distracted by arguing with me to notice you. I'll take you next time too, just in case."

Tammy was obviously regaining her cheer. Freya wasn't sure that *she* was regaining any cheer, and was even less sure that she should be going, next time, but she didn't want Tammy to get drowned by an irritable river god either. Tammy didn't seem to have paid attention to the river god's threats to take Tammy and her power if Freya wasn't there. How many risks had she run already? Freya sighed to herself, and didn't tell Mum why their clothes were still damp when Mum returned from work that day.

Tammy dragged Freya along next time they had a day off together, and the next as well, later in the spring.

"We get more things happening when you come along," said Tammy. "The deities are more talkative. And it usually only works once for every two or three streams or pools I try, but with you there, it's first time, every time. You have to come."

Freya went, but more to protect her sister if need be. However, Freya saw that Tammy did, indeed have fun when the river deity was younger (at least in appearance - who knew how old any of these river deities actually were?) and less irritable.

"Tammy, I know we're descended from a fertility goddess, but are you sure you should be kissing them? And with me right here?" Tammy looked up from her position half in, half out of the stream. The latest river deity was giving Tammy a back massage. Tammy had removed most of clothing to avoid the bother of having to dry it later. Freya sat out of reach of the water, half-turned away so she didn't have to watch, but ready to throw salt if things went awry.

"There's no harm in it. And like you say, we're descended from fertility deities. Dionysus was a bit of a fertility god too, and he was big on rituals as well, you know. So, we're practically born to come up with our own rituals." She stood up and dismissed the deity, though, to Freya's relief.

"I'm sure it's not the sort of thing you should be doing with me around. And I'm bored. So, when do *I* get to learn how to summon things? I want to ask my own questions. It's not fair that you always get them to do what you want. I want to know what they think!" said Freya.

"They'd tell us if they wanted to do things differently. And you can learn when you're older."

"That's not fair. It sounds like you learnt when you were my age!"

"I was older than you are."

"But you said yourself that you get better results with me around. Can't you teach me?"

"Oh, I suppose so. Stop nagging, and bring my bag over here. These clothes have got all wet. I'll teach you next time."

As the spring wore into summer, Tammy and Freya went out most weekends. Their Mum's few extra hours had turned into a regular thing, which was good in terms of having enough food to eat, for themselves and for Mr Fluffbum, and less good because Freya had no-one but Tammy and her cat to spend time with. Freya grew bored being a bystander on their outings. She and Tammy had discovered that the river nymphs in the area seemed to have strong emotions. Tammy enjoyed herself. Freya was not so happy with the situation, but she didn't want Tammy going out without her. What if Tammy encountered a deity that was too strong for her? Freya felt curiously protective of her big sister. Sometimes, Tammy simply asked the water deities they summoned about local happenings. That was interesting, although often what the deities said reminded Freya of the one time she'd decided to try a cryptic crossword. Nothing made any sense, even though the words were all English. Most times, they both ended up soaking wet.

Every time, Freya asked to be taught more.

"Come on, Tammy, you promised. And you said it's our heritage."

"I suppose it could be useful. Maybe. But…"

"You just want me there to rescue you if you need it." Freya was sick of being dragged along to throw salt if something didn't go the way her sister wanted.

"Partly." Her sister grinned. "It *is* helpful not having to worry about seasonings. But this *my* thing. I don't want you taking over. I just want a helper."

"Please, Tammy. It's like you said, Mum never teaches practical things like this."

"I'll think about it."

At long last, at the side of a small river, Tammy made a start on teaching Freya.

"The thyrsus helps," she said. "Dad told me what plants to use. But it's more about layering in your will with your voice," she said. "That's why I use the phone to make a song-web. That way, I get several layers of voice and will, which makes it stronger."

"So can I use your phone?" ask Freya.

"No. If you really have more power than me, you'd better start with just your voice and command."

Freya frowned. That didn't seem fair. But she opened her mouth to sing anyway, wishing she could sound half as good as Tammy did.

The water dimpled almost immediately, forming itself into a proto-deity.

"Yes!" Freya exclaimed in excitement – only to slump with disappointment as the incipient deity disappeared with a splash.

Tammy looked at her with something like resentment on her face.

"What?"

"I just can't believe you got something with a single note. Next time don't interrupt yourself, the deities want surety." Tammy turned away from Freya, tension informing the lines of her neck and shoulders.

Freya hardly noticed, eager to try summoning again. She experimented with humming, singing notes aloud, and with songs. Everything seemed to work, making the river swish one way then another. She settled on a sequence of notes that felt right, and called up the river deity to its full height. This time, she was able to ask all the questions she wanted.

"It's not fair," complained Tammy on the way home. "I'm the one who showed you how to do this. So how come you can do it easier than I can?"

Tammy might not be happy about it, but Freya was thrilled. At last, there was something she could do well. Tammy was so often better than her - able to grow things, better at identifying edible plants, better at attracting friends. This time, she was better. It was a heady feeling. Freya had never felt so powerful.

She had always wanted to be able to do *something* better than Tammy - if she discounted Tammy's ability to attract boyfriends. Freya didn't want *that* ability. Not yet. Maybe not ever. After that, Freya was the one to ask Tammy to go out walking with her on weekends, and sometimes after school, too. Danae didn't seem to notice - on weekdays they were home before she was, anyway. And if they brought foraged foods to help feed everyone, then she was pleased with their thoughtfulness - so long as they didn't bring back anything poisonous.

CHAPTER FOURTEEN

SUMMER

Summer passed in a blur of summoning and occasional sun. Tammy began to get irritable towards autumn, when the water spirits they summoned started talking to Freya before they talked to her.

"You're taking over my deities," she said after the latest water spirit had proved more interested in discussing current events than in a more personal interaction with Tammy. "Stop it, or I won't let you come with me next time." She took off a shoe and poured water out of it. The water spirit in question had gotten excited by Freya's passing on reports of storms in the north that had caused flooding, with the result that both Freya and Tammy were decidedly damp.

"They're not *your* deities, Tammy. They're their own. And I can't help it if they talk to me." Freya wished she'd brought a change of clothes. She hadn't meant to get the water spirit so excited, but they'd heard a news bulletin about the floods last night, and she'd thought it was the sort of thing that a water deity might be interested in. Unfortunately, she'd been correct. She tipped water out of her own shoes, wondering if it was possible to squeeze the water out of them, and how many blisters she'd have when she got home. She'd discovered that wet shoes did that.

"You don't have to get them so worked up that they throw themselves all over us in some sort of flood re-enactment. I think I'll go back to summoning them by myself." Tammy put her shoe back on, and removed the second shoe. Her mouth was a flat line.

Why is she so annoyed at me? I can't help it if the water spirits prefer to talk to me.

"Don't go by yourself, Tammy. You might come across another kelpie who wants to eat you."

"If so, I'll deal with it. I can throw salt as well as you can." Tammy shoved her foot back into her second shoe with some force, but it got stuck halfway on. Tammy hadn't untied the laces. She stamped around a bit until it went all the way on.

"But you said I was better at it," Freya wailed, on the verge of tears.

"Sure, I did. I was trying to encourage you. I didn't realise that you didn't need encouragement. Now let's go home, I'm soaked. And without even a massage to show for it." Tammy turned her back on Freya and started walking away.

"Wait for me!" Freya hurriedly stuffed her own feet into her shoes, picked up her rucksack, and ran after Tammy.

After that, Tammy stopped taking Freya out. Freya was torn. With the onset of autumn, it was chilly walking in the afternoon, and it began to get dark too early for comfortable or safe walking. But she longed to try out her power again – and she worried for Tammy whenever Tammy was late returning from school. What would Tammy do if she came across another grumpy old kelpie, and she didn't have Freya there to throw salt?

When in due course they moved again, the rental period on their cottage having expired, it was to another rundown cottage in a seaside town with few streams, and less access to the hills. Freya had no desire to call any seaside deities, even if she was able to. It seemed her brief access to her demigoddess powers was at an end.

CHAPTER FIFTEEN

THREE YEARS LATER: SUMMER

"Why do we always have to stay on the coast, Mum? It's a terrible place to grow up. There's nothing to do. Couldn't we just move inland? It was great that summer we had in the hills."

"The hills where you and Tammy disappeared all the time? No thank you. That was a nerve-wracking time for me," Danae said.

Freya looked at her mother in surprise. She'd never realised that Danae had noticed all the times she and Tammy had disappeared to summon the deities of small streams and ponds. That had stopped when they moved back to the coast. The only accessible streams tended to be heavily polluted – and therefore at high risk of containing angry deities – or too close to human habitation for safe summoning. Worse, as far as Freya was concerned, anyway, Tammy had long since stopped taking Freya with her when she went out. That had been the beginning of the end of their closeness. Or maybe just the end. Freya remembered her surprise when Tammy had wanted to show her anything. She sighed.

"Are you sure we can't move inland like other people do?"

The family was packing yet again. Danae's current short-term job had finished, and she'd successfully applied for another, further north, though still on the coast. This was the third move in as many years. Freya heartily wished that her mother would get a permanent job so that they could stop moving, even if it *was* on the coast. She still remembered their cottage on the clifftops wistfully, because they'd had two whole years there before its demise forced their move.

"I've told you before why we stay on the coast. We are watchers. We keep an eye on the sea and her deities."

"Yeah, I know that, Mum. But why us? Why not some other family of demis? And we were fine in the hills away from the sea."

Freya's mum expertly flicked out a sheet, then rolled it tightly. Her fingers whitened as they pressed hard on the sheet.

"We weren't in the hills long. And mistakes were made in the past."

"Like what?" Freya was intrigued despite herself. Her mum almost never talked about whatever kept them near the rising sea.

"It's not something I want to talk about. I've told you about your Grandad, and that's all I'm saying. You don't need to know about the bad things that happened to me in my youth. You'll just have to accept that we live by the sea. Have you packed up that cat yet? If you spent more time doing the right thing instead of running after him, you wouldn't be always complaining about where we live." She jammed the sheet into a partly filled wheeled suitcase that sat beside her.

Typical, just when I think I'm going to learn something useful about our family instead of just generalities about demigods, and Mum goes off on a tangent. I wonder if it's because she *made mistakes? She certainly doesn't like to admit mistakes now.*

"You never want to tell us about the important things, Mum. Why do you keep it to yourself? I'm nearly grown-up, and Tammy is an adult, whatever she acts like. You're going to have to let us in on the secret someday, you know." Freya had reached her full growth now - a centimetre shorter than her mother, to her chagrin. She was still trying to convince Danae that she deserved full voting responsibilities in the household. Sadly, Danae wasn't keen on household democracies.

"Today is not that day. Leave it, Freya. And sort out your cat."

"You just wish I'd left Mr Fluffbum on the streets, don't you Mum?" It was hard not to lash out verbally at her mum when Danae was being so obstructive.

"You know that's not the case, Freya. But cat food is expensive. And you moan about not having friends, but don't go out and make any. I can't do that for you, you know." Her mother picked up a blanket and gave it the same tight rolling treatment as the sheet.

"It's not my fault, Mum. I don't know what to say to people. I'm not like Tammy. And when I do say things, people look at me strangely. At least Mr Fluffbum understands me." Freya turned away. She felt picked on. Just because no-one else in the family had a pet, didn't mean they should resent her having one. And she'd make friends if she could. But every time she did make a friend, the family moved on. It got dispiriting after a while, to the point where she no longer tried to make friends. Why bother if she wouldn't get to keep them?

Her mother's voice interrupted her thoughts.

"Come on, Freya, stop daydreaming and finish your packing! We have to be ready to go first thing, you know."

"I know, Mum, but I'm still looking for Mr Fluffbum. Have you seen him?"

"You know I've had too much to do, lining up a new job, finding somewhere better than this demolition-worthy place to live, trying to keep food on the table, to notice your cat."

"Yes, Mum, I just thought you might have. He usually turns up for dinner around this time."

"Sorry, Freya, you'll have to find him yourself. But pack first, please."

Clearly the subject was closed. Freya wished she'd managed to find out more about her ancestors while her mum was on the topic.

Oh well, never mind the past, focus on the real problem.

She went down the hall to investigate her sister's cupboard-sized room, and interrogate her sister while she was at it.

"Tammy, have you seen Mr Fluffbum?

Tammy looked up from the bed where she was arranging lipstick and foundation into her makeup case in colour order. Freya wondered briefly why Tammy bothered with such things – she'd always had great skin.

"No, I have not seen Mr Fluffbum. Not since he tried to sit on my best coat this morning. He objected to being removed and scratched me, so I shut him outside."

"Tammy! Why would you do that? You know I keep him inside!"

Tammy shrugged.

"He's a cat, he'll figure it out. Maybe he'll find a mouse and have the time of his life killing it."

"Tammy!"

"Well, hush about your cat then, Freya. How do you think I feel about this move? I had just started getting a life here, I had friends to see, and now who knows when I'll get to do that again? Now don't interrupt, I want my makeup put away properly at least." Tammy picked up a tube of mascara from the bed and slotted in into her case.

"You're no fun anymore, Tammy. We used to do stuff together, now you just spend hours with makeup. And go out for more hours with people the rest of us don't get to meet. And put my cat outside."

"You're just jealous."

"No, I'm not. I wouldn't *want* to spend time with a bunch of trolls."

"They are not all trolls, for your information. They never are. I don't know why you always suggest that first. And anyway, who are you to talk, still spending all your time with a cat?"

It was hard for Freya to argue with that, so she tried to settle her sister's disgruntled feelings. Maybe Tammy would help her find Mr Fluffbum if she calmed down.

"You never know, your friends might come visit us in the new town. It's not that far away. Have any of them got cars?"

"Yeah. One of them, anyway." A complete rainbow of lipsticks went into the case, each shade precisely aligned with its neighbour.

"Maybe you could persuade that one to give you a lift with most of our stuff," Freya suggested. "Is that one your boyfriend?"

"Maybe."

"What's your boyfriend's name again?"

"I only told you yesterday, don't tell me you've forgotten already?" A set of flesh-toned eyeshadow went in next to the mascara.

"It's not my fault you change boyfriends so often I can't remember their names!"

"I do not! You just don't pay attention." Tammy reached behind her and threw a pillow at Freya.

"Why should I pay attention, if I blink you've dumped one and picked up another." Freya caught the pillow and threw it back, aiming carefully to avoid the makeup case. Tammy might still be up for a pillow fight, but not if it scattered her precious makeup.

"I'm aiming for quality." Tammy caught the pillow and fluffed it up, then replaced it behind her with a soothing pat, as though the pillow was an affronted cat.

"It looks more like quantity," said Freya.

"How else will I find the quality ones, if I don't try them out?"

"OK, so tell me about the latest quality boyfriend?" Freya ventured further into the room and shut the door behind her, in case privacy would help Tammy talk. If she talked, she might give more information about Mr Fluffbum.

Tammy gave an annoyed huff, but relented enough to tell her sister.

"His name is Sigvard, OK? He's Norwegian. And I haven't brought him home because of the endless comments I get from you and Mum." Tammy looked suspiciously at Freya. "Why do you want to know? You don't usually show any interest in my boyfriends."

"*He's* got a car, hasn't he? I saw him dropping you off last week, when you got back at dawn instead of midnight." Freya sidled closer to the bed.

"Oh. You didn't tell Mum, did you?"

"I didn't need to; she was beside me. You know it's worrying when you stay out all night without warning, don't you?"

"It shouldn't be, you know I can take care of myself."

"Come on, Tammy, I'm your little sister, I shouldn't be telling you these things. It should be the other way round, if anything."

"Yeah, but you've always been the goody two shoes in this family. Look, if I do get Sigvard to take some of my stuff, can you and Mum not speculate about his heritage, for a change? 'Cos I'm telling you straight up, he's part-jotunn, and he gets pretty grumpy if people mistake him for a troll or something like that."

"Is it really a good idea to spend time with a grumpy jotunn who could be mistaken for a troll?"

"Oh, it has its advantages. Jotunns are very well-built." Tammy smiled.

Freya groaned.

"If you're talking about anything other than the size of his biceps, I don't want to know. Just look after yourself, OK? Stay safe."

"Yes, 'Mum'," Tammy sneered.

"So, anyway… could you help me find Mr Fluffbum, since you let him out?"

"No. I've still got half my stuff to pack, and if I don't do it now, Mum will make me leave it behind. Go find him yourself." Tammy slotted some peacock-coloured eyeshadow into her case.

"That's not fair!"

Freya made a lunge for the pillow and threw it at Tammy again, this time deliberately jogging the makeup case, before rushing out of the room. Tammy swore at her, the words mostly cut off by the closing door. The sisterly chat had not been illuminating, and she still didn't have someone to help her find Mr Fluffbum.

Freya stepped outside with a shiver. The weather had been quite mild, before the cluster of storms swooped in. However, the storms came from the north, dragging chill air with them as well as howling winds and sleet. The few late summer gardens Freya passed would be devastated once their owners managed to dig them out of the hail. At least that was one worry Freya's family did not have with this move. There would be no crops for *their* family to lose. They hadn't managed to get an allotment in this town and unusually, they had little growing in their pocket-sized courtyard. A year of drought had caused widespread crop failures. Now they were moving, they'd no doubt end up at the bottom of another allotment waiting list in their new town. Maybe they'd be moving to somewhere with a garden. Freya hoped so, even though it was Danae who would be doing the growing if they did.

Freya and Tammy had been sent out foraging often in the last few weeks. Although she was better at identification now than she had been when she was ten, Freya still would have preferred to be able to grow or buy food. Some foraged food was delicious. Other such foods - such as the ubiquitous dandelions - Freya thought would be best left for wild rabbits to enjoy. *She* certainly didn't get much enjoyment out of the bitter greens. This time she wasn't looking for foraged food, however. Freya ran from house to battered house, calling her cat's name and peering through windows.

"Fluffy... Fluuufbum." She was torn between embarrassment at her pet's name, and worry for her cat. The result was an urgent whisper that probably couldn't be heard above the wind, punctuated by louder calls that died away whenever she saw a movement that could mean someone had heard her.

Is Mr Fluffbum hiding in someone's garage? Has he got stuck in a house that had already been abandoned to the rising sea, tempted in by the promise of shelter, or the hunting of mice?

Freya searched the nearest ring of houses, knocking on doors despite her shyness of strangers. While most who answered the door were sympathetic, no-one had seen a stray cat. It seemed no-one had been watching the storm at all, preferring to ignore it so long as the batteries held out for their streamed movies. Freya started back along the waterfront, checking the row of houses closest to the thundering waves, calling out her cat's name as enticingly as she could, with her voice raised to a shout to be heard, her growing fear for her cat overcoming embarrassment. There was no answering meow.

The shriek of the wind increased as the day wore on, another storm front on its way. Freya's ears began to hurt from it. After hours had passed with no sign of her cat, Freya returned home and risked putting a bowl of precious dried cat food outside the front door, hoping that the lure of food outside mealtimes would attract her cat back home. By late afternoon it was soaked, swollen by rain into a gummy mess. A small procession of ants were busily biting off tiny pieces and taking them away, but Mr Fluffbum hadn't appeared. Freya sat by the bowl watching the ants. Each morsel of disappearing food was a needle piercing her heart. She felt empty and cold without her cat.

CHAPTER SIXTEEN

STORMY WEATHER

By evening the increasing violence of the storm forced Freya indoors despite her worry. She sat by a window with a view of the front strip of concrete. The window itself was covered with strips of tape to prevent shattering in the event of a particularly violent wind gust. Her first choice of window had not been available - it was already covered with a sheet of plywood, since a wind-flung branch in an earlier storm had smashed its glass. Freya huddled in a blanket for warmth.

"Can't we turn on a heater or light a fire or something, Mum?"

Danae was chopping onions with a practised hand. Onions were almost always cheap.

"No, Freya. You know the electricity has been off for days. And there's no wood left for a fire."

Freya turned away from the window to look at her mother.

"Why is the electricity still out, anyway? Isn't it someone's job to fix it?"

"Yes, well. That woman who runs the corner store told me that every time they try to fix the lines, they get blown down again. Too many storms for them to cope with. If you ask me, *I* think there's probably some Thor-kins around in this town. They're often associated with storms."

Danae's stormy expression as she searched through the sprouting potatoes for ones that weren't too soft to use suggested she herself might be related to the thunder god, though Freya was sure that wasn't the case.

"You always think everything's due to some demi or other, Mum. Couldn't it just be weather?"

"Not in my experience. There's usually more demi effects around than most people realise. They just don't know what they're seeing."

"OK, Mum, if that's how you see it. Where's the camping stove?" Freya didn't disbelieve in the gods - she'd seen plenty of river gods, after all. But she did think her mother's attitude was rather extreme.

"It's in the kitchen box. But we've only got a bit of fuel left for it, so keep it for hot drinks, after I've used it for the soup."

"Can't I have a hot water bottle, Mum?"

"There's not enough fuel for that, Freya. And you spent too much money on cat food for that cat of yours for us to buy more fuel."

"He has to eat, Mum!"

Freya's family had invested in some camping equipment at their last house when there was a little extra money for a change. It was worthwhile to be able to cook even when the electricity was off, as it so often was. But a camp stove didn't keep anyone warm. Warmth was a luxury item these days. Coal fires had been banned for a few years now, and only rich people had hydrogen or solar heating. Freya kept her vigil in the cold, her head resting on the chilly window.

The potato and onion soup was good, though, seasoned with foraged herbs. Freya felt a little better after she'd had her share.

Mum makes the best soups, even when we have almost no food.

Despite her concern for Mr Fluffbum, she felt happier for being fed.

I just hope Mr Fluffbum has found the food outside. Even if it is all anty, now.

"Are you going to bed, Freya?"

Danae had collected the dishes and left them in the sink.

"No, I want to stay up and see if Mr Fluffbum comes back."

"Are you packed for tomorrow?"

"Mostly." It was almost true. Freya didn't have much to pack, so she didn't think it would take her long.

"Well, finish it off now please. Then, you and Tammy make sure the dishes are done. I'm going to bed."

"Yeah, yeah. Goodnight, Mum."

Freya resumed her watch of the street, without packing, hoping that soon a twitch of an ear or swish of a tail would announce her missing cat's return.

It was closer to dawn than midnight when she awoke, dismayed to discover that she'd slept. Her watch had been unsuccessful. No cat had slunk nonchalantly into view. She checked out the window again, hoping to see Mr Fluffbum waiting outside the window. Instead, her view was unexpectedly obscured. At first, she thought her vision was faulty. Or maybe the night was just really dark. Then she realised that her window had in fact been covered by a layer of leaves.

"Seriously? We don't even have a street tree here."

Freya tugged at the window latch, but it resisted.

Oops. I forgot it's painted shut.

Freya creaked to her feet. Surely, she was too young to feel this stiff. But she'd slept so long in one position, her legs had gotten numb. Wind still battered the house, but she wouldn't do any good trying to see through a dark window. She lurched down the stairs, clutching the banister for balance. Her legs weren't working properly after her long stint at the window. She wriggled her toes until the feeling came back into them, then proceeded in a more normal fashion. The blanket around her slipped off halfway down, and she had to pause to rearrange it scarf-style over her shoulders, or risk tripping on the trailing edge.

I'm sure other demigoddesses don't have to fight with blankets on the stairs in the night. Why does this sort of thing always happen to me?

A few more steps saw her safely to the ground floor and creeping down the hallway. The floor was uncovered - probably it had been polished a couple of decades ago, but it was now returning to its original state. The surface was chilly beneath her feet, and the floorboards creaked in an uneven cadence as she walked along the hall to the front door. Peering out, she was relieved to see that the rain had stopped. However, no cat mewed in grateful greeting. Remembering another night like this one, a few years ago, Freya stepped out of the house and pulled the door closed behind her. The night they stayed in a bed and breakfast, that dreadful day their house had washed away. Back when Mr Fluffbum had been just a kitten, he had led her down to the beach on a stormy night, begging for fish from the wind demis. Had he gone looking for Lio in a storm again? It had been years since that had happened - since they moved to the hills, in fact. Freya headed for the sea, just in case.

There was not much beach in this town, not anymore. Thanks to the rising of the sea, there was now only a concrete seawall increasingly broken up by seas that were rougher and higher than it had been designed for. With many of the streetlights not operating, the streets were dark as well as windy.

"Come on, Mr Fluffbum, this is the sort of night you're supposed to be curled up on my bed, not missing in action."

There was no answer from the streets. On balance, Freya supposed that was just as well. What would she do if she met someone out here in the wild night? Lucky it was so cold, anyone sensible would be at home. Did that mean she was not sensible? She supposed it did.

Freya reached the seafront without sighting her cat, or anyone else. If it weren't for the blue-lit flickering of TV screens from some windows - the ones with household batteries - the town could be empty, ghost ridden. The wind howled through the streets, blowing leaves and old takeaway boxes before it.

Freya leaned into the wind and clutched at her blanket. She looked north first, but could only see endless breakers crashing against the rocks which were exposed at low tide. No cat there. She turned bodily to the south, blocking some of the wind so that her blanket flapped in front of her. She squinted along the seawall. The promenade was scattered with chunks of broken concrete from the wall. Another furious gust, and a chance wave broke over the wall with a smattering of foam. Was that a movement, just beyond the reach of the wave? She hurried in that direction, but stopped, her skin crawling when she saw a figure easing out from beside a building. Distant thunder rolled ominously. The figure laughed cheerfully.

"That is so over-the-top, honestly! Thor has too much sense of the dramatic," said the figure.

Freya felt a rush of relief. The voice was familiar, and so was the skinny, half-clad figure, seemingly lit by red light. Given the night was dark, the effect was startling.

"Lio! What are you doing lurking about here? It's a long way from your normal beach, isn't it? Don't you have things to do, races to run?"

"I always have races to run. Though I've not done that for a couple of years. Family duties, you know. But as for beaches, I go where the wind blows. The world is my home! But I thought I saw you cowering between the buildings, and I was intrigued."

"I was not cowering! It's cold out here, you know. Not that you're dressed for the weather."

Lio grinned.

"I make my own weather. No blankets for me. But you are usually led by a cat aren't you?"

Freya, who had experienced a lightening of heart when she identified Lio, now felt a flood of hope.

"Just the one cat. I've been looking for him everywhere. Have you seen him?"

Lio's face clouded. "I haven't, sorry. But you should know, there's a troll in this town. Nearly full-blood, I heard. They can be partial to cats." Fear clutched at Freya's stomach, hope vanishing like water down a plughole.

"Do you mean..."

"I don't know anything for sure. I only come when there are storms, you should know that. And this storm's from the north, so I've just whipped in on the end of the cyclone, so to speak. I heard about the troll from friend. A troll so nearly full-blood is pretty rare these days, so that gets commented on. As do demi-goddesses who walk out in storms with their cats. Anyway, I hoped I'd see you out and about. Hardly anyone else comes out in storms these days. I haven't seen you for years. You've grown."

"Ugh, you sound like a long-lost aunt! You've grown, too, if it comes to that."

"You should come out more often. I've missed you."

"I guess I've been feeding Mr Fluffbum well enough that he hasn't felt the need to go out. If he doesn't, I don't. Sorry."

"It's not much fun without other demis to talk to, you know. Full-bloods are always holier-than-thou, and humans don't even notice me. Or maybe they pretend they don't, I'm not sure. They look around and through homeless people in the same way. So demis - well, I just wish there were more of you out at night. And out in the weather. It seems like most of you are practically human, these days."

Freya clutched her blanket tighter.

Lio seems much less tied to humans than we are. Maybe his deity-blood is more recent...

"Well, we almost are. Mostly human, that is. Most of us have almost no powers to speak of, so we have to try to look like humans, anyway. Or so my Mum is always telling us. It doesn't seem fair that we should be demis and not ever get to tell anyone, or do much about it," said Freya.

"Unfair, and surely dangerous, too. If you don't do anything with your power, however small, surely one day something will pop, won't it?"

Lio gestured with his hands, miming an explosion. No constrained British body language for him, Freya noticed.

"I guess. Tammy - my sister - she's always using her powers. No fear that she will pop. But I don't even know what my powers are. Apart from water summoning, I suppose. Not that I've done that much recently. I never do near the sea." She shivered. The sea still scared her after all these years near it.

"So, you found some powers then? That's great!" Lio enthused.

Freya shook her head, not denying it, but rather in response to the emotions that came with remembering her lost closeness to her sister.

"Yeah, I did. Water like Tammy. Fresh water."

"That's an odd one. I wouldn't have guessed it from a Norse goddess, Greek wino combo," Lio commented.

"I know, right? I have no idea how Tammy and I ended up with such a weird-yet-similar power. That sort of drove Tammy and I apart, you know. I think she was envious of what I have. She went through some weird stuff when her power came in, and I haven't had anything like she did. Not that I've done anything with power for a while. There didn't seem to be any point in competing with her. But that reminds me. You said there was a troll here. Does he have a name? Tammy knows some part-trolls. And jotunn."

"Sorry, I'm not good with names, I mostly remember faces. But she should probably be avoiding the jotunn too. I've heard it said that jotunn is just an older name for troll."

A particularly strong gust of wind spattered sea spray over Freya. She edged towards the meagre shelter of the battered seaside houses, unwilling to turn her back on the sea. Lio walked with her. He seemed to have no qualms about the stormy sea.

But then he wouldn't, would he? He spends his whole life in storms.

"But aren't the Norse giants and trolls different? That's what Mum always told me."

"Stories change. It's hard to know their truth. Be careful out there. Avoid the jotunn if you can. Your cat should, too." Lio looked around as though trolls might be peering out from the nearby buildings.

"Tammy's not going to listen to me about that. But we're leaving here tomorrow. That's why it's so urgent I find Mr Fluffbum - no, don't laugh. I was pretty young when I named him, you know. And it suits him still, he's got such long fur. If only I could find him!"

"I can look for your missing cat. He may remember me fondly."

"That's true. I don't think we would have got through without you and your fish, that first winter," said Freya, warmth stealing into her voice.

"My pleasure," said Lio. "But I make no promises, now. Trolls, you know. And kelpies."

"Surely there aren't kelpies here, too! I haven't seen any."

"Oh, yes. It's probably a good thing you're leaving. I don't know how long you've been here, but this town is not a healthy one, not for people who like to live long, happy lives without being a meal."

Freya shivered. While they hadn't encountered more than the usual number of dangers in this particular town, hearing how dangerous it *could* be was worrying. But...

"So, how do I know I can trust you? Are you a healthy being to be around? It's not like I know you well anymore."

"Hmm, tricky question! But yes, you can trust me. I always looked out for Mr Fluffbum, didn't I? Still, how do you know you can trust anyone?"

Freya found herself nodding.

"I suppose. But tell me if you see Mr Fluffbum. Please! I miss him. I need him."

"I'll keep an eye out. But I'll only be able to tell you if another storm blows up this way, or if I see him before this storm moves on. You land demis are not the only ones with limited powers, alas."

He seemed genuinely sad about this. Freya too wished she had the powers of her ancestors. Why, the original Freya was said to have had a chariot drawn through the sky by cats! That seemed beyond the achievable in Freya's lifetime. Right now, just one cat curling around her ankles would do.

A sudden gust of wind blew sea spray onto Freya once more and she shivered again, suddenly aware of how bone-deep the cold had become.

"I can't stay out here. I'll freeze. And surely Mr Fluffbum wouldn't have stayed out, either. He's usually inside on nights like this."

Lio looked at her with something like pity on his face, and reached out a hand to gently pat her shoulder.

"I do hope you find your cat. Check for bones, though. Good luck." With those decidedly depressing words, he turned and ran swiftly out of sight. Freya wondered where the other boys were, the ones whom she'd seen sometimes when she saw Lio on a beach. She didn't wonder long though. The bitter cold and the talk of trolls and bones scared her. She turned away from the sea, and started running herself, back to the house that was home for the rest of this night, at least.

Next morning, Freya awoke at first light still pressed against her leaf-covered window. She had spent the night leaning against it in the hopes of hearing her cat come home. She was stiff and cold, and had to stretch her legs a few times before she had enough feeling in them to walk without falling, then went to find her sister.

"Tammy. Tammy, wake up. I need to know; just how much troll is that boyfriend of yours?"

"Mmmf. Why are you waking me up so early?" Tammy rolled away from Freya.

"Because my cat is still missing, and your boyfriend might have something to do with it. Tell me about Sigvard, please," said Freya, jittering from foot to foot with impatience and worry.

"I don't see what Sigvard has to do with your cat. Like I told you, he's a jotunn, not a troll. And he's from Norway. OK? Now let me sleep."

"Are you sure he's really a jotunn?"

"That's what he told me. Why would he lie? Now go away!" Tammy pulled her pillow over her head.

Freya did so, still worried by the dreadful thought that had come to her while she slept.

What if Tammy's boyfriend was also the troll Lio had told her about? What could be easier for a cat-loving troll than to pick off a friendly cat like Mr Fluffbum?

Still, there was not much to be done, since Freya had no way of verifying the species of Tammy's boyfriend. All she could do was keep looking for her cat.

A tour of the streets in the morning light - dreary with a light drizzle that kept threatening to become heavier - failed to turn up any sign of her cat. When she returned to the house, colder than ever, and now uncomfortably damp as well, Freya saw that the leaves on her window had blown partly off. The remaining leaves spelt out words:

NO CAT YET.

Can't you manage anything creepier, Lio?

The wind demi clearly didn't have access to something as simple as pencil and paper. At least, Freya was pretty sure that it was Lio who had rearranged the leaves.

The house she returned to was in a familiar state of semi-chaos, with the usual piles of things they enjoyed having but now needed to pack littering the floor.

"Mum, why do we even bother to keep this stuff?"

"Because it's important to be warm enough at night. Are you saying you don't want blankets?"

"Of course I do, it's just that we have to pack everything so often. Maybe we should just admit we're permanent travellers and live in sleeping bags."

"That doesn't sound comfortable. And anyway, I'm sure we'll find somewhere permanent one day."

"But when, Mum? I'm so sick of moving all the time!"

"Oh well, it depends..."

Freya's mother trailed off, the task of exiting a house taking over her forebrain once more as she piled last-minute things into bags.

"Oh well, same old same old," sighed Freya. Then she rallied.

"But Mum, I still haven't seen Mr Fluffbum. Have you seen him anywhere? We can't leave without him."

"Look, I'm too busy to *think* right now, let alone look for that cat of yours. We have a deadline; buses don't wait for anyone. And we don't have transferable tickets. If you can't find him, he'll just have to make his own way."

"But he's a *cat*, Mum, not some super-tracker dog or haunt or something!"

"I know, I know, but I'm too busy. Please go make sure we're packed up, and hopefully he'll turn up shortly."

Dissatisfied with this response, but powerless to change her mother's mind, Freya set off on her usual exit-tour of the house, collecting essentials that had been left out: portable stove, solar charger for her sister's phone (not often useful in winter, but too expensive to lose), a half-empty pack of painkiller.

She passed her sister arguing on her phone to someone. Not wanting to eavesdrop particularly, but unable not to hear her sister's half of the conversation in the thin-walled house, Freya inadvertently gained more insight into the challenges their family was facing this morning.

Tammy was grumpy because her boyfriend (Freya couldn't help but wonder again, *troll-friend?*) had apparently refused to move any things of hers, claiming a lack of fuel. She refused to discuss the problem with her family, grimly stuffing her belongings into an overloaded suitcase with one broken wheel. Freya suspected that the friend had declared a disinterest in visiting Tammy once she was further afield. That would certainly account for some of the grumpiness.

Freya hastily crammed her belongings into the large rucksack she'd acquired in a thrift shop. It was easier to carry a cat cage if you had a free hand. Her other hand would be engaged in pulling a suitcase full of food and kitchen items. Now though, she wondered if she would need the cage. There was still no sign of her cat, and no more word from Lio. The storm had receded, leaving the usual grey skies.

When the family left later that day, they left without Freya's beloved pet. Freya took the precious cat-cage, though - just in case. No amount of raging or tears could persuade the rest of the family to stay longer. Freya was heartbroken. Surely, no new town was worth leaving behind a loved one. Even if the old town in question was a troll-infested hole full of houses without decent gardens.

If I had found Mr Fluffbum, I'd be happy to be leaving this dump. It's not like I even made any friends here. It's just... I want my cat!

Freya was the only one who looked back as the small family trudged away towards the station. All she saw was rain, lashing the houses where they perched at the edge of the heaving sea. Her tears blended with the rain till they ran unnoticed down her face. By the time the rain cleared - well, stopped for a short time anyway - her tears had dried. And she knew that she couldn't rely on her family to care for the same things that she did.

"Goodbye, Mr Fluffbum. I hope you turn up somehow."

Their bus was missing. Freya stared at the orange text on the overhead signs, willing their bus number to appear, perhaps with a few numbers indicating the minutes until it arrived.

That'd be a handy demigod ability. I wish I had it.

Sadly, no matter how hard she willed, the display continued to indicate a lack of buses.

"What time was the bus supposed to be, Mum?" Freya asked, setting down her burdens and wrapping her arms around herself.

"It's supposed be leaving in two minutes. Right before the bus going east."

"And we're catching the bus going north, right?"

"Yes. The bus that is currently nowhere to be seen."

Freya shuddered as a particularly violent gust of wind blew a wet spattering of rain under the bus shelter.

"It doesn't look like the bus gods want us to leave without Mr Fluffbum," Freya said.

"Act your age, Freya, there are no such things as bus gods," Tammy said, hunching her shoulders against the wind.

"I know, Tammy, it's a joke." Freya rolled her eyes at her sister. "Sort of."

"If Sigvard had been nicer to me this morning I'd stay anyway," Tammy muttered.

"Told you he was a troll." Freya knew she shouldn't taunt her sister about her boyfriend - Tammy was obviously upset - but *she* was too upset about the loss of Mr Fluffbum to care.

"He is *not* a troll. Just making a really poor choice right now."

"That's enough from both of you," snapped Danae. She'd been furiously searching bus timetables on her phone. "We can catch the next bus north, there's one due in half an hour. But I don't have enough money left to get us new tickets all the way to our destination. We'll have to walk the rest of the way. With any luck the storm has done its worst here."

"Oh, Mum, no!" both girls chorused in dismay.

"Yes. It's not so far. And it will be a good opportunity to review your knowledge of northern edibles. They're quite different to the southeast."

Tammy and Freya exchanged identical expressions of horror. Neither of them felt that an extended walk in the rain with their mother drilling them in foraging was an enjoyable prospect. However, there was little choice.

"At least we can get partway on the bus," Freya said. "Will we have far to walk?"

"We'll see," said Danae.

There were still forty kilometres to go to get to their new home when the bus deposited them at another gloomy station. The rain had paused for a while and watery sunlight was causing steam to rise off the asphalt.

"Let's get a move on, then," Danae said briskly. Freya and Tammy, scrambling to pick up their things, ceased glaring at each other long enough to glare at their mother.

"This isn't anywhere near where we're going, is it?" Tammy asked, consulting her phone.

"It's a lot closer than we were. The sooner we start, the sooner we'll be there." Freya crossed her arms.

"We're going to have to camp out, aren't we, Mum?"

Danae shifted uneasily.

"Maybe not, if we hurry."

"I am not camping out. My things would get ruined," Tammy declared.

"Your things aren't as important as my job," Danae snapped.

Freya picked up her empty cat cage and shouldered her rucksack.

Looks like it's time to act like the adult around here.

"Come on, Mum, Tammy. The longer you argue the later it will be when we arrive."

CHAPTER SEVENTEEN

AUTUMN

"Don't make me go to school today, Mum," Freya pleaded. She was standing in the doorway of their rather battered new-to-them kitchen while her mother threw together some food for the day. The grim memory of camping out en route to this place was fading, thankfully. Blisters had made all three of them miserable for the second day of their enforced trek, and the weather hadn't helped.

"Why shouldn't you go to school? It's not a holiday or a weekend." Her mother was abstracted, not focused on the argument.

"Come on, Mum, it's horrible there. There's no greenery, it's all just fences, asphalt and brick buildings. And everyone stands around in huddles, like groups of penguins with their backs to the storm."

"Sounds like a sensible way to keep warm. It's certainly colder here than in the south." Her Mum pressed down the lid on her container of salad and slipped it into the bag standing at her feet.

"It's not sensible if you don't have a huddle to join. And I don't. Come on Mum, one day off won't hurt."

"You know I could be fined for not sending you to school, Freya."

Freya felt that she might be winning her argument. She pressed harder.

"And Mum, the teachers don't even stop people bullying each other. They just stalk between groups. I suppose they usually stop outright warfare, but that's about it."

"Look, Freya, I'm sorry you haven't settled in yet. It takes time though. I'm sure you'll find some people to spend time with sooner or later." Danae picked up her bag and slung it over her shoulder. She was clearly ready to leave, and no closer to letting Freya skip school.

"You always say that, and it hasn't happened yet. The kids at this school pick on me because I'm new, you know. Do you want me to have to go through that?"

"Of course not, Freya, but you must go to school, and I must go to work. That's just the way it is. You'll survive. Think of it as character building."

"I've got enough character for a dozen of me by now."

"Go for the baker's dozen then. Once more into the fray and all that. Off to school with you now." Freya's mum herded her out the door.

That day at break-time her situation reached new lows. The clouds were a bruise in the sky, and the asphalt was dark and wet from earlier rain. People had formed their usual huddles. Freya had yet to fit in to any group. It had been a lonely few weeks, especially with no cat to go home to. She stood uncomfortably to one side of the so-called playground, trying to look casual and relaxed.

"Freya, slayer," chanted one obnoxious boy from a nearby huddle, staring over at her in a challenging manner. Red hair, freckles and broad face identified him as a local.

Well, there goes the casual look.

She hadn't figured out his name yet - admittedly in part because she didn't want to know.

"Did you forget your big sword on your way from Valhalla? No, wait, you don't have a sword and you don't come from Valhalla," he said in a mocking tone.

Freya groaned inwardly. Apparently, he had listened to her last outburst, when she had had more than enough taunting for one day. She'd told off the teasing group in no uncertain terms, trying to educate them about the difference between someone with a Nordic name, and someone who came from the Norse hall of the gods. It was always tricky, trying to tread a fine line between denying the gods - probably a hazardous thing to do when one was descended from them - and telling the truth. She'd always had it drummed into her that telling the truth was simply not an option.

"Freya layer then? Are you easy like your big sister? Down in the valley with someone different every week I hear. Valley-girl, valley-girl! Give us a kiss, valley-girl!"

Freya's cheeks burned, and the blood pounded in her ears. She opened her mouth to make some reply, but couldn't think of one. His taunts about her sister stung all the more for the grain of truth in them. Tammy took her ancestry as a descendant of a fertility goddess seriously. Freya, who had inherited the name, was always trying to live it down. Freya had hoped that now Tammy wasn't at school any longer, she would avoid the unpleasant associations and insults. It seemed that her hopes were unfounded. She turned and ran indoors, trying not to cry in front of the other kids. Maybe she should tell them about the goddess Freya being the chooser of the dead. Except that she'd always hated that idea.

Safely away from the eyes of her classmates in the toilet stalls, she let a few tears slip down her cheeks. Every time she moved to a new school it seemed to go like this. It was hard to make friends when she started off as an outsider. But this school was the worst so far. And she stood out from the locals, who almost all seemed to share the same colouring. Clearly no-one moved far around here.

She emerged from the stalls when the bell rang for the next class, avoiding the eyes of her classmates as she slid into a seat. This school was old-fashioned, with desks and chairs - no beanbags around here. The students slouched into the room in the usual way. The boy who had been bullying her earlier pretended to trip next to her, and dropped a note onto her desk as he did so. She didn't pick it up, but couldn't help but look at it. In large pencil letters, the words

'*Midnight. Oak tree in town square. We know where you live.*' were written.

Now there was an assignation she shouldn't keep. Then she worried - what would happen when she didn't go? Would these bullies track her down to her house?

At least at home she would have the backup of her sister and mother - though only her mother was likely to be helpful. Tammy had recently told her that she needed to learn to stand up for herself. At times like this she wished Dad had stuck around. Surely, he would have stood up for her. She had no idea where he was, these days. She didn't even have a postcard from him to give an indication of where he might be living.

Freya risked glancing around the room. The red-haired boy was staring at her, smirking. She hastily lowered her eyes again. The teacher stood at the front of the class and shouted for attention. It took a few minutes of glaring and shouting on his behalf before the class quieted.

"Listen up, class. As you know, there's a major storm forecast today. Usually, we'd simply keep you in class and have a wet-day lunch hour, but the latest forecast has the storm making landfall directly through our town, with a high chance of building damage, so school is closing early."

There was a cheer, and the teacher shuffled his feet as the class turned their full attention on him.

He probably doesn't usually get that much attention in a week.

"Ahem. We expect you all to go home and help your families to prepare your homes for a potential emergency. This storm is shaping up to be quite out of the ordinary, so please go straight home, no lingering."

The red-headed boy put up his hand.

"Yes, Gareth?"

"What if we want to linger?" Gareth's voice was a sneer of sarcasm.

Another boy interjected.

"Yeah, what if we want to get chips and watch the waves on the seafront?"

The teacher assumed a dignified-yet-responsible air that Freya thought he'd probably practised in front of the mirror - maybe when he was pretending he was principal already.

"I trust that you will act sensibly and go home. Remember that the eyes of the public are on you, and you are expected to uphold the honour of the school while you wear its uniform."

There was muffled tittering. Clearly the class didn't think much of the school's honour. The teacher smoothed his hair sideways.

"That means no eating chips in uniform, and wave watching would be an extremely unsafe activity under the circumstances. I strongly advise against it."

"Are hot dogs OK then?"

The class laughed as Gareth continued his efforts to mock the teacher. This time, the teacher ignored them.

"Now. Since this storm is of unprecedented strength, we are taking the unusual step of giving you advice to share with your families. Here is what the forecasters are telling us. When this storm hits us, there will be gale force winds as well as the usual rain. I'm sure we're all used to rain."

The class groaned. They were indeed used to rain.

"However, given the predicted wind strength, you and your families might be best to retreat into the basement, if you have one. Listen for updates on the radio."

He was interrupted again.

"Radios are so last century. No-one has radios anymore; we have the internet."

"Nevertheless, I hope you or your parents are able to access one. In case of emergency, audio communication is more reliable. Those of you in flats, I hope your buildings are strongly built." There was more laughter, rather nervous from those who lived in flats. The teacher smoothed his hair again. "Er. Yes. I mean, consider using internal stairways for shelter. Please pack up your bags now, and when the fire bell goes, it's time to go home. I will expect you to make up today's work after the storm has passed. I have assigned you all a worksheet on calculus as applied to storm prediction that you can go through. I also suggest that you investigate the principles of transistor radios." He grinned toothily, an unpleasant expression on his usually sober face. "You may find the information useful."

Typical. Go home and look after yourself, but make sure you get this worksheet done and do some electronics. Teacher priorities are all wrong.

Freya started re-packing the few things she'd taken out of her bag, pointedly leaving the note on her desk. It was not the time to consider clandestine meetings, even if she had wanted to go - which she didn't, of course. Even if this was the first invitation she'd had to participate in some sort of activity with her schoolmates.

Freya joined the rush of students out the door when the bell rang. The red-haired boy, Gareth, managed to press in behind her, and she shuddered away from his unwanted touch. The sooner she got away from school, the better. She broke into a run as soon as the press of bodies eased. The wind had risen even in the short time since she'd come inside, dark clouds scudding faster across the sky. Ragged tendrils of cloud reached down towards her, twisting in a disturbing reminder of a tornado. Freya shuddered. Surely the clouds couldn't really reach for her?

She decided to take a shortcut through an alley behind the shops. She didn't like the look of the rising wind. It was almost certainly accompanied by storm sprites, who she never got on with. They seemed to take delight in giving her unexpected shocks. Also, their red colouring currently reminded her of the unfriendly townsfolk. As she pounded past the back doors of shops, shopkeepers were dragging their recycling bins indoors. Some bins had already blown over, strewing the alleyway with refuse. Freya leaped over blown boxes and dodged bottles rattling down the street, enjoying the challenge despite the rising wind. She turned the corner to head up the hill towards their house, and skidded to a halt. Ranged across the street were a group of large, red-haired boys.

CHAPTER EIGHTEEN

ENTER THE WERE-FOXES

All of them looked like the boy who had been taunting her at school, but bigger. Freya took an involuntary step backwards. She'd been so busy worrying about storm sprites that she hadn't paid enough attention to her surroundings, thinking herself safe from the mundane.

As she eyed the group warily, wondering how to get around them, she realised that in fact this was not a mundane encounter. Every one of the large boys in front of her had lengthening hair on their exposed forearms. And curiously, she could see their nostrils flaring as they took a threatening step towards her. She had a sudden wild thought that perhaps this was simply a meeting of the ginger society on steroids, before shaking herself back to reality. She had to find a way home. And she didn't want to get entangled with what was looking worryingly like a pack of weres. Were-what, she didn't know and didn't want to have to find out. She eyed the feral grins of the boys. Were their canines lengthening? One of them stepped closer with a swagger in his step.

"Are you listening, Freya? This information could save your life one day." Her mother's remembered voice made an unwelcome counterpoint.

"So, new girl in town, eh? We heard about you and your sister."

Freya gritted her teeth and forced out a reply (not easy, through gritted teeth, but that was the way these boys made her feel).

"I'm just getting home before the storm. I'm not looking for trouble."

"Don't keep reading your book, you need to know how to deal with weres."

Not helpful, Mum.

"Well, looks like trouble found you first," sniggered the leader. Freya wondered how long he'd been waiting to say that - or if he said it every time he and his friends cornered someone.

"Don't you want to avoid the storm too?" she suggested in a reasonable tone.
"Keep them thinking, not acting."
Good advice, Mum, Freya thought. *How about some specifics?*
"Nah, it's more fun out here, ain't it boys?" The red-haired leader looked back at his red-haired cronies and winked. "If we stay out a bit longer, we can fight the sprites. But-" his attention turned back to Freya. "You are in *our* patch here. And you're not one of us. If you wanna use this way, you're going to have to fight for the right. Yeah, fight for the right!"
"Whatever you do, avoid large groups of weres."
Too late, Mum. Now what?
The group began to clap in time, grinning at each other and chanting. Freya was sure their canines were longer now. She needed to know what they were in order to deal with them. Werewolves? No, none of the re-wilding movements had managed to get wolves approved yet, so anything wolf-shaped that turned up would be shot by angry farmers protecting their stock. Were-polecats? That would be weird. And they'd be able to climb. These guys didn't look especially agile though. Maybe... she cast her mind about, trying to think of what animals were gingery around here. Ah! Foxes. She sniffed, suddenly aware that her movements were being copied by the figures ranged around her. A rank odour met her nose. Yes, foxes seemed about right. Didn't they smell bad? Right on cue, the ringleader wrinkled his nose at her.
"You're not just new, you smell weird. Boys, don't she smell weird?"
His cohort nodded obediently. They didn't seem to bother thinking for themselves.
"Yeah, she stinks. Stinks worse than the singletons round here. What *is* she?"
"We'll have to have a bath after we beat her up, Tobes."
"Nah, Lachy, it's gonna rain. Don't fuss your fur."
"I reckon we'll need deodorant after her."
"Nah, put the deodorant on her, man. Keep it real."
Ugh. She didn't care for their banter. She was pretty sure of her identification now. Were-foxes. *They* stank, not her. It was worrying that they seemed to think that she smelled different though. Could they tell demis from regular humans? That might be a problem, one day. If they were weres, she supposed that they would have a better than average sense of smell. That would also explain the ginger fur starting to cover their arms, and the incipient beards on previously beardless faces. Also, foxes hanging out in an alleyway, how typical. Really, the only thing that was odd if she judged them by fox standards was the way they were hanging out together. Maybe that was something weres did differently.

She couldn't recall. Right now, she needed to know how to escape a pack of were-foxes, and she didn't have hounds and horses to help her out. Or did she?

She snapped her fingers involuntarily, a sudden movement that caught the attention of the whole group. They all focused on her hand. She moved it to the right, and their eyes followed it. She crouched briefly, picked up a random piece of rubbish - a half-eaten packet of crisps, it turned out to be, and tossed it to the side, away from her, hoping to divert attention away from herself. The group pounced after it as one. She was startled by their reaction, but quickly took advantage of it by starting to run back the way she had come. Back one block and over a street there was something that just might help - if she could get that far. The wind was whipping about her face now, the few trees on the grassy slopes above the town being blown by great gusts. The sky was darkening rapidly, although it was not nearly sundown. She pelted down the alley and took the corner faster than was sensible, grabbing the rough brick corner of the greengrocer's building to help swing herself round faster.

Up the street again, the way she obviously should have gone the first time round. The streets were deserted now, shop fronts covered by roll-down frontages or locked metal grilles. Soft footsteps followed her, their lack of sound scarier than the clatter of boots would have been. Her breath was coming in ragged gasps. While she spent plenty of time walking, she didn't do much running these days. She'd need some breath for what she planned to do. Just a bit further...

A clawed hand grabbed at her arm, slowing her as she twisted away from it. But she reached out in one desperate lunge and grabbed the stone fountain with both hands. She vaulted into the shallow water that surrounded the leaping horse sculptures at its centre and started to sing a song-web. She didn't know for sure that anything inhabited this fountain, but it was an unusual thing to grace a square in such a small town. Maybe just once in her life she'd get lucky. And if nothing else, there was a chance of a water deity.

Red-furred weres tumbled to a halt at the edge of the fountain, circling round it and growling. None of them seemed inclined to speak now. She added a couple of extra notes to her song and circled the horses herself. It wouldn't do to have a raging grindylow or nixie grabbing her rather than grabbing her foes. The fountain was only just big enough for this spell. Reaching the end of her circle, facing the ringleader again, she completed her song. There was a tremendous cracking sound as the hooves of the fountain's horses broke free. A smell of chill, dank caves rolled forth, making Freya gasp for fresher air. The stone horses leapt out of the fountain, battering were-foxes with their stony hooves, their mouths opening in silent neighs. Water splashed over Freya, making her gasp. The weres ran back the way they had come in dismay, yelping when those hard hooves came into contact with them. The sound of stone hooves on asphalt was a dull clatter, quickly receding. Freya didn't wait to see what happened next. She climbed soggily out of the pool, muttering a quick thanks, and ran up the street and homewards as best she could. She left a trail of wet footprints at first, but as she ran the storm broke over her, a deluge of heavy raindrops that obliterated her trail. She could smell ozone as the rain hit the concrete. Freya glanced upwards. The clouds were too close now to see if sprites accompanied them. Sprites were mostly found *above* thunderclouds; they only descended to pester mortals when the clouds lowered. She increased her pace. She had no idea how long the being that had inhabited the fountain's horses would keep the were-fox pack occupied, but she needed to get home before the storm reached its full fury.

Of course, foxes were supposed to be cunning, too, so she shouldn't discount further problems from the weres. Hopefully, they wouldn't get in her way now. All she had to do was run a couple more streets and she'd be on the home stretch. Of course, she wasn't used to running far at a time. She could cope with doing school sports within the limits of what was perceived as acceptable (that meant running slowly and complaining about it afterwards). Running from a were-pack was a misadventure that hadn't come her way before, and she didn't feel like she was fit enough for the challenge. Right now, she was gasping for each breath, she had a stitch in her side, and her legs were sending extremely negative messages her way. Assuming she got out of this mess in one piece, she was totally going to add some running training into her weekly schedule. Sadly, the limited repertoire of things that worked for her as a demi did not include superhuman strength or agility. Or growing things. Frankly, she was amazed her song-web had worked, without the support of her sister.

Freya risked a glance back, and was encouraged that she could not see any of the red-haired were-fox boys.

Just one more street now, she told her heaving lungs. A flash of russet glimpsed from the corner of her eyes was the only warning she was given. All at once she was at the centre of a flurry of kicks, bites and punches. The physical assault was stunning, so unexpected and rough. Freya tried to battle her way out of the middle of the brawling weres, with little effect.

How did they catch up with me? I suppose four-legged creatures can run faster than two-legged ones.

For a few, horrible minutes, there was nothing but pain - first individual pain points as one punch was succeeded by a kick. Then there seemed to be no discerning each blow from the next. Were those teeth in her leg?

Yuck, I hope they brush those canines. Who knows what diseases they're carrying?

The thought was irrational, but helped to focus her mind away from the pain. What could she do? She wasn't trained as a fighter, and there were more large were-foxes than she could cope with. Freya was quickly overwhelmed and pinned down by the fighting weres. It was an entirely unexpected relief when a sudden flash of orange light lit up the area, leaving a smell of singed fur in its wake. The were-fox boys sprang back in confusion, out of the path of the being which had burnt its way through them.

"Home time, boys. Leave off, Lachy, Tobes."

"I reckon if the sprite wants her, it can have her."

"Yeah, he might like the smell."

In a burble of voices, the were-foxes retreated.

Ugh! thought Freya. *They think they're funny.* Despite the beating they had given her, Freya watched the sprite, if that's what it was, rather than the weres. She did not trust this last-minute saviour. Also, one of her eyes had been hit, and it was already swelling and hard to see in the direction the weres had gone.

The sprite seemed to solidify, and as Freya struggled to focus, it became apparent that it was a tallish boy, or possibly young man, rather than a sprite, with a pack of assorted dogs on leads yelping and struggling to run after the vanishing weres. The figure held something bundled up in his arms. Whatever it was, was squirming around. And the man was rather familiar. Not a sprite after all.

"*Lio?* Is there a storm you don't turn up with?"

"It looked like you were having a bit of trouble with the locals," said Lio. Was it only her imagination that projected an undertone of thunder to his voice? Lightning flashed over the hills, and Freya decided that yes, it was her imagination. There was plenty of real thunder around, no need to imagine any extra. Lio's dark hair was plastered to his head by the rain, which was now pattering down in huge drops. The bundle leapt out of his arms and disappeared into the unnatural twilight. Freya couldn't quite tell what it had been. Lio's shoulder's slumped.

"Oh, Thor's balls. I'll have to catch him again, now. I've seen those weres off for now, but you should be careful not to go about alone in this town. It's a were-haven, you know."

"That's news to me. Although I was just getting educated about it, I guess. How about next time we move, you let me know in advance what sort of place we're heading into. That'd be much more helpful than *after* I've had a run-in with some unpleasant type or other."

"Maybe if you tell me when you're going and where..." Lio trailed off suggestively.

"Yeah, right. Because you're so reliable in your appearances."

"It's not easy when you're at the beck and call of the storm gods."

"Oh, so that's your excuse? Well, I'm not buying it."

Freya kept up her show of snark in self-defence. She had missed having Lio to talk to, but she didn't want to admit weakness. Why on earth had they moved to a town with weres anyway? Surely their previous experiences should have made this town a no-go area for them - if they'd known.

"How do you always know so much about who lives where, anyway?"

"Oh, you know. The answer is blowing in the wind."

"That is the worst pun."

"It wasn't meant to be one, it's a song," retorted Lio.

"Oh. Sorry. Umm. So, thanks for getting rid of those weres." Apologising to people wasn't like her at all, but then, getting beaten up was a new experience too. Come to think of it...

"How *did* you see them off? All I saw was a flash of light. I thought maybe we'd been struck by lightning; except we aren't dead. And you've never had dogs with you when I've met you before, either." She moved her hand out of the way of a questing muzzle.

She saw Lio's teeth reflect another flash of lightning as he grinned. He had rather a nice smile, she thought, irrelevantly. How come she'd never noticed it before?

"Oh, foxes don't like my dogs. I acquired them recently. Part of growing up in my world, you know. Though they were rather foisted on me when I inadvertently proved that I was capable of looking after another living being. You'll like that part - at least you will when I've retrieved it. These are the hounds of winter, or of war. Storm-hounds. It turns out that no matter what they're called, they still don't get along with cats. As for lightning... I suppose there *was* a bit of lightning as the dogs went after the foxes, maybe that's why you thought of it."

Freya was not convinced - she was sure the light and burnt fur smell were not her imagination - but she certainly didn't want to stand around debating it with Lio in a storm. No matter how dire the situation he had rescued her from, and no matter how nice his smile. The wind was strengthening, pushing her towards her house, and the rain on her face stung as it spat at her, such was its force.

"Well, thanks again," she said. "I need to get home now. Thanks. Er... Bye." Aware that she was repeating herself, Freya backed away a few steps, then turned and ran again, as an enormous peal of thunder split the air. Lio called something after her, which she didn't quite catch. He did not follow.

One last effort took her staggering legs to the door of her house. The wind helped her, pushing at her back and whipping her hair into her face. Hail arrived before she got to the door, stinging her already painful skin. Luckily, she did not have to fumble for a key, as the door proved to be unlocked.

There was nothing worth stealing inside, anyway.

Old houses without storm defences are cheap... thought Freya, as she closed and locked the door behind her, thankful to have walls between her, the weres and the storm.

CHAPTER NINETEEN

A STORM MAKES LANDFALL

There was nothing Freya wanted so much as a bath to wash away the feeling of the smelly were-fox hands on her. Unfortunately, with the storm already beginning to hit the town, and presumably her house still undefended - unless her mum and sister had made some progress with storm defences - there was no chance of doing what she wanted. She slumped against the wall for a moment, before she made her way dripping into the lounge, pausing only to push off her sodden boots and hang her wet anorak onto one of the pegs by the door. It hurt to get the anorak off.

"Mum!" she called, a note of hysteria in her voice now that she was away from the immediate threat. "Tammy! Are you home?"

"Back here." Her mother's voice came from the lean-to kitchen at the back of the house. Freya made her way to the kitchen, every muscle protesting the abuse it had received as she did so. As Freya appeared in the kitchen door, her mother gasped.

"What happened to you?"

Tammy was in the kitchen too, her stiff movements suggesting that whatever she was doing, she didn't want to be doing it.

"I had a run-in with a pack of were-foxes. Did you know there were some in this town?" said Freya.

"I did," Tammy said unexpectedly, in a flat voice. "I've run into them a few times. I didn't think they'd go after you though." There was an odd note in her voice. "I told them to leave my family alone."

"Well, I sure wish they had listened to you." Freya couldn't help the bit of whine that crept into her voice. She was feeling sore, and more than a little sorry for herself. "They waited for me in an alley on the way home. I thought

I'd gotten rid of them..." she paused, not wanting to mention the summoning she'd done to her mum, since that was something Tammy had taught her to do, and Mum had never mentioned the possibilities of summoning. Freya had a sneaking suspicion that their summoning abilities came from their dad, who was never mentioned these days.

"So, what happened?" asked Danae.

"Well, then they jumped me just before our street. I hurt all over. They really had it in for me, even though I'd never met them before. Incidentally, I don't think much of the citizenry in this town. No-one tried to save me until a stranger stepped in. And even he wouldn't say why he did." Freya wasn't sure why she didn't tell her mum about Lio, who was not, after all, a stranger. Perhaps it was just that it would be so awkward explaining all those stormy nights she'd gone out alone or with her cat. She felt an almost physical stab of loss at the memory of Mr Fluffbum. She still didn't know exactly what had happened to him. She'd spent a lot of time in the last few weeks trying to work out how a lost cat might find its way home, when its home had changed location. She hadn't come up with an answer.

"Well, I'm glad someone did help you out. Do you know who he was, so we can thank him?"

"Mum, I told you he was a stranger. And he disappeared pretty much as soon as the weres did. Look, are you going to help me out or just stand there asking about other people?"

Freya's mum stepped forward as though to give her a hug, but stopped short.

"Why, Freya, you're soaking! And some of those injuries look painful. Look, we've got to get the house sorted for the storm, but we'll give you some first aid too. Here, take the frozen peas and put them on your eye while Tammy and I finish boarding up the windows in here. Does anything need bandaging? OK, I'll tear up some curtains, they're not doing much good anyway." Her mother put actions to words, passing Freya a packet of frozen vegetables to use as an icepack, and cutting, rather than tearing, the old, somewhat mouldy curtains from the kitchen windows.

"Ugh, Mum, that can't be healthy to put on a wound."

"We don't have any regular bandages, you'll have to make do. Now, I've decided that since the windows here are closest to the ground, they're probably the easiest to defend. Also, if there's a tornado we don't want to be on the top level of the house." Danae paused, the tattered remainder of the curtains in her hand.

"Those weres. They're not waiting at the front door or anything are they?"

"No," said Freya. "Someone chased them away before I got home. But Mum - they could smell that I wasn't mundane - not just a human. They said so. And they smelled pretty bad too. Even worse than you'd guess for something hanging around in a gross alleyway. And Mum, they beat me up, hurt me, and I couldn't do anything! Why haven't you taught us to defend ourselves? And are we safe here if they know what we are?"

Danae sighed. This time she did hug Freya.

"I guess I hoped you wouldn't ever have to be in a situation where you had to physically defend yourself. I'm sorry you've experienced that. This house had the cheapest rent, and there was a job going. We had to come here. But weres - that's bad news. Weres and demis have never got on well. Maybe because weres always can tell that we're different."

Freya noticed her mum's hands were fidgeting, moving a ring up and down on her little finger.

"Still. There's nothing to be done today. We need to get a move on, I can hear the wind rising out there." As she said this, a tremendous wind gust hammered the windows, which Freya now saw were partially covered with large, flattened cardboard boxes. Someone had evidently gone to the local supermarket or greengrocer for supplies.

"I don't know how much help I'll be. I can hardly move. What windows are left to go? And do we have candles? I don't fancy sitting in the dark during a storm."

"Don't worry about that yet, we're almost out of cardboard, anyway. Give yourself a few minutes. There's the solar lantern if we lose power." The lights were still on, so they hadn't yet lost electricity. However, in Freya's experience, electricity would quickly be lost in a storm this size. She wished they did have a basement to retreat to. Some of the houses she'd lived in had had that, and while unpleasant on a typical day, they were a haven in a storm. The cold outside seemed to reach inside her, and she had a sudden, intense craving for a steaming mug of hot chocolate. She wondered if they had any left, and if there was a chance of boiling water before they lost power.

"Can I get some hot chocolate? Then maybe I'll be up to helping you," she suggested.

"There's a tiny bit left in the bottom of the jar. I boiled the kettle before we started on the windows. You can use that. Hurry though, the wind isn't waiting for us." As Danae spoke, Freya could hear the howl of the wind rising. Rain battered against the windows, louder where they weren't covered with card. Every so often the rain was mixed with hail, making a sharper sound against the glass. There was still half of the kitchen to go. Tammy was flattening more boxes over by the cooker. Freya scooted past her mother to get to that end of the kitchen. It was just about the smallest room in the house, built as a lean-to on the end of an older brick structure.

The kettle was on the cooker, so Freya busied herself getting the chocolate, stepping awkwardly around her sister. The mundane task calming her racing heart. She scraped the powder into three mugs, topping it off with the cooling hot water. Her mother and sister must have been at this a while. There was half a bottle of milk remaining in the fridge, but Freya suspected that they would be low on supplies if the storm kept them inside a while. Best to save that for later. *Oh well, it won't be the first time I've drunk hot chocolate without the milk it deserves.* She replaced the peas in the freezer. They were getting warm, and there was every chance that the family would need to eat them, later. She drank her chocolate, appreciating the sugar rush it gave her, making her feel closer to normality. She offered the other mugs to Tammy and her mum, and took Tammy's place flattening the remaining boxes while Tammy drank her own chocolate.

"I'll have mine in a bit," said her mother when Freya offered her a mug. She was using masking tape in tiny sections to attach the card to the window-frame of the last window in the kitchen. It was dark inside the kitchen when she'd finished, despite the uncovered electric bulb. Done at last, she downed the final mug of chocolate in a long series of gulps.

"Right then. This is our safe place. If the roof lifts, we come in here. Same thing if there's a sprite strike. The walls should hold, they're pretty solid. Do you girls want to bring in some pillows and blankets? We've probably just got time. Freya, if you need more first aid than just those peas and curtains, now's the moment," announced Danae.

Freya wasn't sure what could be done about all her scrapes and bruises, but she definitely felt in need of sympathy.

"Sure, Mum. That'd be good."

When she tried to stand up from her spot on the floor, she found all her muscles had stiffened up. She groaned aloud.

"Ow, ow ow. I am *so* taking up fitness classes after this. I can't even walk without hurting after all that running. Damned weres."

"Freya, mind your language. I know for a fact that weres aren't damned," snapped her mother.

Freya let her head fall backwards against the cooker door, dramatically.

"Come on Mum, they beat me up. Now is hardly the time to debate their theological position."

Her mother gave her a more contrite glance.

"I suppose not, but you know I hate loose language. It can get you into trouble," she said.

"I feel like I've already got into trouble. We're probably OK while the storm lasts, but what do we do now we know we're living in a were-town?" Freya replied grumpily.

"That's too much trouble for one night," her mother replied stiffly. "Let's deal with that situation in the morning. Right now, I want you and Tammy on lookout duty. Get that bedding in here, then check on the other rooms. I didn't have a chance to cover the allotment, not that it was producing much yet. We'll be short on food for a while after this storm. Make sure you bring in any supplies from the bedrooms." Her mother clearly expected action now, whatever state her daughter was in. First aid seemed to be forgotten.

Freya gave another sigh, and levered herself to her feet. She staggered to her room near the front of the house, upstairs, to collect her private supply of snack food. In the last few years they had started to keep a stash of snacks in their rooms, so that if anything happened to the supplies in one room, they had something to fall back on. Life could be detrimental to food stores when the unpredictable powers of three demis were concentrated in one house. Tammy had once accidentally summoned a naiad into the kitchen, which had drenched everything edible in the house, and a fair amount that wasn't edible, too. Freya was sure she'd never done anything like that, but her mum claimed she had induced their firewood to grow into trees when she was a toddler. Privately, Freya thought that if she could do that when she was a toddler, she would be much better at growing things now, rather than the bean-killing failure of a crop and fertility demi-goddess she knew herself to be.

Freya was halfway under her bed when the tree fell. She'd been easing herself out, hoarded snacks in hand, when an enormous crashing, splintering sound made her try to leap up, bashing her head on the underside of her bed.

"Ow, I so didn't need that," she muttered to herself. She had a sudden sense of deja vu, and remembered her last moments in that cottage on the cliffs, so long ago. She was aware of wind tugging at her clothing in the previously still room. Pushing herself all the way out from under the bed, she got her head clear at last.

"Fafnir's breath, lucky I *was* under there!" she exclaimed. The tall oak tree that stood near their front door had toppled onto the house. Most of the front of her room was no longer there, crushed by the weight of the tree. Freya's pillow was pinned down by a branch, and rain was drenching the remainder of her bedding. Slates from the roof pattered onto the floor. Dislodged by wind-sprites, or just by wind? Or by something else? It was hard to know.

"Mum!" yelled Freya. "Mum, did we have a deposit on this house? 'Cos I don't think we're getting it back!" Realising that her mum probably couldn't hear her over the storm - which was even louder now that the walls and roof were breached - Freya clutched her snacks with one hand, gave a tug at the soggy bedclothes with the other, then gave up bedding retrieval as a lost cause. She was lucky there was still a door to exit her room, she thought. She certainly didn't want to try climbing down from her second-storey bedroom window.

Fortunately, the tree seemed to have destroyed only her room at the corner of the house.

It's hard to see my room being destroyed as fortunate.

She was able to descend the stairs, limping a little, and made her way to the kitchen with her meagre supplies. Her mother was back in the kitchen, her own bedding tidily arranged in a stack in the corner away from the cooker, against the back door.

"What happened, Freya? I heard a crash. And you don't have your bedding."

Typical. A tree destroys half the house and she doesn't come to see what happened, just asks where my blankets are. Maybe this is why she never keeps a job long and we're always having to move.

Freya loved her mum, and knew that she was at least more stable than her now-absent father. But at times like this, Freya couldn't wait to be old enough to move out of home. She and Tammy had not been close since what Freya thought of as the summoning summer, but Freya sometimes wondered why Tammy had stuck with the family. Perhaps she didn't find her mother as infuriating as Freya did. She certainly wasn't driven by any obvious ambition, the way Freya was.

"Mum, didn't you hear me yell? I told you, a tree fell on the house. It fell on my bed. I'm lucky I wasn't killed. I would have been if I'd gone to bed the way I want to." Her voice shook a little as the shock caught up with her. Her mother replied apparently casually,

"Oh, sorry. I was trying to get these windows sprite-proof." She indicated some thin wire that criss-crossed the card in patterns. Freya hadn't noticed it earlier. "But if the house has a breach already, there's no point. We may have to make some personal protection instead. If you want to lie down meanwhile, you can use my bedding. But get those wet things off first, please."

"Mum! I'm not stripping naked in the kitchen. My other clothes were under the tree-trunk. I'll just- just- oh, I don't know what to do." To her own horror, Freya found herself sobbing.

It's just the shock, she told herself. *Everyone feels odd after a shock.*

She was ready for this day to be over. If she had a bed remaining to sleep in, she would pull the covers over her head and pretend that the rest of the world didn't exist.

She found her mother giving her a blessedly gentle hug, and wrapping one of her own blankets around her.

"Sorry, Freya. You always seem so resilient, it's hard to remember that you need a bit of comfort too."

Freya allowed herself to relax in her mother's arms for a moment before pushing those arms away. She wiped her wet face on her even wetter sleeve. Not much drying had happened since she made it indoors.

"I'll just sit down for a bit here. Where is Tammy?"

Her mother replied vaguely.

"Oh, she'll be down in a bit. Sooner if the wind gets worse and starts lifting the roof. She was pretty upset, seeing what those weres did to you."

Freya frowned. Something odd was going on with Tammy. It sounded like weres might have something to do with it. But right now it was all too hard to think about. Freya sank onto the pile of bedding and closed her eyes.

CHAPTER TWENTY

ADVENTURES WITH LIO

The wind still howled when Freya opened her eyes to darkness. She wondered what had woken her. With the kitchen windows covered, there was no light to aid her as she peered around. Had she heard something? It was hard to tell, as the wind and rain continued to hammer the windows. She staggered to her feet. There was a warm body beside her, suggesting her mother or sister had also taken refuge in the kitchen. Her groping hand found plaited hair. Mum, then. Tammy's hair was too short to plait.

She felt her way into the hall. Unexpectedly, the front door hung open, letting in the rain.

"Tammy? Are you out there?" Freya called. There was no answer. But as Freya's eyes adjusted, she saw a flicker of movement out on the road. She approached the door with caution.

"Who's there?"

Peering into the stormy night, Freya was half-blinded by the torrential rain. Her clothing was instantly soaked. Unexpectedly, a voice spoke in her ear.

"Don't put yourself out on account of me."

She jumped. There was a smile in the voice, wholly unwarranted in Freya's opinion.

"What are you doing?"

"Just your friendly neighbourhood rescue service."

Freya squinted into the darkness. As she did so, something warm and wet pressed against her hand.

"Ugh!"

The owner of the voice laughed.

"Don't worry, it's just the hounds saying hello."

"Lio, what are you doing here? And what are you, anyway? You've never said. Are you a sprite?" she demanded suspiciously. He might have rescued her, but she had no idea of his intentions otherwise. She had never known that, really, but she found herself more suspicious these days.

"I am visiting with intent to please. But no, I'm not a sprite. Ghastly fellows. I am simply myself."

"Well, what are you, yourself, doing here then? Rescue accomplished, thanks and all that, but it's the middle of the night, I'm being rained on and I want to go back to the pile of rags I'm currently calling a bed."

Lio laughed again, a rich amused sound which was drowned out as a flash of lightning was immediately followed by a deafening rumble of thunder.

"You don't fancy a midnight stroll with me then? I can show you all sorts of interesting things."

"No thanks. I don't go walking in the night with strangers, or near-strangers either."

"I'm hardly a stranger, though. We've met many times on dark and stormy nights. I thought we were friends. I even looked for your cat, which is in fact why I am here. Ah well, I'm not one to push in where I'm not wanted." He looked towards the house windows, mostly covered with cardboard and wire - though Freya was sure he couldn't see the wire.

"And I can see I'm not wanted here." He sighed deeply. "Such mistrust."

"My cat? What about my cat? Do you know where he is?"

"I do in fact. And I have the scratches to prove it. It is both fortunate and unfortunate that I have acquired hounds. They enabled me to find Mr Fluffbum," he began, before Freya interrupted him.

"Where?"

"In a deserted house near the shore, as it happens. Though I don't believe it had been deserted long. There were signs of recent occupancy by trolls, as I had feared."

"But is my cat alright? Do you have him?"

"I did have him. He is alive. But as I said, it was also unfortunate that I have hounds now. They don't get on with cats. I've been waiting on a storm that brought me near you - I hoped that you would be on the coast again. But just after we drove off those were-foxes tonight, Mr Fluffbum escaped me. He hasn't appreciated my hounds in the least. I had planned to follow you and present him to you, but he ran off. I've been scouring the streets for him ever since. By the way, did you know there's a large gathering of were-foxes in the town square?"

"Wait, what? Around the oak tree there, by any chance?" Despite her concern for her cat, Freya was distracted by this news.

"Ah, you do know." Lio started to turn away and Freya put out a hand to stop him. His arm was uncovered, wet with raindrops. Freya wondered for a moment if he ever wore an anorak.

"Do you know what they're doing there?" Had they planned to meet Freya there all along, prompted by the note she'd been given at school? What if they'd appeared at her house? Suddenly, the broken front windows seemed a much greater safety hazard than before.

"No idea. I avoid large gatherings of potentially violent beings on principle. If my brothers didn't automatically fall into that class, my policy would work better."

"You have brothers?"

"Is there one direction to the wind? Of course I do."

Freya was momentarily distracted. Apparently Lio *was* a wind sprite, or maybe a wind demi, after all. She remembered that he hadn't been alone when she first met him, though the weeks he'd brought fish for Mr Fluffbum, his companions hadn't showed up. But those weres... and Mr Fluffbum!

I can't believe Mr Fluffbum is still alive. But where is he now? In a storm in a town full of were-foxes, that can't be healthy.

"Do you think you could help me distract the weres? I got asked to meet someone in the town square at midnight, and they know where I live. But most of all, I want to find Mr Fluffbum. I'm guessing foxes are nearly as bad as trolls when it comes to cats."

"That's quite a rescue you're asking for."

"Well, are you up for it? You've got dogs and thunder, don't you?"

"Hmm. I can but try, since you ask so politely." Lio's sarcasm was thick enough to cut with a knife.

Freya stepped into the rain and closed the door behind her.

"Come on then, let's go," she said.

Lio and Freya set off together in the direction of the town square. Lio's dogs tugged at their leashes, first one way then another as they sniffed at each interesting spot along the way. The rain assailed them as they half-walked, half-jogged through the town.

"Are we safe out here?" Freya asked. Lio didn't answer. That was not reassuring. "Well?"

"It depends on whether the elves turn up, I suppose," Lio answered reluctantly.

"What, the small beings who help humans grow things? That doesn't sound worrying."

"No, those are pretty much a myth these days. I'm talking about weather elves. They usually stay above the clouds though, like sprites, so I guess we're good."

Freya saw Lio looking up at the storm clouds which roiled above them. She shivered.

"Are your brothers up there?"

"Probably. It doesn't matter though, they have their own plans. As I said, I try to avoid them when I can. Let's find those weres and see what *they're* planning. And find your cat, while we're at it. I haven't been plundering the ocean to feed him for a month, only to lose him to foxes. You have no idea how hard it is for someone like me to keep a cat."

"If we get him back in one piece, you have my endless gratitude."

"Well, that's something worth trying for, I guess."

They slowed as they reached the streets surrounding the square. The wind was stronger than ever. Given that the square opened onto the seaside promenade, Freya wondered if this was the most sensible place to be. Then again, she would have stayed at home if she was being sensible. The dogs tugged at their leashes impatiently. Was it because there was a cat nearby, or the presence of were-foxes, that had them excited? At least they didn't bark, and give away their presence.

"What's the plan? Freya had to raise her voice to be heard over the rain. Maybe it wouldn't have mattered if the dogs barked. Though it *would* scare a cat. Lio looked her way.

"Let's see how many weres there are, first. My dogs and I can only take so many. But we'll have to be careful not to be seen." Lio stopped suddenly and held up a hand to indicate that she should stop too.

"They're close."

Freya wondered how he could tell. She could barely see two feet in front of her, now. She stuck close to the railings beside the tall houses here. Lio paused beside a low shrub, crouching so that he was no taller than it. His dogs growled low in their throats, till he turned his head and gave each one a stern look. They subsided.

Well, at least they are well trained. I wish I had Mr Fluffbum, though. He never growled at anyone.

Freya brightened a little, at the thought that her cat was still alive somewhere.

Lio peered around the shrub then shrank back. Leaning close to her ear, he whispered loud enough to be heard over the storm.

"There's a big gathering. Too many to take all at once. We'll have to get them to separate."

"How?"

"If it wasn't raining, I'd run a scent trail. As it is, I'll have to bait them. Lucky thing I've always loved running."

"What-"

But he was gone, racing the wind as he tore around the square and off along the wave-battered promenade, dogs beside him. Freya started up as though to run after him, realised there was a square full of weres around the corner, and decided against it. She didn't want to risk a second mugging. As she hesitated, she thought the sounds of the storm were changing. Was the rain getting harder? A sudden surge of water drenched her feet as it careened off the edge of the building beside her. Before she could react, it drained away again, only to be replaced by another wave.

The sea - it's overtopped the promenade!

But as walls of water went, this was more of a garden edging. She could handle it. The tide must be in, she realised. And the storm pushing it even higher, flooding the low-lying land. But if she was getting wet back here, what was happening in the square, which fronted directly onto the sea?

She risked a look, peering through the darkness, on her hands and knees despite the wet. Whatever Lio had done, a lot of the weres must have followed him. There were just two figures remaining. One was in the tree. The other one seemed to be trying to persuade the tree-hugger to come down. As she watched, another wave surged through the square, making the one on the ground stagger. Surely, she could deal with these drenched individuals? She stepped forth boldly.

As soon as she turned the corner, Freya was buffeted by the wind. She staggered backwards a step before leaning into it and making her way forward. She got quite close to the figures before they noticed her. As she neared, she recognised Gareth from school as the were up in the tree. The other one was a girl who looked vaguely familiar; she had distinctive blue hair.

I'm sure I'd remember that hair.

Maybe she wasn't a were after all? At least she wasn't one of Freya's attackers from earlier in the evening. Freya relaxed a little, but then fought to keep her feet as the next wave made its presence felt.

No relaxing around here. What am I doing? I can barely walk in these conditions.

Gareth's eyes widened when he saw her. He made frantic 'go-away' gestures with his one free hand - the other was holding him in place. What was going on here? Had Freya misjudged the situation? Lightning flashed, and Freya saw the thunderheads outlined in a blue-tinted white light. Bizarrely, there was no answering roll of thunder. Blue-haired girl noticed Gareth's waving hand, and looked around. She spotted Freya and stalked towards her. Freya backed away, unsure what to expect from this new player. She bumped into the railing that surrounded the house.

I guess this is where I'll stand, then.

"Cool dye job," said Freya randomly.

"It's not dye."

Well, that's probably not the best start to this conversation.

Freya wished she could take another step back.

"Why are you hanging around with these weres?" the blue-haired girl asked in an aggressive tone.

Freya had to laugh.

"I can't think of anything I'd rather do less."

"What are you doing here then? This is not the time or place for *children* to hang around."

"I am not a child. And what business is it of yours where I hang out? It's a free country." Freya refused to be intimidated by this stranger - so long as she wasn't being physically attacked.

"Sure, you're free to be mauled, drowned or struck by lightning. What's your preference?"

"How about a civil conversation?"

"At midnight during a storm? No chance."

Another wave swirled through the square. This wave was knee-high. The storm surge was getting worse. Freya stayed in place by clutching the rails behind her. The blue-haired girl lurched sideways but kept her footing.

"OK, why do you look familiar then?"

Blue-hair looked askance at her.

"I've never seen you in my life."

Freya squinted through the gloom.

"You remind me of someone - Lio!"

Lio was indeed looming behind Blue-hair. The girl turned to look at Lio. Lio's dogs were nowhere to be seen.

"Oh, it's you," she said. As they looked at each other, Freya could see the similarities in their faces. They must be related. No wonder the girl had looked familiar.

"Nice to see you too, Nik. Still bothering my land dwelling friends, then?" said Lio. He was acting casual, but Freya noticed that he sauntered between her and the blue-haired girl, Nik. Was she dangerous, then?

"You never told me you had sisters, Lio. Do they all come out in storms? I thought you were worried about elves, not sisters."

Lio looked at Freya, a frown on his face. The effect was spoiled as another wave swept past them, tugging at their legs.

"She's my cousin. And though she affects blue hair, she's a wind demi, not an elf. Luckily. Not to say harpie, of course."

Nik raised a fist at Lio.

"Never let that word cross your lips again, cousin or not."

Lio ducked away from the fist.

"Well then, never threaten my friends. Easy."

"Excuse me, are you two going to argue all night? Because while I don't think I can get any wetter, I actually came to see who was meeting here at midnight," Freya interrupted.

"Vermin," spat Nik.

"Not unless the laws have changed," corrected Lio. The weary tone of his voice suggested that this was not the first time he'd said it.

"Still arguing? What about the kid in that tree? He's from my class at school. Schoolkids are usually not classed as vermin, no matter how hateful they are. Even if they are weres." Freya might not know how to make friends in this place, but she refused to be cowed by this stranger.

"I have no idea what he's doing, other than dangerously antagonising my cousin. If I were you, I'd leave him to his fate." Lio ignored the teasing. "Freya, Nik here is someone you should avoid. Maybe even more than those weres."

"Don't be rude, Lio, it doesn't suit you," Nik said.

Lio ignored her.

"Those weres, by the way, are now scattered all over town. No more ambushes should happen tonight." He looked proud of himself, now. "My dogs have taken care of that."

"Well, thanks for that, anyway. I wasn't keen on a repeat. But I think I should check on Gareth anyway. He's the one who dropped the note on my desk."

"As you wish, then. Nik, can you leave off torturing that were-kid for a few minutes?"

Nik, who had been alternating her glare between Lio and Freya, now turned fully to Lio.

"What's in it for me?"

"I could tell you where I left the rest of them."

Nik smiled, a feral grin that made Freya uncomfortably certain that no matter how wild the weres in this town, there was always something wilder.

"It's a deal." The pair conferred briefly before the blue-haired Nik set off across the drenched square at a splashing run. As she reached the edge of the square, there was another blue-edged flash of lightning, and she disappeared.

"Strange relatives you have, Lio." Despite her desire to find out what the school bully was doing up a tree being tormented by wind demis, Freya was quite prepared to give the wind demi in question a wide berth.

"Tell me about it. Just be glad it was my cousin, not my brothers."

"You are not making me keen to meet those brothers of yours."

"Hopefully you will never need to. They're not as pleasant as me. And they are more powerful, too."

"Times like this, I feel like I was behind the door when the demi-talents were being given out." Freya was sick of feeling like the most broken demi in the box.

"Cheer up, you're probably just missing the obvious."

Freya glared at Lio. She wasn't in the mood to be fobbed off with platitudes.

"*Anyway,* what is your weird cousin doing, going after the were-foxes? Not that I mind, of course."

"Playing, I would guess. She doesn't play nice though, never has. Like I definitely didn't say, harpie. I avoid her, too. Gave me quite a shock when Nik swooped in while I was playing chase with were-foxes. So. Let's go see that fox-kit you were so concerned about, before any older were-foxes slip back past my cousin."

Freya allowed herself to be guided, this time. Gareth the were-fox had begun to climb out of the tree, but he stopped when Lio and Freya approached.

Probably wants to keep the higher ground. This had better not turn into a fight.

Freya decided to try to keep the initiative.

"Care to say why you chose a gang meeting, in what is probably the storm of the century, as a good spot for an evening hangout?"

Gareth looked away and mumbled something unintelligible. Freya continued the offensive - as much as she could while clinging onto the tree to keep her feet. The sea wasn't draining out of the square, now.

"And perhaps you can share why there were dozens of your hairy acquaintances here as well?"

Gareth looked at her properly this time. It was hard to tell in the dim streetlight, but she thought he was blushing.

"My big brother's idea. He found out I was coming here, and he brought his friends. But then him-" he pointed at Lio - "and that weird blue chick turned up and started making threats. At least the girl did, that guy just chased everyone else away with some vicious dogs."

"So why did you invite me out here anyway?"

"..."

"That's all you have to say?"

"I just - I'm not - I have a reputation to keep up at school."

"One that involves insulting newcomers? You might want to do some work on yourself."

Gareth looked away and mumbled something. It might have been an apology. Freya gave up on needling him. It seemed unlikely to improve matters anyway.

"Well, I for one want to get out of the storm. I guess I'll have no choice but to see you round. But if I were you, I'd leave now too." So much for the exciting midnight assignation. While there had been plenty of excitement, seeing the school bully grovel wasn't what she had hoped for. She was about to turn away from the tree when she noticed a movement higher up in it. In the dim light, she couldn't see much, but there was a flash of white fur. "Mr Fluffbum?" Freya asked incredulously.

Unexpectedly, Gareth spoke.

"My big brother and his friends had treed a cat when I arrived here. They sent me up after it, but I didn't want to bring it down for them to hurt. It went too high, anyway. Do you know how hard it is to hold onto a tree in a storm?"

"Not something I've tried. But is my cat alright?" asked Freya.

"I don't know whose cat it is, but it's definitely in one piece. My brother couldn't get up the tree either, he's too big. And I've been between him and the cat the whole time. So yeah, the cat's fine. Probably wetter than I am, though. If it's not rain, it's waves. If I ever try and meet someone again, it's not going to be down here, that's for sure."

"Good. Now hurry up and get out of the way, I want my cat, and he's not going to move while you're there."

To her surprise, Gareth finished climbing down the tree without further argument.

"See you at school," he mumbled, as he sloped off in a different direction to the way Nik and the other were-foxes had gone.

Freya was focused on Mr Fluffbum. She called him enticingly, and to her joy, the cat she'd thought was dead scrambled down the tree and leapt onto her shoulder. She staggered briefly but managed to keep her feet. She tried to pat him, but her hand stuck to his wet fur. She was sure he was purring, though, even through the noise of the wind and waves.

"Oh, Mr Fluffbum. I've missed you so much. Come on, let's get you home." She glanced over at Lio, remembering that he'd said her cat had run from his new dogs.

"Lio, what happened to your dogs? I hope they're not mauling people somewhere. Or drowning."

"I thought you didn't like those weres?"

"Doesn't mean I want anyone mauled."

"Just as well I tied the dogs up back there then."

To Freya's astonishment, Lio led the way away from the square, around one corner, and a little way up the hill and there were his dogs. Their bedraggled tails waved frantically as Lio approached. Freya tightened her grip on Mr Fluffbum. She didn't want a repeat escape, not when she'd just been reunited with her cat. Damp fur tickled her nose.

"Well. I guess that's alright then."

"Home time?" Lio asked.

"It certainly is for me," Freya said with emphasis. The square behind them was thoroughly flooded and seemed likely to get more so. She was beginning to feel sore again, too, now that the excitement was over. The wind helped them up the hill. Freya was pretty sure the gusts were getting stronger. She wondered if Lio's unseen brothers had anything to do with that, but decided she'd rather not know, just now.

At home, Freya farewelled Lio at the door and retreated inside. She considered her wet clothes ruefully. In the end, she stripped them off and left them in a sodden pile on the hall floor. She locked the door and put out her hand to help find her way back to the kitchen, where she rolled herself in blankets once more. Mr Fluffbum kneaded the blankets beside her, and Freya stroked him happily. She was thrilled to have a cat to curl up with once more. Now it would be easier to sleep through the storm.

CHAPTER TWENTY-ONE

AFTER THE STORM

Freya opened her eyes in the darkened kitchen. Despite the turmoil in her mind and the wind outside, she had slept almost as soon as she closed her eyes. While she slumbered, someone had covered her with another blanket, one usually kept in the sparsely furnished lounge. She was glad of the extra blanket. It was chilly in the unheated house. Sitting up, she saw that the warmth on her right was her mother, curled up under another blanket. The warmth on her left was Mr Fluffbum, dry now, and curled up in a tight ball with his fluffy black tail covering his nose. Between them they covered most of the space on the floor of the small kitchen.

Freya felt thrilled all over again as she looked at her beloved cat. She reached out and patted him to reassure herself that he was real and not just a figment born of wishful imagination. Mr Fluffbum gave a small meow, and tightened a paw over his eyes. He was clearly not yet ready to awaken. Freya stretched and sat up.

As she did so, she discovered that just sitting up hurt. She fingered her puffy face and decided not to visit a mirror this morning - assuming it was morning, of course. She levered herself cautiously to standing and draped her blanket around her shoulders, then decided she should leave the kitchen to inspect the house. Her cat ignored her actions.

"Nice to see you, too, Mr Fluffbum. Lio must have been feeding you well, wherever he had you."

Looking at the gaps in the cardboard on the windows, Freya felt bad that she hadn't helped much with the storm defences. Usually, she was the household mainstay with such preparations. Luckily, most of the windows had held. On her way out the kitchen door, Freya skirted a patch of broken glass from one smashed pane. She wondered where Tammy was. Often, if they had to defend a house from a storm, they all slept in the same room.

Freya stroked a gentle hand along the sleeping Mr Fluffbum's back, then headed up to her bedroom to see if her memory of the damage was correct. There was no easy way to get to her chest of drawers, as the robust tree trunk that had crashed through the roof mostly covered it. Her bed was similarly covered in tree parts and the mattress was sodden. Leaves, branches and roof shingles covered her bedroom floor. It was indeed morning, as she could clearly see through the hole in the roof. The main body of the storm had passed, and only swiftly moving clouds scudded past. She could see tree branches down through the valley tossing in the stiff breeze, but the wind no longer howled. She turned away. There was nothing she could do in here without a chainsaw, which she didn't own and probably couldn't operate even if she did.

Tammy's room, across the stairs from hers, was eerily empty of life. It looked like it had been torn apart by an internal tornado in the dim light that filtered through its card-covered window, despite its intact roof. Drawers were pulled out; clothes were strewn over the floor and bed. She wondered what had caused the fury that resulted in such destruction. Something to talk to Tammy about... from a safe distance. Freya picked up a few of the clothes and changed into them. She and her sister were a similar size these days, and she needed something to wear. Hopefully Tammy wouldn't mind too much, if Freya found her.

When I find her.

Bundling the discarded blanket under one arm, she headed back downstairs.

In the front room, there had evidently not been enough card to go round. The front windows had shattered and blown in. Everything was damp. Small branches and leaves had blown in too. Through the broken windows Freya could see the road and houses beyond. The roof of one house was in the garden of the one next door. Branches covered the roads, and the sycamore two doors away had blown down too, though it hadn't hit a house that she could see. Freya tried flicking the light switch on. Nothing happened. There would clearly be a big clean-up required in the wake of this storm. At least no sprites had attacked while she was asleep.

Her whole body was waking up now, and telling her its woes. It was possible that her feet didn't hurt, but everything else did. Actually, come to think of it there was a blister on her heel, from all the running she'd done yesterday.

OK, everything hurts.

Feeling sorry for herself, she limped back to the kitchen.

"Mum, where's Tammy?"

Her mother groaned and opened her eyes, not uncurling from her foetal position.

"I don't know, Freya. Why, do you want her?"

"I just wondered where she is," Freya said.

"We had an argument after you fell asleep. She went out into the storm and I haven't seen her since. I tried to stay up for her, but I guess I fell asleep."

"What?" Freya almost screeched. "You let her go outside in the storm? With those weres around, too? She could be... be - killed! Why are you just lying around, Mum?"

Freya couldn't believe her ears. Her mother didn't seem to be extending any of her usual motherly care to Tammy lately.

Danae sat up, pulling the blanket around her shoulders.

"Oh, I know what it looks like. But I'm exhausted. I was up most of the night, you know. I'm too old to do that. Tammy said she'd encountered those weres that set on you - before now. And that she knew how to sort them out. I couldn't stop her going - I couldn't leave you hurt and alone as well. And you know nothing stops her when she's set her mind on something."

Her mother's explanation sounded glib to Freya, but she couldn't summon the energy to argue effectively. All the same...

"Well, when do we go find her? Let's take our breakfast with us and go looking. It's not like we can do much with the house. We don't even have a house hob here yet."

Freya realised that her mother was crying silently, much to her discomfort. She patted Danae's shoulder awkwardly, wondering when they'd grown so far apart. Surely it hadn't always been like this? Freya felt like she was the mother in the room as she helped her mum up and got the kettle boiling.

"Come on, Mum. We can't just let her go off like this. Even if you did fight, we need to know she's OK." Freya felt more guilty than ever now. Not only had she failed to help defend their house, but her mother and sister had somehow argued so badly that Tammy had run off in the middle of a huge storm - and Freya had slept through it all. Blood pounded in her ears, the huge pressure of worry giving her an instant headache. Picking up her rucksack, she emptied the schoolwork from it out onto the kitchen bench, and piled in portable food from the cupboards. She looked around a little wildly, added a water bottle, and shouldered the bag.

"Come on Mum, you need to get ready. Are you coming with me, or staying here to look after the house? Maybe you should stay here. I suppose Tammy might turn up back here and be worried we'd left without her if we're all gone. But oh, Mum, did you see? I got Mr Fluffbum back last night! But I can't take him with me to look for Tammy, he's not used to the area yet."

Danae looked sourly at Mr Fluffbum.

"Another mouth to feed again, then."

"Oh, Mum, don't be so mean about him. You know how much I've missed him, and I thought he was gone forever. I'll figure out a way to feed him. Er. Somehow. He's asleep now, anyway, so I'll feed him when I've got back from looking for Tammy."

Freya's mum was looking indecisive, twisting a corner of her blanket into a tight spiral.

"I don't know, Freya. I haven't had enough sleep to think straight."

"Look, Mum, how about I have a scout around the likely places, and come back to let you know if I find her. Maybe you can start cleaning up the house. Make sure Mr Fluffbum doesn't get out those front windows, they're cracked. Maybe keep the door shut. See you soon."

Freya felt odd, telling her mum what to do. Wasn't she supposed to be the child still? Picking up a leftover flapjack from the bench to serve as breakfast, she adjusted her rucksack and hobbled out of the house, carefully closing the door behind her - for all the good it did when the windows were broken and the roof had holes in it.

In truth, they hadn't been here long enough for her to have any good ideas about where Tammy might have gone. She was surprised that Tammy had socialised with the were-foxes and not told the family. The mere presence of weres might have made them move on, job or no job.

Freya headed out of town first, partly because she didn't feel like going anywhere near where she'd been set on by the were-foxes, and partly because she thought Tammy might have gone out to find a water-deity for solace or protection. She trudged up the steep hill that sheltered a series of valleys from the storms that beset the coast. The clouds were clearing now, and the wet grass on either side of the road glittered in the sporadic sunshine.

As her muscles warmed up, the walk became almost enjoyable, apart from that annoying blister, and occasional stabbing pains in her leg. Not to mention the constant gnaw of worry for her sister. Small birds sang in the hedgerows, and Freya glimpsed a buzzard soaring away in pursuit of small prey. There weren't many trees out here to be blown over, so there was little evidence of the storm's passage at first.

Cresting the hill behind the town, Freya had a broader view of the landscape. She now saw that the fields of grain and hay, usually punctuated by the occasional spinney or lone tree, were instead littered with roofs blown off barns and houses. The storm had flattened the long grass in un-mown hayfields.

The valleys she sought were soon in view. The first stream she reached had scoured away a large bite on either side of its usual course, bloated with brown, racing water. Freya did not much fancy summoning a water-spirit from such a place, but she didn't know any other way to find Tammy. She wasn't a tracker to be following a scent, and no footprints had survived the battering rains of the night.

There wasn't much in the way of vegetation near the stream where it raced into a culvert under the road, so Freya left the road and followed the stream's path at a respectful distance until she came to a stand of small trees and shrubs. Poking around to find an appropriate species, she selected a few herbs and got as close to the water's edge as she dared before drawing a circle around herself, as Tammy had taught her. Gritting her teeth briefly in annoyance that she had to do this alone, she began the song-web. It took her a few tries to get it just right. She'd been lucky, last night in the fountain. When eventually she managed to summon the local water deity, it turned out to be surly and uncooperative because *she* didn't co-operate with its desires.

"You call that a thyrsus, girl? It's just a bunch of weeds," the nix - one of the many types of water deity Freya had encountered over the years - sneered at her.

"I had to improvise, OK? And you came, didn't you?" Freya tried to keep her temper. Every stand of fennel for miles had been flattened by the passage of the storm. She'd had to make do with a thin stem of yarrow wound about with goosefoot bedstraw. It was not an impressive wand.

"I came because no-one's called me in longer than I care to remember. Well, weeks, anyway. I suppose I should be glad you're not trying to poison me with hemlock."

"Yes, remember that, there are other weeds I could have used," Freya said. "Anyway, I wanted to ask if you'd seen my sister."

"You have a sister? Hmm. Couldn't you have brought her too? I could do with a good warm-up, and two young maidens sounds better than one. Come closer, you. I can't reach you when you're up on the bank there."

"I said I was *looking* for my sister. And I'm quite comfortable here, thank you."

Freya ducked as the nix reformed itself from something horselike into a more human-male-shaped watery figure. It brandished an amorphous, dripping shape at her. Freya could see a thin, silvery fish inside it.

"I could teach you the fiddle. Very popular, fiddle-playing."

Freya avoided the drips and peered at the shape.

"Oh, is that supposed to be a fiddle? I couldn't tell. Times have moved on, sorry. If I wanted violin lessons, I'd sign up online, I wouldn't enter into a dodgy bargain with a water spirit for some tuition."

The nix let its fiddle splash back into watery nothingness, releasing the fish.

"Where's the gratitude in young folk these days? People used to beg for fiddle lessons from me. Come on, just step a little closer and give your favourite old nix a hug for coming out to see you. I didn't have to, after all."

"Thanks for that and all, but I just want my sister. She looks like me, maybe a bit blonder. Shorter hair. Are you sure no-one like that has been here?"

"Oh, *her*. She was fun, not like you. But she hasn't been here for weeks. Such a shame."

Well, at least the slippery nix knew who she meant.

"So, you haven't seen her, last night or today?"

"I already told you, no. Now are you going to be friendly-like?"

"Probably not. Sorry."

Freya was more than ready to end the conversation; despite the efforts she'd made to initiate it. She was satisfied that the watery deity had not seen Tammy, and dismissed it with thrown salt. She wished she knew a better way to end these summonings. Perhaps a more polite way existed, but Tammy hadn't taught her any other method.

Trudging onward, Freya repeated the process with all the small streams she came across, with similar results. At least her song-webs improved, requiring less repetition to work. Perhaps she should have been doing this all along. None of the water spirits had seen Tammy since she first visited them a few weeks ago. That absence rather disgruntled some of them. At least this assured Freya that Tammy's usual actions upon arriving in a new area had not changed. She always liked to maintain a 'positive acquaintance', as she put it, with the local water bodies. It seemed that this had made her rather a popular newcomer. A shame Freya couldn't use similar tactics at school. Not that she would want to. She shuddered briefly at the thought.

At last, hungry despite having eaten all the snacks she'd taken with her, she turned for home, weary and dispirited. The whistle of the wind had begun to grate in her ears, and she was tired enough that her eyes kept closing as she walked. The bruised one throbbed in time with her footfalls.

Pay attention, Freya, you're supposed to be looking for Tammy.

Nevertheless, her eyelids drooped as she crested the top of the last hill before the descent to the sea. A short, yipping bark sounded off to her right; her eyes flew open. A group of were-foxes were congregated at a crossroads, blocking her path. Freya's entire body went tense. This time, Gareth from her school was with them as well as a number of women. Some were semi-familiar faces, perhaps people she'd seen in town. Some were the attackers from last night. Others were completely unfamiliar. She stopped, wishing there was a handy wall she could back up to. None of the drystone walls around here were in good enough repair to be considered as something to provide protection.

This time, a woman stepped forward. She shared the same colouring as the rest of the pack, reddish brown hair and brown eyes. To Freya's surprise, she held out her hands in a non-threatening manner.

"Greetings," she said.

Seriously? Freya thought. *Who* says *that?*

"I understand that you had an... interaction... with some of my family last night. They wish to apologise to you. They were under a misapprehension about you which has now been corrected. Boys? Step up and make your apology."

A number of the taller young men shuffled forward and mumbled variations on 'sorry', 'It was all a misunderstanding' 'won't happen again' before slinking towards the back of the group once again.

Freya was viciously happy to see that some of them also wore bruises.

"I hope you will bear our family no ill-feeling, especially since our two families will be encountering each other regularly in future. This was what we had wished to meet with you about last night, though the storm and the ill-considered actions of our younger members delayed that meeting. I presume you are in search of your older sister?"

Freya's mouth dropped open. She hastily closed it again, not wanting to appear at a loss.

Never act like prey among predators.

"Er... yes. I am," she managed to say. "But I have no idea what you mean about meeting regularly. Is... is there a reason we'd want to do that? I mean, no offence, but I'm not exactly keen to spend time with the 'younger members' I have met."

The woman smiled, a dazzling smile full of unspoken secrets.

"Your sister Tammy is joining our family. Of course we will meet again. Hopefully you will get over your dislike of our boys once you have had time to heal, and they have had time to improve their manners. Won't you, boys?"

The woman's last words were clearly directed to the boys who had been so heavy-handed (and heavy-booted, and possibly heavy-toothed) with Freya the previous night. They shuffled nervously, avoiding the woman's gaze.

Freya didn't know what to think. Had Tammy gone mad? Why would she join a were-pack? And where was she now? Some of her thoughts must have shown on her face, because the woman spoke again.

"Are you not happy with your sister's actions? You will be gaining a whole new set of relatives."

"No! I can't believe she'd be joining a pack of things like you. It's - it's just not like her!"

Freya was sputtering with anger. The pack in front of her stirred, discontented muttering reaching her ears. Realising that she'd better try to be polite - after all, she had no other leads on Tammy, and she really, truly didn't want to be hurt by these weres again - Freya hastened to add, "No offence meant, really, it's just that... she's always been more interested in water-deities. Of course, we hadn't come across people like you before." This was true, now Freya came to think of it. At least, she'd never come across were-*foxes*. "Umm. When did you say Tammy met you?"

The woman smiled again.

"I only met her recently. But she encountered one of our number several weeks ago. I believe it must have been just after your family arrived here. She has spent rather a lot of time with our clan since then. I believe she will be one of us when she returns from the sea."

Freya found it hard to believe the woman. It was true that she hadn't seen much of Tammy since their arrival in this town, but had she really taken up with weres? And what did this woman mean, return from the sea? The latter she could at least ask about.

"What are you talking about? Why would she go near the sea, especially in a storm like last night's one?"

"Because she wanted to become one of us, and the sea is key to that. Or rather, what lies under the sea. Our ancient homeland is there, and to become a part of our clan, she must bring back an appropriate artifact. You didn't think we bite people to turn them, did you?"

The woman's voice was rather condescending.

"Like I said, I really don't know much about your kind," responded Freya. "But biting is what all the books say about weres becoming weres - well, apart from the weird sex-object-obsessed books."

She blushed despite herself. She hadn't meant to mention those books, which she'd borrowed from Tammy a couple of years ago, then wished she hadn't. Some ideas were hard to un-imagine, however much one wanted to.

"And I've never heard of whatever ancient homeland you're talking about. But your clan didn't seem to like the way I smelt, last night. They certainly weren't what you might call welcoming. Why would Tammy be any different? Does she smell any better?"

"She does, as it happens. And she's different enough from you that she has made a union with my son," snapped the were-woman, losing her smile.

Gaia wept, thought Freya. *What has Tammy done now? And how do I tell Mum about this? Or maybe she knows and that's why she's so upset. I bet Tammy doesn't really smell much different from me. Why would she?*

Looking at the woman, she spoke slowly and clearly, as though to someone stupid.

"Tammy is my sister. I want to make sure she's OK, and that she's happy about her choices. Have you seen her? Can you help me find her? Also, what can I call you?"

The woman looked at Freya somewhat icily now. Freya realised she had asked a series of questions without waiting for answers.

"You may call me Lisichka, though I'm sure you realise that's not my full name. And as for your sister, if all has gone well with her search, she should be arriving near the sea-cliffs shortly. The storm surge often helps bring new artifacts closer to shore. If you wish to come to meet her, kindly refrain from insulting my kin. And stay upwind."

Great, now we're on a hunting trip, thought Freya. *But at least I have a name. I'll have to do some research on weres when I get electricity again. And undersea lands, too.*

Aloud, she said, "Alright. I'm ready to go whenever you are. Lead on."

Lisichka did just that, stalking to the front of her pack - no, clan - of weres, and starting the journey down the hill. Freya sighed tiredly, and trudged after her. Evidently these weres had no additional transport, either. Of course, after a storm many roads would be closed due to fallen trees. It seemed unlikely that a handy country bus would come bumping along anytime soon. She started to sigh again, decided they might consider it rude, and walked after the weres in silence instead. The wind was blowing from the direction of the sea, washing

Freya in foxy-scented salty breeze, so she assumed she was downwind, or upwind, or whatever they called the right place to be.

Tammy and a were-fox. How could that have happened? And why would the weres have attacked her, if they were about to be kin in some way?

She had no answers.

CHAPTER TWENTY-TWO

LOOKING FOR TAMMY

Freya was glad when they finally reached the steep stairs leading down the cliffs to the sea. The blister on her heel had been joined by several more. Her wounded leg was protesting continued use. What had she been thinking, to go out again last night after the first incident? Now, her whole body ached, with occasional stabs of pain from bites, for added interest. She was extremely uncomfortable in the presence of the were-foxes who had beaten her the night before, and twitched whenever one glanced back at her. She had no reason to trust Lisichka's control of the youths. The last thing she wanted to do was spend time with them, but she also wanted to see her sister safe.

So near the sea, the strong breeze had increased to buffet them dangerously as they descended. Freya wished she'd thought to bring a tie for her hair, as her tresses lashed her in the eyes while she tried to take careful downward steps. She paused a moment to braid her hair instead. She knew it was a futile effort, since without a tie it would quickly unravel again, but her hands kept going through the habitual movements. It was briefly comforting to have her hair out of her face, at any rate. She then had to hurry to catch up with the were-fox clan.

The last few metres of steps were covered by gigantic piles of flotsam. Large rocks, whole trees, a boat or so, unidentifiable coloured bits of plastic, seaweed, a dead bird, it was all jumbled together in a random assortment. Freya followed the path picked out by the were-foxes, trying not to breathe in the already-strong smell of decay emanating from the pile. Or maybe that was just seaweed.

The beach was covered with detritus from the storm – so much so that at first Freya didn't see the figure washed up at mid-tide. Ragged clothing blended in with torn plastic bags – still a regular feature of beaches despite being banned years ago – and parti-coloured stones helped to disguise the body that lay there. The were-foxes had headed in that direction as soon as they set foot on the beach, so it was several minutes of careful rock-hopping before Freya could see the body that was her sister. Pushing her way through the surrounding weres, heedless now of their destructive potential, Freya reached her sister's side.

Tammy was lying face down on the stones, one hand flung out towards the cliffs. Her hair was dark with seawater. The waves still broke around her feet, and if the beach had had any more slope, Tammy would have been sucked back into the churning, silt-tinted sea within minutes. The tide was coming in.

Clutched in her sister's outflung hand was a curiously shaped piece of flint. Glaring at the weres who circled her, daring them to come any closer, Freya pushed her way to her sister, and gently opened Tammy's hand. The flint was roughly chipped into the shape of a canine. Perhaps, Freya thought numbly, it was a fox.

The hand suddenly clenched around the flint once more, startling Freya into dropping it. Her heart beating wildly, Freya cried out.

"Tammy! Tammy, are you alive?"

She immediately felt silly for doing so. Despite all the fantasy tales she had read as a child, zombies were not a thing. Weres, demis, water spirits and more, certainly. But zombies were things of the imagination. So, no matter how dead her sister had looked, lying on the beach, if she moved, she was most certainly alive. She took a deep, steadying breath, and asked in what she hoped was a more measured tone,

"Tammy, are you hurt? Do you need help? These weres led me here. Um. You should probably tell me more about them. But... maybe not just now. When you're feeling better."

Freya looked uncertainly around. The weres had stopped circling, but she unquestionably didn't feel safe.

"Tammy, come on, speak to me! I've been looking for you all day. Mum will be out of her mind with worry. What's been going on?"

Freya realised she'd been shouting. So much for steadying breaths. A groan emerged from Tammy, and she turned her head towards Freya.

"What are you doing here, Freya? You shouldn't be here. This is my time." Tammy's voice was croaky.

Freya felt rebuffed, hurt. Here she was, having worn out her already beaten body, having tolerated being near the perpetrators of that beating, having thought (however briefly) that Tammy could be dead - and Tammy told her she shouldn't be here? It was intolerable. She opened her mouth to say as much, when another voice intervened.

"Well done, Tammy. It appears that you have brought forth a relic of our ancient sea-covered land. Rise, and join us."

Freya looked up at the speaker in disgust. Lisichka stood slightly in front of the other weres. She was smiling serenely, her eyes focused on the flint figurine.

"How can you do this?" raged Freya. "You're trying to steal away my sister, and you haven't even checked to see that she is OK! And what have you told her? She's my sister, I have every right to see if she's hurt."

"Oh, but I don't need to steal her away. She is doing this of her own free will, aren't you, Tammy?" Lisichka's voice held a faint mocking note. Tammy flopped over onto her back with another groan. She lifted the flint figure so that she could see it, back-lit by the setting sun. Freya was sure a small smile flitted over her face before she cradled it to her breast and sat up. She cleared her throat.

"Look, thanks for checking on me, Freya. Go back to Mum and tell her I'm fine. This is what I've chosen for myself. I want more from life than endless wandering from town to town, never belonging anywhere. You always think I don't have ambition."

"I never said that!"

Tammy ignored Freya's interruption.

"You're just not looking in the right way. I've always had the ambition to find a place for myself. When I met Lisichka... and her son... well, maybe you don't remember much about what Mum told us about weres."

"That's because she told us almost nothing."

"Yeah, she did. I remember even if you don't. Maybe you should have paid more attention. But you know what weres do? They settle down, and they stay put, and they look after their own. I want that, Freya."

"You're not the only one who's sick of always moving."

"Yeah, sure. Moving sucks Loki's ass. But when they said I smelled good... I knew I had the chance to change my life, for the better! They have extremely sensitive noses, you know. It wouldn't work out if I didn't smell right."

"You're abandoning us because of the way we smell?"

"Listen, I'm taking that chance with both hands, no matter what it takes. And of course, I can do things they can't. So I'll have status. No were can summon like I can."

"But you summon better with me, Tammy, don't you remember? You said so yourself, that summer you taught me how."

"I think I've shown today that I can summon pretty well on my own. No-one has ever gone as far into the sea-kingdoms as I have now. So, you go, have a good life, make it your own. Go and be what you want to be, Freya. Don't let Mum keep dragging you around. I'm staying here with the weres. I just wish you hadn't got on the wrong side of my family-to-be."

Finishing her speech, Tammy rubbed at her drying hair, which fell in short tangles down her back.

"Ugh, I so much prefer fresh water to salt."

She looked up at the ring of waiting weres and assumed a more dignified manner, lifting the artefact in her hands above her head. She seemed to swell, become more than herself. A wild gleam entered her eyes. Freya suddenly wondered how well she knew her sister after all.

"Doggerland lives," Tammy intoned.

Freya wondered what on earth she was talking about. It didn't sound pleasant. However, a cheer went up from the surrounding clan (with some suspicious yips interspersed with it). Lisichka stepped close again, and addressed herself to Tammy.

"You have done better than I expected."

There was reluctant admiration in her voice.

"You must be good at wrangling with the powers of the sea. How fares Doggerland, the land of our ancestors?"

Tammy shrugged, then seemed to realise that she should be more formal. She cleared her throat.

"The sea rules over that land now, as you know. But the rivers of old still carve their channels through the seabed, though they are now hunted by sea wolves and squid."

She looked at Freya, and Freya could tell that her sister was trying not to laugh at her own words. That hidden gleam of laughter made her heart ache for her sister, who seemed to think that belonging to this group of others was more important than their own family.

Freya tried one more time to persuade her sister to come back to reality, to normality.

"Come on, Tammy. Just come back home with me. We can talk about what you're doing next. Tell Mum yourself that you're OK. Don't make this the end of our family!"

Freya felt tears leaking out of her eyes, and dashed them away hurriedly. She hated to show that she was overwhelmed in front of the weres. While they might not be close anymore, Tammy was a third of her family, not to mention the only sister she had. Freya didn't want to lose her.

"Please, Tammy. Come home." Tammy was shaking her head.

"Sorry, Freya. This is my chance and I'm taking it. There's all I need, right here. Plenty of water, beings who are prepared to put trust in me, welcome me, value my strengths." She grinned. "I could have children, even. I don't want to risk losing this opportunity. Even you being here is going to cause some issues. You know yourself that some of them don't take kindly to you."

Horrified at this cavalier dismissal of the severe beating she'd received at the hands of the weres that her sister wanted to join, Freya immediately protested.

"Didn't 'take kindly' to me? How can you talk about extreme violence so lightly?! I could have been killed, if Lio - er - if that passing sprite - hadn't done something to stop them! And why leave now? Why did you go out in the *storm*, for goodness' sake?"

Never mind that I also went out in the storm.

Tammy patted Freya on the shoulder.

"I know, I know, and I'm sorry. The storm - well, there are huge currents during a storm like that. I knew I could go deeper with a big swell, get something worthwhile. It's lucky I spent all those years practising with water deities though. I almost didn't make it. There were selkies down there, and they're almost as territorial as weres. Speaking of weres, Lisichka here has assured me that those youngsters will be punished. They'll know not to do it again. Apparently young weres can be easily upset, especially at this time of year. The oldest ones will be moving on to new territories soon. But the poor decisions of a few teenagers don't necessarily reflect the whole society. What I've seen of the rest of the clan is really positive. They work for the good of the group, even though we see a lot of loners around. They come back home to a loving family. Like ours used to be. If you smelt better to them, I'd encourage you to join them, too. As it is..." she shrugged. "I think your best option is to follow your ambitions. Finish school, get a degree maybe. Prove yourself in some way if that's your thing, go do something big. Somewhere else."

There was no stopping Freya's tears now, though she tried desperately to maintain her dignity.

"Somewhere else? Don't I get to choose where to live my life, what to do with it? At least when I'm old enough. I wouldn't have chosen all this moving either, that's for sure. And you're my sister. Can't you stick up for me? You should! Come on, Tammy. Mum and I need you. Don't ditch us at the first opportunity."

Tammy shrugged.

"I'm not ditching you. I'm bettering my position, just like all those Jane Austen heroines. I found a being of good fortune in want of a wife. You should be congratulating me, Freya."

"Yeah, sure. Well done, Tammy. Just what you always wanted." Freya's voice was bitter.

The weres closed in at that point, pointedly avoiding contact with Freya. They lifted Tammy to their shoulders in a sitting position. She put her arms around them for support, and as they bore her towards the stairs up the cliffs like a queen, Tammy looked back and waved at Freya, once. Freya was left behind on the beach, waves thundering on the pebbles, all alone.

The splash of a wave on her foot reminded Freya that the sea was encroaching, and she would have to move or be washed out to sea herself. Without the extra-strong watery connection her sister had, she probably wouldn't survive the experience. With a shaky sigh, Freya started the long, weary journey up the stairs and home.

CHAPTER TWENTY-THREE

BACK TO LIFE

Back in their tree-dented house, Freya was surprised by her mother's reaction to the news. Or rather, she was surprised by her mother's lack of reaction. Danae merely nodded, when Freya explained what had happened on the beach.

Her mother said quietly;

"She's been growing away from us for a while now. I half-expected her to stay back in the last town we lived in. She could have left any time in the last several years. At least weres are probably safer than trolls, or even jotunn. Though when she found that pure human a few years ago I thought that was it. Of course, then we *had* to move. Ah well. The question is, do we stay here, or do I try to find another job further north? It's tricky when there are weres about, but maybe now Tammy has joined them, they won't bother you so much. There are a few things we can do to protect ourselves. Though I doubt wolfbane will work on foxes, it may be worth a try. And it would be nice to be able to see Tammy from time to time, to know she's doing well for herself."

Freya wondered if this was how the mothers of those Jane Austen heroines had felt. Most of the mothers in question didn't get to talk to their 'bettered' daughters.

"You knew she would do this? Why didn't you try to stop her, Mum?"

"She was always going to leave someday, Freya. She's chosen her fate, just as you will. We aren't whole, Freya, we'll always be broken in some way. At least Tammy has found a way to feel more fulfilled."

"Why shouldn't we be whole? Just because we're demi-goddesses - or hemi-demi-semi-whatever-goddesses - shouldn't mean we're not complete in ourselves. Pure-humans don't think they're lacking, do they? Deities certainly don't, they're usually so full of themselves it's unbearable. Why should we be stuck in between and somehow not complete?" Freya found she was shouting at her mother. She'd never expressed her feelings like this before. It was a little frightening just how much of a relief it was to say it out loud. Very loud.

"Oh, Freya. I know it's hard to accept. But it's just the way things are."

"It's not the way things should be!"

"We don't get to choose the way things should be. We just have to learn how to live with them," said Danae.

Freya crossed her arms and glared. Both her mother and Tammy were acting as though they would never see Tammy in the house again. Freya just couldn't accept that - although she had to admit she'd be happy never to see those weres again.

"Well then, if we're losing my sister, and we'll always be broken, useless demis, are we losing this house, too? Or do we repair it so we can at least get our deposit back if we have to leave in a hurry?"

Danae answered quickly, stroking the air as though to smooth ruffled feathers.

"Oh, I suppose we'd better have a go at repairing it. I don't really want to leave my job at the greenhouse here. It suits me. And there's room for advancement, for a change, so I wouldn't be stuck potting on plants for the rest of my days. I'll just pop next door and see if they have a saw or something, so we can get that tree out of your room. Come on, Freya, we've got things to do."

Freya was astounded at the way her mother could simply move on from the abrupt, and probably final departure of her eldest child. She could only trail after her mother like a toddler as they started the long, slow process of reclaiming their home from the aftermath of the storm.

It took the two of them a long time to fix their home. The next-door neighbour did not have any tools. Nor did the one further down the row. The landlord seemed disinterested in managing the repair himself.

"He's probably too busy getting his own house repaired after the floods down the hill," was Danae's explanation.

Freya thought that a landlord should look after his tenant's houses too, but Danae declined to be drawn into an argument about this.

They did manage to get a tarpaulin to cover the hole in the roof before the next major downpour, awkwardly roped under the tree, which was too heavy to move. But Danae's work in the local glasshouse didn't pay well enough to buy a new roof. At least the glasshouse had suffered sufficient storm damage that her mother and the other glasshouse workers were working for much longer than usual hours - meaning more than usual pay, too. The necessity of a local food supply meant that everyone agreed the glasshouse took priority. Most of the crops in the ground had been pummelled by hail when the storm passed through, and other crops had been flooded in its wake. A covered glasshouse meant that there was something to eat.

However, her mother's work hours meant that Freya was on her own a lot, even more than usual - except for Mr Fluffbum, who was more of a hindrance than a help. Left to her own devices, she worked first on restoring her bedroom to a semi-usable state. She swept up leaves, and used her mother's garden secateurs to snip off first smaller, then larger branches from the tree that filled much of the room. She couldn't deal with the large trunk, however, and it loomed menacingly above her bed.

The carpet in her room began to smell like mouldy socks.

I wonder if I smell like that to a were? Freya considered, after being rebuffed at the door to her room by a wall of odour, a few days after the storm.

After a few tries, she managed to lever up an edge of the damp, smelly carpet. She carried it in a roll downstairs and left it outside the back door. The plants out there would surely mind the smell less than she did. The wooden floorboards that remained in her bedroom would no doubt be freezing in winter, but at least they didn't smell bad. And at present, they were pleasantly cool to lie upon, letting Freya gaze up at the sky through the hole in the roof while the tarpaulin was drawn back. The weather had turned warm again after the storm. No doubt the farmers were rejoicing that they had a chance to recover some crops.

Despite the painful reminder of her sister's continued absence, Freya had taken to sleeping in Tammy's room most nights. The smell of Tammy enveloping her was comforting. Freya could almost imagine Tammy was there, telling Freya off for messing up her makeup, or laughing about the latest concoction they'd made from a mix of foraged food and charity boxes. Over the years they'd made a lot of odd combinations. Acorn flour muffins with canned peaches, perhaps. Or walnuts with pot noodles.

Also, while the carpet was no longer there to give off its stench, the small matter of a tree resting on her bed was rather off-putting. Mr Fluffbum generally went to sleep curled up at her feet, but when Freya awoke, he was often sitting on her chest or stomach. The first time he did this, Freya woke up from a dream in which she couldn't breathe.

"Oof, get off me, Mr Fluffbum. It's lovely to have you back, but I still need to breath." She gently tipped him off by turning on her side. Mr Fluffbum put his ears back and glared at her before climbing back on top of her. Freya laughed.

"You must really want something, I guess. Look, I'll find some food soon. But you'll have to get off me in order for me to do that." Mr Fluffbum started to purr in place. "Oh, all right, you can stay there for a bit."

Freya learnt just how little use her demi abilities were when it came to carpentry, as she and her mother laboured to repair the damage done by the storm. No doubt the descendants of that Greek smith-god - Hephaestus, wasn't it? - would do better at that task. Unrealised fertility and wine-making traits weren't much help with building repairs. And of course, she had to go to school during the day. The school had not suffered much storm damage other than a few tiles lost from the roof, and it re-opened after only a few days of closure - with buckets to catch the drips of the inevitable rain.

On her return to school, Freya was once more immersed in local news. It turned out that the local shopping mall had been flooded by the heavy rains and tidal surge the storm brought. For weeks after the event, people in Freya's class were swapping stories with those who had been trapped in the mall (they were viewed as the lucky ones) or those who had merely been *nearly* trapped by the rising floodwaters.

Freya, as one who avoided shopping malls when at all possible - the bright lighting, smooth plastic surfaces and buzz of people annoyed her beyond measure - avoided commenting unless it was overtly called for. She wished that being trapped in a flooded-in shopping centre was the worst thing that had happened to her the night of the storm. She did feel a tiny niggle of guilt, however, when she heard that the floods had been exacerbated, because much of the water had arrived from a previously unknown watercourse that seemed to originate near the town fountain, as well as coming in from the sea. Had her release of the stone horses in the fountain had a knock-on effect to the spring below?

If it *was* her fault, Freya thought, she refused to feel guilty. Despite the damage the flood had caused, most people seemed to have enjoyed the experience. And the people inside the mall had been safe from the storm, which weather forecasters were calling the 'worst of the century'. Maybe she'd done them a favour. After all, her house hadn't been the only one to have a tree drop on it. And many of the houses near the sea had been flooded by the storm surge.

She'd arrived back at school sporting an enormous black eye, in addition to the more hidden hurts and bruises. She wore trousers to cover her hurt leg. It was cold enough that no-one queried her fashion choices - no more than usual, anyway. Freya had expected questions, and had considered blaming the fallen tree in her room. She didn't want to tell everyone how she'd been set upon, and the subsequent events. It was never a good idea to be seen as a victim.

"What *happened* to *you*?" a black-haired girl in her class blurted out when Freya limped in that first morning.

"Some boys up near the shops…" Freya blurted - but she was interrupted, perhaps deliberately, with the first of many loud retellings of the flooded shopping mall story. The storyteller on this occasion was a shorter girl with flowing copper hair, who tended to be something of a ringleader in school.

"I was so frightened. I thought the whole shopping centre was going to wash out to sea."

Freya knew she should ignore this story, but couldn't help herself.

"Why would you think that, Lisa? The shopping centre's not even on a cliff. And it's been in the same place for decades, hasn't it?"

Lisa replied scathingly.

"Didn't you see the news about that place over in Wales? *They* weren't really close to the sea, and they were swept away in a landslide."

Freya shuddered internally at the idea.

"I didn't see that; I don't have a TV," she said.

The chatter immediately swung to how poor you'd have to be to have no TV. Freya tried not to feel embarrassed, and avoided further participation in that conversation.

She tried to talk to the black-haired girl who had questioned her about her storm-day experience during break-time, but found herself constantly interrupted by thrown balls, accidental bumps and loud nearby conversations. It began to feel deliberate.

At lunchtime, the black-haired girl introduced herself as Aisha. She looked like she might say more, but at that moment someone bumped into Freya with a full lunch-tray, spilling half their soup in Freya's lap.

"Tell me later," the girl said. "Not here."

Freya gave up the attempt to communicate, and retreated to the bathroom once more, this time to clean up her clothes. At least she might have an ally in the minefield of high school, one person who did not seem associated with the were-fox clan.

Later that day, as they were leaving school, Aisha passed Freya a note. Freya read it in the school bathrooms, where she would not been seen reading the note.

'Meet me at the station cafe. 4pm.' it read.

Thank goodness it's not another midnight meeting suggestion! I could do with a friend here - especially someone who is not connected with those were-foxes.

She resolved that this time, she was going to try to make a friend. Maybe they would move again, but it was too miserable to be friendless amid the were-clan. A friend would be helpful.

CHAPTER TWENTY-FOUR

MAKING A FRIEND

The station cafe was deserted at 4pm. Freya wondered if she had the right place - though there was only one station in town. Then she wondered if it was deserted due to the were-fox influence. There was no-one with even the slightest hint of ginger frequenting the cafe. Of course, she'd be really easy to spot if anyone else did turn up. Oh well, she could hardly be more disliked by the foxes. And why should they spoil her potential friendships as well as her family unit?

Freya walked boldly up to the counter, which was staffed by a short, dark, grey-haired woman with smile lines around her eyes. Freya ordered a cold drink - the cheapest thing on the hand-written menu on the cafe wall. She made a face. She preferred warm drinks. A grey cat sat at the end of the counter, probably flouting every health and safety rule there was. It blinked at her, rose, and presented its chin for scratching as Freya neared.

"You're a favoured one, then," commented the woman behind the counter. "Isis here usually scratches rather than purrs."

"That can't be good for business."

"Ah, well, it depends what sort of custom you want. We're usually happy with Isis's choices."

Freya gave the cat its requested scratch then sat in a corner with her back to the wall. She surreptitiously put her injured leg up on a chair, under the table where it wouldn't show. That made it throb a little less. There was no escape route other than the way she came in, but at least she could see if anyone else came in. She felt a little paranoid, thinking so seriously about where she sat, and placing her back to a wall. However, her recent experience with weres had made her much more anxious than usual. A few precautions did not seem unreasonable, or so she told herself.

Happily, the first person who entered the café after Freya was Aisha. She waved at Freya, patted the cat, who purred loudly, then ordered something from the counter before sliding into the seat opposite Freya. Evidently, *she* had no qualms about putting her back to the entrance. Freya watched her enviously. Aisha seemed full of energy and confidence in this place – more so than at school, where she tended to blend into the background.

"Hey, Freya! Glad to see you here. I figured it would be easier to talk outside of school. The walls have ears, there, whereas here, no-one cares what you say. Also, this is my family's café, so the gingers don't frequent it, racist bunch that they are." She paused for a quick sip of her milkshake, then plunged on. "So, what did happen to you? You look like someone gave you a real working over. Are you OK?"

Freya sipped her own drink, finding that she wasn't quite ready to talk after all. There was a lump in her throat when she remembered the night of the storm, and the day that followed. Aisha chattered on reassuringly.

"It's OK, you can tell me anything, I won't tell a soul unless you want me to. Not even the cat." She nodded over her shoulder at the grey cat, who had curled up, tucked its tail around its paws, and appeared to be asleep with its nose on the counter. "It's not like I'm overwhelmed with besties in this town. In case you hadn't noticed, I don't have red hair and freckles, so I don't match the local landscape. But my family's been here for generations, so they have to live with us."

Freya had indeed noticed that Aisha's olive skin and glossy black hair didn't fit the local trend – indeed, it was a big part of the reason Freya had followed through with meeting Aisha today.

"Er, yeah, I had noticed that," she said.

"So, want to talk about it?" pressed Aisha.

Freya nodded. "I guess. I need to talk to someone who knows this town."

"Well, that's me for sure," smiled Aisha. "Like I said, generations! What I don't know about this town isn't worth knowing. And if I don't know, one of my aunts or cousins will."

"Alright, then," Freya said slowly, pressing the cold glass of her drink against her aching cheekbone. "The night of the big storm, I was attacked. And all of the people who attacked me were red-haired. And... rather hairier than you might normally expect. I'm not even really sure how I escaped, except maybe they got hit by lightning, because there was a burning hair smell – really awful – and they suddenly ran off.”

Freya wasn't giving Lio away to Aisha yet.

“But even though I was totally soaked by the rain by that time, I didn't get shocked. Luckily. There was a man standing there, when they ran off, but he went off too, afterwards.” Freya wasn't sure why she didn't want to explain Lio or his help. Maybe it was just that she didn't know Aisha well. “So, I just ran home as fast as I could. Um...” She didn't want to discuss the further events of that night. “But then, the next morning there was a tree in my room – I mean it had crashed into the house, it only just missed me – and my sister was missing. We found out later that she'd gone off and joined the people who had hurt me. I just can't understand how she could do that to me. She's my big sister! She's supposed to look out for me, right? And I'd spent all day looking for her, even though I could barely walk. She didn't even wait for the storm to die down, as far as I can tell – just up and left us in the middle of the night. And I saw her, that day – after the storm, I mean – so I know she's alive – but she just told me she was leaving our family and it was for the best. How can she possibly say that? Everyone seems to leave my family.” Freya's voice wobbled, and she closed her mouth tightly, unable to say more without bursting into tears. She blinked rapidly. She didn't want to cry in public, in front of someone she barely knew.

Unexpectedly, Aisha nodded.

“That's pretty tough,” she said. “My family's had a few people leave, too, and it never feels good. As for the other... it sounds like you've met The Family. They can be pretty rough if they decide you're in the wrong place at the wrong time. You were lucky to get away. Most of us who aren't part of The Family run up against them from time to time. They pretty much run this town – but not every part of it.” She added the last bit proudly. “Usually, people leave, or they stay and avoid confrontations. My family stays on our own terms, though.” She paused. “So, the ginger-hairs attacked you, but mysteriously stopped. And then your sister went off and joined them. That's almost unheard-of. Maybe she was trying to help you, after all.”

Freya made a face, then wished she hadn't - it hurt too much.

“It's hard to see how leaving our family to join a bunch of violent thugs is helpful,” she said.

“I know,” replied Aisha, “but if your sister has any sway with them, they are less likely to hurt you again. In any case, if you and your mum are sticking around, you should probably know some more about the town. Do you have a dad here, too?”

"No," said Freya shortly. Aisha nodded, and thankfully didn't ask further questions about her dad. Freya didn't feel up to relating that sad tale today, on top of everything else.

"OK then, just the two of you? Plus your sister, who presumably is looking after herself."

"Yes, just us," choked out Freya. She took a deep breath and let it out slowly. "Actually, just us and my cat. He was lost, but I got him back on the night of the storm."

"A cat, that's great! Cats are very important in my family. And yours was lost? You must be really happy to get him back then."

"I am," said Freya.

"Alright, then. I should introduce you to my grandma first. She's the one who served us. And Isis, she's the cat." Aisha called out suddenly, "Nena! Nena, come and meet my friend Freya."

The old lady appeared from behind the coffee machine, and hobbled over to their table.

"Pleased to meet you, Freya," she said.

"Nena," Aisha interrupted. "Freya's sister just left her family, and Freya's had some problems with *The* family. She has a cat, though. Can we do anything for her?" The woman addressed as Nena considered for a moment, then nodded.

"Isis welcomed her when she arrived, so I expect we can. Isis's gone to sleep now, though, so we won't get anything useful from her till she wakes up. No-one here wakes a sleeping cat." Nena's voice was unexpectedly serious. "Let your friend finish her drink - and you finish yours, too, Aisha. I don't make drinks to have them wasted, you know."

Thus admonished, Aisha screwed up her face.

"Yes, Nena." Aisha took a large gulp of her drink. She waved at Freya to do the same.

At that moment, the squeal of a train braking to a stop filled the cafe.

"Oh, bother. I was expecting it to be late again. Come another time," said Nena. She hastened back to the counter in anticipation of customers.

"There you are Freya," said Aisha, "You've got my family at your back now too. Whatever else happens, we've got this. By the way, did you say you have a tree in your room? I might just have a solution for that." Her twinkling eyes said that whatever the solution was, it was probably not an orthodox one. "If we go now, I can probably sort it out for you before the next storm. Would you mind if I came to your house?"

Feeling rather as though a whirlwind had whistled through the room, Freya nodded.

"Sure. Mum won't be home yet - she works at the glasshouse, you know. And I have to find something to feed Mr Fluffbum."

She gulped the rest of her drink and rose. Aisha took the glasses back to the counter, and whispered something to her grandmother, who rummaged around behind the counter and handed a small package to Aisha.

"Nena says you're welcome back anytime, and if The Family give you any problems, you're to call Bastet." The cat looked up at Aisha, and transferred its gaze to Freya before blinking and looking away. Freya saw that the cat had one blue eye and one green.

"Bastet, that's the Egyptian goddess, isn't it?" she asked.

"That's right," said Aisha. "We usually call on the cat goddess Bastet, and save Isis the cat for serious emergencies and cafe visitor vetting. You know some mythology then?"

"Do I ever," groaned Freya. "You have no idea how many extra lessons I have had in mythology."

Aisha laughed.

"Me too. But mostly Egyptian mythology. My family is pretty focused on that. I even have a brother who's gone back to Egypt to do archaeology there before the dust storms get so bad they cover up what's left out there in the desert. It would be way too hot for me there, though. I've spent all my life here, in cooler climes. I don't know how he stands it."

Freya looked at Aisha consideringly. Was she not a pure human? Extra mythology lessons were a good clue, as was the suggestion to call on a cat goddess. Not to mention the willingness to let a cat sleep, although that on its own wasn't a giveaway.

"So, does your family have any particular ways of dealing with the gingers? The Family, I mean?"

Aisha laughed again.

"We sure do. You might figure it out when we get to your place and see how I deal with the tree." She giggled, apparently vastly amused by her private joke.

Aisha hustled Freya to the front door of the cafe. A light drizzle misted the air. Aisha looked at it resentfully before marching staunchly into the rain. They walked uphill from the station, out through the grimly layered houses till they reached Freya's own house, right on the end of its row. Out here on the edge of town, houses stuttered out into countryside, but Freya's house clung agoraphobically to the buildings beside it. The mighty oak that had toppled was still sticking half-in, half out of the roof. From this angle, it was evident that Freya had barely touched the surface in her efforts with the secateurs. Great branches reached skywards, and broken ones reached into the roof of the house. Tiles were scattered on the roof, and a few had fallen in front of the house. The remaining leaves on the tree were wilted and sad. Aisha whistled.

"Wow, that's quite a tree. Lucky you weren't in your room when that one fell in!"

"Oh, but I was! I was rescuing supplies from under the bed! I couldn't believe it when I came out and it was spearing my pillow with one branch. Pretty creepy, when even the trees seem to be trying to kill you."

"Don't worry," said Aisha. "I'll deal to this killer tree in seconds, just wait and see."

Freya led her inside. Mr Fluffbum met Freya at the front door, mewing frantically and weaving around her legs. She almost tripped as she tried to walk down the hall far enough to let Aisha in. Mr Fluffbum glanced briefly at Aisha and narrowed his eyes a little before returning his attention to Freya.

"I know, you're hungry, aren't you, Mr Fluffbum. I'll try and get some money from Mum tonight to buy you some food, alright?"

Aisha cleared her throat.

"I might be able to help with that. Nena gave me this for you." She held out the small package. Freya took it cautiously, and peeled back the newspaper that wrapped it.

"Thanks! That's so thoughtful." Her eyes misted a little as she took the tin of cat food.

"No problem. It's important for us to look after cats."

Freya deployed half the cat food, to Mr Fluffbum's evident delight. She put the remainder in the fridge for later.

"Well, now that you've won over my cat, perhaps I can show you my other problem." She led the way up the stairs. At the entrance to Freya's room, Aisha stopped.

"No need to ask if this is the right room, is there?" she asked rhetorically. The room was half full of branches and wilted leaves. "Can you wait here? And don't make a sound, alright? Even if you really hate bugs."

This sounds ominous. Have I done the right thing, inviting her here?

But it was much too late for second thoughts.

Aisha raised her arms above her head, and cried out.

"A sacrifice, great Bastet. Take this mighty oak as your due."

A great humming filled the air, as of a thousand locusts. In fact, Freya realised, it *was* a thousand locusts, chewing their way through the tree from above. The large insects worked with incredible speed, and before many minutes had passed, the tree was gone, branches, trunk and all, eaten alive by thousands of tiny mouths. The locusts rose up in a swarm, and disappeared in the direction of the sea.

Freya was momentarily speechless. She drew breath.

"Well. That wasn't what I expected. I thought you would call a few of your family with chainsaws, or something. Or maybe an army of cats to scratch the oak to bits. Though I think oak's the strongest wood we have, so that might take a bit longer."

Aisha laughed again.

"Oh, in a way I did." She winked. "Cousins, sort-of. Super distant ones. With miniature chainsaw mouths. It's a family connection, anyway. A Bastet speciality." She looked worriedly at Freya. "You don't mind, do you? You seemed like the sort who can deal with a few out-of-the-ordinary solutions."

Freya swallowed. She was used to out-of-the-ordinary, but less used to swarms of locusts.

"I guess I'd much rather not have a tree in my room. Thanks. I'll be able to work on the hole in the roof now. And yeah, I guess I have seen a few unusual... things in my life."

Aisha punched the air, startling Freya into jumping backwards, where she bumped into the wall of the hall. At least she hadn't fallen down the stairs.

"Yes! I knew it!" crowed Aisha. "I thought there was something different about you as soon as you joined our class. But you know, you can't just blurt these things out, can you? So, what are you? Some sort of demi? Scandi, I'd guess, given your name. Am I right?"

Freya took a few seconds to absorb the shock of being recognised. Had she been *that* obviously different? She'd have to figure out what was giving her away. Aisha seemed friendly, but it wouldn't do to be picked out so easily as a demi. Her mum had drilled that into both Tammy and Freya since they were tiny. To be recognised as different was to be perceived as a threat, and *that* was yet another thing that led to them having to leave.

"Er. Yes. Some, anyway. Er... what do you know about demis?" Freya managed to say.

"Oh, what don't I know? Obviously, I'm one. And my family are too, of course. We trace our heritage to the original Bastet, as you probably guessed already. My dad's from a different family, with djinn roots, we think. Anyway, it's my mum who wears the pants in our family, so we mostly consider her heritage, not dad's - and it's my mum's mum, Nena, who you met in the cafe. Honestly, I don't get to tell many people about it, because it's mostly weres around here. They're so insular, practically xenophobic. That's why I was so surprised they took in your sister. Um. Sorry, I wasn't going to talk about that. Anyway, my family settled here ages ago, so they've mostly gotten used to us, or avoid us, anyway. Some of Bastet's little tricks help us out there. You should see what happens when I summon fleas to a were!" She giggled again. After a moment, Freya laughed, too. She couldn't help it, imagining that thugly group of fox-boys scratching uncontrollably.

"That does sound like a handy trick. I wish I had anything that useful. You're right that I do have some Norse in my family tree. Probably a few other things too. My sister was - is - really good with water deities, freshwater ones, anyway. But she's always been pretty focused on the fertility aspects of our heritage. She taught me a bit, but there's a few years between her and me. I think she would have been better waiting till I was older to show me some of that stuff. Anyway, lots of watery affinity for her, so we think there must be something wet in the family heritage that we haven't been told about."

"Isn't that always the way? You'd think people would keep better records, given the effects of being a demi. What about your Mum then?"

"Mum mostly works with plants. I keep trying with plants, but you saw that tree - they're more likely to kill me than grow for me. My dad had Greek heritage though, and he was a wine salesman, before he left us. So, Dionysian background from him. All in all, we're a real mix. But - how did you pick me out? We try so hard to act mundane. How did you know I wasn't?"

"Oh, as to that, that's easy," said Aisha. "One of the things my family is good at is spotting demis. Something to do with catlike observational skills, maybe. My out-of-school training was in demi-spotting. That's why we have the station cafe, so we can spot who comes and goes. We don't want too many demis coming here, because of the weres. No-one benefits from outright warfare, and that's what it would be if the weres thought they were being flooded with demis. Other demis, that is - even though weres don't think they're the same as the rest of us, they are really. Just descendants of a lupine god, or a fox one, or whatever other animal they shift into."

"Really? I never heard that. We try to avoid them - or at least we did in the past."

"I don't know why they think they're special. But they *are* touchy, so we - my family, that is - try to avoid a situation where they see too many other demis.

We're gatekeepers, that way. We don't stop people coming in, but we do warn them, if they come through the station. Your family can't have come through the station, though, because the first I knew of you was when you turned up at school."

Freya was astonished by this flood of information. She'd hardly ever met other demis, and they were usually just as focused as her family were on staying undercover. Also, weres as demis? That was hard to accept. She'd been taught that they were a totally different branch of non-mundane. But Aisha's take on them did seem to make sense. After a pause, she replied to Aisha.

"Oh, yes. We walked in. We didn't have much to bring from our last town. So, we just headed out along the cliffs. It took us days. You have no idea how uncomfortable it is to sleep 'under the stars', especially when you don't have enough blankets to go around, and no mattress, and it's drizzling - of course." She shuddered at the memory. It seemed as though life had been going downhill in one huge spiral, ever since her house fell off the cliff all those years ago. Then her dad had left, drawn elsewhere by the promise of a better life, or a different wife, or something. A huge well of bitterness threatened to overwhelm her, and hurriedly she moved her thoughts along. There was no climbing out of that well, if she once succumbed to it. She still wondered sometimes if Dad had left because of something she or Tammy had done. Finally, they had come to this town, driven by the need for a job for her mum, school for her, and a direction for Tammy - only to find herself assaulted and have Tammy leave the family circle mere weeks after they'd arrived. At least Mum still had her job. It was hard not to rage though. Some of her powerful emotions must have crossed her face, because Aisha put out a hand and patted her shoulder.

"Hey, Freya, it's OK, you survived. And now you know me, you won't have to rely on random strangers appearing to drive off weres. That is *so* weird, you know. Just as weird as your sister being accepted by the weres. Even if they are demis too, they're *different* about smells. She must have some mad good perfume."

Freya laughed, shakily.

"Not that I ever noticed. But then, I'm more likely to notice colours, not smells. And I'd be happy to avoid any future confrontations with weres. Whatever their family history."

"So, you didn't come through the station, we didn't have a chance to warn you, but here you are. With a now-treeless bedroom, and someone to call if you run into a pack of rabid weres again. Just think of them with fleas and call on Bastet. And hope I'm nearby, of course. I have no idea what calling on a goddess not your own would do. Probably nothing. Anyway, I should be going home now. I haven't done any of that maths our hideous teacher set us before the storm, and he's just the sort to get sarcastic. I hate sarcastic teachers, don't you?"

Aisha seemed almost unbelievably cheerful to Freya - but then, it sounded like she'd had a settled life, notwithstanding living in a were-infested town. Freya walked down the stairs with Aisha and waved her off at the door.

"Thanks for getting rid of the tree. See you at school tomorrow." She went into the kitchen and got herself a cup of hot chocolate, then sat down on the back doorstep to watch the sun setting over the hills.

CHAPTER TWENTY-FIVE

SCHOOL DAYS

"**Y**ou have no idea how much better school is, now that I don't have to huddle alone," Freya told Aisha during a break between classes. She cast a surreptitious glance at Gareth, the red-headed were-fox. Despite the demeaning names he had slung at her before the storm, nobody seemed inclined to make fun of her afterwards - not even Gareth. Their midnight meeting seemed to have achieved that much.

"Happy to be of service," said Aisha with a grin. "You'll notice it works out well for me, too."

"Or maybe everyone's too busy comparing their family's storm damage, and they don't have the mental room to be mean," suggested Freya ruefully.

"Or they're too hungry to think up names," said Aisha.

Freya nodded gloomily. Most people didn't have the foraging skills her Mum had taught her, supermarket foraging being much more popular with anyone who could afford it.

The storm had damaged several roofs, and more than a few farms and allotments had been destroyed in addition to the glasshouse damage, so food was in short supply. The proximity of the sea had previously meant that food could be imported relatively easily, but the pier had also been damaged, and the cliffs were more than usually unstable. Some of the big houses on the waterfront had been abandoned, and the pier repair was on hold until the construction materials could be imported over land.

"I heard some of the houses near the sea are going to have to be abandoned," said Aisha, chewing on a hank of her hair.

"Sucks for them," replied Freya.

"I think most of them have city houses they can go to," said Aisha. "The ones on the beach are just for summer visitors."

Freya's sympathy shrunk abruptly.

"I wish we'd had another house we could just go to if we lost one," she said. "It doesn't seem fair."

"I agree. But Mum says we need the summer people's money. And with the pier shut down, we won't get so many tourists in. Mind you, anyone who does come will have to go through the station." She smiled, reminding Freya of a cat who'd just had a satisfactory meal. "That means more traffic through the cafe, so it's a win for us."

"Isn't the pier mostly for fishing and imports anyway?"

"Yeah, but now *everyone* has to go through the station. Of course, we can't get stuff from Europe now. That sort of sucks. I prefer the European chocolate to the stuff we get here," said Aisha.

"That sounds snobbish," Freya said.

"Who are you calling a snob? I thought I was your friend," Aisha rebuked.

"Sorry, no offence meant," Freya hastily assured Aisha. She didn't want to lose the only friend she had here.

"Good. Look, I'll bring some of the good stuff tomorrow so you can taste the difference. I bet you just have the cheap chocolate, right?"

"There's nothing wrong with cheap chocolate," said Freya defensively. She enjoyed chocolate in any form.

"Not if you don't know any better. Which, to be fair, most of the kids here don't." She gestured at the clusters of teens dotting the area. "If they're lucky, they'll just be buying in bulk from that factory inland. There's practically no cocoa at all in those chocolate bars they make."

"I would be thrilled in be able to buy chocolate in bulk, wherever it was from," said Freya.

"Cheapskate. Or maybe I mean greedy-guts."

"Guilty as charged, if it's chocolate."

Freya smiled a little as she saw Gareth edge around the playground, clearly trying to avoid getting too close to her.

Now that is an improvement.

The next day, Aisha brought in two small squares of chocolate, individually wrapped in foil, and gave one to Freya in the lunch break. The brand name was scrawled across the packaging in a flowing, illegible font.

"Must be fancy if you can't read the name, right?" said Freya.

"You're a chocolate connoisseur already, I can tell," giggled Aisha. "This isn't the best one, but it's the best we have. Turns out we need the pier operational, too."

Freya peeled off the wrapping and inhaled the rich aroma.

Mmm, chocolate. Even if this type turns out to taste terrible, it smells so good.

"You don't sniff it, Freya, you eat it," Aisha said, her voice full of suppressed laughter.

"I will, I'm just appreciating it properly first."

"Carry on, then."

Freya wasn't sure she liked this expensive chocolate on the first bite. It was much stronger than the milky chocolate she was used to. But as she rolled the melting morsel around her mouth, trying to draw out the experience as long as possible (who knew when she'd get to try it again), she began to appreciate the depth of flavour. She took a second bite, and tried to make that last even longer. The third bite was the last. When it was gone, she sighed.

"You've gone and ruined regular chocolate for me, Aisha. Is that the action of a friend?"

Aisha laughed.

"Only the best. But that's all I can get for now, Mum said there's no more. I don't know if she meant till the pier is fixed, or something else. I know there's some sort of chocolate tree blight."

"That's the worst news I've had all day," said Freya. "First you ruin the cheap stuff for me, and now you say that you don't have more expensive stuff, and even worse, all chocolate is doomed? I don't think life would be worth living without chocolate."

"Hey, I didn't say it was doomed. Just that we don't have more!"

"*And* then you bring up some blight. Whole species have disappeared from blight, you know. *My* Mum taught me that."

"OK, now I'm depressed too."

The bell rang, summoning them all inside again.

"And that just tops it off. I hate my life being dominated by bells," said Aisha.

"Me too," agreed Freya.

"Did you hear, Freya?" Aisha was leaning against the wall beside Freya at break-time the next day. They watched the huddles of people form and re-form.

"The were-foxes have offered to rebuild the pier. Of course, they want a cut of any future trade that comes through."

"You're kidding!"

"Not even. They're going for a power move. If they manage to take over the port, they'll rival us at the station. At the moment we're pretty much on an even keel. Well, almost. If they get the port, they'll definitely have an edge."

"Will that make much difference to you? Or to me?"

Aisha shrugged.

"Who knows? Hopefully it won't happen, and we won't have to find out. But maybe it has something to do with your sister. You know, now they have someone who can maybe deal with the water deities a bit better."

Freya looked around. No-one was particularly near, but she was uneasy all the same.

"Are you sure we should be talking about this at school?"

"Probably not. But I thought you'd want to know, since it means your sister might be around a bit more."

"Thanks. I think."

"So, on a totally non-controversial topic, what do you think about these storms then?"

Freya blinked at the sudden change of topic, saw that Gareth was nearby, and shrugged.

"My whole life has been dominated by storms. It's nothing new."

"So, you don't think they're getting worse?"

"They probably are. My family tries not to live right on the shore these days, but the winds are just as bad inland."

"Yeah, they are. My cousins lost their roof in the last one. And I don't know how we're supposed to keep trees alive to fight climate change, when they keep getting baked in summer, drowned by floods in winter, and get blown over in spring and autumn. They don't seem to have much chance, do they?"

"You're talking to the world's worst gardener. You know those bean experiments they get five-year-olds to do? Mine never grew."

"Wow. Okay, yeah, that's pretty bad. So, we keep you away from growing trees, then?"

"Definitely. You know, my Mum's got these super-green fingers. She can grow anything - that's how she got the job that brought us here. And here's me unable to even grow a bean. Some fertility goddess, huh?"

"Don't worry, Freya. There's plenty of people out there who can't grow stuff. Most people our age don't care about growing things, you know. I'm sure there's something else you'll be better at."

"I sure hope so. I just wish I knew what that was."

The other people at school were worried, too. Word was that storms like the last one would get more common, and stronger, too. How would the town withstand the repeated battering? Many of the students came from homes that had been damaged, and all of them knew someone who hadn't yet managed to repair that damage. Before science class, Freya overheard some of her classmates openly discussing their safety options.

"My cousins in America have storm-cellars. We should make our basements into storm shelters."

"That's the best suggestion I've heard. But we don't have a basement. We live in a bungalow."

"Bad luck. Guess you'll be blown away then."

"Nah, we'll open up the old bomb shelters. There's bound to be some around here. We should find them."

"Or caves in the cliffs. That could work."

"Except that you'd have to get past the waves, idiot."

"Oh, yeah."

Freya smiled to herself. While her classmates were trying to find solutions, it didn't sound like they were close to a good one yet. Her smile faded as she realised that *she* didn't have a good solution either.

CHAPTER TWENTY-SIX

ENCOUNTER WITH TAMMY

Freya hoped that she would hear word of Tammy at school, especially since many of the kids there had red, ginger, or copper-toned hair - indicators of belonging to The Family. But her hopes proved to be unsubstantiated. Her sister was not mentioned. Of course, she'd never spoken much to any of the kids at school except to defend herself, so not hearing gossip was pretty much normal.

One Friday after school, Freya made a detour on the way home, to buy food for Mr Fluffbum from the discount supermarket. She thought she might visit Aisha afterwards. It was a long walk. She was trying not to let the distance bother her, but the wounds on her calf were making her whole leg ache. She wished she'd managed to get Mum to make one of her herbal concoctions for it. But it had been weeks since she saw her Mum for more than a quick goodnight.

Aisha's whole family lived near the station, so the station was an easy place to meet her, and also to feel safe from the attentions of weres. Freya had realised since meeting Aisha that the were-foxes tended to congregate around the shopping centre and the bus station - both of which were well separated from the train station. She did wonder how many other demis she'd been missing, since she hadn't realised Aisha was one. Freya was on high alert as she strode along the street, eyes scanning for any sign of ginger hair - or indeed, any sign of demi-ship in the passers-by. She was fairly confident that she could now spot the were-fox clan reliably. She had daily practice in class, after all. But the town was not so small that she knew everyone yet. She was looking for unusual weapons, questionable fashion choices, and tell-tale odd-coloured irises. It was hard to do this while maintaining a normal walking pace. More than once, Freya had to apologise to someone because she'd bumped into them. The third time, she apologised to a lamp pole. After that, she decided that her approach wasn't working, and was in fact more likely to get her in trouble than not. As she was dusting herself off from her lamp pole encounter, she caught a glimpse of a familiar profile. Tammy!

Freya burst into a run, calling after her sister, who miraculously didn't seem to have any attendant were-foxes. Her sister appeared not to hear her, but turned into a wine-shop. Freya ducked in after her, not caring that she was under-age for such an establishment. The smell of dust and wine enveloped her, evoking memories of her Dad. The memory of loss made her angry.

"Tammy, where have you been? Why haven't you been in touch?" she burst out.

Tammy turned from the aisle of bottles she was gazing at.

"Freya."

Freya paused, startled by the lack of warmth in her sister's voice.

"What, Tammy? Why aren't you happy to see me?"

"I told you to move on. I'm making my own way, here. You make yours."

"I am, but I'm still your sister. Get real!"

Tammy went on as though Freya hadn't spoken.

"Besides, I told you the weres don't like the way you smell. If I touch you, they'll smell you on me. And I have enough trouble keeping them in line as it is." Her voice softened momentarily. "Look, Freya, I'm sorry you're upset. But this is the right move for me. I just can't let anyone ruin it. Maybe in a few years I'll be running this town and I'll be able to call the shots. But right now, I have to be careful. So, you see, I can't be seen talking to you, and I can't give you a hug." She looked up, and quietly indicated the shopkeeper's eyes on them. "You shouldn't be in here, you're too young. See you again one day, Freya, but don't come looking for me. Promise?"

Freya couldn't say anything. Her throat felt like there was a band around it, choking any words she might have said. Tammy blew her a kiss, and turned back towards the bottles. Freya stumbled to the door.

It was hard for her to contain her hurt. It seemed like her sister had found an ambition at last, but that ambition precluded being with her family. Her sister's abandonment of the family, of her, felt like a knife wound to the gut. Every time she saw her sister not respond, the knife twisted a little. Why would Tammy think that running the town was more important than giving her little sister a hug?

CHAPTER TWENTY-SEVEN

MEETING KARIM

Freya reeled out of the shop door without looking around. Just outside the door she cannoned into a tall figure.

"Woah, slow down there!"

"Sorry." Freya tried to get around the person. She wanted to get as far away as possible from the uncomfortable scene behind her.

"Excuse me. You dropped your bag."

Flushing with embarrassment, Freya turned around. The person holding out her bag was a tall young man, dark-haired and dark skinned.

Not from around here was her initial assessment. Most people who lived in this town appeared to belong to a few distinct tribes as far as looks were concerned. Dark and handsome wasn't one of those tribes. He smiled at her, and Freya was first glad to see that he did not possess overly long canines - it was always good to avoid vamps and weres - and then noticed that his smile was rather attractive. And... familiar?

"Er... are you related to Aisha, up at the station?"

The young man's smile grew broader for a moment.

"Yes, she's my sister, actually. I take it you know her?"

Freya grew shy again.

"Yes, she's a friend. Anyway, thanks for my bag." The man held out his hand to Freya, dangling the bag by its strap. She took it, and was about to turn away when the man, leaving his hand sticking out, introduced himself.

"Karim."

"Huh?"

"My name. It's Karim. What's yours?"

Freya shook his hand briefly, feeling like someone playing at adulting.

"Freya."

His hand was warm and dry. She turned resolutely up the hill. She wanted to tell her Mum that she'd seen Tammy, but Danae would still be at work. Perhaps she should tell Aisha about it. Aisha knew the background of Tammy's abrupt departure from Freya's life. She'd be a good person to sympathise.

Freya had taken several steps uphill before she realised that Karim was still walking beside her. She glanced at him out of the corner of her eyes. Was he following her? After her experience with the were-foxes, Freya had been rather paranoid about being followed. She supposed someone who was blatantly out in the open couldn't be described as following, but it was unnerving all the same.

"I hope you don't mind me going this way too. It's just that I'm heading home, and that happens to be in this direction," Karim said.

Freya belatedly realised that she'd been walking towards the station, to find Aisha - which was no doubt his destination too.

"Oh. Er. No problem, I guess." Given how upset she was, maybe it was a good thing to have someone around who looked like they could take care of themselves. She certainly couldn't, it seemed. She'd enrolled in a self-defence class, the first week after the were-fox assault. But she was still learning the basics.

Karim walked along without chattering like Aisha would have done. Freya was grateful for that. She needed some time to compose herself after the encounter with Tammy.

After a while, however, Freya felt obliged to speak.

"So, are you the brother who works in Egypt?"

"Yeah, that's me. Aisha's told you all about me then?"

"No. Just that she has a brother."

"Oh. Well, I'm back for a bit of education. Though it's a shame to miss winter in Egypt, that's the best season there, cool and dry. Well, relatively cool anyway."

"Are you an archaeologist then?"

"Well, sort-of. I don't have a proper degree yet, so I'm helping on digs, not directing them the way I want to. But it's an amazing place. So much depth of history. And so many gods they've been through. Every place has their own versions. I suppose it's even worse here, but over there it's written down in a clear hierarchy. I like that, it's restful."

Freya was interested in spite of herself.

"So, what do you want to achieve, over there?"

"Oh, I want to find the cat statues and mummies, and restore them to their proper places. They've been ignored far too long, I think. But I have to get to be the leader of a dig, or higher, before I can do that. So, it's a long-term goal."

This sounded like an entire life-time goal to Freya. She was pretty sure that archaeology didn't move fast.

"What about archaeology back here, do you do that? Or just Egyptology?"

She hoped she'd got the word right. She hadn't had an opportunity to use it in conversation before. Karim laughed.

"Well, Egyptology is where I really want to focus. But my family is here, of course. They want me to do some digs here too. And there *is* some interesting stuff happening just offshore here."

"Around here?" Freya's disbelief showed in her voice.

"Yeah. Undersea archaeology is supposed to be the cutting edge of archaeology these days, and Doggerland stretches from just south of here all the way to Denmark. You probably know it as the North Sea of course."

Freya must have made some noise, because he looked at her curiously.

"You've heard of Doggerland? That's unusual, most people haven't."

"I've heard the word, recently. That's all. But what is it?"

"Oh, it's a bit like Atlantis. A land lost beneath the waves. Tidal waves, actually. Apparently, humans lived there even before the pyramids were built, but then the seas rose. Like now. What will they call this land when it's sunk beneath the waves, I wonder?"

"You say that like it's not a problem. Aren't you worried by the idea of our country, our homes, sinking beneath the waves?"

"I suppose so - but then, there's not much *I* can do about it. One man trying to stop the sea is one of those biblical tales, right? It just doesn't work. I prefer to look back, not forward. Forward is depressing."

"Well then. Can we learn anything from those ancient submerged lands? From Doggerland?"

"Yeah, don't build your civilisation in a valley."

Freya snorted despite herself.

"Not very helpful, then."

"Well, it all depends on your perspective. I mean, the people who lived in Doggerland were pretty advanced for their time. And they lived there because that's where the food was. Maybe we just need to figure out better places to get food. You know, away from the lowlands. But that's outside my area of expertise."

"So, how many people do know of Doggerland?"

"Oh, a fair few must do, I guess. It's just that it's mostly talked about by archaeologists, not your average person on the street." He gave her a somewhat conspiratorial smile. "But you're clearly *not* the average person on the street!"

Freya's cheeks heated. She hastened to change the subject.

"So, tell me about Egypt. I don't know anyone who's been there. What's it like, over there?"

Karim grimaced.

"It's a mixed bag. I actually love it there. But the worst thing is that there's so much poverty. There are just so many people. Luckily, I work out in the desert, where nobody in their right mind spends long – except the Bedouin, of course – and even they don't spend as long as they used to, since the climate got drier. Did you know one of the old governments built wells along the coast to try and keep them out of the desert? It didn't work, of course, but it's an interesting idea."

"It seems an odd thing to do. Why did they want to go into the desert, anyway?"

"Oh, you know, tribal lands, heritage, that sort of thing. Anyway, we go out into the desert from a big city, so we have to go through all the slums. I don't think it helps that I look like I belong there. I don't know the customs, so I'm always making mistakes. Looking at people wrong, that sort of thing. 'Course then I discovered I was like, looking into their houses, being rude. I nearly got beaten up, the first time I went out!" He chuckled.

Having recently experienced being beaten up, Freya did not laugh.

"You're lucky to have avoided that," she told him. "Getting beaten up hurts." Karim stopped laughing and looked at her.

"Are you OK? You look really white. Have – have you had experience with that sort of thing?"

Freya drew in a shaky breath and let it out before she replied. "Yes. Recently. Turns out you don't have to go to Egypt for that experience." She found she couldn't say more without bursting into tears, and she didn't want to do that in front of this handsome stranger - or any stranger. Karim stepped in with his own commentary.

"That's terrible! I hope the bastards got time for it."

Freya gave a short bark of laughter, almost a cry.

"I wish. No-one would listen to me. I'm just glad they haven't tried it again." Karim whistled.

"Wow, that's just awful. I wish I could offer to do something, but I'm not much of a fighter. Hmm. What did he look like, the guy who attacked you?"

"It was not just one guy. It was a whole gang. As for what they looked like, they were all red-haired. Aisha said they were 'The Family'. It sounds like those guys have a lot of influence around here. So, I guess I don't have much hope of justice. Or retribution." Freya tried not to sound miserable about that, but it was an uphill battle.

"Oh. The Family. Hmm. That does make it difficult. Well, at least Aisha's on your side. That's another good reason for me to work over in Egypt. I'd much rather deal with crocodile-headed gods and the like, than deal with The Family." Karim fell silent, apparently depressed at this thought.

"Crocodile-headed? That sounds off-balance," Freya said.

"Most of the ancient Egyptian gods are like that. Their descendants are something else. Weirdest bunch of powers ever." Karim narrowed his eyes at Freya for a moment. "You *are* a demi, yes?"

"Are all your family so up front?"

"Ha, sorry. I forget all the time we're not supposed to ask. My mother says I'm too much the product of a protective matriarchy."

"What's that like to live with?"

"Oh, it's not too bad. I'm used to it, though. Mind you, after living in Egypt for a bit, I can see why my family didn't stay there. Matriarchies go down much better over here."

Freya found herself wondering what it would be like if matriarchies were more of a thing in her own family – then realised that to an outsider, her family probably did look like a matriarchy.

She and Karim walked in silence for a while. Freya still felt self-conscious, walking beside a strange young man. What would people think, if they saw her? Turning a corner, they passed a pub which still had dead plants in its hanging baskets – had they been re-hung after the storm? Freya wondered idly. The dead plants made her think of her own ill-fated gardening attempts. With her mother so gifted at growing things, she'd always felt that it would be a foregone conclusion that she too would be good at growing plants. Unfortunately, her efforts so far suggested that this was not the case. She'd sown bean seeds every week for a month in spring, at their last house. The first lot hadn't come up at all. The second sowing had been eaten off at the base by slugs just after unfurling their first leaves. The third sowing had grown a pair of leaves which promptly shrivelled and turned brown. The final sowing, Freya had found half-eaten by mice after a single night. She'd given up after that. If her own skills were anything to go by, it was no wonder the world was short on food.

"Do you get anything green to eat, in the desert?" she asked Karim. He looked at her, surprised by the seemingly random question.

"Oh, we start off with fresh food, but by the end of the third day, it's almost all cans. Everyone longs for fresh, crunchy food after a while out on the dig. Maybe second only to a hot shower. Sand and grit gets into everything, even the food. And that's without a sandstorm. Those things are terrifying."

"More terrifying than a storm coming in over the sea? I'd have thought it would be restful, not having waves to worry about."

"Well, you can see the storms coming across the desert, of course – there's nothing to get in the way. But if you've been concentrating on unearthing something promising, and you look up, and there's this tan-coloured cloud just filling the sky, you have to get what you were working on covered up, and all the while you're hoping that you've still got time to get to shelter, and that this storm isn't going to be the one that destroys that shelter. I really hate that. And of course, when the storm's over, you have to redo all your work again, assuming it hasn't been destroyed. Experiences like that make you appreciate solid walls. So, I'm looking forward to being home for a bit, living in a building, not a tent."

Freya considered what he'd said.

"So, are you going to do a degree in archaeology?"

"Yes, that's the plan. That's why I'm home now. I need to make sure my application is all sorted, and figure out student dorms, all that sort of thing. It seems a bit odd after being away and in charge of myself all summer." The station came into view. "Ah, here we are."

Freya and Karim both turned towards Aisha's house, one of a row of similar brick buildings - much like Freya's, but in better repair - and Karim laughed again.

"I didn't realise you were coming here too. Thanks for putting up with me taking over the conversation. It's been a while since I've spoken much but Arabic, and I'm not as fluent in it as I should be, or so I'm told. It's so much easier to talk in one's first language."

As he said this, Karim opened the front door, calling out as he did so.

"Hi everyone, I'm home!"

CHAPTER TWENTY-EIGHT

DINNER WITH KARIM

A stream of cats appeared before any people made it to the door. Black, tabby, grey and ginger forms threw themselves at Karim. Several cats peeled off to greet Freya with similar verve. She knelt and scratched chins and patted backs. When Aisha and her mother appeared, clattering down the stairs to greet the newcomers, Freya hung back, feeling uncomfortable at being an extraneous part of this homecoming. However, Aisha spotted her, and called out in her usual cheerful voice.

"Freya! Did you come in with Karim just now, or did he race you for the door? Have you met each other already? Karim, I thought I'd see you coming in from the station, why didn't you come through there?"

"I met Karim down near the high street," said Freya.

Karim interrupted sunnily.

"We literally bumped into each other! Freya said she knew you, so I came on up with her. And you wouldn't have seen me come through the station because I didn't come from there. I took a ship to get back this time – thought I'd see how that went. And I tell you, I am not doing that again. I had no idea it was possible to feel that seasick. Sure, planes might be dangerous and expensive, but days of retching has got to be bad for your health too. And it still wasn't cheap. I don't care how much smaller my carbon footprint is, it's just not worth losing my breakfast for that many days straight. Plus, did you know there are pirates in the channel these days? My boat was lucky to get through!" Apparently, Karim was as much a talker as his sister was.

"Pirates?! No way, you have all the luck. Did you use your tricks on them?" queried Aisha. Freya looked at Karim.

"What are your tricks?" she asked. "I've seen Aisha's bugs. Do you do something similar?"

Karim's mouth fell open.

"Woah, you know all the secrets. How long did you say you've known her, Aisha?" he asked.

"I guess it's only a few weeks," said Aisha. "But they've been really *busy* weeks. Did you hear about the storm we had? Freya was nearly squashed by a tree in her own bedroom. I could hardly leave her with a branch spearing her pillow now, could I? Plus, she had some trouble with The Family, so she's a natural ally. And you haven't answered her question, Karim."

"Oh, well," he said. "If you know about Aisha's bugs, and you're not aligned with The Family, then I guess I can tell you. But it's a bit embarrassing – not masculine, or anything. That's what comes of being descended from a goddess like Bastet. I kind of wish Aisha had it, and I had her tricks. But, yeah. I make ointments. Or potions, that sounds better. Good ones. I can make potions that preserve stone, even. That's what got me interested in archaeology. But it turns out that I can't put any potions on artifacts without 'full and rigorous scientific testing', or my dig supervisor said. So, I need to get my degree, then I can use the potions the way I want. Meanwhile, every time I come home, this lot get me to whip up a few first aid potions. So, yeah. That's my trick."

Freya, who'd been smiling to herself while he described his non-masculine abilities, thought that as tricks went, it sounded useful – probably more useful if not applied to archaeological finds. But since she had yet to figure out what power she had herself, other than summoning water spirits like her sister, she wasn't going to judge.

"That sounds useful. Got anything for were-bites?" she asked.

Karim goggled at her. "Wow, you really *did* have a run-in with The Family, didn't you? I've never tried making anything for were-bites, but I guess I can try. We've avoided getting that close to the weres in this town. Do you have some bites at the minute?" He sounded curious.

Freya shrugged, and pulled up her trouser leg a little to show the unhealed bite on her calf.

"It's been there for weeks. It just doesn't go away."

"Freya! Why didn't you tell me about that?" demanded Aisha.

"Sorry, I guess I didn't think you could do anything. And it doesn't bother me all the time," Freya apologised. "Usually, I'd show my mum something like this, but she's been so busy at the greenhouse, I barely see her." Freya paused, then added half-jokingly, "And this town wouldn't survive without tomatoes, so she's doing vital work."

"Oh yes, go the tomato-lady, we all need tomatoes!" said Karim enthusiastically.

"In actual fact," interrupted Aisha's mother, "I think that this town would fall apart at the seams without the food from the greenhouse. But speaking of food, Karim, have you had anything yet? Surely it is nearly time for a meal. We didn't know you'd be coming today, so it's just falafel and rice. You'll feel like you've hardly left Egypt! But we do, in fact, have fresh tomatoes. Freya, will you stay for mealtime?" Unwilling to interrupt a family homecoming further, Freya mumbled an apology about being expected at home.

"But you just said your mum was working all hours at the greenhouse. She's not at home, is she?" Aisha interjected.

Freya was forced to admit that Danae was unlikely to be home.

"So, you should stay! After all, it will be dark soon, and it's better not to walk home alone in the dark. Right, Mama?"

Aisha's mother looked sternly at Aisha.

"Please don't pressure your friend to stay if she does not want to. Freya, you are welcome to stay if you wish, but I will not be offended if you wish to get home before dark instead. And if you do want an ointment for those wounds, I will send Karim over tomorrow with something, once he has consulted with Nena. She is as good as he is, you know, and she certainly has many more years of experience. Please do consider an ointment. Were-bites are nasty things."

Freya now felt more in-the-way than ever. But she would like to have her leg whole and healed again.

"I should get home and make something so that Mum eats when she gets home. Sometimes she's too tired to eat, when she gets in after a late session at the greenhouse." Freya made a face. "Then she's unbelievably crabby." She covered her mouth, realising too late that she shouldn't criticise her mother in front of others. "Oops. Guess I shouldn't say that."

Aisha's mother smoothly covered Freya's gaffe.

"Well, if you are going home simply to cook, perhaps you can stay for dinner here, and take home some extra for your mother?" Correctly interpreting Freya's facial expression, Aisha's mother added;

"Don't worry, the chilli is mostly added separately to this meal."

Freya had not reacted well to her first major encounter with chilli at Aisha's house. Bowing to the inevitable, she thanked Aisha's mother, took off her boots and moved into the house after Karim.

Karim disappeared to the kitchen to start talking ointments and potions with his grandmother. Aisha muttered that her grandmother usually appeared a few minutes before the meal was set on the table, just after closing the station cafe. Listening at the door, Freya was surprised that Karim did not dominate that conversation. He only spoke to answer questions put to him by his mother or grandmother.

Aisha and Karim's father appeared late, and was duly scolded. Freya had seen him a couple of times - a stocky man with heavy grey eyebrows and a bald head. He seemed generally amiable, and indeed, on other visits, Freya had only ever seen him acquiesce to any demands from his wife.

"Sorry, sorry my dear. I was busy in the shop. Wouldn't you rather we had customers? But I'll try not to be late in future. If I'd known Karim had returned, I would have turned the customers away. How are you, boy? Still able to make yourself understood in the old country?"

"'Course, Dad. Every time," said Karim.

"Are you ready for your stint of higher education, then?"

"Yes, Dad. I got my acceptance ages ago. It was just a matter of getting back in time. So here I am, and I'll head off to uni in time for the start of term." Karim turned to his mother.

"Any letters from the student halls yet?"

She turned away from the table long enough to locate an unopened letter, which she put in front of Karim. He tore it open eagerly, but his face fell as he read it.

"They don't have a place for me. What do I do now? I don't know anyone in the city."

"Are you sure, Karim?" asked his mother. "I thought they had to keep halls for first year students."

"No, it says they're over-booked."

"You'll have to go flatting then. Some poor person will have to share your cooking space. I wish them luck," Aisha chipped in.

Karim seemed unconvinced, leaning his arms on the table and placing his head in his hands dramatically.

"My university career is doomed before I even start. How can I study with nowhere to live?"

I'm sure things will work out," said Nena reassuringly.

"Yeah," said Aisha, "and even if you do have to find a flat, at least you won't have to dodge pirates. York's only got a river. The worst you'll face is flooding.

Speaking of which, did you hear about the flood we had here?" Aisha launched into the now-familiar recount of the flooded shopping centre.

After dinner, Freya rose to take her leave. Aisha's mother had packaged up some extra falafel and rice. The rice was something of a luxury to Freya - the price of rice had increased dramatically after the flooding of Bangladesh, and no other rice-growing country fully made up the short-fall. The difference in available food choice at Aisha's house made her achingly aware of her own family's poverty.

No use worrying over that now though. One day I'll be in a better position.

"It's a shame you don't wear knee-high boots," said Aisha as she surveyed Freya's mauled calf while Freya prepared to leave.

"Then my legs would have just been bitten higher up," Freya groused in response.

"Fair point. But they'd look good," countered Aisha.

"Glad to know you're more concerned with fashion than with my welfare," Freya said.

"Can't I be both? One of these days, I'm getting you to a decent thrift shop."

"I tremble at the thought."

"Leave off, Aisha," said Karim. "I'm ready to go."

The plan was for Karim and Aisha to walk Freya home, so that Aisha didn't end up walking home alone, either. The three of them set out as the moon was rising through a drizzly sky, shining through occasional breaks in the clouds. The temperature was dropping as winter grew closer. Aisha took the lead, both in pace and in questioning.

"So, Karim, did you really have to dodge pirates in the Channel?"

"I did have to dodge pirates, but it was in the North Sea. The pirates had a demi with them, but I wasn't sure which type she was. She had a dog, which kept on barking whenever it smelt us. It was super-irritating. In the end I made a few smell-bombs and threw them out into the water, to try and throw it off. I had to use rotten fish, 'cos that's all the captain would let me throw overboard. Mind you, by that time throwing it overboard was the kindest option. We'd have had to eat it otherwise - we didn't catch anything on the way, and it turned out they hadn't brought enough food to go round. So, it could have been sea sickness or food poisoning that had me feeling so rough. I hadn't eaten anything for a couple of days, when I got here. Bastet knows, I was glad Mum had dinner ready for us."

Aisha was quiet for a moment, digesting this information.

"You didn't tell Mum most of that."

"No, and I won't either. She'd just worry, and try to feed me up. So long as I figure out a place to stay while I study, I'll be fine - now I'm on dry land, everything seems better." Karim stretched his arms above his head as he walked. "I'll be glad to sleep on something that's not rocking, too," he said. "Hey. What's that light up on the cliff? Is there a new house built up there since I left?" They all looked across the town's roofs to the dark cliffs.

"No, it's all reserve land on the cliff edges. You know that, Karim." Aisha was dismissive. A light flashed up there, once, then again, a few seconds later.

"It was orange - maybe like flames," said Karim uncertainly. "Who'd be up on the cliffs with flames on a night like tonight? The wind's getting up, and those cliffs aren't fenced."

Freya considered the light as it appeared again.

"It's too regular for flames, not flickering so much," she said. "It could be one of those old-fashioned lanterns - with a wick. Though why anyone would be up there..." she trailed off. Could it be the were-clan, getting up to some mischief? "Is this a smuggling sort of place?" she asked, trying not to feel like she'd been thrown into a Famous Five adventure yarn. If it was weres up there, the absolute last thing she wanted to do was go anywhere near them. But she did feel a little braver with Aisha and Karim walking with her. "Tell you what, let's drop off this food at my house, and then maybe we should check it out? It's not breeding season for the seabirds, so it's unlikely to be some twitcher after something rare."

Aisha and Karim both looked at her.

"What? You've lived here all your lives, surely you know what twitchers are like?"

Aisha spoke up.

"I think we're just not used to other people knowing what twitchers are. I mean, they're the birding world's version of a piranha, but a lot of people think it's a computer programmer or a tree or something."

Freya laughed at this description.

"I think I know most of the birdlife around here. It's hard to avoid noticing the birds and animals when you're competing with them for food," she said.

Aisha nodded understandingly, though Karim still seemed surprised.

"I used to spend a lot of time birdwatching up here, before I went to Egypt," he said. "There are some pretty amazing birds in Egypt, too. Like those black and white striped kingfishers, they're pretty cool. Do you still go birding, Aisha?"

"I've stuck with field-based birds for the last little while," she said. "The gannets always look like they want to peck an eye out."

Freya looked from one sibling to the other in wonder.

"So, you're both birders, then?"

"Sort-of," said Aisha. "Not hugely serious - I mean, I don't have those huge spotting scopes or anything. Just a good pair of bins. I think it comes from the cat goddess. All cats love watching birds. I've even seen one of mine pounce on a bird's shadow, when it couldn't get outside to try and catch one. It's easy to see the attraction."

"Does that mean I should keep you away from birds in case you want to pounce?" asked Freya.

"Don't worry, I've always managed to restrain myself so far," said Aisha with toss of her head. "And it's not like we're weres, we don't become our goddess's spirit animal or anything weird."

"I guess you're going to go do biology or animal behaviour at uni next year, then, Freya," said Karim. "Sounds like you know half the stuff already."

Freya, who'd been privately admiring Karim's green eyes earlier during dinner, suddenly felt out of patience. Why should Karim assume he knew so much about her and what she would do with her future? They'd only just met.

"What about Aisha's bug army?" she asked defensively. "You seem to know plenty about them."

Aisha patted her arm.

"It's OK, bio-buff," she said. "We like people who know stuff. As for the locusts, I know about them because they're my speciality. Maybe your speciality is just a bit less specialised. There's nothing wrong with that."

Freya felt like a cat whose fur had been brushed backwards before being patted in the correct direction. It took more than a bit of patting to calm down.

CHAPTER TWENTY-NINE

HEARING THINGS

The trio trudged on up the hill in silence for a while, till they came in view of Freya's house. There were no lights gleaming from its cracked windows. The headland above it was shrouded by rain.

"You're a long way from the waterfront here."

"Yes, thank Frigg. We haven't had much luck with seaside apartments. Oh, will you look at that, now?"

Freya's efforts with the tarpaulin on the roof were being undone by a rising breeze that lashed the light drizzle into their faces. "I'll have to fix that tarpaulin again. In the morning, though. No way am I getting up on that roof at night."

"Good call. I don't miss this weather when I'm in Egypt," said Karim.

"I don't usually mind the rain," replied Freya, "when I'm properly dressed for it." She wasn't, having gone out in the much warmer, drier morning to get to school. It had been a long day out already.

Aisha gave an exaggerated sigh.

"It's just typical that it would rain when there's a chance of something interesting happening in this town. Freya, if you go in and your Mum's home, will she make you stay in?"

"Very likely. Especially since it's dark and raining. She'd say this is plant-growing weather, not people-growing weather."

"Drat. Well, I want to go see what those lights are. Do you want to come?"

"Er... can I say no? I know it was my idea..." hesitated Freya. She rubbed her leg through her trousers. Although she was curious about the light on the cliff, the old bites on her leg were hurting after the walk up the hill, and probably needed a change of dressing.

"Why would you do that?"

"It's just my leg. It's a bit sore."

"You can say no, but that would be super-boring. And I'd miss your company. So would Karim, isn't that right, Karim?" Aisha bossed.

"Sure, but who said I was going anywhere but home? You're assuming a lot, little sis," Karim replied, refusing to be bossed, or to be drawn about missing Freya's company.

Freya intervened before a sibling squabble could break out.

"Look, I'll take the food in. If Mum's there, I'll stay in. If she's not, I'll come out with you, but only to stop you going up there by yourself. You know that's not sensible, no matter how powerful Bastet is."

Aisha accepted this compromise as though it was a heartfelt acceptance.

"All right, we're on for adventure!"

When Freya glared at her, she relented a little.

"Yes, yes, I know, you're only coming if your Mum isn't there. But *you've* had interesting times, lately. I've just had second-hand storm stories. The only excitement we had was a lack of trains through the station for a few days while that mudslide was cleared off the tracks. And believe me, that's the dead *opposite* of excitement. Anyway, I am ready for something interesting happening in my life. You got were-fights and lightning and mysterious strangers, and I got distant views of mud. *So* not fair."

"You're welcome to some of my awful luck, if you don't mind assault. I wouldn't recommend it, myself. But I guess I was lucky with the lightning," Freya said somewhat wryly. Somehow, Lio had always felt like a secret friend.

"Excuse me, ladies," interrupted Karim, "but are we going to stand out here in the rain all night, or is Freya going to deliver her mum's dinner?"

Freya hastened to unlock the door – that probably meant her Mum was not at home, but it wasn't a total assurance, since Danae had started locking it while she was in sometimes, after the were-attack on Freya. Mr Fluffbum threw himself at Freya's legs, twining around her.

"Yes, yes, Mr Fluffbum, I'm happy to see you too. I got you some food." Freya turned to her companions. "Come in for a moment," she told Aisha and Karim. The siblings followed her suggestion, only too glad to get out of the cold drizzle for a time. Karim bent to greet Mr Fluffbum, who sniffed Karim's hand with a series of huffs, before giving it a long smooch. Aisha patted Mr Fluffbum's back, confident in her welcome as an already known friend.

Once inside, Freya tried turning on the lights with the switch by the door.

"Frigg's chariot, we've had a power cut again." She picked up the solar lantern they'd been keeping by the door and pressed its 'on' button. A dim light illuminated the hall. It looked like the lantern hadn't been charged enough lately. However, it gave them enough light to see the stairs leading up to the bedrooms, and the short passage that led to the kitchen and lounge.

"Mum! I'm home, are you here?" When no-one answered Freya continued. "I guess she's still working. I'll just put this food in the kitchen, then. Aisha, Karim, do you want a cup of hot chocolate or something before heading out? I'm freezing after being out in that rain."

"Are you kidding? I want to go see what those lights are!" Aisha was waiting near the door, clearly itching for something exciting to do.

"Oh, well. I guess we can always have a hot chocolate when we get back. It'll be easier if the power's back on, anyway."

"Yeah, let's do that. Come on, let's get going now. Karim, I'm sure you want to investigate."

To Freya's surprise, Karim pondered for a moment.

"I'm not sure it's a good idea in the dark, and with Freya injured. And I promised Mum I'd see you home, Aisha. I'd rather head up tomorrow morning. Do you have school?"

"It's a Saturday tomorrow, Karim, of *course* we don't have school. But what if whatever it is, isn't there tomorrow?"

Karim looked briefly confused as he worked through this muddled statement. He opened his mouth as though he was about to argue in favour of a delay when there was a penetrating scream from outside.

"What was that?" they asked each other in unison.

"It came from the north," said Karim.

"That's up by the cliff! We *have* to go investigate now!" cried Aisha.

Freya shivered.

"I hope that wasn't weres. I wish Mum was home safe. When I hear sounds like that, I wonder what's going on."

"Come with us, then. At least we'll be together," Aisha suggested.

Freya looked around the kitchen, which had lost its cosy feel. The dark night seemed to press in through the windows. The scream repeated. Was it further away? No, she didn't want to stay here alone. Freya made her decision.

"Alright, let's go. Someone might be in trouble."

CHAPTER THIRTY

CLIFFTOP MYSTERY

Freya hurriedly stuffed a few flapjack bars and some small apples into her pockets. Karim looked at her curiously.

"Feeling peckish?" he asked.

Freya blushed, but continued her preparations.

"I like to have supplies. Just in case," she said. Karim shrugged.

"Go ahead," he said. "I brought something to snack on myself."

Well, that's unusual. I'm usually the only one taking snacks.

Prepared for weather and unforeseen emergencies, Freya decided she was as ready as she would get that night.

"OK, let's go."

The three of them shuffled out the front door into the rain once more. Freya's house was just about the last before the countryside began, so there were few streetlights under ordinary circumstances. Tonight, with the power off, the area was pitch black. There were a few lights in the town behind them, other people with solar power, torches or candlelight. Freya had a sudden image of how villages must have seemed at night before gas and electricity were widespread - so dim, huddled together against the terrors of the night, a few flickering lights together in a sea of darkness. She shivered. What terrors were out in this night? Probably were-foxes, if nothing else. And the night-loving descendants of hundreds of gods and minor deities. Sometimes she wished she didn't know as much as she did about the seen and unseen possibilities. She turned her attention outward once more as they left the comforting familiarity of the town.

"Do either of you have a torch?" Freya asked, as the night grew blacker. "Mine broke just after we moved here, and I haven't got a new one yet. Wish I'd brought that lantern."

"I'd use my phone's light, but it went flat while I was still on the boat. Too many rainy days for my solar panels. I left it charging at home," said Karim.

"My phone has a flashlight, and battery too," Aisha volunteered.

"That'll do fine."

The three shared the phone's light as they followed the cliff-path up the hill. The path had been moved again recently, to avoid the site of a landslide - the cliff in one long stretch having fallen prey to the sea. That meant that although there were markers from time to time, the track was not well-worn, and they kept having to stop and swing the torch wide to figure out the direction it took. Up here, it wasn't wise to stray from the path. There were sudden drops and steep gullies in most directions. Occasional muttering sounds, squeals and grunts came from the direction of the cliffs.

"That's just the last few gannets that haven't left for winter," Freya commented.

"Yeah, I do know that much, nature-girl. I *have* lived in this area all my life," said Aisha. An odd squawk sounded off to their left.

"You're welcome to reassure me on that one then," said Freya.

Karim chuckled, the warm sound dispelling Freya's worry.

"That's just a little owl," he said. "Not a native, but they live pretty much everywhere, these days."

The sound of waves crashing at the foot of the cliffs overlaid everything, and ensured that they did not stray close to the cliff-edge - something Freya had worried about when she thought of venturing onto the cliffs at night.

So far, they had seen and heard nothing out of the ordinary. The rain had not relented, so it was a cold and weary trudge along the cliff-path.

"I don't think we're going to find anything tonight," Karim said in a tired-sounding voice. Freya was reminded that he had just arrived from a wearisome sea journey involving pirates and seasickness that afternoon. "How about we turn back? I don't think we'll be able to find anyone in the dark."

Freya was about to eagerly second this plan when another scream rent the air. It was not far from their location, but inland. They swivelled to face the sound, which continued for a second or two before dying away.

"That does not sound good," said Freya.

"It sounds like someone in pain. We'd better find them," exclaimed Aisha, always a people-person.

"Yes, I guess we'd better look," agreed Karim.

Leaving the path, they headed in the direction they thought the scream had come from. Before they found anything, a large hairy four-legged body came crashing towards them through the low shrubs. Aisha swung towards the sound, and they all caught glimpses of the approaching beast as it leapt over patches of brambles and pushed through stands of willowherb and hemlock grown tall and rank. Reddish fur gleamed on its shoulders, and eyes reflected the light in an eerie glow as it looked their way.

"Backing up now," said Karim.

"No!" said Freya urgently. "Stick together!"

Aisha gripped Freya's arm tightly with the hand that wasn't holding the phone, but she kept the light pointed towards the were - no easy task as it kept moving.

"I think it's a fox. Do you think I should point the phone away?" she asked in concern. "Might it go away then?"

Freya shuddered at the idea of an unseen were-fox attacking them.

"Please, I'd rather see an enemy than not. Keep doing what you're doing. Karim, do you happen to have any knowledge about how to deal with were-foxes, having lived in this area all your life, as Aisha says? I'm pretty sure regular foxes don't act like that unless they have rabies. And *that* one is rather large."

Karim laughed, a despairing sound rather than an amused one.

"I guess I should have told you before," he said. "Another reason I'm going *away* to study and work is because the were-foxes hate me. I have literally no idea why, or how to stop them. I spent my entire school career here being either bullied by them or avoiding them."

Friends are great and all, thought Freya, *but couldn't I have made some friends who were more effective against were-foxes?*

The beast was closing in on them fast. Larger than a fox by an order of magnitude, Freya could see its long sharp teeth now.

Why can't they be the size of regular foxes? Surely conservation of mass should be superseded by magical ability... This is why I don't like physics. It holds true when you don't want it to.

Freya, Aisha and Karim clutched at each other and backed up as fast as the rain, the dark and the uneven footing would allow. The sound of gannets was drowned out by the growling of the were-fox as it bounded closer to them, then paused.

It eyeballed Karim and let out a series of yipping barks, which, terrifyingly, were answered from their left with another, deeper yip.

"Quick, back towards the town, there's more than one!" cried Freya. She didn't want to risk those canines again. Although she wasn't sure if these were the same were-foxes that had attacked her before the storm, did it matter? Probably not, if they were out for blood.

"But what about that person who screamed?" Aisha protested. "They might die of exposure if they're out in this rain all night."

Unfortunately, Freya knew she was correct.

"OK, emergency plan. Has anyone got a weapon? Karim, any potions or leftover rotten fish? Anything?" Freya asked desperately.

Karim shook his head.

"Nothing I can think of." He put his hand in his pockets to check. "Nothing but an extra falafel from dinner." He pulled it out. Freya was disappointed. She'd somehow thought that a person who survived the wilds of Egyptian archaeology digs in the desert would pull out a bullwhip or saber - something like Indiana Jones. Also, Karim had clearly not seen the same ancient movies as she had.

"Put it back in your pocket, Karim, did you never see that old movie?" hissed Freya.

Karim looked confused, but replaced the offending falafel.

"Frigg. And there aren't any water courses up here, so there's nothing I can use," said Freya. She turned to Aisha.

"Can you do anything with those locusts of yours?"

Aisha made a face.

"They're vegetarians. And they don't like the rain," she said. "Also, I only do locusts and fleas, before you ask for hordes of were-eating mosquitoes." She tried to smile, but it didn't quite come off.

The glimmerings of a plan came to Freya. Not a great plan, but at this point anything seemed worth a try.

"That falafel will do fine, Karim," she said. "Get it out again. And when I tell you to, can you throw that falafel at the were-fox, as close as you can manage. Then Aisha, can you send your locust swarm after the falafel, even for a few seconds? And then summon fleas to the other one?"

But Aisha was shaking her head.

"I can only manage one summoning per day," she explained. "I was showing off, when I got your tree dealt with. It's not often a locust summoning is so useful. I can manage either fleas or locusts now, but not both."

Freya made a small sound of irritation, though she was not truly surprised. All demis had limited powers, and many had far less than Aisha had displayed.

"That'll have to do, then," she said. "Get the locust swarm to consume the falafel when it gets really close to the were-fox. They should come for a few seconds, shouldn't they?"

"Well yes," agreed Aisha, "but I have no idea why you'd want them to eat a falafel. I thought we were trying to fend off a were-fox. Wouldn't fleas be better for that?"

"Just give it a go - and we'll see if it works. I'm betting that foxes are pretty used to fleas - I mean, wild ones almost all have fleas, and it doesn't kill them," said Freya. She didn't know what to do about the second were, but at least they could try to scare off the first.

The were-fox was now stalking a handful of metres away, eyes fixed on them. It was clearly not worried about them escaping. They could all hear the thunder of the sea, disturbingly close behind them. There was nowhere to run in that direction.

"OK, Karim. Give it your best shot - as close to the were as you can, maybe a bit over its head. I hope you have good aim."

"Now that, I do have, luckily," said Karim.

"Aisha, are you ready?" said Freya.

Aisha, with her hands raised, phone still in one of them, nodded.

"Now!" said Freya.

Karim threw the falafel. Aisha called out her summoning phrase.

"Bastet, take this sacrifice."

Karim's aim was true, the falafel catching the light just above the were-fox's head. Dog-like, the were-fox leaped high after the morsel, its back curved, legs tensed. Almost at the same moment, a swarm of locusts flashed into being around the falafel. A heartbeat after that, the were-fox snapped the falafel out of the air like a dog catching a ball, still surrounded by locusts. There was a crunching sound. The were-fox opened its mouth again with a yelp of distress. Small, glowing grasshopper-like locusts poured out of it, more than could possibly have fitted into its mouth - and certainly more than had initially appeared. The were-fox whimpered again, scratched ineffectively at its nose with its paws, then turned and ran away from the small group on the cliff.

"Wow," said Aisha, admiringly, "Bastet's offerings shouldn't be crunched, that's clear."

"That has got to be the best falafel effect, ever. A bit like bonfire night in miniature," said Karim.

"Well done, you guys. But come on, quickly now! We shouldn't just stand around admiring our work. We need to find that injured person and get out of here before the other weres arrive, and that one recovers!" Freya dragged Karim and Aisha by the elbows in the direction of the groan they had heard a few terror-filled minutes earlier.

Snapping out of their astonishment, they followed her, Aisha providing phone-light, all of them staggering through the long grass. The threat of the unknown weres kept them going despite the uneven ground and the rain now lashing their backs, blown in from the sea.

"But how did you know that trick with the falafel would work?" panted Karim as they ran.

"I didn't," answered Freya shortly. She didn't have much breath for talking as well as running. "But I thought that having something thrown at it might distract it - after all, foxes are in the dog family - and then maybe the locusts would be more of a distraction." She grinned. "But it worked out even better than I imagined. Great teamwork, guys!"

CHAPTER THIRTY-ONE

SKY RIVER

In the midst of their self-congratulation, Aisha was snagged by a straggling bramble, and fell heavily. The phone flew out of her grasp to lie face-down on the wet grass.

"Oof. Did I mention I'm not keen on running? Especially not through dark wet bramble patches?" she panted.

Freya puffed out a laugh.

"Funnily enough, that didn't come up in any of our previous conversations."

Aisha pulled herself to her feet, picking up her phone in the process. However, the damage was done. The phone, their source of light, no longer worked.

"What now?" groaned Karim, who had also paused when Aisha fell. It was hard to run without seeing where to go.

Freya was momentarily stumped. When had she become the leader of this expedition?

That's where sharing your bright ideas gets you, unwanted leadership.

"Umm. Er. Call out? Maybe the person out there has a light?"

No-one seemed to have any better ideas, so Freya called.

"Hello? Who's out there? Are you hurt? Where are you?"

To her astonishment, a familiar voice replied from quite close by.

"Freya! What are you doing out here?"

"Mum? I could ask the same of you! But where are you? It's as black as pitch up here."

A tiny flicker, no more than a spark, lit up a patch of shrubs a short way away.

That must be what the flames were, thought Freya. *She has her flint with her.*

A few years ago, her mother had invested in a prepper-style flint and steel, attached by a short rope. It was ridiculously hard to get a fire going with it, but it had seemed like a good idea at the time, as they'd had a series of power cuts in winter, and kept running out of matches for the wood-fires they'd used to keep warm. Her mum had taken to keeping the flint in her pocket then, and evidently hadn't lost the habit.

"Again, Mum!" Freya called. "We don't have a light."

There was a pause, where nothing seemed to happen, and Freya imagined her mother trying to strike the steel and flint at just the right angle. Finally, there was another flash of light. Freya caught the barest glimpse of her mother's form, huddled by a patch of longish grass. Taking hold of Aisha and Karim's arms, she advanced cautiously in that direction. It was even harder going in the dark, and she stumbled more than once. However, after what seemed like an eternity, with rain dripping down under the hood of her anorak and pelting cold against her back, Freya's feet hit something more solid than tangled vegetation.

"Ow!"

"Sorry, Mum, I didn't see you there. Are you OK?" She let go of her friends and reached down, feeling for her mother in the dark. Her mother reached up and grasped her hand.

"Freya, thank Gaia. We've got to get off this headland. It's were territory through and through. But my leg's hurt. Who is it you've got with you?"

"It's me, Aisha. Freya's friend. And my brother Karim's here too. I'm sure we can help you. We're pretty keen to avoid any more weres, too. Besides, you don't have any more falafel, do you, Karim?"

"If only! I just managed to pocket one before mum spotted me. Such a waste, though it was effective." He sighed. "Er... Mrs? Freya's mum? There's more falafel at your place, from my mum."

"Why, thank you," said Freya's mother dryly. "In that case, call me Danae. Should we make it off this headland alive, I look forward to your mother's falafel." Her voice sharpened as she addressed her daughter. "Freya, why are you up here on the cliffs at night with no light and no food? I thought I'd taught you better than that."

Freya flushed in the darkness, embarrassed and therefore annoyed by her mother's words in front of her friends.

"I do have food; I just didn't want to waste it as were-bait. As for a torch - well, you won't let me have a phone, and the solar lantern hadn't been charged. It's usually Tammy's job to charge it." She tried not to whine the last sentence, though it was hard not to. She hadn't yet become accustomed to taking over the jobs her sister had done around the house. However, her mother latched onto that topic, though not for the expected reason.

"Tammy's absence is exactly why I am here. I can't let her just go off with a pack of weres and not keep us updated on how she's doing. She hasn't sent a single message. When I saw a few weres coming up here while I was on my way home from the glasshouse, I thought I'd find out about Tammy from them. They looked human at the time, of course. Unfortunately, they weren't prepared to share any information, and they turned on me when we were out of sight of town."

"That's terrible, Mum. Didn't you think of asking when other people were about?"

"I had to take the chance I had. For all the good it did. As for phones, they're not all that useful when they run out of battery. Which mine has. And I don't have anyone to call in this town yet, anyway."

"But you could have called emergency services!" said Freya.

"I don't trust them. The weres control almost everything other than the station where your friends come from."

Aisha and Karim spoke simultaneously.

"We control more than just the station!"

"Well, a bit more. A shop or two," said Aisha.

"Yes, exactly," said Danae. "Not emergency services, am I correct?"

"Well, not exactly. But one of my uncles is a waterfront manager."

"Hardly enough to make a difference. When Freya was injured, I tried to report it to the police. They wouldn't record anything, said there were no witnesses. After that, I knew the authorities here were biased. So, no emergency services. Speaking of which, the leg bite seems to be a popular target for these were-foxes. I would appreciate it if you could help me up, and down the hill. Before any weres return."

"Yes, let's go," said Freya.

"Good plan," said Karim. "Aisha, you and I aren't injured, so we'll offer a shoulder each to Freya's mum. Freya, any idea which way to go?"

Freya was pleased not to have to be leader for this. It was too embarrassing around her mother. But she was concerned about her mother's injuries, whatever they were.

"Do you need us to figure out some bandages, or something?" she asked.

"No, without light you can't see what to do, and I'd rather get somewhere safe first," Danae said.

"Alright then. Light. Hmm." While she was trying to work out which direction led homeward, there was a brilliant flash of light as lightning struck out to sea. It was quickly followed by a rumble of thunder that shook the ground. Freya automatically counted the seconds between the lightning and thunder. It didn't take long.

"That's all we need, an electrical storm on the way! At least I saw the right direction. That way!" Freya felt somewhat foolish as she pointed, then realised that without the flash of lightning, the others couldn't see her hand. The sea roared periodically on one side though, punctuated by the occasional raucous gannet. They stumbled along painfully. Aisha and Karim soon began to complain about sore shoulders. Apparently, supporting her mother wasn't the easiest choice they could have made.

"I'm right here, you know," said Danae. "And I'm trying to take my own weight as much as I can."

"Sorry."

"There! I see the lights of the town," said Freya. They had reached the cliff-path that headed down towards Freya's house now, and with the sparse lights from the town she was able to see enough at last. She stopped and waited for Aisha, Karim and her mother to catch up. All three of them wore grim, pained expressions. Aisha and Karim had swapped sides, presumably to ease their sore shoulders. Behind them, the headland was still shrouded in black. While she looked, another flash of lightning lit up the area. There was no gap before the thunder, this time, and the rain abruptly redoubled.

"Knowing my luck, the storm sprites will turn up now too," Freya muttered to herself, thinking of her early experiences with sprites and the dangerous not-a-harpie-Nik.

"What was that?" said Aisha.

"Nothing. Let's just get out of here as soon as we can." Now was not the time to share her private fears. Not with her mum listening, too.

"Yes, we'd better keep moving. We're at risk from lightning strikes here, and those weres could be anywhere. They live in town too, remember," said Karim. He was clearly no longer enjoying this adventure.

Karim's words seemed almost prophetic. They had only taken a few steps down the hill when they encountered a new and unwelcome challenge: a line of were-foxes arrayed across the path below them.

Honestly, here we are on the home stretch, and we have another *obstacle to overcome? This is like some drawn-out nightmare.*

Freya stepped towards her tormentors with fists clenched at her sides. The faint pain from over-long fingernails reminded her that this was real, no dream.

"What do you want?" she demanded.

"I've told you what I want." Her classmate, the red-haired Gareth, called out from one side.

Freya ignored this as the catcall it was. Evidently his reputation was at stake again, since he felt obliged to give smart remarks.

"This storm is right above us, we're all at risk here." On cue, another flash of lightning highlighted the russet hues in the human hair of the weres facing them. Freya thought she felt her own hair frizzling with the nearness of the strike. Storm sprites around for sure. "Look," she said. "We don't want a fight. We just want to go home. We need to get out of this storm. Let us past." She scanned the faces she could make out in the gloom. More lightning helped her in this identification effort, though it didn't help her nerves.

No Tammy. No Lisichka. All males. Is this pack under control?

Unexpectedly, her mother spoke up, her voice strained but clear.

"Your pack has one of my daughters. Be glad of her, and leave me and my remaining daughter alone. Go back to your lives and leave me to mine."

Yeah, go Mum!

Unfortunately, the weres seemed less impressed. Their voices overlapped in loud complaint.

"We don't agree with Lisichka's decisions."

"We've decided to mete out our own justice. Maybe it's time for a new were-haven."

"This town is getting crowded - we can't even go out for a solitary stroll on the headland without finding foul-smelling demis in our territory."

"Then don't keep my sister!" Freya snarled back at them. She was trying to make this town home, at least for a while. The last thing she wanted was for these arrogant weres to take over - especially since they clearly had no love for her or her kind. And what about Aisha and Karim? She glanced back at them. They were still ostensibly supporting her mother, although Danae appeared to be standing straight now. Maybe she was simply trying to appear stronger to these predators. Did her mother feel like prey right now? She'd already suffered a were attack tonight... Suddenly, Freya wondered how her mother had escaped the first attack. Maybe their unexpected presence had interrupted it. But how would she and her companions escape the new threat? With steep cliffs to one side, and dark farmland to the other, not to mention weres behind, they seemed to be trapped between... what was that old Greek story? Yes, between the Scylla and Charybdis. Stories... maybe that was the way out. Get them talking, at least. It had to better than having them attack.

"So, you want to form a new pack. But I thought foxes lived alone. And you're were-foxes, aren't you? How come you're working together?" said Freya.

One of the not-very-much older weres gave a barking laugh. "Everyone seems to think foxes are solitary. That just goes to show how little you know about us. For a start, we're weres, not foxes. So why should fox behaviour define us?"

"You don't seem to be letting human behaviour define you," muttered Freya. Her comment was ignored by the spokesfox.

"Let me tell you, both foxes *and* were-foxes are quite happy to live in groups. Usually we avoid being seen together, in case someone leaps to unfortunate conclusions. It's handy to have a reputation as loners. But out here, no-one can see us but you. And *you* are trespassing."

Freya shivered at the menace in his voice. The cold rain didn't help either, she told herself.

Sure, it's just the rain making you scared. Keep them talking, Freya.

"OK, so you're just socially inept, is that right? I can believe it. Any group that repeatedly attacks lone females can certainly do with some extensive social retraining. No wonder Lisichka doesn't let you out unsupervised if she can help it. Your behaviour must be quite the embarrassment for her."

I wish I didn't feel like such a hypocrite calling them socially inept. Pot, kettle, black?

Freya was trying to get the weres to lose cohesion, but she didn't think she was managing it terribly well. Currently, they'd all drawn closer together, and was that a growl she heard?

"Freya!" Aisha whispered urgently at her. "What are you *doing*? I don't think getting them angry is a great idea right now. Remember, I've used my summoning for the day. I can't do anything else!"

"Can Karim summon anything?" Freya whispered back.

"Not that I've ever seen. He's a potions expert, remember? He works in a quiet room with beakers of goo! But we're all together here, and I want to get out of this alive. Please don't make them any angrier!" Aisha finished her whispered tirade.

No help there. I'll have to come up with something else.

"Mum, can you do anything? Get us past these guys somehow?"

Her mother replied with depressing predictability.

"No. I can't. If I could have, I would have done so when they attacked me up on the headland. Even fast-growing plants don't grow fast enough in this cold weather. If they don't listen to reason, the best we may be able to hope for is the return of the matriarch to get them back in order. But it sounds like they are renegades anyway. She may have no control over them anymore."

Freya let out her breath in a huff.

"There must be something we can do. Aisha, didn't you say I should call on Bastet if I had problems again?"

"Er, yes. But actually, I don't know if that will work for you. I mean, it's not like you're a priestess of the cat goddess or anything. I guess you could try. But I'm not promising anything. And if she does send help... well, she's not exactly... I mean, she always has a price. And the bigger the request, the bigger the price."

"Have you got any better ideas?" asked Freya.

"Freya," Karim spoke up at last - he'd been sagging rather, wilting in the rain perhaps. "I don't think you should try Bastet. As Aisha says, she's not your goddess, and she's particular. But more than that, she's not that strong. People will do anything for their cat, but most of them have never heard of the cat goddess. I'm not sure that she'd be able to do anything for us even if she did come. Plus, cats, you know. They're self-centred. Bastet is *very* catlike. If it's not in her interest to help you, she won't. I can't summon her, and Aisha's already used up her summoning for the day. Isn't there anything from your own heritage you can call upon instead?"

Freya looked at her mother, and shook her head. She didn't want to summon any water deities in front of her mother, even if there was one nearby. Of course, she didn't want to be set upon by weres again, either. It was looking more like she'd have to do a summoning with every passing second. But summon *what*? The rain streamed down her face, making snakes of her long hair. Freya thought frantically.

Stories, stories. There must be something I can use.

"So, once upon a time I read that there are rivers in the sky. It sure feels like one of those is here tonight. I expect there will be flooding again if it keeps up like this. Funny, isn't it, the way a river in the sky can turn into a river down here. And there *was* flooding last time we met, wasn't there?" Freya couldn't see her opponents faces clearly enough to read their expressions, but she saw them take a step away from her.

That's right, keep backing up.

"In fact, I would expect this evening's sky-river to burst its banks quite shortly. Say, in the next minute. What would *you* do if it did that? Seeing as you are downriver of us, so to speak?"

The weres took another step back. Alright, summoning it was, they seemed to feel threatened by that. The only streams here were indeed in the sky, so she'd have to improvise.

She knelt, and patted around blindly for long grasses. She came up with a handful of stems, and some bramble snagged her hand. She gingerly wrapped that around the grass, gaining a few more scratches in the process. Raising her handful high, she paced out a circle and began to sing, picking her words at random.

"Ooh, scary, Valley-girl is singing."

"Do you wanna be a social media star, Valley-girl? Shame you can't keep a tune."

"You need to upgrade your microphone, Valley-girl,"

Freya tried not to listen as the weres mocked her efforts. She needed some help.

"Can you be a chorus, Aisha, Karim? Mum? Just sing what I do?"

"Er. Sure. But I warn you now, I am *not* a good singer," said Aisha.

"That's OK, join in anyway. I'm trying to do something different," said Freya.

She sang again, the voices of her friends trailing after her, a note or two behind in ragged chorus. After a few moments, she heard her mother's voice join them. The rain increased in intensity. This must be what they meant when they said it was bucketing down. There was another flash of lightning, and for a moment it felt as though they would all be swept down the cliff by the surging torrent of rain. Water pounded on Freya's head and shoulders, surprisingly painful. She put her arms over her head, trying to protect herself. The trickle of water down her back became a flood, and rivulets made their way over her face. She struggled to draw breath, there was so much moisture in the air.

I guess there really are rivers in the sky. Thank goodness for that.

Freya tried to lift her feet, and realised that her feet were ankle-deep and more in a stream of water. The water rose quickly to her knees, tugging her downhill. She clutched at Karim's arm, afraid of being washed away. She couldn't see the were-foxes anymore, though they had been only a few steps away. Surely that meant the water had done its job?

How do I stop the rivers of the sky, now I've called them?

"Lio!" Freya shouted, hoping against hope that he would be around, and hear her. A wind demi might know something about weather control. "Lio, help!"

Someone cleared their throat behind her. Freya's already pounding heart redoubled its pace as her adrenaline spiked. Both Nik and Lio were standing there. Lio's storm hounds lunged eagerly forward, only to be stopped by their leashes.

"Well, that was different," said Lio. "I've never seen anyone summon with brambles, grass and blood before. Innovative. Well done."

Freya felt her face heat, unseen in the darkness.

"Thanks. I think. But how do I make it stop?"

"Good question. Luckily my brother owes me a favour," Lio said cryptically. "Just a moment." He splashed out of sight. Given the heaviness of the rain, that didn't take long. Freya wondered what was going on out in the deluge. Then it was over, the rain easing abruptly to the merest mist.

Lio jogged back into sight, looking a trifle smug.

"Job done," he said.

Aisha and Karim turned to stare.

"Do we know you?" asked Karim.

"Oh, I do hope not," said Lio. "It would be terribly rude of you to have met me and forgotten, after all."

Karim didn't seem to know what to say to this.

"If you want to walk around us, please do. We're helping an injured woman here, so we can't leave the path, such as it is," said Aisha.

"Oh, no. Far be it from me to inconvenience an injured woman," said Lio, politely. "Nik, I believe you and I are not needed just now. Freya has taken care of her problem. But there may be something of interest to you down the track."

Lio took a wide berth around them, his hounds tugging at their leashes. The air around him smelled faintly of ozone. He looked at Freya and one eye fluttered in a half wink.

"Beautifully done," he said to her.

Nik followed Lio down the hill, keeping her distance. She sent a pointed glance at Freya though.

"Fancy summoning, but don't do it again when I'm around." She did not seem happy to be there.

As Lio and Nik rounded their group, Freya saw that the were-foxes were further down the slope, scattered about across the field, apparently having been washed off their feet. As the wind-demis got close enough for the weres to identify, a number of groans went up from the pack.

"Not them again!"

"Tobes, I don't think we're going to be spraying any deodorant tonight."

"Lachy, you may be right, old boy."

"Come on, you lot. Nothing to see here."

They struggled to their feet and straggled swiftly away into the darkness, the wind-demis and storm-hounds disappearing after them.

There was a damp pause.

"That was enough excitement for me for one year. Can we go home now?" suggested Karim.

Aisha laughed a little hysterically.

"Yeah, me too."

"I think we're all in favour of a quick return home," said Freya.

Danae said nothing. When they looked at her, they realised it was because she'd fainted, sagging slightly between her helpers.

"Mum! Wake up!" yelled Freya.

Karim and Aisha gently lowered her to the soggy ground. Freya reached out and put a hand on her mother's injured leg. It was warm and wet. In the darkness, Freya could not see much, but she thought it was bleeding. She tried to apply pressure, the way they'd been taught in school first aid classes.

"Ow!" exclaimed her mother, waking from her faint. "Stop it!"

Well, that worked, sort-of.

"Alright, let's get her home where we can treat her wound," commanded Freya. "Aisha, do you need me to spell you? I'm sure my leg can take it for a little while. Sorry, Karim, there's only one of me so you'll have to keep going."

"I knew I should be doing more weightlifting," remarked Karim. "Looks like tonight is the night to make up for all those missed opportunities."

"Yes, please," said Aisha. "I'm exhausted. Sorry."

They traded places, Aisha scouting the smoothest route, Karim and Freya staggering along with Freya's mother limping between them. As they slowly made their way down the hill, the storm moved away from them, as evidenced by the flashes of lightning further inland. Freya wondered if Lio and Nik were going with it. They seemed to appear with storms, after all.

When they reached Freya's house at last, they all collapsed.

In the light of the solar lantern, Aisha looked blue with cold.

"So do you," retorted Aisha when Freya mentioned it.

Freya's clothes were clinging unpleasantly to her. Aisha and Karim looked to be in a similar condition, and Danae's trousers wore torn and reddened with blood.

"Mum, you better lie down while we get your leg sorted. Aisha, Karim, you can borrow some of my clothes if you want. Er. They're upstairs in my room. They probably won't fit, though. Um. Have a look and see what you can find. On the floor."

A shame I didn't tidy up before inviting them in. I finally invite friends home and I have to send them into my messy room by themselves. There must be something wrong with the way I'm going about this.

"I'll make that hot drink now. At least - in a minute, when I've got Mum comfortable."

Danae had got herself to the lounge and was leaning back on the faded blue sofa. Its cotton cover was growing darker as the water from her clothes soaked in.

"Come on, Mum, let's get you some dry clothes, at least."

"Give me a hand, then, Freya. My leg hurts too much to move."

Despite her proclamation, Danae stripped off her own top. Freya cringed inwardly - she was used to privacy around bodies.

Come on, Freya. You know she needs help, don't get side-tracked by embarrassment.

She closed the lounge door though. No need for her friends to see. Then she found a long t-shirt for her mother to change into, and helped her put it on, dropping the sodden clothes on the floor. She hissed in sympathy as the removal of trousers showed the lacerations on Danae's leg all too clearly. Blood dripped onto the discarded clothes.

"Go get something for me to use as a bandage, Freya. We should have stocked up when you got attacked."

"It wasn't the first thing on my mind. Mum, you'd better put pressure on those bites while I get a bandage. They're getting blood everywhere." Freya swallowed uneasily. She'd been dealing with her own leg wound for a while, but she could see this one much too clearly, even by dim lantern-light. She hastened upstairs and found one of Tammy's old t-shirts to use as a bandage. It would be soft, at least. Aisha and Karim emerged from Freya's room, clad in a wild assortment of Freya's clothes. It looked like Karim had painted his t-shirt on, it was so tight.

"Sorry I don't have anything to fit you better," Freya said.

"I'm just happy to be dry," Karim assured her.

Downstairs, Freya finished dressing her mother's wound.

"Leave me alone for a bit, please Freya. Although I'll want to know more about this summoning business you did, later," said Danae.

"Tell you what," commented Karim as Freya boiled the kettle a few minutes later - the power having mysteriously returned. "Next time we see flashes of light and you feel like a night in, we're going with *your* plan."

"All in favour say 'aye,'" suggested Aisha. They all echoed a resounding "Aye!"

"That was a night to remember," said Freya, "but in the way that you remember nightmares."

"Yeah."

"Just as well we did go, though. I mean, since it was Mum in trouble."

"True enough."

Eventually Karim and Aisha left for their own home, saying they'd have to reassure their parents that they were still alive. Karim assured Freya that he'd be back the next day with a suitable potion for wounds. After giving her mother tea and falafel, avoiding direct questions about summoning, and cleaning a few scrapes and bruises of her own, Freya sank into bed, exhausted.

CHAPTER THIRTY-TWO

TAMMY'S AMBITIONS

Freya had expected to sleep late into the morning. She'd been looking forward to it, in fact. So it was with extreme irritation that she found herself awoken while it was still dark. Someone was shaking her.

"Freya. Freya, wake up! Wake up now, I haven't got much time."

Tammy? Freya opened her eyes and sat up, bumping into the person's head as she did so. There was a light by her bedside. Freya reached out blindly and switched it on. It *was* Tammy, now rubbing her forehead ruefully.

"Tammy, what are you doing here? I thought you'd done with us." Freya's words were bitter, but she felt a leap of gladness in her heart at seeing Tammy in their house again.

"I know. I'm sorry. It's all a bit complicated. But I had to come and see if Mum was OK, after those idiotic teenage wannabe rebels came back to the den-house with their tails between their legs, and said they'd done a job on her."

Freya looked up at Tammy resentfully. "Mum was pretty badly hurt. It was just lucky that Aisha and Karim saw lights on the headland and wanted to investigate. We nearly didn't go. We nearly didn't get back, either, thanks to those 'wannabe rebels', as you call them. We only got back in the end thanks to some off-the-cuff summoning I tried. And someone I know who turned up, I guess."

"Is that your mystery man? He sounds useful. Maybe you should try to keep him."

"He's a wind demi. Not for keeping. He only seems to show up in thunderstorms, anyway." She brushed her hair out of her face impatiently. "Look, why don't you have a look at Mum yourself? And why do you stick with those weres, they are just... just *horrible!*" Freya nearly obliterated her own questions as she thought of the murderous were-foxes.

"I *have* looked in on Mum. She's asleep. I didn't want to miss the chance to talk to you in private."

"Couldn't you have talked to me before? Like, any time in the last few weeks?"

"It's all been a bit sudden for you, hasn't it?" Tammy sat down on Freya's bed. "The teenage kits are pretty hard to keep in line. But the older ones - the weres I know better - they're so kind. I wish you'd run into them, instead. But of course, you wouldn't have noticed if you had, because they're very subtle, and wouldn't have attacked you at all." She sighed, and took Freya's hand.

"I would so have noticed, if anyone had been nice to me in this town! I noticed when Aisha was. And she's no were." Freya crossed her arms.

"I just want you to know that I'm doing OK, and I hope that those teen weres get sorted out soon so that you can do OK too. I'm still your sister, I still love you and Mum. But it's all a bit political at the moment, which is why I won't be talking to you in the street for a bit. I thought... I thought maybe you should know that I'm pregnant."

"You're *what*? Tammy, I know we're descended from fertility goddesses, yada yada, but you're not that much older than me. Isn't this all a bit sudden?"

"I've always wanted children. And maybe you don't know, but were-foxes are extremely protective of their families. Once I have children, I'll be fully a part of that family-"

"But why would you want to be? Aren't we your family?"

"I want a family that's mine, not just one I'm part of by accident of birth. Hopefully everything will settle once I'm family for the weres. And the older teenagers will be going off to find new homes soon, too. They won't be here breathing down your neck so much. OK?"

Freya felt tears sliding down her face.

"How *can* that be OK, Tammy? I don't know how you can think that. I guess I'm supposed to say congratulations or something."

Her sister leaned forward and gave her a hug, awkwardly. It had been a long time since they'd hugged.

"I know, Freya. I know. It's going to be tough for a bit, but we'll get through it, and come out the other side. Hold on to your dreams, and get that university entrance. I know you want that. Get it and go. I'm getting what I want.'

"Yeah, I can see that," muttered Freya.

"Like I told you before, I've always wanted stability. Stability and children. And enough to eat without having to forage for it. I'm doing what I have to do to get that. Look, I've got to go, now. They'll be out looking for me otherwise. And I need to shower before they smell you on me." She rose and went to the door, paused and looked up at the not-quite repaired ceiling. "Nice work with the tarp. Love you." And with that, she turned and left.

CHAPTER THIRTY-THREE

KARIM'S POWERS

Freya did get to sleep in, after all. She was awake for a long time after Tammy's unexpected visit, trying to imagine what Tammy thought she was doing. She fell asleep still wondering, and lightning flashed through her dreams, highlighting unlikely scenes in which rain, rivers and wind-demis featured heavily.

Her next awakening was also unpleasant in its own way. For a while, she dreamt that her mother was calling her and her family to breakfast, that there were pancakes with lemon juice waiting on the table. Freya wasn't sure if this had ever actually happened, even on Pancake Day, and it was the unlikeliness of the dream that roused her in the end. Her mother was indeed calling her, but alas, no pancakes or other family materialised. With a start, Freya remembered the events of the night, and hastened down the stairs to check on her mother's injuries.

She was kept busy for a while making tea, finding something edible for breakfast, and re-bandaging her mother's wounds, which looked much worse in daylight. After that, she was sent outside to check on the potted plants her mother had set up when they first arrived at the house.

"Don't touch them, just make sure they got some water overnight," said Danae.

Great, even my own mother doesn't trust me to grow plants now.

Freya was glad when Karim arrived with the promised potion. She had never had any aspirations to be a nurse, and dealing with her mother's pain-induced crotchetiness would have put her off if she had. She had watered those plants that had missed the night's rain through being too close to the house when the easterly storm had come through. She'd moved other plant pots in the exact order specified by her mother – wondering all the while when her mum had had time to pot up all these things. Hadn't she been working late for weeks? And they'd only had a few weeks in town before the big storm hit. Grumbling to herself, Freya had prepared breakfast for both of them, going back for several different herbs that her mother wanted on her eggs. Sometimes, having a mother who knew everything there was to know about plants and herbs was just a touch irksome.

"Who cares if oregano is better than marjoram for wound-healing? They taste practically identical." She had made more herbal tea again as directed. The smell had just about put her off her breakfast, though she was sure it was very wholesome. All things considered, she supposed that she should be glad that her mother hadn't made *her* drink the same thing, after the first were attack.

I guess that tells me how worried Mum was when Tammy disappeared. Even though she didn't seem to be.

Which reminded her…

"Mum. About last night. After we got back, you fell asleep – actually so did I. But anyway, Tammy came back. No – she's not here now, sit down." For her mother had tried to get to her feet, regardless of her mauled leg. "She said she couldn't be seen with us in public. Which is incredibly rude of her. But anyway, she said to tell you that she was OK, and that she loves us. She said it's only for a while, till she gets to the top of the pack power structure, I think that's what she meant, anyway."

Freya stopped, horrified by the silent sobs that were wracking her mother.

"Mum, it's OK." Freya patted her mother's back, then tried giving her a hug. "Oh, alright, it's not OK. It's horrible and I miss her even though we haven't really talked in years." Tears were sliding down her own cheeks now. Emotion was contagious. "I don't know what deal she's got with the weres, but she said she saw the ones that attacked us come in, and they were boasting about what they'd done, which is why she came to check on us. I wish we'd never come here!"

The quiet knock on the door sounded like a bass drum to Freya's oversensitive ears. Leaping up from beside her mother, she scrubbed her face with her sleeve.

"I'll answer it," she announced, as though there had been any doubt.

Karim stood at the door, looking fresh and well-scrubbed. Freya sniffed. Aftershave? It was a bit early in the morning for that wasn't it? She glanced at the clock in the hall.

Oops. Not early morning anymore.

The smell of aftershave was overpowering.

"Good morning," she said politely.

"Hey Freya, nice nightie."

Freya looked down at herself. What with one tea or another, she hadn't had a chance to change out of the long t-shirt she'd worn to bed. It was rather short these days, and bore the picture of a curled-up cat with a thought bubble across her breasts. It declared in large letters 'Cats have better dreams'. She blushed.

"It's been a busy morning," she said defensively.

"Nah, I like it!" Karim declared, grinning.

Typical. Of course *the descendant of Bastet likes a cat nightie.*

She decided the only way forward was to change the subject.

"So, did you have any luck making a potion yet?"

Karim became serious at once.

"I've made a first attempt. When Aisha and I told the family - that's my family, no capitals, right? – about what happened, they got pretty upset. That's why Aisha's not here today. They wouldn't let her out of the house. Apparently, since I've been taking care of myself overseas all summer, I'm allowed to brave the streets of our hometown. Anyway. Can I come in?"

Freya realised she'd been standing in the doorway, and Karim was still on the step.

"Oh, yes. Sorry."

She led the way into the hall, then hesitated. Where should she take him? She wanted to hear what else he had to say before taking him in to her mother. Danae was in the lounge, which left only the kitchen or the bedrooms. She was somehow uncomfortable about taking him to her room. While she'd admired his eyes the night before, she felt uneasy with him this morning.

Probably because you're not dressed, she told herself.

"Come into the kitchen. Do you want tea? I've just finished making some for Mum. You probably want something different to her though, hers was pretty medicinal smelling."

"Sure thing," Karim replied easily, as he followed her the short distance to the kitchen. "Just promise me we're not going up on those cliffs again afterwards, alright?"

"Absolutely! Though they're probably safe enough in daylight – after all, the place is swarming with birders in spring, isn't it?" commented Freya.

"Let's wait for spring, then. Even the birds couldn't tempt me right now," said Karim.

Freya had to laugh.

As Freya made yet more tea, she asked Karim, "So, you said you'd made an attempt at a potion. Did your grandmother figure anything out? Or you?"

Karim held up a small glass pot in answer. It contained something yellow, like beeswax.

"It was a joint effort," he said. "Nena made up the base and I added the good stuff. It should work against whatever's keeping the wound from healing. Probably some sort of bacteria, but I included anti-fungals as well, just in case. And it's been blessed by Bastet, of course." He glanced towards the lounge, where her mum was no doubt straining her ears to hear what was being said. He lowered his voice. "Better get this potion on you and your mum as soon as you can. I don't know what other effects were-bites have, but you don't want to start howling to the moon, I'm guessing."

Freya shuddered at the idea of becoming like her attackers.

"They did tell me you don't become a were by being bitten," she said aloud. "And nothing like that has happened to me in the last few weeks."

"Well, I don't know," said Karim. "All the folklore says you do, so there must be something in it. And while I haven't heard *you* howl yet, I only met you yesterday. Anyway, even if that's not the way it works, there's clearly something unpleasant in their bite. Do you want me to put the ointment on you?"

Freya hesitated. Did she want Karim's hands touching her? She wasn't sure.

"I'll just put it on, no funny stuff," he assured her, perhaps reading the doubt in her expression.

"Alright, then." She sat down on the sole kitchen chair and stuck out her bare leg. She'd had it covered with bandages, but they'd been soaked and dirty after last night's adventures, so she'd peeled them off and left them on the floor by her bed.

Karim knelt by her feet, glanced up at her, and grinned again.

"Your wish is my command, oh Queen," he intoned mock-seriously.

"Karim!"

"Sorry, sorry. I just couldn't resist." Opening the small ointment jar, he dipped two fingers into the golden goo inside, and smoothed it gently onto the raw patches on her calf, holding her leg still with his other hand. She watched his dark hand against her fairer skin. It might have been sensual if it didn't hurt so much. He repeated the process until all the wounds were covered and glistening.

"Nena said you shouldn't cover it up. Besides, the ointment is greasy, so it might make marks on your trousers. When you've put them on," he teased. He got to his feet, and offered her a hand - not the grease-covered one. "Shall we get the rest of this onto your mother's wounds, now?"

Freya gratefully agreed. Taking his proffered hand, she let herself be hoisted to her feet. Sore or not, she was feeling off-balance after having Karim hold her legs. It had felt so intimate, and although they'd gone through a harrowing experience together last night, she'd only met Karim yesterday.

Standing in the door to the lounge, she addressed her mother.

"Mum, this is Karim. You met him last night, remember? He helped get you home. He's good at potions, and he's brought one over for your leg. OK?" Her mum was slumped against the pillows on her couch-bed, but she opened her eyes when Freya started talking.

"Oh yes, Karim. I heard you come in earlier. Thank you for your help last night. May I smell your ointment first, please?"

Freya wondered how much Danae had heard of her conversation on the doorstep with Karim, and her cheeks burned. Small houses were so public! Then, she wondered how her mother would smell anything over the over-done aftershave.

Meanwhile, her mother was sniffing the opened jar that Karim held out for her, nose close.

"Hmm. Oregano, calendula, goldenrod, and... is that yarrow? Good choices. Alright, go ahead and put it on." Danae had a good nose for herbs. She nodded sharply, uncovering the leg she'd had covered by a thin blanket. Despite Freya's efforts, the blanket was blood-stained. Karim didn't make any smart remarks to her mother, fortunately. He simply applied the ointment quickly and efficiently and stood up, wiping his fingers on a small rag he pulled from his pocket.

"My grandmother said you should apply the ointment every day for the first week," he said. "There's only enough there for a couple of days treatment for both of you, so I'll make up more and bring it around tomorrow."

Karim turned to Freya.

"Aisha's grounded till Monday, so it will be me bringing the ointment. She said to tell you that she wanted to come, and also that if you need fleas, she's happy to oblige." His eyes twinkled as he passed on Aisha's offer. Freya grinned back.

"I'm sorry she got in trouble," she said, "and let her know that I'll be sure to call if fleas are what I need. Or locusts, though I hope there aren't any trees left to fall on our house."

She escorted Karim to the door, and impulsively gave him a quick hug, though she didn't usually do that sort of thing.

"Thanks for helping us last night. We couldn't have made it without your falafel!"

"Sure, you could – you had a pocket full of apples, didn't you?"

Freya felt her mouth fall open, and shut it again with a snap.

"I didn't want to waste more food."

Don't let him know you forgot about it...

"I'll take your thanks and run, then," Karim laughed. "See you in a day or two." He walked away, then turned and waved before continuing.

Freya stared after him a moment, then went inside.

"That seems a reasonable young man, apart from the unfortunate application of scent," commented Danae from her position on the couch, as Freya closed the door.

"Mum!" Freya protested, not liking her mother's easy acceptance.

"Well, the balm he brought is soothing," said her mother in a placating voice. "Look, can you bring me my phone? I want to read if I can't be gardening. And I don't think I can be today. I need to be well enough to get back to work on Monday."

Freya knew this was true - her mother's income from the glasshouse was the only thing paying the rent. She gathered all the books she could find - a random selection of battered, so-old-even-the-second-hand-shops-wouldn't-take-them tomes - as well as her mother's scratched old phone, and put them by Danae's bed. If her mother was reading, that would give Freya the time she desperately wanted, to think about Tammy's late-night secrets.

In many ways Tammy's 'unfortunate condition' shouldn't be a surprise, Freya thought. Tammy was several years older than Freya, and the school-kids taunts had not been so far wrong, in that Tammy really had wanted children. That fertility-goddess focus again. However, while Freya was sure that children would be fine, sometime in the future, she didn't see the urgency. And she especially couldn't understand why Tammy would choose to have children with a were. Come to think of it, she didn't even know which were-fox it was that Tammy had selected. Somehow, Freya was certain that it would have been Tammy choosing, rather than the other way around.

She shook her head, mentally closing off that train of thought. It was clear that Tammy had made her choice, for better or worse. The question was, what should Freya do? She could see the attraction of being settled, but she wouldn't want to settle here. Too close to the sea, too many weres. And more than that, Freya wanted to see more of the world. She wanted to be better educated than her parents, to have better opportunities, not to be scratching a living along the uncertain coast.

She sighed aloud. There was no quick fix to this problem. She still had to finish this year at school, do well enough to get into university, and then get a degree, and a job. The future stretched out before her, an endlessly long road. She wished she knew all the stops on that road.

CHAPTER THIRTY-FOUR

SCHOOL WITH COWED WERES

School was different on Monday. Freya noticed quite a few people missing - all russet-headed. It looked like the were-foxes had kept their older offspring at home today. Without their subtle menace in the background, Freya almost enjoyed school. Aisha was back, and Freya was able to review the weekend's events with her friend.

"I'm not allowed back to your house yet," Aisha said. "Since I 'irresponsibly went off in the night' from there. Honestly, what will they do next year when I'm an adult and can legally do what I want?"

"It's just because they care about you," Freya said. "At least your family want you around."

Danae had limped off to work that morning, impatiently telling Freya to get herself to school, and no 'buts'. Freya had only wanted to help her mother to work, so she didn't injure herself further, so she was feeling more than a little rebuffed.

"My family want to see more of you, if that helps," Aisha said. "Karim does, anyway." She nudged Freya with her elbow. "You've made a conquest of my brother already. Better not abandon me for him."

Freya laughed and blushed at the same time.

"He said he'd come by your place this afternoon with a fresh batch of whatever he and Nena have been concocting. Otherwise, I'd suggest you come over to the station cafe. You wouldn't believe how strongly our house smells of herbs at the moment. It's almost unbearable. I'd forgotten how much his potions stink the place up. It'll be a relief when he heads off to uni. At least I'll be able to breathe again at home then."

Freya grinned.

"I thought he was wearing aftershave when he turned up on Saturday. But then the smell lingered all day, so maybe it was the potion after all."

"Oh, he was wearing aftershave, too. I told you you've made a conquest," Aisha said.

"Don't be silly, Aisha, no-one ever falls for me. And I hardly know Karim."

"Yeah. It's a bit fast, seeing as he only got back on Friday. But you'll have to work quickly if you want to do something about that. He goes to uni in a few weeks."

"That's faster than ever I've worked in my life. And I'm not that sort of girl. It doesn't seem likely."

"Just as well, it would be pretty weird if you got together - my friend and my brother, ugh!"

"No fear!" Freya exclaimed, but she wasn't sure she meant it. She did like Karim. But was it a good idea to try form a relationship with someone who was so clearly going elsewhere? Of course, Karim wasn't going far away just yet - and he'd be home to see his family in the holidays. But she didn't want to lose Aisha's friendship, either.

Freya's train of thought was interrupted by the school bell. It seemed tame to be going to classes after the weekend's dramatic events. Maybe tame was an improvement, though. She and Aisha trooped into class together.

Technology was the most interesting subject of the day. The topic of the term was storm shelters, a surprisingly appropriate choice, Freya thought.

"Thank Frigg we're doing this topic," she told Aisha. "Better than at my last school. We had weeks of yoghurt flavouring compounds, there."

"That doesn't sound so bad. I like yoghurt," said Aisha.

"It's OK, I guess, but I'll never get those weeks of my life back. And I can still taste the acorn-flavoured one when I think about it."

"Don't think about it, then, easy."

"You say that, but every year when I see the green acorns forming on the oak trees it comes back to me."

"Excuse me, young ladies, I'm trying to tell you about the study break project, *if* you don't mind." The sarcastic voice of the tech teacher broke into their conversation.

"Sorry." Freya assumed a listening attitude, eyes on the board at the front of the room where the teacher was standing. Aisha sat up straight at the desk beside her, hands poised on her notebook - the model of an attentive student. As the teacher began to speak again, she did a quick sketch of the teacher cowering in front of a giant yoghurt pottle, an acorn decorating its side. She turned the paper towards Freya, who had to smother a snigger. The teacher glared at them, but continued.

"As I was saying, in light of the storm we all experienced a few weeks ago, and the high probability that we will see more storms like it, I've decided to launch a competition for the senior class. Your task is to design and create a prototype for an in-place storm shelter, capable of withstanding winds of up to 100 miles per hour -"

"But wind is measured in kilometres per hour," said one student.

"Or in knots, when you're in a boat," said another, whose family owned a fishing boat.

"You can apply your mathematical skills to converting my measurements, then." The teacher glared at the interjecting students. "Your shelter should also be rainproof, and able to support the weight of, say," he looked directly at Freya, "a large oak tree. There will be a prize for the best design. I expect you to include working drawings, and calculations supporting the design of your project. Now, are there any questions?"

As a babble of voices rose around them, Freya turned to Aisha.

"That was creepy. Why pick on me? And how does he know about the oak tree falling on my house, anyway?"

Aisha shrugged.

"Mr Smith always picks on someone. Maybe he noticed my drawing. Or else he heard about your tree on the news. I guess an oak tree through the roof is a pretty public accident. I wouldn't worry about it. Anyway, this is a good project, better than making metal lunchboxes or something, like Karim had to do when he came through this class. Although I think he still uses that lunchbox."

"I guess I don't need a metal lunchbox. But I don't know where to start with a storm shelter. Can we work as a team?"

"Sure thing."

Thank goodness for a friend.

CHAPTER THIRTY-FIVE

KARIM MAKES HIS MOVES

That afternoon Karim appeared on the doorstep, freshly groomed as always. As Freya opened her mouth to greet him, he patted his hair into place, not quite satisfied with the way it sat. Freya couldn't help it - she laughed.

"Finished preening yourself yet?" she teased. Karim pretended not to hear her.

"Nena sent me over with something for your mum," he said.

Freya quickly sobered.

"Thanks. She's not home from work yet. But she was limping badly when she left this morning."

"Nena wanted to invite you and her over to dinner, but Dad's not happy with all the time I've been spending out since I've been back. So instead of being polite and agreeing like he's supposed to, he's demanding that I eat at home for 'at least the next three nights' before he'll agree to anyone else coming over. Honestly, I think he's forgotten I've been making my own way for the last year."

Freya shrugged. She wasn't that keen on her mother invading her social life anyway. Not now she actually seemed to *have* a social life. It was a novelty she wanted to keep to herself for a while.

"That's OK. At least you're here now," she said.

Karim smiled, an appreciative grin spreading over his face. That had clearly been the right thing to say.

"Come in," said Freya, leading the way to the kitchen.

"Just for a minute, I'm expected back."

"I wanted to ask you about your other potions." Freya was thinking about their still-unpatched roof. Karim was dubious at first.

"I haven't done much with them yet," he said.

"Look, I'll show you, and you can tell me if there's anything you can do," said Freya. She led the way up to her room, feeling self-conscious at inviting a male into her private space. Probably she should have tidied up, first.

"I suppose I could come up with something waterproof," Karim said, gazing up at the tarpaulin in her room. "I guess the real problem is that the wind keeps moving the tarp. You need a builder in. Shouldn't the landlord organise that?"

"I know, but our landlord is terrible. And we would get a builder in ourselves, it's just the money…" There wasn't a good solution to that problem.

"Well, I guess I can make you some glue to keep the tarp in place. Temporarily." Karim seemed a little doubtful, but he brightened up as he thought about it.

"That would be useful on the dig as well," he considered aloud. "Hmm… tell you what, I'll come back tomorrow with something, I've got some ideas to try. Meanwhile," he extracted the next jar of wound-healing potion from somewhere in his clothing, magician-like.

"Your healing balm, your majesty." He knelt before her again, and suggested, eyes twinkling, "Take a seat, so that I may apply it like a gentleman."

The only seat available up here was her bed. Freya sat on the edge, only to slip off with a thump as her bedclothes - never well ordered - slid off the bed when she shuffled around awkwardly. Freya found herself blushing furiously. Karim laughed as he offered a hand to help her up again. Freya had to laugh too. She supposed it *was* funny. However, she sat well back on the bed this time, determined not to embarrass herself with clumsiness again.

"Take two?" Karim suggested.

"Er, yes." She was wearing trousers, as usual. Karim lifted both her legs onto the bed, then gently pushed back the fabric of her trousers on the injured one. Freya could still feel the tingling trail of his fingers on her skin after they had passed.

"Your leg's looking better today," he said, sounding pleased. "But you've missed a scratch at the back, see?"

"Well, no, I can't," countered Freya. "That's probably why I missed it."

Karim stroked more ointment onto her leg. It didn't hurt so much today. Perhaps his ointment was doing some good.

"I can come and put it on you every day if you like," he suggested, his voice almost a purr. "To make sure all of you heals well."

Freya couldn't resist teasing him.

"I hope you don't make that offer to all your patients."

Karim made a face.

"I'm into archaeology, not medicine. You're just lucky I'm working with you." He had finished smoothing on the ointment, but continued to stroke her leg, sitting on the edge of the bed beside her, but facing her. He leaned forward, his eyes intense. "But I would like to keep working with you a little more, if I may?" Freya nodded. Was he going to kiss her? She felt the blood roaring in her ears. Anxiety or excitement? Maybe a bit of both.

"Freya, are you home?" The sound of her mother's voice destroyed the moment. Karim scrambled up, putting the lid on his potion jar. Freya leapt off the bed, hastily rearranging the blankets. *Not that I've done anything illicit,* she thought ruefully. *Just the usual disorganisation.*

"Coming, Mum," she called back. "Karim and I were just looking at what can be done with the hole in the roof."

They clumped downstairs, where Karim offered his pot of balm to Freya.

"This will be enough for you and your mum today. I will bring you more tomorrow." His eyes promised more than balm as he took his farewell.

"Freya," said Danae. "You'll have to make dinner tonight. I made it through work, but I'm too sore to move anymore."

Freya followed her lead into the kitchen, where she spent the next hour following exacting instructions while her mum sat in the chair. She was perfectly capable of preparing dinner herself, but apparently her mother wanted her in sight. They ate silently in the kitchen. Eventually, Freya remembered that she had to put potion on her mother's leg - only to have her mother brush her off.

"No, I can do that for myself now. Pass me the pot. Good. Thank you for making dinner. Now, we need to review your knowledge of were mating systems before you do your school homework. Since Karim was here when I arrived, I'm guessing you haven't done your homework yet. Am I right?" Freya grudgingly had to admit that this was indeed correct. What with one thing and another, windspeed calculations hadn't appealed.

Later, after an intense session of reviewing the different types of weres and their putative mating systems, Freya asked her mum a question that had been bothering her.

"But is all this information based on observation? Or does it come from the weres themselves?"

"Why do you ask?" said her mother suspiciously.

"Well, it seems to me that it might look different from the inside. I mean, we're always told that foxes are solitary, but then we see those were-foxes in packs. And they said something about that themselves. Something's got to be wrong with what we know. So... I'm just wondering."

Her mother scowled.

"Please do not start trying to find out from the inside yourself," she said. "It's bad enough losing one daughter to those... those vulpine creeps."

"Maybe Tammy can tell us herself, one day," suggested Freya. "After all, she's the one who is going to have were-fox babies."

"What?" shrieked Danae.

Freya realised too late that she had never got around to telling Danae that part of Tammy's news.

"Sorry, I thought I told you. She said she was pregnant when she came that night."

"I cannot believe you neglected to tell me the most important thing she had to say. Freya, I expected better of you."

"At least I'm in no danger of following in Tammy's footsteps, Mum. I mean, I like my information accurate, but I'm not *that* desperate for knowledge. I just thought that maybe if we see Tammy again, we could ask her, that's all."

"Enough wondering, then. I'm tired. Can you help me to bed?"

Freya assisted her grumpy, limping mother into bed. She wondered how her mother had managed to get to work that day - and if she'd manage it again the next. If she didn't, Freya would have to look into getting an after-school job. Somehow.

The next morning her mother was up and ready for work as usual.

"It's not so bad in the mornings," she explained, "when I haven't been standing all day." She trudged off in the direction of the bus stop when Freya left for school.

Karim met Freya as she turned out of the school gates that afternoon, a rucksack slung over one shoulder.

"How's your leg?" he asked.

"Getting better slowly, I guess. It hurts today," she said. *She* was limping a little today too. They'd had PE at school, and Freya was determined to become fitter, so that next time she was chased by a pack of rabid weres - if there was a next time - she wouldn't be puffed after the first block. That meant she'd exercised harder than usual, and her leg was feeling it.

"I'll come with you and get some potion on it, then."

Aisha, who had come out with her, rolled her eyes.

"Come to the station cafe tomorrow after school," she suggested. "Karim can't hog you every day."

Freya tilted her head apologetically at her friend.

"It was mostly my mother hogging me last night," she said. "She's decided I need to review my folklore. Again. But I'll come tomorrow before she gets home from work."

"See you tomorrow, then," said Aisha, before striding off in the direction of the station.

Karim walked beside Freya, chatting amicably about the work he'd been doing in Egypt, and how he'd found a website that advertised student accommodation at the university he planned to attend.

"When do you go?" she asked quietly. She was feeling conflicted again. She was enjoying Karim's company, but he was clearly not planning to stick around. Karim looked at her with a frown, perhaps hearing the slightly hurt tone in her voice. He took her hand, rucksack clinking as he adjusted it. She extricated her hand gently. She didn't want the town's rumour-mills whirring too fast.

"In another two weeks. But it's not far by train. You and Aisha can come visit me, if you like."

Freya shrugged noncommittally. In a world where she had enough money for trains to go wherever she wanted to go, she could indeed visit him.

Despite her limp, Freya and Karim made good time to Freya's house. Inside, Karim's green eyes seemed darker.

"Let's get the roof looked at first, then look at your leg," he said. "Unless it's really sore?"

It was, but Freya suggested working on the roof anyway. She wasn't yet sure what she wanted to happen after that.

Karim had clearly been working hard on his magical glue ideas. His rucksack turned out to be filled with several re-purposed jars, each half full of a different goo.

"I suppose I should be doing chemistry at uni," he said. "But I've never heard of chemical archaeology, so I guess I'll just have to muddle through." He directed Freya to hold the tarp just so, as he applied each different mixture to the edge where it met the roof tiles, with a brush he'd brought along for the job. Finally, he covered the whole tarp with another mixture.

"When that one's dried, the whole thing should set like stone," he declared. "No builder required." He seemed pleased with his efforts.

"Thanks," said Freya. "It'll be good to have that temporary roof a little more solid, with winter just around the corner."

Karim turned to her, brushing off his dusty clothes. The tarp had not been terribly clean. The room seemed suddenly smaller, and Karim very close.

"Look, I want to make sure things are clear between us," he said. "I like you, Freya. I like you a lot. But you know I'm heading off to uni soon. I can't change that, and to be honest I wouldn't want to. But I know you've only got a year to go. Maybe you could apply to York, too?" he rushed on. "But even if you don't want to do that, I'd like to spend more time with you. There are holidays, Christmas break, that sort of thing. I mean, I wanted to say…" he trailed off.

"Not just a holiday romance, do you mean?" asked Freya, a little snippily. "Oh, Karim. I don't know what to do. You'll be entering a new world. Going to do your thing. I'm a bit jealous of that, you know. I mean, I'll be doing it soon too, but a year feels like a long time. And who knows what will happen between now and then. Let's just…" she shrugged. "See what happens, I guess?"

Karim took a step closer to her, and took both her hands.

"Could I be a thing that happens?" he asked.

Freya closed the remaining distance between them.

"Maybe?" She put her arms around him and lifted her face. She liked the feel of him in her arms - he seemed solid, dependable. As his face descended to meet hers, she thought,

This is it. This is when I find out what drew Tammy out to sea, away from us.

However, their kiss was not explosive, but rather clumsy. Freya bumped into Karim's jars of roof-glue after a second or two of fumbling, off-balance once again. The height difference between them made it rather awkward to remain standing. Karim broke off the kiss somewhat guiltily.

"I haven't even seen to your leg, yet!" He released her hastily. "I should have applied your potion first." Evidently, he thought her stumble was due to a sore leg.

Freya arranged herself on the bed so that Karim could apply the ointment again. She was glad to be sitting. She wanted to think about their kiss. It hadn't been the world-shattering experience she'd thought it might be. Had she expected too much? Karim once again sat beside her on the bed. He reached out to apply the ointment and looked at his dirty hands.

"Can I use the bathroom?" he asked ruefully.

Freya directed him across the hall. While he washed, Freya wondered at herself. Was she throwing herself into this potential relationship because she'd lost her sister? Was she simply curious? She knew Karim was leaving soon - perhaps that made it easier, since there seemed little chance of a long-term relationship.

However, Karim seemed worried when he returned.

"There's a crowd out the back of your house," he said. "I saw them through the bathroom window. It's The Family."

"What! Show me!" said Freya. Her voice quivered. After several run-ins with the were-foxes, she was not keen to encounter them in force again. Running to the bathroom, she peered through the clouded glass.

"I can't see a thing through this," she complained. "How did you manage it?" Karim pointed to the upper window, which was open a crack.

"What on Gaia were you doing up there?" she demanded.

"I heard something, so I looked. I'll boost you," he said, offering his hands as a platform.

"Just make sure I don't fall," she said. "I'm not exactly graceful."

"You won't fall," he assured her. "And you seem graceful enough to me." Freya smiled. She could get used to flattery, even if their first kiss hadn't been a runaway success. Placing a bare foot in his hands, she let him lift her towards the window. She braced herself against the wall with her hands, leaning away from the bath. Falling into that would be painful.

Freya gasped as she peered through the thin crack of the open window. She could see a large gathering over the back fence. There were russet hues, ginger, red and auburn, all shades reminiscent of fox-fur. What were they doing here? As she stood watching on Karim's hands, were-hands started pointing in her direction.

"I think I've seen enough. Or perhaps I mean I've been seen enough. Down, please."

Karim lowered his hands so that she could step to the ground. She turned to face him again.

"Any bright ideas, if they attack?" she asked.

"Er, no?" he replied. "I'm a soon-to-be-student archaeologist, not a warrior."

Unexpectedly, a knock sounded at the back door.

"Better see what they want, I suppose," she said grimly. Karim followed her downstairs. She found she was acutely aware of him behind her. She wished they hadn't been interrupted, but she was glad of his presence - however non-warrior-like - as she opened the door. It seemed strange to be opening the back door for someone. Since it opened onto the concrete pad that served as a yard, only residents came through it as a rule. The were-fox matriarch Lisichka stood in front of Freya.

CHAPTER THIRTY-SIX

WERE-FOXES ASK FOR HELP

The rest of the weres hung back, to Freya's relief. Lisichka spoke at once, not waiting for a formal greeting.

"Freya. Good. Is your mother home?"

When Freya answered in the negative, Lisichka looked momentarily distressed - an unexpected expression on her stern face.

"In that case, let me ask you. Have you powers of summoning, or better still, of childbirth? You *are* descended from your namesake, are you not?"

Freya didn't know what to say.

"Er. I can do a little summoning. Water summoning, like Tammy. I don't know anything about childbirth. You'd need a midwife for that, wouldn't you?"

Lisichka tapped her foot impatiently.

"Of course, I'd prefer a midwife," she snapped. "But finding one in this small town who is able to deal with those of us who are not mundane is not possible today. The one we usually use has travelled South for training. If you have summoning, then that is better than nothing. Come now. This is for your sister, you understand."

Freya's mouth dropped open.

"But... but she only told me she was pregnant a couple of nights ago. She wasn't even showing. She can't be having a baby already!"

Lisichka nodded once.

"Indeed. And that is the issue. It is far too soon, and she is not a were-fox as we are. We had thought that as the descendant of a fertility goddess, she would be able to overcome the problems of crossbreeding. We had pinned our hopes on it. But now she is in trouble. Don't waste more time - come." She transferred her gaze to Karim, her face turning sour.

"Leave your cat-boy here."

Karim gazed back at Lisichka with equal dislike.

"That doesn't seem wise for her," he said. "Since your young hooligan friends tried to lynch us on Friday night."

"They will not touch Freya tonight," Lisichka replied icily.

"No, since I'll be going anywhere she does," Karim reacted angrily.

Lisichka transferred her gaze to Freya.

"If you want to help your sister, come now. There is no more time." Ignoring Karim completely, Lisichka turned away, clearly expecting Freya to follow her.

Freya looked at Karim.

"It's my sister," she said. "I have to go if she's in trouble. Even though I can't see how I can help. But - maybe I should leave a note for Mum." There was a notepad in the hall. Freya scrabbled around the kitchen drawer, looking for a pen, and eventually came up with a pencil. Halfway through writing the note, the lead broke.

"Fafnir's teeth. That will just have to do. I hope she sees it - I'll put it on her bed." Freya suited action to words, grabbing her boots as she raced down the hall again, and stuffed her feet into them without doing up the laces. Lisichka was back over the fence now. Freya considered her options, then went back through the house, out the front door and around it to the back once again. Now was not the time for heroic fence-leaping. Getting caught halfway over the fence, which seemed the likeliest outcome, would just slow her down. Karim followed her without comment.

The weres set off as soon as Freya appeared, half-jogging up the cliff path. *Not up there again,* she thought. However, they veered off before Freya was too much out of breath from the fast pace they set, and took a path away from the cliffs half-way up. They followed a narrow trail that Freya wouldn't have considered a proper path, had she been walking there in the usual way. It was too narrow, more like an animal trail. It wove around some small shrubs and through tall, rank, end-of-season vegetation before disappearing under a weeping willow tree that sat down in a hollow. Ducking under its low hanging branches, already bare of leaves, Freya saw the last of the were-foxes disappearing through the dangling branches on the far side of the tree. She followed. On the other side, a large cottage stood within with a well-kept garden, bursting with late season blooms. A small ornamental pond took pride of place.

Mum would love this garden.

Lisichka waited for her by the door.

"Did you expect a hole in the ground?" she asked acidly, as she took in Freya's astonished expression. "We are not simply foxes, you know."

Freya hastily schooled her expression as she stepped inside. Lisichka led the way to a bedroom at the back of the cottage. She looked at Karim at last as she paused by its open door.

"You stay out here, since you've ignored my wishes by coming along," she ordered. "The rest of the family are in other rooms. You are not required in this room, and your presence here is unwanted. Understand, cat-boy?" Taking his assent for granted, she swept in, beckoning for Freya to follow.

Even given the surmises she had been making as she walked, Freya was astonished when she saw Tammy crouching, white and sweating, on the bed. Her arms were wrapped around her stomach. A strawberry-blond male were-fox stood beside her, stroking her back. He looked up as Lisichka arrived. Tammy didn't. She emitted a low moan.

Freya stopped in the doorway. She didn't know what to do in this place, or what she was expected to do for her suffering sister. Lisichka saw her hanging back, and gave a peremptory gesture to come closer. Freya wondered how Tammy could stand having this woman order her around. She'd never been one to take orders well. However, since Freya couldn't think what else to do, she gingerly approached her sister.

"Tammy? What can I do?" Tammy didn't reply, but put out a hand, which Freya took. Tammy squeezed her hand hard, then whispered.

"Get Mum. She might help."

"But Mum's not home!" Freya said, despairing in the face of this pain-ridden Tammy, a Tammy she didn't recognise without her light-hearted smile. Lisichka appeared in her peripheral vision.

"I will send the cat-boy for your mother. You try summoning. Nehalennia is the one you want." Lisichka named a Germanic goddess of the North Sea. Freya recoiled, recognising the goddess who her mother had blamed for the loss of their house to the sea many years ago.

"But I've only done rivers. *Small* rivers," she protested. Lisichka shrugged.

"I assume you want your sister to live. So try." She turned away towards the door, presumably to try and order Karim after Freya's mother. Freya, looking at her back, noticed that her shoulders - no, her whole posture was tense. Perhaps she was not as unfeeling as she appeared. She'd come to find Freya, after all. Another moan from Tammy claimed Freya's attention.

"Tammy, they're telling me to summon Nehalennia. She's a sea goddess, salt won't banish her. I don't even know how to call her. What do I do?" Her question was almost a wail.

Tammy looked at her, eyes dull with pain.

"I don't know, Freya," she whispered. "It wasn't supposed to happen like this. Please try, try something."

Freya thought, frantically. She was descended from a fertility goddess, too, and most fertility goddesses were associated with childbirth - it went with the territory, so to speak. It just wasn't something Freya had ever been particularly interested in. She'd assumed if any of them ever had a child, it would be in a hospital. What did sea-summonings have to do with childbirth - or miscarriage? What safeguards should she use if she tried to summon a sea-goddess? She couldn't think of anything that tamed the sea or changed its nature. Unless...

"Can we go outside?" Freya requested. "Into the garden? Also, I need a magnifying glass if you have one." After the man at Tammy's side and Lisichka exchanged a look, Lisichka nodded. The man lifted up Tammy bodily, and Freya noticed that Tammy's skirts were stained with blood. She looked away, feeling sick. Lisichka disappeared for few minutes, and returned with an old-fashioned school-classroom type of magnifying glass, round with a short black handle.

Karim had gone from the doorway when Freya walked through it. She hoped he'd gone to get her mother from work, though part of her resented being abandoned. Freya felt woefully under-qualified for any of this.

The ornamental pond in the garden would have to do as a water source, one that might help her to call the more unfamiliar sea-goddess. If she listened hard, Freya could hear the sound of the not-too-distant sea. The man carrying Tammy set her down by the pond's edge. Freya snapped a twig from the hanging willow, earning a glare from the were-foxes. She drew a circle around both herself and Tammy. It was hard to make the circle show through the grass with the bendy twig.

At least it's not high summer, a circle would be impossible to draw then.

Wincing at the sting from the old leaves, she wrenched off a few stems and wrapped them around the willow twig. Tall, barely-seeded umbels of fennel completed the thyrsus. It was not a traditional Dionysian wand, but then again, she wasn't trying traditional magic. She had a sudden memory of Lio commenting on the blood from her scratches, when she had summoned the sky river. Grimacing at the sheer grossness of it, she picked at one of her scabs till it bled once more, and pressed a few drops of blood onto the wand.

Ugh, I hope I never have to do that again. What now? I wish I'd been taught how to do this properly.

She started singing her song-web, unsure though she was. She hummed a few tunes at random, trying to get a feel for what would work here. Something with an unexpected twist, perhaps. Freya glanced around. Several were-foxes had gathered around the edges of the garden, and every one of them was watching her or Tammy. Or possibly Tammy's boyfriend, who was holding Tammy's hand and whispering to her. Freya caught his eye and put a finger to her lips. She didn't know what stray voices would do, and she didn't think the unexpected twist she needed in the song should come from a were-fox.

Ah, maybe that song about the two sisters. It seems appropriate somehow.

More confident now, she began to sing an old song about sisters warring for the same man's attention.

Not that we are, but never mind...

At first nothing seemed to be happening. But Tammy joined in on the last verse, their voices twining together, a semblance of harmony where there had been none before.

"I'll be true unto my love..."

As their voices faded away, the centre of the ornamental pond seemed to dimple. The water level rose until it was overflowing the edges of the pond, lapping at Freya's feet. Just as she remembered from that long-ago summer with Tammy, the pond seemed to invert, drawing up more water than could possibly be contained in it. A figure formed, rippling and brown with flecks of pond weed dripping down its back like hair. Instead of legs, the figure's body flowed out from the hips down to the pond, a little like a dress.

"Watch out, it may be connected to the Gypsy Race," murmured Tammy, pausing to take a pained breath.

"What's that?" asked Freya.

"Just an underground river round here. Never mind, keep doing your thing," Tammy waved away the issue.

Freya took a breath, then let it out. What could she say?

"Er. Greetings. I need help. I need to summon a sea goddess."

The water column turned its humanoid head towards her. Freya was sure it was regarding her with contempt.

"Truly?" it asked her. *"Why?"*

"Look, I don't know why. I just got asked to help my sister, here. The were-foxes told me I needed the North Sea goddess. Nehalennia. Can you help?"

"Perhaps. For a price." The water deity seemed to be unwilling, swishing to and fro, the pond weed tumbling about.

Freya tapped her fingers against her leg.

"What sort of price?"

The deity indicated Tammy.

"The first litter."

Freya was confused.

"What do you mean, litter?" She had a sudden internal image of an overflowing rubbish bin.

"Your sister. She will lose this litter without aid. Let me have it, and I will deal with Nehalennia."

Freya, still disturbed by the idea of her sister carrying a 'litter' replied firmly.

"I can't make that promise. My sister's children aren't mine to give away."

"They are not for you," said Tammy unexpectedly, addressing the water deity. The sisters looked at each other in unusual accord.

"All I want is to call Nehalennia. That shouldn't cost so much," Freya bargained.

"Very well. I will take my price from your *future."*

Freya blinked. That sounded ominous.

What is this, Rumpelstiltskin?

"Not if it's lethal!" said Tammy.

"It won't be, for her," the deity assured.

"I don't want to agree to an unspecified promise! You could be asking for anything!" objected Freya.

"You've already turned down my first offer," the deity replied.

"Because it was unreasonable."

"You are hardly in a position to quibble."

A future price seems so huge. What could a water deity want from me? Freya shivered. Beside her, Tammy moaned.

"Do something, Freya. I hurt. I don't want to die."

And here I am acting like the big sister again... but what else can I do?

"You're not dying, Tammy. You'll be OK."

And I sure hope I'm right about that.

"Make your price specific. I'm not agreeing to anything so vague," she said.

"I can't give away something I don't have."

"But you can give away something you might have. You are young. You have time for many things. Grant me this one thing. It will not hurt you, and in return I will help you get help for your sister."

"Well... I guess so, then," Freya agreed at last. "But just one potential. Not many. Help me call Nehalennia."

The deity nodded her agreement.

"It is decided," she said.

I hope I haven't just sacrificed my future, thought Freya. *I have no idea what 'one potential supernatural child' means to a goddess.*

The deity raised watery hands, and they all heard the sound of the sea grow abruptly louder. The sound of waves crashing on the shore grew closer, and with a splash that drenched them all, a large wave surged through the garden, flattening plants and drawing at the legs of those standing. Freya shuddered as the wave overtopping them reminded her of her tsunami dreams. Instead of departing like a normal wave, this one stayed, swishing through the garden with a soft seething noise. Out of the wave rose another deity. This one was definitely female. Another, smaller wave coursed through the garden and became a dog-shaped lump of water at her side.

"Almighty Bastet, not her again," muttered Karim, forgotten until now.

Freya spared him a glance, remembering his tales of a goddess on his sea voyage. Where had he sprung from, anyway? She'd thought he was fetching her mother. Before she could ponder his re-appearance further, Lisichka and the other weres sank to their knees in the water.

"Our lady," they all intoned. Freya looked at them uneasily. She'd brought them their goddess, it seemed. But at what cost to herself? Lisichka arose and addressed the sea goddess directly.

"We are seeking to return to your lands, Lady Nehalennia. With the soon-to-be-born children of this water-summoner" - she gestured towards Tammy - "we will have regained our water affinity. But they need your help to be born alive."

The sea goddess looked at Tammy, then back to the weres.

"A worthy endeavour. And my dominion is growing with every passing season. I would welcome new denizens in my realm. But I can only do so much," Her voice was like waves playing on seashells, rough, but with unexpected tinkles. *"Not all may live."*

This sounds worrying. Does Tammy know what they plan? Freya didn't trust this goddess an inch - and she trusted the were-foxes even less than that.

Nehalennia transferred her attention to Freya.

"I understand you have already bargained with your future." She smiled. It was not a pleasant expression. *"I will take my price elsewhere."* She splashed into wave form once again, her dog following suit. The waves rolled improbably towards Tammy and Freya, and faster than thought, broke through Freya's circle. The waves sloshed around Freya for a moment, then surged over Tammy, who had collapsed to lie on the grass, clutching at her stomach. Her water-covered form writhed and twisted. A drenched scream bubbled forth, then she was still.

"Don't!" Freya cried, and throwing salt at the nameless pond-deity, she dismissed it without ceremony. Pulling out the magnifying glass, she glanced towards the sun - thank goodness it had come out from behind the clouds for a change - and angled the glass to catch the light. A small white circle played upon Nehalennia's waves, and slowly but surely the waves began to steam. Sunlight - the only thing which could change the nature of the sea. Sometimes high-school physics *was* worth knowing. Although, now Freya saw how small her circle of light was, she realised that it must feel like a mere pinprick on the surface of Nehalennia's bulk. Nevertheless, as abruptly as she had surged forward as a wave, Nehalennia reared back into her person-form.

"You've made your point," she said, quite pleasantly. *"But you're too late. I have helped the litter live and taken my price."*

"No!" Freya's mother was suddenly there, splashing heavily across the small garden towards her daughters. Dropping to her knees beside Tammy, Danae looked vengefully towards Nehalennia.

"You. You did this. You have overdone your price."

Nehalennia shrugged, a ripple running through her watery form.

"I was called. I came. Anything more I do is surely a bonus."

"A life taken is not a bonus. Give it back." Danae was fierce in her grief.

"You know I can't do that," said Nehalennia carelessly.

"Then take another in its place. Make it mine."

Freya was horrified all over again.

"No, Mum!"

Nehalennia merely laughed, the sound of waves crashing on beach. She looked at Freya again.

"I have a new companion. You have dismissed the water-spirit who brought me here. I am bound no longer. Farewell. Enjoy my gifts."

She collapsed into waves once more, and the waves drained quickly back towards the sea. Beside Tammy, Danae cried out as her older daughter was dragged with the receding tide. She reached for Tammy, and Freya left her useless circle to clutch at Tammy too, but to no avail.

The two of them ran after the departing wave, grabbing frantically at Tammy. Freya managed to snag Tammy's hand for a moment, only to have it torn from her grasp. But in that brief moment, Freya felt Tammy's hand grip hers.

"She's alive, Mum!' Freya gasped. Stumbling over rocks and roots, they reached the edge of the sea all too soon. But the grey waves surged back and forth, unbroken by Tammy's figure. Freya and her mother collapsed together onto the gritty shore, for once aligned in their sorrow.

CHAPTER THIRTY-SEVEN

AFTER THE FLOODS

Freya and Danae sat for a long time together on the shore, eyes searching in vain for Tammy. The sun shone thinly down, and gulls called harshly to one another. Freya felt empty, too shocked for simple grief.

"I always worried it would end up like this," said Danae.

Freya looked at her in surprise.

"With Tammy taken by a vengeful sea-goddess? Seriously, Mum?"

"Well, maybe not exactly like this, but yes, I've been afraid of vengeful sea-gods for many years. Since I was about your age, in fact," said Danae.

"What happened to you, back then?" Freya was somehow sure that something *had* happened. Perhaps the something that had sentenced their family to life on the coast all these years.

"I suppose it doesn't matter if I tell you now." Danae's voice cracked.

Mum must love Tammy after all, despite all the arguments.

"Mmm?" intoned Freya cautiously, not wanting to stop any helpful reminisces.

"Well... I was very naive at your age. Much more so than you, I think. I lived on the shore, lived and breathed seaside life. But - well, there was a boy. I thought he was a full human, but now I wonder... Anyway, he was handsome, but he never noticed me. So I struck a bargain with the sea-gods. I'd just started to realise I had power, but it was so little really. It couldn't help me get that boy, and that infuriated me. So, I went to the sea, and I asked for help. As you've seen, the sea-gods can do all sorts of things, but there's always a price. I didn't care, I just wanted him."

"You agreed to a future price, didn't you, Mum?" Freya was disapproving, frowning at the thought of her mother's carelessness.

"Frigg help me, I did. And how I have paid, and paid, and paid."

"Looks like Tammy has paid, to me," said Freya, then wished she hadn't. Danae started to cry again, harsh sobs that shook her body.

"Oh, Mum...," Freya trailed off. What was there to say? She patted her mother's back, then realised that she did want to know more. "What happened to the boy, then? The one you paid so much for?"

"I had him for a night. It was - well, you don't want to hear about that. The next day, he announced he was leaving, he had a job over in the gun states. I would have followed, but there was no way I could afford to go. I got offered a short-term job over here, which I took mostly to show that I wasn't heart-broken - just to show him, you see."

"That's not a great reason, Mum."

"I know. At least, I know that now. Of course, then I discovered I was pregnant with Tammy and met your father. I ended up stuck here, and stuck on the coast, hoping that the sea-goddess wouldn't take her price too soon, or that the price would not be more than I could pay. At least you were noble in bargaining away your future, to save someone else."

Freya didn't feel particularly noble. She heartily wished that Tammy hadn't needed rescuing, and that no price had been required. She digested the revelations from her mother slowly, picking up handfuls of grey sand and sifting them through her fingers. The sand was wet and claggy from the recent waves.

"Wait, you said you were pregnant, *then* you met Dad? Tammy isn't even my full sister?"

"That's right. Dion suspected, of course. That never helped our relationship. But he's long gone, now."

"You should have told us, Mum."

"Would it have made a difference? You're sisters all the same."

"I know, but it might have helped explain our differences." Freya thought of the years of conflict between her and Tammy - petty sibling conflicts, perhaps, but they hadn't helped anyone. She found a shell in her handful of sand and cracked it into tiny pieces.

"Perhaps I should have, but there never seemed to be a right time. I suppose now it's too late," Danae said.

"Yes. Much too late."

Karim appeared at last, avoiding the puddles that remained. Freya smiled a little despite herself.

'Cat-boy' had clearly not been a totally unwarranted name for him. He knelt and put an arm around Freya, ignoring her mother's sudden sharp glance.

"Are you OK?" he asked her.

Freya considered the question with rather more care than it probably deserved.

"No. No, I am not OK. But I don't think I want to talk about it now. I want to go home."

"Come on then. Let's go see how it survived that wave," Karim suggested.

Freya groaned. She hadn't considered that her home might be in the path of that improbable wave of water.

"You go ahead, Freya. I'm going to stay and sort out what's happened between Tammy and these... people." Danae cast a flinty glance at the were-foxes who hovered awkwardly behind them.

Freya still hesitated. Was her mum safe with these weres? Danae must have seen the uncertainty on Freya's face.

"I've kept myself alive for longer than you've been around, Freya. I'll be fine."
I guess if she doesn't want me to stay, she feels safe enough.

Freya and Karim hurried through the edges of town to her house. It was still standing, to Freya's relief. At least this house was far enough from the sea that the storm surge had not washed it away. The garden was another matter, utterly destroyed, battered by waves and water.

"Mum is going to be so mad when she sees this!" Freya gasped. The front door had been washed open. Debris - flotsam and jetsam was what they called it, Freya thought, dazedly - decorated the hall. Everything was wet.

"Don't turn on anything electrical," Karim warned unnecessarily. He was busy texting on his phone. She wondered how he could do something so mundane at a time like this.

"Don't take any photos, please. I couldn't bear this to end up on someone's Flimflam feed."

Karim looked up at her, dark eyes wide but unreadable in the dim hallway.

"Don't worry. I'm just letting Aisha know what's happened. I don't do social media except with my archaeology group. And this is several hundred years too young to interest them. Now, bury it in sand for a thousand years, and I'd have something to photograph."

"Oh you. Don't tease, I'm not in the mood." Freya continued up the hall. She glanced into the kitchen and wished she hadn't. Seaweed decorated the floor, complete with a couple of crabs who scuttled for cover as she looked in. Bits of someone else's garden gnome poked out from under the seaweed. The cupboards hung open, their contents scattered and soaked. The fridge was emitting buzzing, sparking noises.

"Karim!" Freya called. "Can you find the fuse box? It should be near the front door. We need to get everything turned off before we have a house fire to deal with as well as a flood."

Karim poked his head into the kitchen before taking two long strides back along the hall to the fuse box.

"That doesn't look good. Just a minute." There were some clunks as Karim found the fuse box, and tried to open it. Freya grabbed a butter knife from a kitchen drawer - miraculously still closed - and retreated to the hall.

"Here. It's usually painted shut in decrepit old houses like this." She handed over the knife.

Karim wiggled the knife under the edge of the box.

"Yeah, that's done it. You know a lot about decrepit houses, then?"

Freya gave a half laugh, then stopped, feeling guilty for laughing when she didn't know if her sister was even alive.

"Do I ever. I think every house I've ever lived in - and there have been a few - has had several decades of misuse before we arrived in it. And you would not believe how many storm surges have hit houses I've lived in." Tears pricked her eyes as a wave of self-pity overcame her. "Honestly, I don't know why it always happens to us. You'd think my family would have moved away from the sea before now. It's not like it's an easy place to live. But no, every time we move, we're always close to the sea. It's like a fatal attraction." She stopped talking abruptly, unable to continue. Taking a deep breath, she struggled to regain control of her voice.

"Anyway. Maybe after today, that won't happen anymore. Let's see if the upstairs is any better than down here. One house we lived in, the middle level was the best - the roof leaked, the basement flooded, but the middle was quite posh. If we're lucky, this house will be a bit like that. Except without the basement. Are you coming?"

"Sure. I'll just make sure every thing's off down here."

Freya took the stairs to her room two at a time, forgetting her weariness and despair. Safe! The water had not touched the upstairs portion of the house. Her strengthened tarpaulin still covered the roof, her bed was still a haven. Relief flooded her. This house was still home, even if it was now in even worse repair than before. After what had happened to Tammy, she needed something to stay permanent.

Karim appeared in the doorway as she sank onto her bed.

"Aisha got back to me," he said. "She'll come over when she can. It might take her a while though. Those waves went through town too, and there's more damage closer to the beach. I wondered... how you want to pass the time?" Freya looked up at him. His eyes were dilated as he watched her.

Catlike, she thought. She should probably start cleaning up the house, see what could be salvaged from the kitchen and lounge, wash the saltwater off the plants in the garden. But right now, more than anything, she wanted some semi-human companionship. She held out her hand to Karim.

"Come over here and let's find out."

Karim took her hand and let himself be drawn down beside her.

CHAPTER THIRTY-EIGHT

TAMMY'S SURPRISE

Freya stood at the bottom of the stairway down the cliffs. The looming rock faces made her feel shorter than she was. The wind whipping her light hair painfully against her face was also making her nose run. She sniffed, then wished she hadn't, as she was assaulted by the stench of rotting seaweed.

Fenris's teeth, I wish I had packed a handkerchief to cover my nose with. Now I know how Bilbo Baggins felt. Who knew handkerchiefs were so vital?

She surveyed the rocky beach before her, searching for any sign of her sister, as she had done every day of the past winter.

Freya knew that there wasn't much chance that her sister would turn up here again, but she felt that she had to try. She shifted uncomfortably on her rocky perch. She was going to have to get closer to the sea if she wanted to survey the whole beach. Gritting her teeth, she leaped from one slab of rock to another, wishing the grey stone wasn't quite so slippery and the sea not so close. She didn't want to risk being taken herself, no matter how unlikely that was. One foot skidded on landing, and she lurched, trying to regain her balance. A step sideways, an unbalanced rock teetered, and she fell, her muscles tensing painfully in anticipation of the impact. Unexpectedly, she landed on gritty sand, coarse and brown under her outstretched fingers, but infinitely preferable to landing on rock.

"Oof. I need chocolate."

Lucky I have some, these days.

Freya turned around so she was sitting on the damp sand, fumbled in her pocket and found a somewhat battered square wrapped in gold foil. She brushed a few crumbs of sand off the precious package and peeled the foil off, the thin metal delightfully smooth to her fingers after the sandy landing. Biting off an edge of the chocolate, Freya savoured the morsel as it melted on her tongue. Cocoa overriding a hint of caramel, vanilla, a touch of salt that might have come from the nearby sea or from the chocolate itself.

This is why I don't want to survive off foraged food all the time. Chocolate is much better than salad in a crisis.

Her chocolate-aided recovery was interrupted by the unwelcome splash of waves on her trouser-covered legs. She scrambled to her feet.

"Alright, I'm looking. No need to get watery with me." Freya no longer felt silly addressing the waves. She *knew* there was a goddess there – and maybe her sister, too. Pocketing the remaining chocolate, she resumed her slithery progress towards the far end of the beach, where a long-fallen piece of cliff blocked her view.

Rounding the obstacle at last, Freya paused in shock. She had not found her sister this time. But she had found... puppies? A thin whimpering reached her ears. Or was that far-off gulls? It was hard to tell with the constant rumbling of the sea telling its tale of unseen tumbling rocks.

Freya bent over the pile of puppies. Surely it was too cold here on the beach for such young animals. Her hair immediately fell forward into her face, obscuring her view. She pushed it back impatiently, and it fell forward again. Freya gave an irritated huff, and shoved it behind her ears once more.

Maybe I should just cut my hair off, if it's going to be so annoying. Except then I'd look more like Tammy. I guess I'll leave it.

She transferred her attention to the small beings in front of her.

"What are you little ones doing here? It's a lonely place for puppies. And where's your mum?"

She looked around. No sign of a dog anywhere. Or... she looked more closely at the small heap of wriggling, whining bodies. They stilled and looked back at her with shining dark eyes. Their large ears twitched towards her. *Not puppies.*

"Are you fox kits? I'm sure you don't belong on a beach, whatever you are."

Fox kits might also mean she was in danger – were they true foxes, or were-foxes? She had no way of telling unless an adult turned up. On cue, feet crunched on the sandy strip of the main beach. Freya backed away until she tripped on the ubiquitous rocks.

Ow.

She shuffled behind a larger than average rock.

I hope the seaweed smell overwhelms the smell of me.

The rock didn't provide much camouflage, but some cover was probably better than none. She peered around the edge of the rock. The figure who appeared was somehow familiar, a big man with red-blond hair. A were-fox from the local clan. She tried not to breathe, though she thought she'd probably been spotted - or smelt. All the same, Freya felt insulted when the blond man totally ignored her, striding directly to the kits. He crouched over them as Freya had done, sniffed loudly two or three times, and began gathering the kits up into his arms.

Freya decided that being ignored was worse than any alternative right now – after all, this was just one were. And his hands were too full of baby fox for him to attack her, if he didn't abide by their uneasy truce. She stood up and picked her way over to him.

"Excuse me? Are those yours?" she asked.

The man looked at her at last, and Freya was startled by the grief evident on his face. He was relatively young, but deep lines marred what had probably been a handsome face. Freya suddenly remembered where she had seen him before: supporting Tammy before the sea-goddess took her. *This is Tammy's were-fox boyfriend, the one she abandoned us for.*

"You must be her sister," he said.

"If you mean Tammy, then yes."

"I smelt you earlier."

Way to make a girl feel special. I am so going to change deodorants.

"Well, good for your nose then. I asked if the kits were yours."

The big man nodded.

"More mine than anyone's. But can't you smell your sister on them?"

Freya stared.

"No. Around here, I smell the sea. And a bit of fox, I guess."

The man shook his head.

"They smell of her. She must have been here, and I missed her." He bit off his words, mouth turned down, his anguish apparent. Freya found herself thawing in the face of such strong emotion. He seemed to be genuinely sorry about Tammy's loss.

"You and me both. Did she leave these kits then?"

"She must have done. They smell of her," he repeated. "I will raise them in her memory." The blond man clutched the kits closer to him.

"But what about Tammy? If she was here, where is she now?" Freya looked around wildly, as though her sister would appear magically.

"I can only guess she has gone back to Nehalennia," he sighed.

"That b- that goddess has seriously mucked up our lives," said Freya.

"On that, we are agreed," he said.

Freya looked around more closely. No sign of a goddess here. But a short line of footprints led away towards the sea. Freya followed the prints, and found a patch of wet sand inscribed with words and pictures.

"There's a message here," she called. "Something about shared care, I'm guessing from the pictures of foxes and humans. And... I think it's from Tammy. You should see this."

Juggling kits, the blond man looked at her as though she were a person, at last. Clutching the kits to him with difficulty - they squirmed - he hastened over to her. Together, they puzzled over the message.

I wish Tammy was better at drawing. Though I guess it's hard to draw messages in the sand.

A series of line drawings were scrawled across the sand. There was a foxy-looking thing, then an arrow, followed by a similar thing but with lines on its neck. Two stick figures towered over the foxy thing. Only one of them had a tail.

"Looks like we'd better work together," Freya said.

"Yes. Will you help me carry them home?" asked the blond man.

"Of course." Freya picked her way over the rocks and held out her hands. When she grasped one kit, it tried to nip her.

Why couldn't Tammy have left kittens?

"Does this mean I'm an aunt to foxes?"

"*Were*-foxes. They only change when they're older," he said.

I don't remember that in Mum's teaching. All that time spent on the non-mundane, and there's still big holes in what I know. It must be so much easier to be a mundane, pure human. Maybe when I'm officially an adult I can go away somewhere and pretend to be one. That would be peaceful.

Once all the kits were secure, Freya and the blond were-fox set off along the beach towards the stairs. Behind them, a larger than average wave curled into the small bay, caressing the pocket in the rocks where the kits had been and washing away the drawings in the sand.

EPILOGUE

Rain was hammering on the roof. The weather forecast predicted another large spring storm would hit that night. Right now though, it was warm and dry inside. Freya was glad this house was up the hill and away from the edge of the sea. She looked up when Aisha knocked on the open door to her room.

"Come in."

Aisha sauntered into the room like one of her cats.

"Your Mum said to come up here. Oh, they're so cute," she said, looking at the small furry pile on Freya's bed, "even if they are going to grow up into foxes. I mean, were-foxes."

Freya had to agree. When the sea-goddess had talked of a litter, she thought Nehalennia had been making a snide joke. But here she was, playing with her sister's fur-babies. Freya hoped that meant that Tammy was alive and well somewhere out there. Maybe she'd get her longed-for stability out in the ocean.

"They might not be were-foxes, exactly," she felt compelled to inform Aisha. "There was a note of sorts, from Tammy. Or possibly from Nehalennia. More of a picture in the sand. I think... I think they might be visiting their mother when they're older. Once their gills have grown in."

Aisha looked at Freya with an expression somewhere between curiosity and horror.

"Gills? Seriously?" She ruffled the kit's neck fur, where no sign of gills was in evidence. "Umm. How would that work? Surely they're mammals."

Freya shrugged. "I don't know. It's hard to interpret a pictogram left in the sand by an ancient sea-goddess I've only met once. Or even one left by my sister, she never was much of an artist. They might not get gills. Maybe they'll just shapeshift like regular weres, but into something different." Freya flopped back on her bed, making the small furry bodies protest as they had to find her patting hands again. "School's been feeling pretty tame in the last few months. But I wish Tammy had stayed away from the were-foxes. No matter how much she wanted a home and babies, surely it wasn't worth... well, everything."

Aisha came and sat down on the floor. She lifted one of the kits down from the bed, and cuddled it for a moment.

"Yeah," she said quietly. "It's hard to see how it could be worth everything." She looked up at Freya. "You know," she said, "if ever I get all gooey and romantic over someone, and declare I'm going to start - oh, I don't know, a new breed of locust-flinging pond-cats - please remind me what a bad idea it is."

Freya tried to laugh, but it came out as more of a sob.

"Sorry," Aisha apologised. "Bad joke. But do tell me;" she hesitated a moment. "Who's going to look after them?".

"These little guys?" Freya answered in a careful voice. "Mum's going to take them when she's not working. Overnight. Lisichka and her son, what's-his-name. Todd. They're taking them during the day. Apparently, stockbrokers like them can work with small furry bodies around their feet all day." She looked at the pile of kits scrabbling over each other. "I always knew Tammy wanted children, but this lot seems a bit many all at once. I wonder if that's what she expected?"

"And when do they turn - well, into whatever species they're going to be?" Aisha asked, curiously.

Freya shrugged again. "Nobody seems to know. Apparently, it was an experiment of sorts. They're trying to breed selkie foxes, or something like that. Because Tammy had- has- such a strong water-connection, they thought it might work out. Especially since she's the descendant of a fertility goddess, too. Not that that worked out well for anyone," Freya's voice wobbled, and she stopped, pressing her lips together, struggling for control of her vocal cords. She hated the way her emotions threatened to overwhelm her at the moment. Aisha rescued her.

"Fertility, rubbish. Bastet was a fertility goddess as well, you know. Honestly, they're a dime a dozen. Goes with the territory I suppose - I mean, it's a pretty big evolutionary advantage, isn't it, to have lots of kids? Sometimes I think our ancestors had nothing else on their minds when they thought of goddesses."

Freya laughed aloud, grateful for the distraction. "You have been paying more attention in biology, haven't you?"

Aisha looked momentarily embarrassed. "Well, that new biology teacher's pretty cute. It helps me focus," she mumbled.

"Is that gooey and romantic?" teased Freya.

"No! That's just... Well, you know. Helpful," retorted Aisha, before resuming her former strident tone. "If you ask me, I think your sister just fell in love, and the rest was an excuse her lover's family made so they could accept it." Aisha was obviously frustrated. She'd been furious about being grounded, and when it turned out that as a result, she hadn't been on hand to help Freya save her sister - and that Aisha's brother had been on hand and hadn't got Aisha to come help somehow - she was beyond upset.

Aisha put the kit down with its littermates on the bed, and looked curiously at Freya.

"Do you mind? Them being alive, I mean?"

Freya shook her head, slowly. "It would have been such a waste of life if no-one had survived," she said. "But I can't wait to finish school and get away from here. Even if Tammy is out there, I am so over the seaside." She looked at Aisha. "I'll miss you, though, if you don't go to uni, too."

"Yeah, well. I don't know what I'll do, yet," said Aisha with an uncertain laugh.

"I guess Karim's visiting next week, then?" Freya asked in what she hoped was a casual tone of voice. Aisha's knowing look told her she'd failed at casual, but she answered anyway.

"Yes, he managed to find a flat not far from the uni. But maybe you knew that already. He asked me to tell you he'd come by later. Nena's got him making a shedload of potions before he leaves. Apparently, he improved his potion-making skills while he was away, and Nena's just twigged that she won't have him at her beck and call while he's off studying. She wants to grow her online business to pass on to Mum, and Karim's much faster than he used to be. You should have heard her crowing - it was all 'ooh, Karim's grown up at last, he's so useful now, what do you mean he's going away again?'. It was pretty funny. Especially Karim's expression when Nena started listing all the potions she wants made before he goes. The house stinks awfully."

"Do you think he'll actually get away then?"

"Oh, yeah. I mean, who wants to spend all day doing your Grandma's bidding? Seriously though. I want to know. Have you got a thing for my brother?"

"Er... we're just trying things out at the moment, if you know what I mean."

"Good, do spare me the details. Only - I thought you should know that he's not really a settling down type. In case that's important to you. Oh, this is hard! Look, what I mean is, I want you to stay my friend even if you and Karim don't work out. OK?"

Freya nodded.

"Of course. And thanks for the warning." Then, trying to change the serious mood, she picked up the nearest kit. "Can you imagine this little guy as a teenager?"

"I don't even want to try. They're cute now, but my brain superimposes that idiot Lachy's face on him, and I get a bit of a shudder. D'you know what I mean?"

Freya shuddered herself. "I wish I didn't. I see Tobes. And I don't want to see that face on anything related to me."

"Ugh, change the subject, please!" exclaimed Aisha.

Freya obligingly complied. "So, what do you want to do after school finishes?"

"Well, with Karim going off, my family want someone to stay here and take on the business. It's all I've ever known, and that's pretty comforting, some days. But other days I want to scream with the sameness of it all. It's been much more fun since you came along. Apart from recently, of course," Aisha added hastily. "Are you sure you want to leave?"

"Yes! There's nothing to be gained by staying. I can't bring Tammy back from the sea, and I'm not strong enough, or inclined, to join her there. I suppose these little furballs are my nieces and nephews, but I don't feel much connection to them right now. Maybe if they were kittens instead of fox kits it would be different. I guess... I just want to find something that I'm good at. Figure out who I am. That sort of thing." She looked at Aisha uncertainly. "Don't you ever feel that way?"

Aisha laughed. "Sure. But not in any way that leaving is going to solve. This is my place; everyone knows me, and I know everyone. But I sure will miss you if you go. Come back and visit if you do leave. Which reminds me, I haven't told you. Isis is expecting kittens."

"Oh! I haven't seen a kitten in years. Not since Mr Fluffbum was small." Freya smiled. It was such a novelty and a relief to have a friend. And potentially kittens too. Not that she needed another cat right now. She glanced up at Mr Fluffbum, who was sitting on her battered wooden dresser, well out of reach of were-fox kits. He blinked slowly at her. She blinked back, exchanging love.

"Come see them when they're born, then. Though goodness knows we have enough cats about the place already," said Aisha.

"Would Bastet like to hear you say so?" teased Freya, half in earnest.

"Nah, I'd better keep quiet about that. Moving right along."

"So, who do you think will win the best storm-shelter competition?" Freya assisted the change of subject again.

Aisha smirked. "Me, because I borrowed a load of Karim's special potion that he made for the tarp on your roof. No-one is going to beat my shelter for light and strong!"

The two girls grinned at each other. It had been a hard year. But at least Freya now had a friend - no, two friends. Maybe more. After all, Lio had been around a lot this year too. She hadn't seen him since the last big storm, but her window had been covered with leaves in a pattern again this morning. There had been a note stuck among the leaves. When she'd peeled it off and read it, she'd found herself smiling as she read.

'Midnight meeting tonight? Open your door to see what's in store. We'll stay away from the waterfront'.

Bad poetry or no, I think I will see who's there at midnight.

THE END

Afterword

I hope you enjoyed Freya's adventures. If so, please leave a review! You can read more about Freya in Heat Wave, Book 2 of The Weather Gods. Order from your favourite online store. You can sign up for my newsletter at www.melissagunn.com for updates and a free prequel story in the Weather Gods world.

While you're unlikely to meet were-foxes and storm sprites in daily life, the weather problems in the Weather Gods series are based on real predictions for climate change.

Acknowledgements

This book would not have been possible without the help of many people. My family who withstood years of 'sorry, I'm writing right now, ask me about dinner later', and my children who listened to the whole thing and offered encouraging remarks and critical analysis. My friend Jen started the process when sharing writing prompts on social media during a Nanowrimo season. Thanks to writing mentor Ellie, and the members of the Auckland Writers Café Novel Writers Club, who provided great support and critique sessions; to Julie D, Laura and Anne for reading the whole novel and being honest & helpful with feedback. Julie F did a wonderful job of copy-editing it (any remaining mistakes are my own). My craft night friends (you know who you are) were great for bouncing ideas around and providing suggestions at key moments. My sisters Claudia and Pipiana were infinitely enthusiastic and my family were encouraging. It's been fun. Let's do it again!

ALSO BY MELISSA GUNN

Weather Gods series:

Flash Flood

Heat Wave

Short stories & novellas:

Treescape

Feels Like Heaven
(in Aftermath: Stories of Survival in Aotearoa New Zealand)
First Pav on Mars (in Pav Deconstructed, Pavlova Press)